FLYING
WITH FELIX

FLYING WITH FELIX

ANDREW BASS

PALMETTO
PUBLISHING
Charleston, SC
www.PalmettoPublishing.com

Copyright © 2025 by Andrew Bass

All rights reserved

No portion of this book may be reproduced, stored in a retrieval system, or transmitted in any form by any means–electronic, mechanical, photocopy, recording, or other–except for brief quotations in printed reviews, without prior permission of the author.

Hardcover ISBN: 9798822973169
Paperback ISBN: 9798822973176
eBook ISBN: 9798822973183

This book is dedicated to Marissa and Ryan Bass.
May all of your dreams come true.

Contents

Chapter 1: Mayday! Mayday! Mayday! 1
Chapter 2: Burials Abroad. 32
Chapter 3: Repatriation 59
Chapter 4: The Auction. 92
Chapter 5: Discovering Felix 100
Chapter 6: Growing Up 142
Chapter 7: Fish Scott. 205
Chapter 8: Life as an Aggie 233
Chapter 9: Sidelined in San Saba. 307
Chapter 10: Pre-flight at SAAAB. 322
Chapter 11: Finally Flying. 369
Chapter 12: Wings 435
Chapter 13: Florida Flyboys 491
Chapter 14: Completing the Mission 518
Bibliography 551
About the Author 555

CHAPTER 1

Mayday! Mayday! Mayday!

Prior to joining the military, Felix Ernest Scott was enrolled as a student at the Agricultural and Mechanical College of Texas. Everyone referred to the school as Texas AMC at the time. He began his college career there on 16 Sep. 1938. At that time, the school was serving as a major university, but it also had a well regimented cadet program. Felix felt that this environment would prepare him if one day he should decide to join the ranks of the military as a pilot. Growing up in the small town of San Saba, Texas, had given him the background and work ethic to become a farmer. However, Felix felt that his dream of becoming a pilot could be fostered with the organization, drills, and training that college life at Texas AMC would provide.

The aggression in Europe and in the Pacific was beginning to become more of a world problem in 1939, just as Felix was getting acquainted with college life. Many parts of the country were still feeling the effects of the Great Depression. Felix came from a rather successful and hardworking family. Going to school during a time with so much discord in the world was hard. It was difficult to stay focused on school and life in general with the possibility of the United States getting involved in these conflicts. During his first three years at Texas AMC, Felix had below average grades, and it was apparent that a farming or an agricultural degree wasn't meant to be. However, Felix had adapted to the militaristic lifestyle that he found to be so prevalent while at college. During his final semester, which ended on 29 Jan. 1942, Felix ended up with 3 F's, 2 D's, and 2 B's. He clearly saw the writing on the wall that he wasn't going to graduate. Felix was frustrated, and he knew that his family would be rather disappointed once they found out that he had decided to drop out of college. Although his spirits were down, his head was still up as he headed back to San Saba to determine his next steps.

The surprise attack on Pearl Harbor, at the hands of the Japanese, hit Felix hard on 07 Dec. 1941. He, like many of his classmates, was eager to retaliate against Japan in the days soon afterward. Felix felt that he could and should do something to honor the lives of the dead servicemen. He wanted to avenge the dreadful sneak attack which cost so many lives that December day.

It was February of 1944, and Felix was glad to be finally wrapping up his pilot training in Sarasota, Florida. Felix had received his orders that he'd be reporting to an Air Base in India. In military terms, that part of the world was known as the CBI. The CBI was otherwise known as the China, Burma, India theater. Felix had only left the safety of the United States once for a short trip to Mexico with a buddy. He had heard about the CBI during his training, but he had a hard time envisioning in his mind where exactly on the globe he'd be going. Felix and his fellow pilots had been receiving briefings mostly related to the European and Pacific conflicts. With the war raging across the globe, he figured that he'd be heading to Europe or to the islands of the Pacific as a replacement pilot. Finally, and most importantly, Felix would have his opportunity for payback. Feeling surprised and uncertain, Felix and a few of his pals went to the Flight Room there on base to have a look at a world map to see exactly where Dinjan Airfield was located in India. He noticed that India was located almost right between Hitler's Germany and the mainland of Japan.

Felix and his pals were thoroughly trained and ready for war. They despised the reference to them being called "replacement pilots." "Why are we replacement pilots?", Felix asked himself. Maybe the pilots who had fought before him had been so successful that they were coming home. He tried not to think of the other possibility that maybe they were getting killed right and left, and he was next to fill in for those who had fallen.

Just like that, Felix was en route to his new base of operations in a faraway land. He was told to expect a journey that could take several weeks. When a soldier sails away from United States shores, he or she is embarking upon a journey with an unknown and yet to be determined ending. A situation like this can be exhilarating, but yet can also bring profound sadness to that person, who is wondering if he'll ever get to hug and share good times with his loved ones ever again.

This Valentine's Day for Felix was going to be spent at sea, and far away from his girlfriend, Elsie. He'd met Elsie while stationed in Santa Ana, California, and he'd give anything to be back in her arms. Felix sat on a bench near the dock wondering what he was getting himself into. As the sun rose, he extinguished his pipe, and boarded a large transport ship, laden with other pilots, soldiers, cargo, planes, and supply personnel. The ship sailed south to Puerto Rico, Trinidad, and on to Brazil. From there, they stopped at Ascension Island, and then continued on to Liberia, Morocco, Libya, Egypt, and Iran. Each country was so unique, and Felix really enjoyed the camaraderie in being around his shipmates. At times, he felt like a tourist on a remarkable worldwide cruise. However, the cramped conditions and rough seas humbled Felix. The journey was already long and arduous, but he remained focused on his mission to become a successful pilot, and to make his family proud.

After departing Iran, the next stop was Karachi, Pakistan. Up until Karachi, Felix had been unable to purchase many trinkets and souvenirs, as there wasn't much room on the ship to store bulky items. Karachi was an interesting city with camels and elephants roaming about. Horses and donkeys could be seen pulling carts and carriages. There were both dirt roads and paved roads for the trolley cars and double deck buses to traverse. It was a bustling city with bicycles and motorcycles speeding up and down the streets.

There were many shops and street peddlers playing host to a boat full of soldiers with money in their pockets, which made for a quite a scene in town. Felix and his pals were granted an unusual three-day leave pass, so there was plenty of time to see the sights. Felix loved his family, and knowing that they felt that they'd probably never get to this part of the world, he wanted to send some of it to them. He was excited to explore the city to see what treasures he could find. Shortly after disembarking, Felix found a group of youngsters on the Lady Lloyd Pier. He traded some chocolate candy bars for an opportunity to join them in fishing off the pier. Felix really enjoyed fishing back home, so this was a special treat.

Felix found that trading cartons of smokes was almost as valuable as using actual cash. Felix had won many cartons of cigarettes while playing cards during his time aboard the boat. He preferred a pipe over cigarettes, so he naturally found a way to profit off his winnings. Some places took the American dollar, but Felix was able to convert some cash to Rupees while on the Karachi Air Base. He found some fancy silk tablecloths and exquisite shawls for his sisters and for Elsie. Felix discovered an ornate salt and pepper shaker made of ivory. He fell in love with a set of eight napkin rings also made of ivory, and he just had to buy a handcrafted leather holster for his father. Felix was able to get these items boxed up and shipped at the APO station there on the base before heading out for Bombay.

It was nice having the few days off the ship. However, Felix was excited and anxious about getting to his new base so that he could begin flying the P-51 Mustang. The P-51A was going to be a new plane for Felix, since he had recently spent most of his time flying the P-40. Felix knew that he'd be getting additional training at his new base there in Dinjan, and he was certainly eager to get back into the cockpit! The last leg of Felix's trip aboard the transport vessel was a rather quick two and a half days journey, with the final stop being at the harbor in Bombay, India.

As Felix's ship sailed into the Bombay harbor, he stood on the top deck along with many of his shipmates. The water was a bit choppy, but the views of the lush mountains ringing the harbor were spectacular. Felix quit counting the ships because there had to have been more than 100 military, commercial, and personal fishing vessels moored in the harbor. Felix felt that the Bombay harbor reminded him of his recent time spent in and around the harbor of San Francisco. While training in California, he had spent a wonderful weekend in San Francisco with his beautiful girlfriend, Elsie. As his ship neared the dock in Bombay, there were many tall buildings, some of which possessed very ornate architecture. There were religious and palatial looking buildings as well.

Double decker buses and electric trolley cars could be seen all around the city streets. Cargo was being loaded onto merchant ships, while many of the military ships were off loading cargo. Felix was told that his footlocker would be delivered to his new base. Therefore, he prepared to exit the ship with his duffel bag slung over his shoulder, and with his B-4 bag in his right hand. Before heading down the gang plank to the dock, he paused and felt a bit sullen. Suddenly, he wondered if he'd see the end of the war to be able to reboard a ship back to America. Would he ever step aboard a ship again? He gripped the railing tight, and gave a little kick to the deck wall before disembarking.

Felix and his shipmates were ordered to proceed down the long wooden dock to a row of "deuce and a half" trucks that were lined up by the dozens. Each of the large cargo trucks could carry more than a dozen men along with their belongings. There were signs, and officers were directing the men where they needed to go. Some of the men would be taking long journeys on the trucks to their new area of operation. In Felix's case, it was a rather short ride to the airport for a flight to the CBI. He'd finally end his journey to the other side of the world upon his arrival at his new base, Dinjan Air Field. Just as Felix pulled up to the airport, he heard the whizzing of a flight, which consisted of P-51As in a finger four formation. As the P-51s flew over him in formation, Felix looked up and waved his cap and yelled out loud, "Go get 'em boys!"

The primary function of the fighter pilots based at Dinjan was to provide protection for the cargo aircraft flying frequent re-supply missions over the Himalayan Mountains to China. The pilots referred to this route as "Flying the Hump." The four-hour flight on the C-47 plane to Dinjan wasn't the most comfortable ride. However, anytime that a pilot or soldier survives a flight during wartime without being shot down would be considered a success. The seat was hard and dusty, and there was certainly no in-flight snack service. Felix was a very jovial guy, and he had a great time sharing stories about home, and cracking jokes with the other servicemen during the flight. They were flying from Bombay, one of India's most southern cities, to the city of Dinjan, which was near its most northern tip. Dinjan was located in the Dibrugarh District of Assam, with China being to the north, and Burma to the east. As his plane touched down upon Dinjan's single runway, Felix was ready to begin the next chapter in his life as a pilot with the US Army Air Forces. After stepping out of the plane on 10 Mar. 1944, he was now officially part of the 311th Fighter Bomber Group.

It was about supper time when the propellers on the C-47 finally stopped turning. Felix and his three fellow replacement pilots deplaned into an evening where the temperature was about 80 degrees. The humidity smacked Felix right in the face, just as if he were back home in Texas. The men were greeted in a formal, yet friendly manner by Captain Sean Edwards, and Base Commander Kevin Hickenbotham. Captain Edwards was a tall fellow with a neatly trimmed mustache. Commander Hickenbotham was a big man who looked stronger than an ox. Their uniforms were clean and neatly pressed. After the introductions, Captain Edwards said, "Let's get some chow, and get inside before it rains."

After finishing their supper, the men hopped into several jeeps that were parked out front of the mess tent. Captain Edwards led the group for a tour around the base. There were about 280 men on base, which consisted of both officers and enlisted men. Although it was now dark, Felix got an idea as to where the key things were located. The base wasn't enormous, and he was told that it was only a few years old. The buildings were mostly adorned with thatched rooftops, although the hospital was a good size and built more modernly. The hospital gave Felix some comfort, knowing that it was there in case he should ever need it. Local villagers worked on the base, and they could be seen walking shirtless along with their carts led by oxen. Swampy areas were a common sight around base, and monkeys could be seen at every turn of the head. Captain Edwards showed the men where the movie theater and tennis courts were located. They also drove past the nine-hole golf course, the library, and of course, the post exchange. The tour ended at the barracks. Captain Edwards wished everyone a good night, and ordered them to be at the flight line at 0700 hours.

Felix had been told that he and the other new guys might be treated a little differently by the other men on the base, since they were replacement pilots. He'd had similar experiences at his previous bases, so he wasn't really all that worried. Many of the men on the base had lost friends during the war, and they were a bit hesitant to make new ones, for the fear of losing them too. When Felix walked into the barracks with his good friend, Ray Simon, he knew that they'd look after one another. He had trained with Ray back in California at the Santa Ana Army Air Base, and in Arizona, at Luke Field, and also in Florida, before boarding the ship to India. Felix knew that being roommates with Ray would be a blast, and he figured that he'd do his best to make other new friends quickly.

The next morning brought the start of a day that Felix had been looking forward to for more than a year. Felix was now part of the Tenth Air Force. More importantly, he was finally going to be flying over foreign soil, and he was one step closer to actual combat. Being an early riser, Felix awoke and ventured outside to do some PT while the air was still cool. After a good workout, he made his way to the mess tent for breakfast. Felix was satisfied with the food choices, which were more robust than what he'd been served on the ship. There was also plenty of fresh, locally grown fruit for the taking.

As Felix was finishing breakfast at a table all by himself, another pilot sat down near him. The pilot introduced himself as Bucky Davidson. Felix reciprocated by introducing himself, and the pair enjoyed a short conversation. Felix was ready to go, and since he could tell that Bucky was a friendly fellow, he asked him if he could provide for him the quickest path to the flight line. Bucky stood up, and said, "I'll do better than give you directions, I'll take you there myself." Bucky grabbed some fruit and his biscuits, and the pair headed out. After a short walk to the flight line, Felix recognized Captain Edwards who was conversing with a few other pilots. He picked up the pace, and made it with a few minutes to spare. Felix was really excited about getting back into the cockpit for training that day. He hoped that it would be in one of those brand new P-51As that he had noticed the night before. Felix was chomping at the bit to fly the latest and greatest war machine available to the United States at that time.

Several folding chairs were lined up neatly in a row facing Captain Edwards. Felix took a seat next to Ray and the other two replacement pilots. Captain Edwards then began the official orientation and reviewed the base protocols. This session seemed to be mostly a get to know each other better gig. The pilots were given aerial maps to study, brochures on local culture, safety guides, and a brief outline of their training regimen for the upcoming weeks. Felix spent the morning of 11 Mar. 1944 back in the cockpit of the all too familiar P-40K. There were some barren areas, but he saw much more greenery than he had expected to see. There was a nice view of the Brahmaputra River, which was close by. Flying up and over the lush green hills, and speeding through the valleys was quite a treat. Felix was disappointed that he wasn't yet flying one of those new P-51As, but he was certainly glad that enemy planes weren't yet shooting at him. He was just happy to be flying, and the new environment made it exciting for him. Felix continued to fly with Captain Edwards for several more training flights to complete his first week there at the Dinjan Air Field.

The next few weeks were spent flying the P-40 and AT-6 as weather would permit. Not seeing actual combat, and with the intermittent weather problems, it was as if Felix was on vacation with a bunch of his buddies. By the end of March, it had rained more than half of the time he'd been there in Dinjan. For a bit, there was plenty of lying around, relaxing, socializing, and even some drinking. Felix thoroughly enjoyed flying both day and night training missions, but he and Ray found it rather laughable that they'd have to attend more ground school courses. They began to really wonder if they'd ever get a chance to fight in the war. There was a refresher session in Navigation, and they found that the courses like Conditions in Combat Zones, Aircraft Identification specific to the CBI, Intelligence, Armament, Escape Tactics, and Communications were actually quite interesting. The young pilots kept their skills sharp by strafing practice targets, and by dropping practice bombs near swampy tea fields. Felix was amazed to find out that three of the Chinese pilots who he had trained with at Luke Field were now on the base with him in Dinjan. Air superiority really began to strengthen for the Allied forces in March of 1944.

Felix would find a few moments each week to write letters to his family and loved ones back home. Felix had been corresponding back and forth with his mother over trying to find the perfect gift for his girlfriend's upcoming birthday. When he was back at Texas AMC, he had really enjoyed spending time at the nearby Blue Bonnet Roller Rink. He and his pals would skate for hours on many Sunday afternoons. Felix wanted to get Elsie a pair of roller skates, so that she could enjoy some fun in the sun while skating up and down the sidewalks of her favorite Orange County beaches. He was bummed when his mother let him know that roller skates were among the many things that were no longer available in the Sears catalog, since the materials were desperately needed for the war effort. Alternatively, Felix provided his mother with Elsie's dress and shoe size. He asked that she pick out the cutest outfit that she could find in the catalog. He hoped to get this war over with soon, so that he too, could be home to skate with Elsie. Felix thoroughly enjoyed receiving letters from Elsie. She wrote thoughtful letters that were supportive and encouraging. Every time Felix would open an envelope from Elsie, he'd get a whiff of her perfume. He wasn't in her arms or by her side, but it was the next best thing.

Felix's thoughtfulness as evidenced by an Easter card sent to his sister Johnnie Mae in April of 1944.

It was Tuesday, 04 Apr. 1944, and Felix was now officially assigned to the 529th Fighter Squadron. Their squadron worked closely with B-25 pilots from the 490th Medium Bombardment Squadron and from the 12th Medium Bombardment Group. Felix thought it was awesome to receive a really cool squadron patch that would go on the chest of his A-2 leather flight jacket. The patch had a big yellow tiger on it with fangs and claws. He also received a large blood chit patch that would go on the back of his jacket. The blood chit provided instructions in Chinese, so that villagers could assist him in case he ever crashed, or if he had to eject behind enemy lines. Felix and Ray made a trip into town that afternoon, and they took their new patches, jackets, and laundry with them. They visited a local shop that had a great reputation for quick, yet professional work with military uniforms. Felix and Ray were told to return on Saturday to pick up their jackets and freshly laundered clothing. They spent the rest of the week flying longer missions to become completely familiar with the territory. Felix and Ray also spent a fair amount of time in the pilot briefing room, learning about the advancements that the Japanese were making in the area.

Letter that Felix sent to his sister Pauline and her husband Ted. It has the official military postmark and examiner's stamp.

On the morning of 06 Apr. 1944, Felix once again made his way to the flight line. This time, there were five P-51As lined up side by side just east of the runway. The planes were painted with an olive drab color scheme, and featured the Air Force star on the fuselage. Felix could hardly contain his emotions, but he somehow kept his cool, and his eye on the planes. He was ecstatic to hear that they were about to be assigned their own plane. He never thought that he could top the excitement from the day that he got his first car, a 1937 Ford Coupe. That car was fast and stylish, but to Felix, getting the P-51A was even more gratifying.

Captain Edwards reminded the group of the importance of wearing their backpack style parachute each and every time they were going to be in the air. Stressing the importance of safety while flying,

Captain Edwards approached each pilot to ensure a proper fit, and he checked that the straps were in good order. Taking the extra precautions made sense to Felix, since they were about to fly a plane that could reach a top speed of just under 400 mph. Next, they were given a pilot training manual for the P-51 Mustang. The book had a tad more than 100 pages, which included everything that the aviators would be expected to know and follow. Captain Edwards instructed the men to read the manual from cover to cover, and to be prepared for a quiz within the next 48 hours. After tidying up other housekeeping items, he directed the pilots to their aircraft. They'd soon be in the air for a routine flight in order to get acquainted with the new plane. Captain Edwards let the pilots know that the Mustang could go as high as about 30,000 feet. They wouldn't be flying that high just yet, but would instead be practicing takeoffs, landings, and routine maneuvers for the next hour or so.

As Felix walked around the Mustang, he saw that his tail number was 36269. After a peek into the ammunition boxes, Felix estimated that there had to be around 1,200 rounds, ready to feed the two .50 caliber machine guns on each wing. He also noticed the racks that could hold two 500 pound bombs. Felix then climbed into the single-seat cockpit from the left side of the aircraft. He was eager to get the engine started while staring at the three blade propeller. Felix felt the gun trigger on the control stick, and peered through the gunsight. He turned his head to the left and right to admire the remarkable aircraft. Felix familiarized himself with the controls, knobs, and switches. All of his fluid levels looked fine, and his other gauges were operable. Felix fastened the lap belt, and adjusted the shoulder harness to ensure a proper fit. He then cranked the canopy down, and made sure that it was completely closed. Felix was grinning from ear to ear with excitement as he flipped the ignition switch to start the 12-cylinder Allison engine. He could feel the capability of the 1,200 horsepower engine that was just waiting to be unleashed into the sky above. Just as Felix adjusted his leather helmet with a built in microphone, he could hear Captain Edwards providing instructions through his radio headset. He and the other pilots then maneuvered their planes towards the runway.

Felix moved into position on the runway, and he was suddenly piloting the most advanced war bird that he'd ever flown. Visibility at takeoff was somewhat limited due to the early morning cloud cover, so the group flew at a fairly low altitude in order to see each other well. The view of Dinjan, and of the surrounding areas became more improved as Felix was about to make his final landing of the day. Before exiting his plane, Felix made sure that he had stopped completely under the camouflaged screen netting that provided some protection from potential enemy planes. He'd had the time of his life in the P-51A, and he was glad that there had been no issues or concerns during the flight. He found the plane to be fast, easy to handle, and very responsive. It climbed quickly, and dived effectively. Felix couldn't wait to get back in the saddle of his Mustang.

After waking up, and performing their typical round of PT and chow, Felix ran into town with Ray to pick up their laundry and jackets. It felt like Christmas morning when Felix unwrapped the paper that covered the good-looking leather jacket. He ran his finger around and around the circular patch, and felt honored to be part of the squadron. The jacket looked terrific, and even though it wasn't cold, he wore it all the way back to the base because he felt that he looked cool.

One of the best treats for the group came later that day on 08 Apr. 1944. After their flight was complete for the day, Captain Edwards addressed the pilots by saying, "Now that you've proven you can fly my planes without crashing them, I'm going to allow you to decorate the nose of your plane if you so choose." Felix blushed a little bit every time he saw the nose art on Captain Edward's plane. The nose on his P-51A Mustang was adorned with a scantily clad woman who was clutching a machine gun in each of her hands with the words, "get some," above her head. Felix didn't have to think about this opportunity for very long.

Felix knew that if he had an image of a woman like that on his plane, his mother, sisters, and girlfriend would whoop him good if they found out. Felix then remembered back to his childhood days when he was around seven or eight years old. Felix's father, Ernest, had built him a toy plane made out of wood, and metal scraps taken from around his tire business. Mind you, this was no ordinary toy plane, and it wasn't your typical hand held toy. It was similar to the size of an average automobile from the time. The plane was designed for years of fun, and it was also used in several rodeo parades during his childhood in San Saba, Texas. The overall shape of the fuselage looked like a pecan, and there was plenty of room for young Felix to sit inside. This was Felix's first recollection of his ambition to become a pilot. There was a two blade propeller on the front, and, of course, it even had a "stick" that he could use to navigate and maneuver his craft just like a real aviator. The wings were decorated, and it even had real rubber wheels so that it could "fly" smoothly around the yard. When those strong Texas winds whipped up, Felix often wondered if his plane would really fly. Young Felix was decked out in a brown jacket, a leather flying helmet, and he even had goggles to boot. All of that was entirely cool, but the best part was that the nose art on his toy plane read "Spirit of San Saba."

Felix envisioned something fun and cool, but not sexy. Just like that, Felix decided to go with the "Spirit of San Saba" motif from his childhood toy plane. He reviewed his vision with Captain Edwards, and received permission for the project. With a plan hatched in his head, and pencil sketch in his hand, Felix headed over to the base maintenance yard. He was told to ask for Bobby Applewood or Charlie Donaldson. These two guys weren't pilots, but they sure knew their way around a mechanic's shop, and they were very artistic. Upon arriving at the yard, he ran into a young, burly man with a cigarette in his hand. Felix introduced himself, and asked the man if he could speak to Bobby or Charlie, just like Captain Edwards had advised. The man opened a door to a nearby building, and yelled out for one of them to come outside. Before you knew it, Bobby came out from the back, and asked how he could be of service. Felix explained that Captain Edwards had sent him, and asked about the nose art for his new Mustang. Bobby advised that he'd be glad to help during his free time, but it would cost Felix $10.00, and two cartons of smokes. Felix inquired, "Would you paint both sides?" Bobby replied, "Definitely. I can paint anything you dream of. I've been painting planes ever since I got here." Felix showed him the sketch, and Bobby took good notes on exactly what was needed to be done. He advised that it would take a few days, and Felix agreed by shaking his hand.

The excitement for the day wasn't done yet, as Felix and his pals had gotten permission to go into the town of Dibrugarh. Felix had become good friends with several pilots with whom he flew regular training missions with. He was going to take the train to Dibrugarh along with Second Lieutenants George Thompson and Ray Simon. Being that it was a Saturday, and Easter weekend, the men were given an abbreviated two day leave pass. They were told to be back on the base on Sunday evening. The train ride took about an hour, and they arrived in Dibrugarh around noon. They ventured into the heart of the city to find some chicken fried rice, tarkari, and a cold falooda to drink. Felix seemed to enjoy the Indian cuisine, and his sweet tooth continued to draw him into many of the local bakeries.

After dinner, they visited a nearby rain forest, and Felix was excited to see some wild elephants, and even a few tigers. The foliage was thick, green, and not at all what he had expected India would be like. The men headed back into town to spend the rest of the day shopping. The local craftsmen and villagers were very skilled. There were all kinds of unique things to purchase for the folks back home. Felix stopped completely in his tracks when he saw this small, circular table that he felt would be a nice piece for his parent's living room. It had wood carvings, and multiple inlays throughout the entire piece. The table was primarily made of teak wood, but it appeared that other types of wood were used on it as well. The legs were the most unique part of the exquisite table. Each leg was carved to resemble the trunk of an elephant, and they were curved to look like a typical elephant's trunk. There were eyes on each leg, and two genuine ivory tusks protruded from the elegant, crafted trunks. Finally, each leg had two floppy ears made of wood on each side of the elephant's head. The table embodied the true characteristics of India, and it must've taken many hours to craft this one of a kind piece. It was most definitely heavy and built to last generations. The merchant was asking $20.00 for it, and he wouldn't take any less. Felix realized that he'd be pretty broke if he bought it, but he just had to have it. Arrangements were made for the seller to meet the group at the train station the following day for their return trip to Dinjan. Felix was super excited about the purchase, and he just knew that his parents would treasure it for many years to come.

Top view of the table that Felix sent home to his parents from India. "Mother and Dad, India 1944" engraved in center.

Waking up on Easter Sunday in a faraway land was rather depressing for Felix. He read from his pocket sized Bible, and recited the Lord's prayer. Back home, Felix knew that there would be church, a fine ham with all of the fixings, and lots of family gathered together. He imagined that his mother, Viola Scott, would be wearing her favorite dress, hat, and high heels with black stockings. His father, Ernest Scott, would be wearing a suit along with his favorite tan cowboy hat. Felix's girlfriend, Elsie, was probably back home praying for his safe return. India wasn't home, but it was home for now, and he was happy that he wasn't all alone. Felix and his pals decided to go out, and enjoy time on the Brahmaputra River, which ran right along the city. They rented a boat that came complete with a local villager to pilot it. The river water was mostly brown in color due to the recent heavy rains. The experience reminded Felix of being back home fishing on the Colorado River. There were plenty of fishing poles aboard the boat. The skipper took the group to some of the best local fishing holes for them to try their luck.

The boat had been anchored about a mile upstream for about an hour, when Felix felt a big tug on his line. The tug then pulled him right up and out of his chair. Felix battled this fish for about 15 minutes, slowly reeling him in closer and closer. As the fish got closer to the boat, it began to thrash wildly, in and out of the water. Felix was enthralled with the developing situation, as he had no idea that there could be a fish of that size in the river. Again, the fish leapt high into the air, and back down into the swift moving water. This time, the weight of the big fish pulled Felix overboard. He'd been unable to grab the railing of the boat, and he ended up going head first into the river. It was quite a sight to see, and now Felix was also thrashing about, and frantically trying to get back on board. Luckily, George was able to grab Felix's fishing pole, and Ray picked up a long pole with a net in order to help Felix get back onto the boat. The skipper then yelled out, "You caught yourself a Brahmaputra bull shark, and you're lucky that you didn't get eaten by one of his buddies." Ray took a moment to snap a few pictures of Felix holding his bull shark, before he tossed it back into the river. Felix had inadvertently swallowed some of the river water, and he had banged his legs on the side of the boat during the fall. All in all, he had survived the harrowing ordeal, with quite a fish story to share with his pals, father, and grandfather back home in San Saba.

The young pilots had a nice time relaxing in the sun and fishing up and down the river. George told stories about growing up in Michigan, and Ray shared his experiences as a young man from

North Dakota. Felix was certainly happy to talk about many of his adventures from San Saba County. It was around dinner time when the men decided that they'd seen enough of the Brahmaputra River. They gathered their luggage along with all of the trinkets that they'd purchased, and it was then time to disembark from the boat. Felix and his pals then headed to the train station to meet up with the man who was to deliver the ornate table that Felix had purchased. The craftsman was patiently waiting there for the group. As agreed, Felix settled up with the man, and he also thanked him for the nice inscription that he had added to the top of the table. The fellas loaded the table onto the train, and they had just enough time to sit down before the train left the station heading back to Dinjan.

The men enjoyed a relaxing return trip on board the train to Dinjan. Felix gazed out of the windows on the railcar, looking at the people going about their day in a world so ravaged by war. Before turning in for the night, he took a few moments to write some letters to his loved ones back home. He was eager to share the experiences he'd had with his new plane, the nose art, and his sightseeing trip. This is part of what he wrote to his folks. *"Tomorrow is Easter Sunday. Just another day for us to wipe out more Japs, and help get things over with so that this time next year we can observe Easter like it should be observed. There isn't much I can say about where we are, and what we are doing…but the guy that said war is hell wasn't very far off from right. Please try not to worry about me. Personally I haven't anything to fear with God as my copilot on one of the sweetest planes ever built, the little P-51 Mustang."*

Since Felix got back late on Easter Sunday, he had to wait until the next morning to visit the APO station on base. Right after breakfast on Monday morning, Felix made the arrangements to box up the table ,and several other gifts to be sent back home to his parents and sisters. He was told that the crate would take a while to get to San Saba. Felix also mailed the letters to his family while he was there. He then added a few final thoughts for a letter to Elsie. Felix sealed the envelope, and then placed it upon an exquisite piece of handmade artwork. Her special item was framed in teak wood, and it possessed a fine grouping of silk flowers with an abundance of color. The clerk boxed everything up, and Felix then headed to the pilot briefing room.

Letter written by Felix to his sister Pauline.

During the morning briefing, Captain Edwards notified Felix and his fellow pilots that this was going to be their final week of transitional training. The pilots were very glad to hear this information. Felix was excited that they were going to be practicing longer, and more realistic combat missions, which would include aerial dog fighting exercises in their P-51s. He was eager to get up in the air, so he was the first one out of the pilot briefing room. Felix couldn't exactly run because he was wearing the backpack parachute, and he had to carry his B-4 pilot's bag. He made it to the flight line, and climbed into a P-40, ready to tackle the mission for the day. His P-51 was still over in the maintenance yard, and he was getting very anxious to see how the nose art had turned out. Felix felt a great deal of relief knowing that his training, which had lasted for more than a year, was nearly over. He felt elated, yet a bit anxious that actual combat missions were just days away.

Upon returning from his one hour training flight, Felix ran into his pal, Bucky, who told him that Bobby, over at the maintenance yard, had been looking all over the base for him. Felix surely knew what that meant, and after dropping off his things back at his barracks, he ran as fast as he could over to the maintenance yard. Felix found Bobby, and he confirmed that the nose art on his plane was now indeed finished. The pair jumped into a jeep, and they headed directly to the rear of the maintenance yard. As they got closer to the plane, Bobby asked Felix if he'd heard about the accident that had happened in his plane a few months earlier. Felix looked puzzled as he shook his head, and he told Bobby that he had no idea what he was talking about. Bobby then asked, "Didn't you sort of wonder why this was one of the planes without any nose art?" He began to explain further with, "As I was painting the nose on your plane, I realized that this was the one that was just returned to us by the 3rd Air Depot Repair Group. They recently completed some extensive repairs on your plane, and she came back to us with this brand new paint job."

Felix was listening attentively as Bobby continued on with, "Back on 14 Jan., a lieutenant colonel from this base had just returned from a combat mission with a few other P-51s. As he was "S"ing on the taxiing strip towards the dispersal area near the south end of the runway, he collided with an L-5 Sentinel that was heading out on a mail run. The P-51 dragged the L-5 for a bit until the planes came to rest in the grass. Luckily, there were no injuries, but the L-5 was totally wrecked, and there was major damage done to your plane. The left wing along with its aileron and trim tab were completely destroyed. It was ultimately a lack of vigilance while taxiing on the part of the lieutenant colonel, but the tower had some responsibility for failing to notify the flight of P-51s that the L-5 was taxiing in their direction." Feeling dumbstruck, Felix rubbed his chin for a moment, and said, "It looks like they got her all patched up though, eh? Do you think that she's safe to fly?" Bobby reluctantly replied, "They did a great job, and the plane looks as good as ever. However, who really knows? She's only been up in the air a few times since returning to us here in Dinjan." Felix began to have an unsettling feeling in his stomach, but he chose to focus on the fabulous nose art that he was about to see.

The jeep pulled up right next to the plane, and Felix got out, trembling with excitement. He stood with his hands on his hips, and shook his head in amazement while gazing at the beautiful artwork. He was awestruck to see that his nut bomb concept had come to life. Adorning both sides of the nose, there was now a big pecan with a tail on the back, resembling a 500 pound bomb. Felix was feeling a bit homesick as he stared at the "Spirit of San Saba," the slogan located right above the pecan bomb. He thanked Bobby for a job well done, and they settled up on the finances. He left by giving Bobby a high five and a handshake. Felix maneuvered his P-51A back to the flight line by slowly weaving back and forth in a pattern resembling an "S." He then sat outside of his plane, admiring the nose art for the next hour or so until it was time to take off for the second flight that was planned that day.

Tuesday, 11 Apr. 1944, was a pretty chill day for Felix. He couldn't fly that day due to weather related issues. Felix decided to find a comfortable spot where he could just relax, and wait for the scattered rainstorms to stop. There was plenty to do on the base to keep busy, but the morale among the men was rather gloomy due to the lack of interactions with the Japanese. He decided that it would be a terrific opportunity to write some more letters to his loved ones back home. In part, one letter went like this.

Dear folks,   *11 Apr. 1944*

When the package I sent as I passed through Karachi gets there, take the table cloth with the peacocks on it, fill up the fruit bowl with the elephants holding it up and the two crows looking on. Then think of the Old Crow and me.

Most of the Burma country is pretty rough looking stuff boy! I'd sure hate to go down in there. A guy kinda mutters a prayer to the effect for that old prop to keep spinning. I'm not any too anxious for a meeting with any Japs on the ground. So far, so good. Just don't ever worry about me because I'm gonna be o.k.

If you can get any chocolate bars, you know where to send 'em.

                                                   Love,

                                                   Felix

The evening of 12 Apr. 1944 was typical in many ways, but it seemed to feel extra special to Felix for some reason. He had returned safely from a two hour flight earlier that day, which had by far been the most exhilarating yet. He was having the time of his life in the barracks with his buddies playing checkers, cribbage, and, of course, poker. They played hand over hand of Texas hold 'em. Felix felt that he was more lucky than skilled at playing poker, but he certainly enjoyed the thrill of winning. After Ray had won everyone's money, the group headed outside to shoot marbles before it got too dark to see. Felix was a skilled marble shooter, and he enjoyed taking advantage of his less talented squadron mates. Shooting marbles took a keen eye, and it required excellent hand eye coordination, which also helped to make Felix a great pilot. The sunset looked so brilliant, and it was a nice way to wind down the evening. Downtime during wartime didn't come too frequently, so the time spent with friends was always cherished. After the sun had finally set, the men returned back inside for a few rounds of Canadian Club whiskey. Before turning in for bed, Felix read a letter that he had received from his sister Pauline. Felix called her Polly, and he loved getting care packages from her. She had sent him a few Hawk Shaw comic strips, magazines, some family pictures, candy bars, and a bag of shelled pecans from their own trees there in San Saba.

It was Thursday, 13 Apr. 1944, and the day started out just as ordinarily as all of the other days that Felix had spent in India. However, in war, is there really such a thing as an ordinary day? Felix knew that soldiers were dying while fighting in combat, and many pilots had encountered the same fate while flying their combat missions. All throughout his training, his flight instructors had reminded him that there was always a chance that he wouldn't return home from war. Felix was undeterred, and he was going to do his very best to buck that trend. He was glad to be a pilot, and to serve his country. He was living out his boyhood dream, and he knew that his family was proud of him back home.

Felix had awoken earlier than usual that morning. He was restless and anxious about the training schedule for the day, and he was the first one to get seated in the pilot briefing room. He was eager to hear the plan for the morning flight, and figured that there was going to be plenty of dog fighting, advanced acrobatics, and maybe even some practice at the bombing range. For some reason, Felix suddenly began to feel apprehensive about the training schedule for the day, but he knew he had to persevere in order to get one step closer to an actual combat mission.

The pilot briefing room was a bit more crowded on this particular day, and the pilots were informed that there would be eight ships on this flight. Felix was thrilled to hear that news, since he loved flying in large formations. (From the earliest days of flight, most folks referred to planes as airships. Over the years, pilots kept the lingo for the most part, but they began to refer to their planes as ships instead.)

The time was about 0600 hours as Felix and his pals walked out to the flight line. The pilots were all wearing tan slacks, white t-shirts, and tan long sleeve shirts. Most of the group had rolled up their sleeves, since it was already getting humid and muggy outside. Their leather flight caps were fitted snuggly on their heads, and their goggles sat squarely on top of their caps. Captain Edwards planned for their takeoff to be at 0645 hours, and the flight was scheduled to last about an hour and a half.

The wind speed was three to five miles per hour out of the South, and the weather was CAVU. In military terms, this meant that the ceiling and visibility was unlimited. Felix thought to himself that it was finally a nice day to fly. The whining and hissing of the other planes already in the sky that morning made it hard to hear one another. He gave a high five to all of his fellow aviators, and they patted each other on the back. They wished each other good luck for the mission, and quickly made plans for what they'd do for dinner when they returned. Once Felix got to his plane, he admired the seven other P-51As lined up in a row. It was quite an awesome sight to see such air power and military might. To be involved in a flight with this group was so thrilling for Felix. He began his pre-flight check of the aircraft, as did the other pilots. Captain Edwards did the same check of his plane, while keeping an eye on the others to ensure compliance.

Felix first inspected the tires to make sure that they were properly inflated for takeoff and landing. Next, he checked the landing gear to ensure that it was structurally sound. He then checked that the gas and oil caps were properly closed. Finally, he inspected the covers on the gun hatches to be sure that they were securely fastened. The pilots had all been taught to approach the plane from the front, and to then go around it in a clockwise motion so that he'd end up at the left wing ready to climb into the cockpit. Felix had his backpack parachute on, and he checked all of the straps to be sure that they fit snuggly. He proceeded to have a seat in the somewhat cramped cockpit. Luckily for Felix, he was neither a tall nor heavy set man, so his slender body fit like a glove within the cockpit.

Once on board, there was a rather lengthy checklist of things to review to ensure that the aircraft was ready for takeoff. He first checked that the ignition switch was in the OFF position. Felix pulled form 1-A from its case to check that the plane had been released for flight. He ensured that the maintenance crew had serviced it with gas, oil, and coolant before initialing the form. Felix then looked at the fuel and oil gauges, and he also positioned the flap handles to an UP position. After positioning the propeller control full forward to

INCREASE, Felix ensured that the throttle was open to the START position. He checked that the bomb and rocket switches were OFF. Next on the list, he ensured that the alternator was showing ZERO, and he also made sure the gyro instruments were operational. After setting the parking brakes, the supercharger was set to AUTO, and Felix then selected the fuel shut off valve to ON. He was now ready to select the ignition switch to BOTH, and the battery and generator switches were selected to ON. Finally, he primed the engine for a brief second, and then held the switch at START.

As he looked over to his right and then to his left, Felix could hear the engines roaring, and he felt the combined power of all the nearby Mustangs. Captain Edwards was the flight officer, and Felix was the number two man in his flight. He was proud to be in the number two slot, which was a coveted assignment among the pilots. The other wingmen were his buddy, Ray Simon, and one other experienced pilot named Tom Mahoney. The second flight was led by Captain Ferguson, and he had two replacement pilots along with one seasoned pilot. At Captain Edward's command, the P-51s raced down the runway there at Dinjan, taking off one right after another at 0645 hours.

The eight ship flight flew over the Brahmaputra River, and they headed west until they reached the mountainous Pakke Tiger Reserve. Captain Edwards then led the ships in a line abreast formation over the Sakteng Wildlife Sanctuary before proceeding east along the mountains near the Chinese border. The final leg of the mission involved making simulated bombing and strafing passes over the range at Majiali Chapori (a.k.a Lali Chapori). The range was located near a small village in the middle of the Brahmaputra River, which was about 24 miles to the north of Dinjan. The men in both flights made repeated passes over the targets until Captain Edwards was satisfied with their efforts.

On the way back to Dinjan, Captain Edwards directed the men to climb above 4500 feet. Captain Edwards maneuvered the flight into a right echelon formation, and he then peeled off to begin the acrobatics practice. Each ship performed two slow rolls in trail formation, and then Captain Edwards performed an Immelmann turn from about 4500 feet. This maneuver was named after Max Immelmann, a German Ace from World War I. Essentially, this move starts with the pilot flying level into the wind. Next, the pilot begins a loop, and at the top of the loop while inverted, he rolls the aircraft left or right until upright to continue flying straight in the opposite direction. After successfully completing his Immelmann turn, Captain Edwards ascended to about 6500 feet to oversee the other pilots while they performed the same maneuver. He then directed Felix to move into position to begin his Immelmann turn.

Second Lieutenant Felix E. Scott, callsign "Scotty," acknowledged the order over his radio headset. "Roger that," crackled over the radio as Felix proceeded into the loop to begin his Immelmann turn. At the top of the loop, where Felix was now inverted, he quickly became disoriented. With a speed of about 300 mph, he somehow overcorrected, thrusting his plane into a right spin. He momentarily brought his ship out of the spin, but further overcorrection then caused him to fall into a secondary left spin. As Felix was spinning out of control, his life began to flash before his eyes. He saw his mother holding his cowboy hat as he left for war, he saw his father working on his truck with him back in the shop, he saw his sisters in their bright colored dresses enjoying life with no worries, and he feared that he might never hold Elsie in his arms again. Within seconds, Felix realized that he was losing control of the aircraft, and he radioed out, "Mayday, Mayday, Mayday." Felix was now dizzy from all of the spinning, and he had completely lost his bearings. He was being tossed around the cockpit with his head banging against the glass canopy as he tried to regain control of the aircraft. He couldn't find the emergency release handle, what with the ongoing struggle that was ensuing within the cockpit. Felix disconnected his radio headset and oxygen hose while preparing to eject as he continued to try and recover from the uncontrolled left spin. He couldn't figure out how to eject quickly enough with all of the twisting, turning, and just from being plum scared. At that point, he might even have blacked out. His altitude had quickly fallen below 1000 feet, and within a second or two he crashed into the rocks along the Brahmaputra River.

Felix went down in a rocky area near the river, which was about two miles downstream from Kobo. It was a very peaceful and remote area nestled among a collection of small rolling hills with lush green foliage. Second Lieutenant Scott was killed instantly, and there now lay in the smoldering ruins, Felix's newly minted P-51A's fuselage, adorned with the burnt and mangled image of Felix's pecan bomb nose art, all completely demolished. Just like that, his life was lost, his candle had been blown out, and the curtain had fallen on Second Lieutenant Felix E. Scott.

Captain Edwards circled the crash site a few times after having observed the whole thing from his position above. He saw some smoke rising from the bigger pieces of the aircraft, but there were parts strewn everywhere. He didn't see any sign of a parachute, nor did he see any sign of life. Captain Edwards then radioed the coordinates back to the base before leading the remaining ships in the flight back to Dinjan. Of course, there was an investigation since a life and a plane were both lost in the accident. The Aircraft Accident Investigation Committee found that Second Lieutenant Scott was "To a major degree responsible for the accident due to very poor technique in an attempted spin recovery. This is brought out by the fact that

Lieutenant Scott broke his spin to the right, but over controlled to the extent that a spin to the left resulted, which proved fatal." The board also found that Captain Edwards be held partially responsible for leading his flight in acrobatics under the required minimum altitude of 5000 feet.

Felix had been a new replacement pilot there in India, and now he was needing to be replaced. He had just recently completed his operational training unit (OTU) training program in fighter type aircraft, and he had nearly completed his transitional training for operating the P-51A. However, he was still a relatively new pilot in a new type of aircraft. The military blamed Felix for the crash, and his fellow pilots were left scratching their heads wondering, was it just bad luck, bad timing, mechanical failure or a less than thorough training program with the new plane? His best friend Ray was left speculating what could've gone wrong with Felix's final flight. Was he not able to orient himself to the ground objective that he had chosen before beginning his Immelmann, did he not have enough speed as he made his climb, or did he fail to maintain horizontal and level flight during the half roll near the end of his maneuver? Either way, they had all lost a dear friend and fellow aviator. Felix probably would've blamed himself more than anything else for the crash. His family was left wondering what had really happened, and who was ultimately to blame? Elsie was left broken-hearted, and she couldn't help but think what could've been had Felix returned to her safe and sound.

CHAPTER 2

Burials Abroad

Ray felt miserable as he returned to the barracks following the crash. He was heartbroken to find that men were already beginning to pack up Felix's belongings into a footlocker. Ray insisted that he be the one to finish packing up all of Felix's things. Their pal, George, said to Ray, "What happened out there?" Ray replied, "We were just doing our routine Immelmann turns. Somehow, Felix began to struggle with regaining his proper positioning after being inverted, and then he just spun in. One moment, he was there to my left, and now he's never coming back." After Ray had finished packing the footlocker, he took it over to the APO office so that it could be sent home to the Scott family in San Saba, Texas. The clerk advised Ray that he'd wait for the bag that contained all of Felix's personal effects from the accident before he'd ship the footlocker back to the United States.

As Captain Edwards exited his plane after landing with the other six ships, many things were already in motion pertaining to Felix's crash. He immediately worked with the field recovery team to ensure that they had the proper coordinates for the crash site. It was determined that the crash site would need to be accessed by boat, followed by a hike to get to the debris field. After loading some supplies and equipment onto a truck, the recovery team quickly left the base. Once the boat arrived near the crash site, the recovery team was met by some local villagers, who were eager to help lead the way to retrieve Felix's remains.

The villagers provided donkeys and carts to assist in the excursion to the crash site. Felix's plane had crashed at a high rate of speed, causing wreckage to be strewn about the area. As the group got closer to the point of impact, they could see that a horrific accident had taken place. It took the crew more than an hour to access, and pull Felix's remains from the charred wreckage. There were thick pieces of the fuselage and wings protruding from the rather shallow river. His body was intact, but there were obvious signs that he had died a traumatic death. There were severe burns to the extremities and to his entire upper torso. The recovery team ensured that Felix's dog tags were still around his neck, and they worked diligently to secure his personal effects. They had noticed something shiny on the chain next to his dog tags. Upon a closer look, they saw that it was a simple gold ring, and not big by any means. Felix's sterling silver pilot wings were still attached to his shirt. The crew took care in unfastening the somewhat charred piece from his shirt. They then checked the pocket on his shirt to find a tattered picture of a good looking woman. On the back of the picture, the crew could only read, "To Felix, with love, El." The men wondered what her name was, but they couldn't quite make it out due to the fire damage on the picture. Felix's broken watch, his wallet, and his United States Army Air Forces (USAAF) bracelet also went into his personal effects bag. The bag was sealed and attached to the stretcher. The crew then placed the stretcher onto a cart, and secured it properly before beginning the return trip to the boat for transport back to Dinjan.

The recovery team made their way back down the Brahmaputra River by boat. After rounding the southwest tip of the Dibru-Saikhowa National Park, their return trip ended once they arrived at the village of Miri Gaon. As the boat pulled closer to the shoreline, the team could see a deuce and a half truck, along with its crew standing nearby.

One of the soldiers was waving an American flag that was attached to a six foot tall wooden pole. The other two crew members were standing straight as an arrow, while saluting the incoming boat as it carried the flag draped stretcher of Second Lieutenant Scott. Great care was taken as Felix's body was loaded onto the large truck. The crew then rumbled along until they reached Dinjan Road, which took them right past the Dinjan Air Field. Their journey ended when they reached the Panitola American Military Cemetery.

At the cemetery, the official action of burying a fallen soldier had begun. Positive identification was made by the base mortician. The official "report of death" paperwork was completed and sent to the Adjutant General's office, which was located in Washington, D.C. Felix's cause of death was officially labeled as "death by airplane accident," and marked as "died non battle" (DNB). His body was then cleaned, and wrapped snuggly using a shelter half blanket. The blanket was made of cotton, measured about 7 feet long and 5 feet wide, and it had a greenish-brown color to it. Rope was used near his shoulders and also near his ankles to keep his body wrapped securely inside the blanket. Felix's body was then placed into a simple wooden coffin and sealed. Shortly afterwards, a group of soldiers came into the building where the coffin was located, and began to carry his remains over to plot O-10. A chaplain wearing a white cassock, along with a red tippet, led the procession to the gravesite. Felix's coffin was then placed upon a bier next to the grave. Nobody would have imagined it at the time, but this was going to be first of several burials for Felix E. Scott.

There in India, it was around 1600 hours local time on 13 Apr. 1944. It hadn't even been 10 hours since Felix had died, but his funeral was about to commence. The military wasn't messing around with waiting to bury him. With the humidity and warm temperatures, it made sense to take care of the burial as soon as possible, since there were no morgue freezers on base.

A small crowd had arrived from the base at Dinjan. Captain Edwards, his pals George and Ray, and about 20 other servicemen came to attend the ceremonial burial for Felix. He deserved a funeral with military honors, and that is what he got. Considering the location, and the fact that no family members were present, the service was going to be rather low-key. The chaplain read passages from the Bible, and his buddies each took a few moments to talk about what Felix had meant to them. All the while that this was going on, an honor guard stood at attention with three men on each side of his coffin. The honor guard was a mixed bag of servicemen from the base. Some were wearing shorts while others were wearing pants. The men were not formally dressed, but they showed their respect, nevertheless.

About 30 yards away, and off to the left of the gravesite, there were seven service members holding M-1 rifles at their side. They were uniformly dressed in tan shorts with belts, and they wore light colored long sleeve shirts with neatly rolled up sleeves. The men all wore the same style hat, and they had knee high socks with black shoes. All of a sudden, their rifles were pointed towards the sky, and each soldier fired three shots in unison over the casket. The momentary silence ceased when a bugler was heard playing taps, while everyone stood at attention. The honor guard then raised the flag off the coffin. They held it tight for a few moments before beginning the process to fold it up. Since there were no family members to present the flag to, it was taken back to the base to be used again at a future funeral for another fallen soldier. Just like that, the service concluded, and the six members of the honor guard lowered Felix's coffin into the ground to a depth of five feet. Each grave was uniformly spaced four feet apart from one another.

The cemetery crew made quick work to cover the coffin with the dirt which was neatly piled off to the side. A concrete cross was placed firmly into the ground, and a metal nameplate was then affixed to it. The nameplate read "Second Lieutenant Felix E. Scott," and it listed his serial number and date of death. One of his id tags was buried in a bottle at the head of the casket near the marker. The other id tag was buried with Felix's body inside the coffin. As the sun began to set, this episode in the life of Felix E. Scott was coming to an end, but his story was far from being over. By 1700 hours local time, all was wrapped up at the cemetery. However, 13 Apr. was just beginning back in San Saba, Texas.

It was 0530 hours in San Saba, and the sun was just beginning to rise up and over the house where Ernest and Viola Scott lived on South Live Oak Street. Viola had awakened during the night, and she just couldn't go back to sleep. She went out to the front porch to try and find anything that would calm her, but the restlessness wouldn't stop. Ernest had come out to check on Viola, finding her on the front porch clutching her Bible. As he approached her sitting in her chair, he could see pieces of her broken coffee cup smashed among the unforgiving concrete floor. Ernest asked, "What happened here?" Viola replied, "I heard what sounded like gunshots, and it startled me. I must've dropped my cup, and I didn't even realize it." Ernest then asked, "What's wrong?" Viola lifted her head up, and turned towards him, and said, "Our Felix is gone." Ernest was confused, and he asked, "How do you know? Did someone come by and give you the news?" Viola started sobbing as her head dropped back down. She simply said, "A mother just knows." Ernest reached for her hand, and he helped her back into the house. He then poured her a fresh cup of coffee, and he offered to fix her some breakfast.

Felix's parents should've woken up on 13 Apr. 1944 to a peaceful morning, and to a day filled with joy, happiness, and time spent with family. It was supposed to be a very special day for Ernest and Viola since it was their actual 31st wedding anniversary. It was also the seventh wedding anniversary for their eldest daughter, Johnnie Mae, and her husband, AJ Blanton. There was a big celebration supper planned at AJ's sister Wynona Lewis's home in Cherokee, with everyone in the family attending. Viola, however, was just not in the right frame of mind to celebrate. The sinking feeling in her stomach told her that something terrible had happened to her only son, but she didn't know what, and she didn't know whom she could ask. This was 1944, and there was no FaceTime, no cell phones, no texting, no internet, and no way to get ahold of anyone in the military who'd know. The United States was at war, and a great deal of soldiers were dying in many parts of the world every day. The War Department did its best to try and notify families as soon as possible if a soldier went missing, or if he had been killed in action. However, it could still take many days, and perhaps even a few weeks before a family would hear the bad news about a loved one.

Ernest poured Viola another cup of coffee as she sat at the kitchen table staring out the window. Viola was always the talkative one, and for her to be speechless and motionless was an odd sight for sure. Outside, the weather was nice, and there wasn't a cloud in the sky for the eye to see. Inside the house, it was eerily quiet since the Scotts lived by themselves at that time. Ernest sat down beside Viola at the table, and he offered her some scrambled eggs for which she refused. Her Easter lilies were still in bloom, and Viola had combined a few with some freshly picked Texas Blue Bonnets in a simple glass vase. The vase sat squarely in the center of the kitchen table, and it had two small American flags protruding from the center. Viola was a proud soldier's momma, and Felix's entire family was certainly patriotic. She sat stoically at the table clutching a framed picture of Felix dressed in his military uniform. Ernest could tell that Viola was busy reciting prayer verses in her head as she continued to rub a small wooden cross that hung in the kitchen. It's safe to say that a mother worries all of the time about a son fighting during war in a faraway land. Call that normal, but call it mother's intuition when something is wrong.

Unable to get much change in Viola's demeanor, Ernest called his daughter Johnnie Mae to let her know what was going on. He asked if she could come over to try and cheer Viola up. Johnnie Mae advised that she'd be happy to come by. She told her father that she'd grab her sister Pauline, the Scott's second oldest daughter, on the way over. Ernest then made a call to Viola's eldest sister Jessie, who lived in Bend, a little country community about 20 miles away. Jessie said of course she'd come, but she'd first go pick up another one of their sisters, Betsy, who also lived in Bend. Both of them lived on farms, and probably had many chores to do, but if their sister Viola was needing them, they'd get there as fast as they could.

Once everyone had arrived, the house started to fill with conversation, and even some laughter. After a short while, Viola began to respond to her family members' attempts at conversation. However, it was clearly evident that she was still not her usual self. Everyone sat out on the front porch, and congratulatory hugs were shared to wish Viola and Johnnie Mae a happy wedding anniversary. Everyone tried to reassure Viola that if something terrible had happened, she would've been notified via telegram. As her family members enjoyed themselves, Viola kept an eye fixed upon South Live Oak Street, hoping that a Western Union driver wouldn't venture down her street. She did her best to remain optimistic, and she put on a good face for her family. Viola finally agreed with everyone that the celebratory dinner would be postponed until Sunday after church. Most folks in Texas refer to the noon meal as dinner, rather than lunch, and the evening meal is typically referred to as supper. The family began to leave before dinner time since they could tell Viola was in no mood to partake in any further festivities.

Friday and Saturday came and went, and there was no word from Felix, or about Felix. Viola and Ernest were glad that there was no visit from the Western Union guy either. Viola was starting to feel better about the situation. She even began to doubt that the event that had violently awakened her just a few days back was related to Felix in any way. When describing the experience, she felt that it was as if someone had dropped a huge boulder on her chest along with the feeling that she was drowning. Viola got out of bed early that Sunday morning to get breakfast started, and she even completed a few mundane chores around the house. She wanted to be sure she had enough time to get dolled up in her Sunday best.

It was supposed to be a fabulous day for Viola on 16 Apr., since she loved going to church and spending time with her family. After church, Ernest and Viola drove south to the little town of Cherokee, which was about 16 miles away. Mr. John Lewis and his wife Wynona were hosting the big wedding anniversary get together. Johnnie Mae brought her husband AJ Blanton and their little boy, Felix Wayne, along with her sister Pauline, and her husband, Ted Burnham, were also coming for dinner from San Saba. Their younger sister, Aletha, couldn't come since she was studying for exams at King's Daughter's Hospital nursing school in Temple, Texas.

The Blantons, the Burnhams, and the Scotts all arrived at the Lewis home at about the same time. If there was one thing that this family wasn't late for, it was for a Sunday dinner. As they walked in the front door, the smell of fried chicken and fresh biscuits filled the air. The time was about 11:30 a.m. as they sat down at the table for the blessing.

All of a sudden, the Lewis's dog, Dynamite, started barking up a storm out in the front yard. Mr. Lewis got up from the table, and he went to the front window, and saw a black Ford Coupe parked out front that had a Western Union sign on the door. Wynona said to John, "Who is it?" John replied, "It's the telegram guy, and he's walking towards our front door." When Viola heard that, she dropped her fork, and her heart started to sink all over again. She reached for Ernest's hand as John approached the front door. Why should she worry though? This wasn't her house, and how would they think to find her at the Lewis home? Nevertheless, Viola was anxious about what the man had to say.

Mr. Lewis opened the front door just as the man started to knock. The man said, "I was over at the home of Ernest Scott, and I was told that he wasn't home. Their neighbor, Dixie Jackson, was outside, and she told me where I might be able to find him. I have an important telegram for Mr. Scott." By this point, Ernest was walking to the door with Viola. He was clutching her arm to support her as she was already trembling. Ernest got to the door, and said, "I'm Ernest Scott, and this here is my wife, Viola." The man handed Ernest a slip of paper for them to read that would change their lives forever. As Ernest looked at the telegram, his mind ran wild, and he was only interpreting a few of the key words. While reading each informative word, it felt as if he was getting punched from the left and the right over and over again. Viola could hear him read the telegram out loud, and she began to cry uncontrollably. Some of the key words that Ernest spoke included, "Secretary of War," "deep sympathy," "loss of your son Felix," "killed in action," "04/13/44," and "plane crash." Viola's knees buckled, and she slumped to the ground. She repeatedly screamed, "Felix, my son, not my Felix!" Mr. Lewis thanked the man for coming and closed the door. Johnnie Mae, Pauline, and Wynona all tried to console Viola, but how can one really help the inconsolable?

Clearly, the dinner celebration was over before it had really begun. Ernest thanked John and Wynona for their hospitality, and he let them know that he needed to take Viola home. Johnnie Mae asked John if she could use their phone to notify Betsy and Jessie of the news. Ernest headed for home, and Johnnie Mae wasn't that far behind after conveying the bad news to her aunts. Back at home, Ernest was able to locate the phone number for the dormitory where Aletha was staying. The news hit her hard, as anyone could expect, and she told her father that she'd get home as soon as she could. Ernest was able to check on Viola in their bedroom, and she was still crying uncontrollably. He then reached out to Viola's sisters, Vada and Veo. They also said that they'd get to San Saba just as soon as they could, since they lived in other cities within Texas. Before long, the whole family, and much of San Saba, had heard of Felix's death.

Viola had spent the rest of that Sunday and most of Monday in bed, trying to convince herself that somehow this was all some sort of a bad dream. Before supper on 17 Apr., Viola hopped out of bed when she realized that someone needed to tell Elsie. She went directly to the kitchen to ask Ernest if he had called Elsie to share the horrific news with her. He said, "Darling, I haven't reached out to her yet. I didn't want to disturb you, nor did I know where you kept that list of addresses and phone numbers for the folks whom Felix wanted you to contact in the event of his death."

Still overcome by Felix's death, Viola somehow had to come up with the strength to reach out to Elsie. She considered writing a letter, but she felt that Felix would think that to be too impersonal. Viola retrieved Elsie's phone number from the address book she kept in the telephone table drawer, that was located by their front living room window. She mustered up the strength, and initiated the call just after 7:30 p.m. Viola was hoping that Elsie would be home from work out there in California, and that she'd be able to answer the phone. She wasn't sure exactly what to say to Elsie, but she figured that she'd speak from her heart, and she hoped that it would be coherent.

Elsie answered the phone with her typical cheerful personality, not knowing what was about to hit her. Viola then said, "Good evening Elsie, this is Viola Scott." Before she could continue, Elsie quickly replied, "Oh hello, Mrs. Scott. It's so nice to hear from you. Felix had written to tell me that you had helped him order this very nice dress and fine pair of shoes for my birthday. The package arrived on Saturday, which was perfect, since that was my actual birthday. I got a very nice card and a wonderful letter from him on Friday." Finally, Viola took the brief moment of silence to say, "Elsie dear, I hope you had a wonderful birthday. You are such a sweet thing, and I'm so sorry to share this very sad news with you. Just yesterday, we were notified that Felix was killed in a plane crash on Thursday. We don't really have any details yet, but I wanted to let you know, just as soon as I could." There was an awkward silence, followed by Elsie crying uncontrollably and struggling to speak clearly. Elsie's tone and perky demeanor quickly changed when she said, "Is he really gone? Is my Felix really dead?" Having had nearly the same reaction the day prior, Viola replied, "We found out he had died after we got a telegram informing us of his death. I truly wish that this was all a big mistake, but sadly, my heart tells me that he's gone." It seemed that Elsie was now being consoled by her parents. Elsie was still crying when she said, "Thank you for letting me know, Mrs. Scott. This isn't what I had expected to happen, and I don't know where I'm going to go from here. Please let me know if you ever hear anything more." Viola closed with, "Felix truly loved you, Elsie, with all of his heart. You're a very special young lady, and he was very lucky to have known you. I'll let you know more if we learn anything new. Goodbye, dear." With that,

Viola disconnected the call, and she once again returned to bed to continue crying until she fell asleep.

As the next few weeks went by, Viola took comfort in reading her Bible, her family, and by listening to music. She really enjoyed listening to "Bringing in the Sheaves," "Shall We Gather at the River," and "What a Friend We Have in Jesus." Viola recalled the good times that they had when Felix had sung a parody on the hymn, "At the Cross," that was written in 1916 by Mrs. Mary Hudson. The parody itself, "At the Bar," was written by Austin and Alta Fife for a character in their book called Heaven on Horseback. Viola certainly cracked a smile or two when remembering Felix loudly singing the parody, with Ernest laughing and singing along with him, while playing the piano. While at the local Five-and-Dime store one day, Ernest purchased a record with the song, "We'll Meet Again," by Vera Lynn. Viola had no idea when she'd meet her son again, but she figured that she'd find Felix singing and dancing with the Lord when the time came.

The horrible month of April 1944 had finally ended. The grief stricken Scott family was left with a dilemma. How could they have a proper funeral for their son when they had no body? Would the remains of their son ever be sent home? Would it be soon, years, or never? These were all good questions that made the next steps in planning some sort of a memorial service difficult. Ultimately, a decision was made to have a memorial service for Felix on Sunday, 14 May 1944. That day happened to be Mother's Day, and it was to be held at the Bend Methodist Church. However, as time got closer to 14 May, the memorial service was postponed indefinitely. Some would ask, why was it postponed? Was it because the family was just not emotionally ready to handle it? Were they still holding out hope that this was all a big mistake, and that Felix would let everyone know he was alive and well?

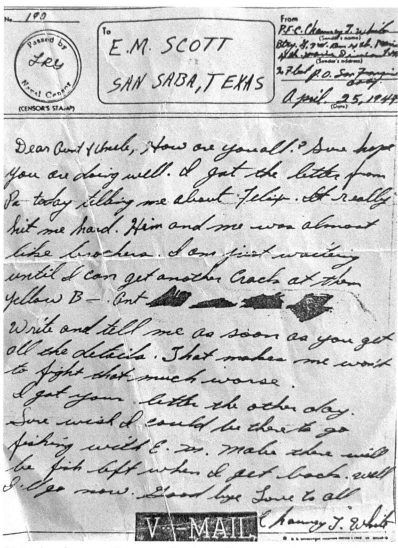

A letter from Chauncey White, one of Felix's favorite cousins, to Ernest and Viola Scott.

A clipping from The San Saba News *regarding Felix's death.*

Ernest made his usual daily trip to the post office there in San Saba on 15 May 1944. He pulled the mail out of his PO Box and proceeded to leave. The postal clerk spotted Ernest, and he whistled for him to come over to the counter. The clerk mentioned that a large box had arrived, and it was addressed to Felix. Ernest was unsure exactly what to think. He had just recently received a large box containing the carved wooden table and other goodies from Felix. As the clerk wheeled the box around the corner on a dolly, Ernest became quite despondent when he saw that the box appeared to be Felix's footlocker. He noticed that the footlocker had been sent by Lieutenant Ray Simon. Ernest recognized Ray's name, as he had met him at Luke Field when Felix had earned his wings. He also knew that Ray was Felix's roommate there in India. Ernest figured that Felix's clothes, belongings, and other personal effects were probably packed within the walls of the wooden box. The men loaded the box into Ernest's car, and he headed for home.

The Scotts sat staring at the box for about an hour or so as it lay in front of them on their living room floor. The slight breeze outside caused the wind chimes to clang about on their front porch. The sound was soothing and peaceful as they debated who would make the first move upon the footlocker. They weren't all that eager to go through its contents, but they decided that they needed closure. Ernest proceeded to cut the lock, and he lifted the lid to find the box to be nearly full of items. Viola began to pull out the items, and she then handed them to Ernest after inspecting each piece carefully. She pulled out Felix's flight jacket and held it to her nose. She began to cry as she could smell the faint scent of her only son. Next came his military uniform and various articles of clothing. She placed her fingers upon the silver wings, which were still firmly attached to his service coat. Viola then pulled out his camera, an assortment of books, magazines, and his bag of marbles. Finally, there at the bottom of the trunk was his personal effects bag. Ernest and Viola looked at one another wondering who was going to be the one to open it. Viola ended up opening the bag to find his broken watch. The crystal was cracked, and the time had stopped at 7:53. At last, she now knew when he had presumably crashed. She handed Felix's wallet to Ernest, and he found some American and Indian currency tucked neatly inside. After they found and began looking through his flight log, they remembered how proud he was to have recorded each of his missions within the pages of this book. The tears began rolling down Viola's face again when she spotted the chain with her golden wedding ring still attached to it. Viola was sure glad to get her ring back, but not under this set of circumstances. When she found the burned and tattered picture of Elsie, she just knew that she'd have to mail it off to her. The picture, and also the blackened pair of pilot's wings that would've been attached to his shirt, were both painful mementos of Felix's untimely death. The bag was now empty, and there was no sign of Felix's Aggie ring. They both knew that Felix treasured the ring, and he would've proudly worn it at all times. The inventory of effects form mentioned just one gold ring. The Scotts were left to wonder what on earth could've become of his Aggie ring. Was it taken by the villagers who had first found his body? Did someone on the recovery team steal it? Was he possibly buried with it there in India? Regrettably, the Scotts would probably never know where Felix's Aggie ring ended up. However, the priceless things that they did have were with Felix at the time of his crash, and Viola vowed to keep them safe. Ernest moved the trunk to his workshop, and Viola proceeded to place some of the items into a cedar chest that was located in what had been Felix's bedroom.

Actual footlocker used to send Felix's effects home from India. Currently on display at the San Saba County Historical Museum in San Saba, Texas.

Just when things seemed to return to some sort of normalcy for the Scott family, another tragedy struck. Viola's sister, Vada White, had a son named Chauncey White. Chauncey was sent off to the Mariana Islands in the South Pacific to fight for his country as a private in the United States Marine Corps. It was July of 1944, after the Battle of Saipan, fighting the Japanese, that Vada and Lynn White received a telegram advising them that their son, Chauncey, was missing in action. What does a parent do when they are told that their son is listed as missing in action? A subsequent letter received from the War Department in August of 1944, confirmed that he had been killed in action on 10 Jul. 1944, while battling for the island of Saipan. Viola was still devastated over the loss of Felix, and she was now having to deal with the loss of her nephew, Chauncey. Felix and Chauncey had always lived in or near San Saba or Bend, and they were inseparable as they grew up together.

Two Grandsons Killed Overseas

BEND, Dec. 18 (Spl.).—Two grandsons of Mr. and Mrs. W. J. Millican were killed overseas this year.

Marine Pvt. Chauncey T. White, son of Mr. and Mrs. Lynn White of Georgetown, was mortally wounded in action on Saipan last July 15.

Second Lt. Felix Ernest Scott, son of Mr. and Mrs. E. M. Scott of San Saba, a Mustang fighter pilon based in India, was killed in a plane crash on April 13, the wedding anniversary of his parents.

White was reared by his grandparents and associated with his grandfather, former president of the Texas Pecan Growers Association, in operating his River Bend farm.

Clipping from The San Saba News.

Chauncey was about four years younger than Felix, and their birthdays were pretty close together every May. The term Gold Star Family refers to the immediate family of a fallen service member who died while serving in a time of conflict. Unfortunately, Vada now had to join her sister, Viola, in being a Gold Star mother. Her son Chauncey's burial circumstances, in a faraway land, and being very similar to Viola's son Felix's, had both Viola and Vada guessing when, or if, their son's remains would ever be returned home.

Vada and Viola would talk to each other at least once a week on the phone, and they'd gather as a family about once a month. They had come up with a plan to have a memorial service to honor both Felix and Chauncey at the same time. Although neither one of their bodies had been sent home, the families felt that it was time, and fitting, to memorialize them. The date had been set for Sunday, 29 Oct. 1944, and the service was to be held at the Bend United Methodist Church at 3:00 p.m. Viola had already notified all of the people on the list that Felix had given to her in the event of his death. However, she decided to write letters to everyone who lived relatively close by, notifying them of the upcoming memorial service. She even sent one to Elsie, who lived in California. Although none of Felix's former girlfriends showed up, Viola was glad that many of his friends were able to come.

Bend was just about a one hour drive to the southeast of San Saba. The Bend Methodist Church sat at the bottom of a small hill, with the Bend cemetery located on the knoll above. The church was white with rectangular windows on each side of the building, adjacent to the main entry door. A small wood burning stove sat in the corner near the door, and it was fired up that day in order to keep everyone warm. All of the pews in the small country church were full as the memorial service was just about to begin. Folks filled in where they could find a place to stand, and, as expected, there were many friends and members of the family in attendance. Even though it was a bit chilly that day, the windows in the church were pushed up so that the folks attending outside the church could hear some of what was going on inside.

The church itself was built around 1910, and it had been the setting for many sad and joyous occasions in the lives of Ernest and Viola and their extended families. Many weddings, baptisms, and, unfortunately, funerals had taken place there. It wasn't a big church by any means, but the guests at the memorial service sure could feel the love and warmth radiating within for two of San Saba County's finest young men. There was an 11" X 14" framed picture of each fallen soldier placed near the altar. There was an abundance of flowers spread neatly across the entire area in front of the first row of pews. The smell of fresh flowers was calming, but there wasn't much that could be done to alleviate the sadness pervading amongst the families.

The clock struck 3:00 p.m., and Pastor W. L. White made his way to the pulpit to welcome everyone to the memorial service. He asked the audience to participate in singing "The Star Spangled Banner." The sound was uplifting as folks both inside and outside joined in. Next, the San Saba Methodist Choir and the Bend Chapel Choir joined together in singing "America, the Beautiful." The audience was moved at the powerful vocal rendition, and tears began to roll down many of their faces. Pastor White then took a few moments to read from scripture, and he led the audience in prayer. The Keeney Quartet then performed a vocal number, and there was a special reading for the audience given by Mrs. W. E. Cantrell. Mrs. J.A. Mays sang a special solo "Give Your Best to the Master."

The Scott and White families took turns addressing the audience with eulogies for their beloved sons. W. J. Millican, grandfather to both Felix and Chauncey, delivered a heart wrenching tribute to honor his fallen grandsons. He ended his speech with, "Gone are the days of seeing my grandsons laughing, the long afternoons of horseplay, and the tireless work that they put in around the farm. The Lord has taken them all too soon, and I'm just plain sad that He didn't take me instead. I know that my boys are sitting under the shade of a giant pecan tree cracking pecans and jokes. Save me a spot, boys! I'll meet up with y'all again one day." Next, several friends of both Felix and Chauncey shared special memories from when they were growing up. The final song sung by the choirs was the "Battle Hymn of the Republic."

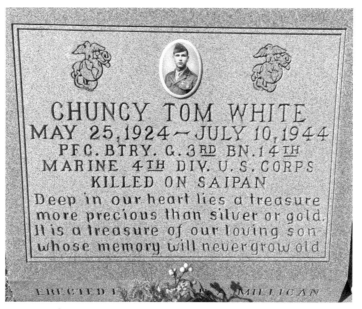

Chauncey White's tombstone in the Bend Cemetery.

Being members of a Gold Star family, it was fitting that there was a lighting ceremony with two golden candles. Ruvonne Underwood, Felix's and Chauncey's first cousin, and Felix Wayne Blanton, Felix's nephew, lit the candles that had been placed on the altar. It was very moving watching the youngsters light the candles. They were just little kids beginning their lives, and sadly, Felix and Chauncey had just recently lost theirs. It was certainly a day that Ruvonne and Felix Wayne wouldn't soon forget. Sobbing could be heard throughout the crowded church as the children returned to their seats. Pastor White said a closing prayer, and he then took a moment to hug the family members sitting in the front rows. Before dismissing the congregation, he asked the audience to go outside. Pastor White then proceeded to lead the group up the small hill to the Bend Cemetery, which was located about one hundred yards away. Attendees were given the opportunity to be the first folks to see the newly crafted, granite memorial tombstones for both Felix and Chauncey. Mr. W. J. Millican, the boys' grandfather, paid for the tombstones as a token of his love for them. Chauncey was especially dear to W. J. and Polly Ann since he had lived with them for most of his life. Since they didn't have any sons of their own, they raised him as if he was their son, and they enjoyed calling him Chuncy. W. J. told Chauncey's father, Lynn White, that since he was paying for the tombstone, he was going to put Chuncy on it, being that is what he liked calling him. W. J. was just devastated by his loss. He wanted both of his grandsons to be remembered by all of the people who might visit the Bend Cemetery in the future.

When most folks are buried, the general assumption is that the person would remain in their final resting place. However, in times of war, sometimes things change out of a necessity, or as a directive from a higher authority. In Felix's case, he was first buried at the Panitola American Military Cemetery as a means of convenience. It happened to be a cemetery close to his base, and it was relatively close to the site of his plane crash. The United States military was made aware that the cemetery at Panitola wasn't suited for long term internment of the soldiers who were buried there, due to the marshy nature of the grounds in that area.

The process to remove the remains of those interred at the Panitola American Military Cemetery began in early December of 1945. The grounds at the cemetery were generally saturated due to frequent rains, especially during the monsoon season. The soggy conditions had certainly helped to expedite the degradation process of Felix's body, and even his coffin had started to deteriorate. His remains were exhumed, and special care was taken to ensure that all of his bones were collected from the mud and debris that had filled the wooden coffin. Felix's remains were carefully unwrapped from the blanket that he'd been covered with, and they were placed onto a screen to dry.

It was right about mid-December of 1945 when Felix's remains were re-wrapped in a fresh blanket and placed into a new wooden coffin. His remains, along with those of many others, were then flown from Panitola to the city of Kalaikunda. Kalaikunda was approximately 950 miles from the Panitola Air Station, and it was in the West Bengal region of India. On 17 Dec. 1945, at around 1600 hours, Felix E. Scott was re-interred at the United States Military Cemetery at Kalaikunda. For Felix's second burial, there was no color guard, no honor guard, or not even a chaplain, for that matter. However, the process was very orderly and respectful. Each coffin was carefully placed into a freshly dug gravesite, based on a map that the Graves Registration Service (GRS) team had prepared. And just like that, Felix was put back into the ground in Kalaikunda. A concrete cross with a new metal nameplate affixed to it was embedded into the earth next to him to mark his location. One of Felix's id tags was once again buried with his body, and his other one was buried in a bottle next to his grave marker.

Profound sadness overcame the Scott household upon the passing of Viola's mother, Polly Ann Millican, on 18 Oct. 1946. The family called her "Ma," and she was going to be missed by her children, grandchildren, and even her great grandchildren. Still reeling from the death of Felix, Viola felt terrible about the loss of her mother, and she wondered why the Lord kept taking her most precious loved ones into His kingdom. She knew first hand that death was a part of life. Viola felt blessed, and she was happy when her granddaughters were born in 1946. Gayle was born on 1 Feb. and Mary Jane was born on 22 Sep. She vowed to keep her faith, and she planned to march on.

It was now late July of 1947, and things were looking up for Ernest and Viola Scott. They were now grandparents to one grandson, two granddaughters, and one on the way. Their son-in-law, Wallace Louis Stephenson, had thankfully survived fighting in the war over in Germany in the Battle of the Bulge, and they were very glad that he was back at home with their daughter Aletha. Everyone called him Steve, and, as an officer in the United States Army during the war, he was the recipient of two Bronze Stars and a Silver Star for exceptional valor during combat operations. Steve was also awarded two Purple Hearts for injuries suffered during combat. His medals and ribbons, and even a few special things he brought back from Germany, were certainly nice to have, but he was just very glad to be alive and still be in the Army, and be at home with his young family. Steve was glad that tragedy had avoided his side of the family, who were from Palmersville, Tennessee. He felt blessed that his brothers, Frank and Ralph Stephenson, and his brothers-in-law, Claude Oliver and Dalton Glover, had returned home safely from the war. The deaths of Felix and Chauncey only four months apart, had rocked the entire Scott family to its core. Everyone in the family was certainly glad that no one else in the family had died during the war. Chauncey's brother, Dimmitt, returned home safely, as did Dardon Scott, the son of Felix's Aunt Betsy, who was Viola's sister. Dardon's brothers-in-law, Jimmie Pittman and Joe Rome, also returned home from meritorious service in the war. Viola figured that God must've had a reason to call Felix and Chauncey into His kingdom, and she needed to learn to live without them.

Business at Ernest's tire repair shop, and at the family's filling station, was thriving once again. Gone were the ration coupons, and it certainly helped that key materials, like rubber and gasoline, were more readily available, since they were no longer needed to support the war effort. Family members who were close by, and even those who were far away kept the Scotts chugging along. Ernest had a daily routine where he'd venture down to the post office in his Studebaker during the hour that he'd close up his shop for lunch. One day, after he had opened his mailbox, he pulled out a letter from the War Department. Ernest had sent multiple letters to the War Department over the previous few years, asking for information about Felix's current internment. He was really hoping for a picture of Felix's tombstone, but at least one of the cemetery. Ernest wondered what could be in this letter, and why would he be receiving something from the government at this point?

Perhaps, maybe, the answers to his questions had finally been answered. Ernest pulled out his pocket knife, which had shiny yellow handles, and he slit open the envelope. With anxiety rushing through his veins, he pulled out the letter.

Dear Mr. Scott: *23 Jul. 1947*

The War Department is most desirous that you be furnished the latest information regarding the burial location of your son, the late Second Lieutenant Felix E. Scott, A. S. N. O 736 719.
The records of this office disclose that his remains were originally interred in a temporary cemetery established near the place where he met his

death, but were later moved to a more suitable site where constant care of the grave can be assured by our Forces in the field.

The records further disclose that his remains are now interred in the American Military Cemetery Kalaikunda, plot 2, row J, grave 926, located seventy-seven miles from Calcutta, India.

The War Department has now been authorized to comply, at Government expense, with the feasible wishes of the next of kin regarding final internment, here or abroad, of the remains of your loved one. At a later date, this office will, without any action on your part, provide all legal next of kin with full information and solicit their detailed desires.

Please accept my sincere sympathy in your great loss.

Sincerely yours,

T. B. Larkin
Major General
The Quartermaster General

As Ernest finished reading the letter, it brought back many of the emotions that both he and Viola had tried to harness over the last three years. This was the first time that he had heard about Felix's remains being re-interred at a different cemetery, and the part about his "final internment" intrigued him immensely. Did this mean that Felix's remains could finally be brought home to San Saba for a proper burial near his loved ones? Ernest grabbed the other mail from the box, and he rushed back home to share the good news with Viola. All of his letters to the Quartermaster General's office had gone unanswered until now. Ernest was very excited about what future communications might show up in his P. O. box in the coming weeks and months.

Ernest made the short trip to the post office nearly every day with the hope of finding another letter from the War Department. A little more than a month had passed when another letter arrived. His hands were trembling as he quickly tore open the envelope. The letter was dated 27 Aug. 1947, and read:

Dear Mr. Scott: *27 Aug. 1947*

Enclosed herewith is a picture of the American Military Cemetery Kalaikunda, India, in which your son, the late Second Lieutenant Felix E. Scott, is buried.

It is my sincere hope that you may gain some solace from this view of the surroundings in which your loved one rests. As you can see, this is a place of simple dignity, neat and well cared for. Here, assured of continuous care, now rest the remains of a few of those heroic dead who fell together in the service of our country.

This cemetery will be maintained as a temporary resting place until, in accordance with the wishes of the next of kin, all remains are either placed in permanent American cemeteries overseas, or returned to the Homeland for final burial.

Sincerely yours,

G. A. Horkan
1 Incl   *Brigadier General, QMC*
Photograph   *Chief, Memorial Division*

CHAPTER 3

Repatriation

After retrieving the rest of his mail, Mr. Scott once again raced home to show Viola the latest letter from the War Department. Viola looked through the window, and she noticed the dust cloud that Ernest had kicked up as he came to a stop in their driveway. He hurriedly went inside, anxious to share the letter with Viola. Ernest showed her the letter, and she was equally excited that they were now one step closer to bringing Felix back home to San Saba. Viola then phoned Pauline, Johnnie Mae, Aletha, and then all of her sisters to share the latest news about getting Felix brought back home. Viola's best friend and neighbor from across the street, Dixie Jackson, decided that she was going to come on over to see what all the excitement was about. The Scott family and their friends were all excited about the possibility that Felix's remains would finally be returned to San Saba, but they were actually rather skeptical that it would really happen. To actually have his body back on American soil would be magnificent, and it would give them some much needed peace. Finally, his remains would be paired with the granite marker already placed in the family plot over at the Bend Cemetery.

On 13 Sep. 1947, the Scotts received the most important letter to date from the War Department. This time, Ernest didn't just get a standard size letter in a legal size envelope, but instead, the contents were housed neatly within a much larger envelope that was heavier and thicker than any of the previous mailings. Ernest couldn't harness his excitement any longer as he reached for his pocket knife. The uncertainty of what was inside the envelope was mind-boggling. The tape used to secure the envelope was tough, but Ernest managed to prevail. He then emptied the contents onto a round oak table located right next to the rows of P. O. Boxes. There were multiple pamphlets, forms, a return envelope, and, of course, a letter addressed to him. Ernest was so excited that he took the time to go through the packet of information right there on the spot. The letter had pretty much the same format as the others, but this one provided the specific steps needed to bring his boy home.

2nd. Lt. Felix E. Scott, O 756 719
Plot 2, Row J, Grave 926
American Military Cemetery
Kalaikunda, India

Dear Mr. Scott: *08 Sep. 1947*

The people of the United States, through the Congress have authorized the disinterment and final burial of the heroic dead of World War II. The Quartermaster General of the Army has been entrusted with this sacred responsibility to the honored dead. The records of the War Department indicate that you may be the nearest relative of the above-named deceased, who gave his life in the service of his country.

The enclosed pamphlets, "Disposition of World War II Armed Forces Dead," and "American Cemeteries," explain the disposition, options and services made available to you by your Government. If you are the next of kin according to the line of kinship as set forth in the enclosed pamphlet, "Disposition of World War II Armed Forces Dead," you are invited to express your wishes as to the disposition of the remains of the deceased by completing Part I of the enclosed form "Request for Disposition of Remains." Should you desire to relinquish your rights to the next in line of kinship, please complete Part II of the enclosed form. If you are not the next of kin, please complete Part III of the enclosed form.

If you should elect Option 2, it is advised that no funeral arrangements or other personal arrangements be made until you are further notified by this office.

Will you please complete the enclosed form, "Request for Disposition of Remains" and mail in the enclosed self-addressed envelope, which requires no postage, within 30 days after its receipt by you? Its prompt return will avoid unnecessary delays.

Sincerely,

Thomas B. Larkin
Major General
The Quartermaster General

Ernest made darn sure that he'd collected all the contents of the envelope, and he quickly exited the post office. He certainly left some burnt rubber in the post office parking lot as he sped home to show Viola the exciting documents. The next day was Sunday, and there just happened to be a preplanned family supper scheduled at the Scott home. Ernest and Viola thought the timing was perfect to share this information with the rest of the family who'd be coming over. The Scott household was certainly bursting with energy as Viola's sisters and their families, including Betsy's new baby granddaughter, Bobbie Lynn, arrived. Pauline and Ted, Johnnie Mae and AJ, and their children, Felix Wayne and Gayle, arrived as well. Everyone was very glad to see that Aletha and Steve were already there with their daughter, Mary Jane. Of course, Pa Millican was there too.

Viola was just tickled pink as she spread the contents of the envelope that they'd received from the War Department upon the little round table that Felix had sent home from India. She felt that it was appropriate for everyone to gather around the table to review the very important documents. Pauline grabbed the "Disposition of World War II Armed Forces Dead" pamphlet, and she briefly thumbed through it. The pamphlet was nearly 20 pages long, and she began at the dedication page. *"In deep and everlasting appreciation of the heroic efforts of those who, in keeping their country free, made the supreme sacrifice in World War II-the entire Nation has been dedicated to disposing of the mortal remains of those honored dead, in a manner consistent with the wishes of their next of kin."* The passage was signed by Harry S. Truman, President of the United States. Pauline continued to read the rest of the pamphlet so that everyone could hear the important details. Ernest clutched Viola's hand as they sat on the couch, listening intently with their eyes fixed on Pauline's face. After Pauline had finished reading all of the relevant parts of the pamphlet, she then picked up the next one regarding American Cemeteries. After seeing what Pauline had picked up, Viola abruptly got up off the couch, and said, "Hon, there is no need to read that one. My boy will be coming home to me right here in San Saba."

Johnnie Mae had been rifling through the paperwork trying to make sense of it all, and she found a document entitled "Request for Disposition of Remains," which she held up for Ernest and Viola to see. Ernest then had Johnnie Mae sit next to him at the kitchen table to take a look at the two page form. They noticed that the top portion of the first page had already been filled in by the Quartermaster General's office, listing Felix's name, rank, identification number, his specific grave location, and the date, 08 Sep. 1947. Ernest reached into a drawer and grabbed a pen with black ink. He began by filling in his name as next of kin. Ernest then chose the box that said, "*Father.*" Next, he selected option II that said, *"Be returned to the United States or any possession or territory for interment by next of kin in a private cemetery."* Ernest could hardly contain himself as he wrote "*Bend Cemetery located in Bend, Texas*" on the line that asked for the name and location of the intended cemetery for burial. Ernest then looked at Viola, and reached for her hand, as he said, "We're finally gonna get our boy home." Page two was rather simple to complete. There was a section asking for the name and address of the funeral home that the Scotts wished to use. He then listed the location of the nearest railroad station, and he filled in Viola's information as the person next in line of kinship.

The section at the bottom of the second page on the form would have to wait to be filled out on Monday morning, 15 Sep. 1947, when Ernest would venture down to the County Courthouse to have the document notarized by the County Judge, Burns Lane. That Sunday night, all the guests sitting down at the Scott's supper table were smiling, and it seemed that they'd had their spirits lifted that afternoon. They now had something to look forward to. They raised their glasses in a toast to Felix, and to mark this glorious day. Ernest could hardly sleep that night, and even though there was a chill in the air the next morning, he decided to walk the few blocks to the courthouse to help clear his mind, and to ease the anxiety that had been building. The clerk opened the doors to the courthouse right at 9 a.m., and it didn't take too long to get the county judge to complete his part and sign the document appropriately.

When Pauline had read the "Disposition of World War II Armed Forces Dead" pamphlet, Ernest recalled the part which stated that this process would be a huge undertaking. It also went on to say that the process could take many months, and probably even years to complete. Ernest was thinking to himself that there had to be hundreds of thousands of families in his shoes doing the very same thing. Ernest was trying to be as expedient as possible, so he headed directly over to the San Saba Post Office, which was located within easy walking distance from the Scott home. As Ernest walked briskly down the street, he recalled many of the occasions when he'd gone to the post office to mail letters or packages to Felix. This time, he wasn't mailing a letter from the folks at home, but rather, it was paperwork to get Felix home. He and Viola had written to Felix often while he was stationed at his numerous training bases, and even when he left for his deployment to India. After arriving at the post office, Ernest walked up to the counter, and said, "Harriet, it's really important that this envelope goes out in today's mail," and Harriet replied, "No problem, Ernest, I'll take care of it personally for you."

Ernest and his family had no idea what would happen next after mailing the paperwork back to the Quartermaster General's office in Washington, D.C. He was rather emotional as he walked out of the post office and headed home. The Scotts were rather patient people, so they planned to go about their normal routine, and hope for the best. Their objective was to get Felix back home, and they were content to wait for updates to come at some point. The repatriation process moved rather quickly for Felix, although the Scotts had no idea as to what was going on behind the scenes. Felix was disinterred from his grave at the Kalaikunda Cemetery on 15 Oct. 1947, which was exactly one month from the time that Ernest had mailed off the paperwork. That was really quick, considering the enormity of the overall project, and the many different theaters of war that were involved. There surely had to be a great deal of families going through the same arduous process. The remains of fallen soldiers would certainly be coming back to the United States from many different countries around the world.

Once Felix's body had been disinterred, his id tags were checked, and both were placed into a new temporary casket. His skeletal remains needed to be prepared for shipment, and they were taken to a warehouse for processing. It remains unclear as to what exactly took place between 15 Oct. 1947 and 02 Mar. 1948, which was the day that Felix's remains were placed into a permanent steel casket. The GRS inspectors signed off on the paperwork after ensuring that the casket was properly marked. Felix's casket was then placed inside a rectangular steel case, which would make storage and shipment easier, due to the large quantity of caskets being shipped at the same time.

The exact date is uncertain, but at some point after 02 Mar. 1948, Felix's remains were transported from India to the island of Oahu in Hawaii. His casket was stored for a short time at Schofield Barracks, which was a US Army installation there on the island. On 24 Apr. 1948, the case containing Felix's casket was loaded onto the USAT Cardinal O'Connell, a United States Army Transport ship, for transport to the West Coast of the United States. On 3 May 1948, Ernest received a telegram that indicated that the remains of his son, Felix E. Scott, were en route to the United States. When Ernest shared the great news with Viola, plenty of neighbors heard the singing, screaming, dancing, and cheering coming from the Scott home on South Live Oak Street. On 7 May 1948, the Cardinal O'Connell sailed through the fog, and under the Golden Gate Bridge. The large transport ship docked at Fort Mason, located on the waterfront near downtown San Francisco.

Felix's remains were among the stacks and stacks of steel cases that were offloaded from the Cardinal O'Connell. The cases were then taken to a nearby warehouse for further processing. The servicemen who were assigned to handle the influx of fallen heroes were inundated.

However, they went about their business diligently and respectfully. There was no laughter, no loud music, and no boisterous conversation out of respect for the men who had just recently been fighting for their country. There were Airmen, Marines, and members of the Navy, and of the Army inside of those cases. They realized they had a job to do, a job to do for the family members and loved ones back home, who were waiting for the return of their lifeless soldier. Once at the warehouse, the cases were organized into groups, depending on where they would be shipped to next. Felix's case was grouped with many other fallen soldiers from the great state of Texas. On or about 10 May 1948, the cases holding the caskets were stacked neatly, one on top of the other, and placed inside a group of box cars that were lined up on the railroad tracks. The outbound train, which consisted of too many box cars to count, left Fort Mason later that evening. The train may have made a stop or two along the way, but this particular train was bound for the Quartermaster Depot in Fort Worth, Texas.

Felix's remains were officially received into the Fort Worth Quartermaster depot on 17 May 1948. There were plenty of caskets arriving at the depot nearly every day from the Asiatic Area, South Pacific theater, and also from the European theater. Deluged with the arrival of so many caskets, it had to be a challenge to get the correct set of remains to the proper family. The military promised that great care would be taken to ensure accuracy.

The Scott family was still anxiously awaiting the day that Felix would be back in San Saba. The Quartermaster General's office made an exceptional effort to keep the family and funeral home aware of the progress made along the way. Telegrams were received regularly at the Scott residence, and also at the Howell-Doran funeral home located there in San Saba. Final word regarding the shipment of Felix's remains was received at the funeral home on 03 Jun. 1948. The telegram stated that his remains would be arriving on train number 53, leaving out of Fort Worth at 10:55 p.m. on 07 Jun. 1948. Felix's casket, encased inside of the steel case, and accompanied by a military escort, was set to arrive at the San Saba station at 10:17 a.m. on 08 Jun. 1948. Finally, the telegram asked the funeral home to be prepared to accept the remains at the train station, and they were asked to notify the family as well. Ernest was very glad to answer the phone that evening when Mr. Howell called with the good news.

Body Of San Saba Flier Is Returned For Burial There

SAN SABA. June 7. (SC) — County Commissioner Ernest Scott and Mrs. Scott of this city have been advised that the body of their only son, Lt. Felix E. Scott, is scheduled to arrive here Tuesday from Inida where he lost his life in a plane crash on April 13, 1944. The body will lie in state at the family home and will have an honor guard from the American Legion and the Veterans of Foreign War Posts until time for burial in the Bend Cemetery Wednesday when full military honors will be held at the graveside.

Lt. Scott, native here, graduated from the local high school, and completed three and one-half years of work in Texas A&M College, when he volunteered for service in the U. S. Air Corps.

His death occurred on the 31st wedding anniversary of his parents, and was also the wedding anniversary of his oldest sister, Mrs. A. J. Blanton of Crane. Two other sisters survive, Mrs. Ted Burnham of Goldthwaite and Mrs. Steve Stevenson of Killeen. The young man was one of two grandsons of W. J. Millican, pioneer pecan man of Bend, who gave their lives in the last war.

Article from The San Saba News. *June 7, 1948.*

The morning of 08 Jun. 1948 was both joyful and somber at the same time. Viola got dressed in a bright colored dress, and she wore her best stockings and hat. Ernest was dressed in his brown Sunday suit, complete with a tie. They wanted to look their very best as they prepared to head over to the Santa Fe Train Station. It was right about 9 a.m., and both Viola and Ernest were feeling restless at home, so they decided to head over to the train station. The station was built of red bricks, and it had many large windows facing the tracks. The architecture of the structure was very appealing to all of those who had traveled in and out of it. The return of Felix's remains had made the front page of *The San Saba News and Star*, and word quickly got around town that there was going to be a grand celebration for his arrival at the train station. The Scotts wanted to be there early in order to greet the family, friends, and members of the honor guard that would meet the train when it arrived.

Viola was quivering with emotion, so she proceeded to walk away from the crowd that had begun to gather. She walked along the tracks in the direction that the train was expected to arrive from. Viola walked a few hundred yards until she could no longer hear the conversations being bantered about. She then stood solemnly under the shade of a large oak tree. The beautiful scenery and tranquility of her location allowed her to recall the last moments that she had spent with Felix. They had been together at the train station prior to him leaving for Florida to attend his final training before heading off to war. Viola recalled Felix holding her hand in front of the station, just steps away from the train before he boarded. Felix told her that he loved her very much, and he promised her that all would be fine, since God was his copilot, after all. Viola recalled how she had hugged him, and that she didn't want to let go of him. Their hug finally ended, and she remembered Felix giving her the keys to his truck and his brown cowboy hat. He asked her to keep them safe, and to look after them until he'd meet her once again at the train station, after returning gallantly from his service in the war. The recollection seemed so vivid to Viola, and she began to cry. She wiped the tears from her face, using one of Felix's handkerchiefs which she had found in his footlocker that had been sent to their home after his death. This was certainly not the reunion that she had longed for; however, after having waited more than 1500 days after learning of his death, Viola was now just minutes away from being near her boy Felix once again.

Viola suddenly began to hear the train whistle blowing on the outskirts of town. She looked down at her watch that read 10:15 a.m. Viola hurried back to the station, where she could see that the crowd had grown even larger. She found Ernest standing next to their daughters Pauline, and Johnnie Mae and Aletha, and their families. Viola was trying to catch her breath as the mighty Santa Fe Railroad engine pulled into the station with its brakes squealing, as the engineer slowed the train to a stop. The caboose couldn't be seen due to the volume of boxcars and passenger cars attached to the locomotive. The conductor hopped off the train in order to assist a man dressed in a full military uniform, who had also gotten off the train. The Scotts had been told that Felix's remains would be accompanied by a military escort. Ernest led his family members towards the gentleman to introduce themselves.

As soon as the conductor stepped away from the sharply dressed military man, Ernest said, "Hello, my name is Ernest Scott, and this here is my wife, Viola. Would you happen to be First Lieutenant Michael Alba?" The gentleman replied, "Yes, I'm Lieutenant Alba, and it's a great pleasure and honor to meet both of you. I'm the military escort who was assigned the distinct privilege of accompanying the remains of your dear son to San Saba today." Meanwhile, the conductor had opened the heavy steel door to the boxcar carrying Felix's remains.

The members of the Scott family began to congregate around the boxcar, and they were in awe of the number of stacked steel cases piled on top of each other. As the crew prepared the ramp to offload the casket, Lieutenant Alba introduced himself to the members of the Wiley B. Murray American Legion post, and to the members of the local Veterans of Foreign Wars post 4376. Ernest looked to his left, and then to his right, and he mentioned to Viola that Felix would be glad that so many folks had turned out to welcome him home.

The color guard stood at attention, proudly displaying the United States flag, the Texas flag, and various other military flags. There was a slight breeze that revealed the full beauty of the colorful flags. There were six pallbearers waiting at the base of the ramp, ready to receive the heavy steel case. The railroad crew members softly guided the case down the metal ramp to the pallbearers who were waiting ever so patiently. Once the case had reached the bottom of the ramp, the pallbearers grabbed ahold of it, and began a slow march to the hearse waiting nearby. As they marched towards the hearse, there were two students from the band at San Saba High School playing a somber, yet rhythmic piece, on their snare drums. Much of the crowd either saluted, or placed their hand across their chest, as the procession passed by. Many folks were seen wiping their eyes, and some were just flat out crying, as the case was loaded into the back of the hearse.

As Viola stood there in disbelief that Felix had actually returned home, Ernest climbed on top of a bench outside the train station to thank everyone for coming. He raised his left hand into the air and whistled loudly, using the fingers on his right hand. After catching everyone's attention, he said, "Viola and I just wanted to thank y'all for coming out here to support us this morning. This has been a long and painful journey, and we really appreciate all of your kindness, love, and support during this time of incredible sadness. We're very pleased, and blessed to have Felix home once again. It means a lot to us, and we're sure that Felix would be pleased as well to see how many of y'all turned out for the celebration this morning. Please come and join us out at the Bend Cemetery tomorrow at 3 p.m. for the graveside service."

Lieutenant Alba looked as if he didn't know what to do or where to go. The train station wasn't that far from the hotels and restaurants of downtown San Saba. Ernest noticed Lieutenant Alba standing by the tracks, so he asked him if he'd like to join them at the funeral being held the next day. Ernest also let him know that he'd be welcome to stay the night with them as their guest in their home. Lieutenant Alba graciously accepted the offer, and he thanked the Scotts for their hospitality and kindness. They all climbed into Ernest's Studebaker, and they headed home. Just as the hearse left the parking lot, the train left the station with its whistle blowing. There was no doubt that it was heading to the next small town to repeat this process for yet another family in mourning. The hearse slowly began to make its way to the Scott home, where Felix's remains would lie in repose from noon that day until 2 p.m. the following day. The crowd began to leave as well, and just like that, Felix had finally made the long and arduous journey home.

Ernest and Viola arrived at their home with Lieutenant Alba to find their large family, and extended family already mingling throughout the front and back yards. There were cars lined up and down South Live Oak Street, and some were even parked on many of the nearby side streets. Friends of the family, and the members of the honor guard, were also there. Once the hearse arrived, the members of the honor guard navigated the casket into the Scott home, and they placed it upon a table in the corner of the living room. Viola's sisters, and some of her friends, were in charge of placing the floral arrangements around the casket. It took nearly an hour to situate all of the flowers around the casket. It would be fair to say that there weren't very many flowers left in the florist shops around town that day. Guests and visitors also brought fresh cut flowers from their gardens, and there were even some people who brought potted plants as well. Viola knelt down in front of the casket to add the final touch. She placed an 11" x 14" framed picture of Felix, dressed in his military uniform, upon the floor directly in front of the casket. She kissed the glass covering Felix's face before standing back up to admire what the ladies had accomplished.

Felix's flag-draped casket sitting among the beautiful floral arrangement in the Scott's living room.

The honor guard members had received permission from the Scotts to provide continuous watch over the casket until 2 p.m. the following day. They had come up with a schedule in which there would be one person to the left, and one to the right of the casket. The men would rotate out every two hours all throughout the night.

Their efforts and actions were very much appreciated by Ernest and Viola. While the ladies had been tending to the floral memorial in the living room, their husbands, and others were busy fixing a fabulous BBQ dinner outside. Everyone brought food, so nobody was going to go hungry. As the day wore down, most of the folks had gone back home, yet the honor guard was busy keeping their rotations. Viola figured that the best way she could thank them, was to keep them fed, and to keep the coffee pot full. Lieutenant Alba seized the opportunity to listen in on all of the stories being shared about Felix by those who were still there at the Scott home. The day had been so surreal and emotionally draining for Viola. She was sad at times, and she was happy at times, since her boy Felix was finally back in her home. When most of the family had gone to bed, Viola stayed up late into the night, staring at the flag-draped casket. She was comforted by the fact that Felix had died so quickly in the plane crash, and he didn't have to suffer a long and painful death. Viola was also glad that he wasn't missing in action, and that he wasn't tortured or held as a prisoner of war. She looked over at the piano, fondly remembering how much fun Felix had had with Elsie, singing and dancing around the living room. Ernest found Viola asleep in her rocking chair early the next morning, clutching a photo album in her arms.

Certainly nobody would ever be emotionally prepared to have a funeral for their child. However, the Scott family had been through quite an ordeal, and they were ready for their emotional roller coaster ride to end. They also felt like Felix finally needed to rest in peace, since this was about to be his third burial. There were plenty of folks who helped to load the bountiful floral display into multiple cars for transport out to the Bend Cemetery. Mr. Howell, from the Howell-Doran funeral home, arrived around 1:30 p.m. to begin preparations to move the casket to the cemetery. The final honor guard rotation was completed promptly at 2:00 p.m., and the other honor guard members had returned to the Scott home. With the American flag still draped atop the casket, the guardsmen proceeded to carry it to the awaiting hearse. Viola was out on the front porch watching as Felix's casket was slowly carried down her front steps. She proudly showed off some of Felix's childhood marbles that had been encased into the concrete footings supporting the front porch. The shiny and colorful marbles served as a wonderful reminder of her only son on an otherwise dreary day. The casket was then placed into the steel case for transport to the Bend Cemetery.

The hearse deviated a bit from the typical route to the cemetery as it made its way through San Saba. The procession had quite a number of cars, and the local police department helped ensure that the caravan would be unabated as it passed by the high school where Felix had played football. The high school band had lined up in front of the school to play their fight song as the hearse slowly drove by. There were many people on the streets of San Saba waving American flags as the procession made its way out of town. The trip took just under an hour to reach Bend. Upon reaching the cemetery, Boy Scouts from the troop that Felix had once belonged to, were busy directing guests as to where to park. The scouts also served as valets, by parking cars for many of the older guests down near the church at the bottom of the hill. This was a generous gesture for those who might have had difficulty walking up the somewhat steep gravel road to the cemetery.

The Bend Cemetery had just about two dozen permanent residents at the time of Felix's burial. Several cars belonging to the family members followed the hearse as it traversed the short country dirt road leading to the cemetery lawn. There was an area close to the fence line, and close to the gravesite, that was roped off for the immediate family and the hearse to park. There were two deuce and a half military trucks in the procession as well. One truck carried members of the honor guard from San Saba. The other truck was equipped with a large antennae on the cab, and it carried soldiers who'd be participating in the funeral service. This group of servicemen were from the Goodfellow Air Force Base located in San Angelo, Texas. The noisy diesel engines caused smoke to blow from the exhaust stacks, which irritated the senses of some of the guests. As the cars continued to pass through the open gate, there was a member of the honor guard to the left of the gate, standing at attention, holding his M4 rifle. To the right was a sailor holding an American flag attached to a wooden pole.

The six members of the color guard stood at attention near the gravesite with their beautiful flags blowing ever so slightly. Two of the men were wearing their white naval uniforms, while the other four wore tan army uniforms. The honor guardsmen stood at attention as they watched the funeral director open the back door of the hearse, revealing the flag-draped shipping case with a bouquet of yellow roses laid atop it. The sound of men rhythmically tapping their drums could be heard as the honor guard got into formation, ready to accept Felix's remains. Viola and Ernest felt proud and thankful for the honors being bestowed upon their son. The funeral, with full military honors, that they had so longed for, had finally become a reality.

The color guard at Felix's burial at the Bend Cemetery.

Terrance Walker, Post Commander of the local American Legion, was the officer in charge of the funeral proceedings. As such, he pulled the shipping case from the hearse so that the honor guardsmen could move it to where the crowd had gathered around the burial plot. There was precision with their footsteps as the men marched slowly across the grassy hilltop. Felix's large family was seated in the first few rows of chairs that had been staged around the burial plot. The family members watched stoically as the casket was removed from the shipping case one final time. The steel casket was shiny, and the sun's reflection upon it was striking. The American flag was once again placed upon the casket, which was now resting on the lowering stand. The lowering stand was wrapped in a deep blue fabric which made for a remarkable presentation.

Reverend W. L. White, pastor of the Bend Methodist Church, welcomed everyone, and he thanked the guests for attending the service. Reverend T. K. Anderson, pastor of the San Saba United Methodist Church, also assisted with the funeral service. Reverend Anderson then began the service with a prayer, and continued with selected readings from scripture. Reverend White then invited the guests to join him in the singing of "Amazing Grace" and "The Old Rugged Cross." Following that, Ernest and Viola each took a few moments to express their love for their only son Felix. It had to have been a heart wrenching thing to watch, and to listen to, the Scotts do their best to speak without breaking down. Their adult children, Aletha, Johnnie Mae, and Pauline, stood behind them for emotional support. Although they too were broken-hearted, they took turns sharing funny and memorable stories of the great times they had shared with their brother.

Finally, Felix's maternal grandfather, W. J. Millican, took a few moments to speak as well. W. J. spoke from the heart, and he ended with, "So farewell, Felix, your place can never be filled. Your name will forever be on the church rolls in San Saba, and is recorded in heaven by Him, that doeth all things well. It's wonderful that a boy can win and woo so many friends in life by living a clean, honorable life. Our eyes are blinded with tears over this sad incidence, but only tears can give relief. Our prayers are to the Almighty God that my boy, Chuncey, will someday come home too." After W. J. sat down, Reverend White read a few more scriptures from the Bible, and he then asked the crowd to join him in reciting the Lords's prayer.

Mr. Walker then directed the honor guard to begin the folding of the flag ceremony. He stood at the end of the casket while the honor guardsmen lifted the flag towards their chests. A group of soldiers with rifles stood off to the left of the crowd near the far corner of the cemetery. A loud voice suddenly rang out with, "Ready, aim, fire!" All seven men immediately followed simultaneously, with shots fired high into the air from the barrels of their M4 rifles. The birds must've been startled by the volleys of gunfire, as they could suddenly be seen flying out of the nearby trees. Each consecutive volley even seemed to startle some of the guests. After the last volley of shots, the crowd turned to the sound of a lone bugler, Mr. Arnold Behrens, as he performed a moving rendition of taps, which certainly brought a few more tears to the family.

There was a soldier who had been sitting in the cab of the truck from San Angelo with a radio headset during the ceremony. Shortly after the bugler had started playing, a group of four bright yellow planes could be seen heading directly towards the Bend Cemetery in formation. The soldier in the truck had been in constant communication with the commander of this flight, which consisted of four North American AT-6 airplanes, and which also happened to be the type of plane Felix had flown during his Advanced training course.

The soldier relayed information as the service had been progressing, so that this group of planes flying overhead, with the objective of performing the "Missing Man Flyby," could achieve a precise time on target just as the bugler finished. It was quite astonishing to see the second plane from the right pull up, and fly high towards the sky as the other three continued on straight with the one plane missing. This was a very poignant display, and it signified the fact that Felix was no longer flying or living. There wasn't a dry eye in the crowd, and many could be seen rubbing their arms from the chills they felt as the planes flew directly above them.

Honor guard preparing to fold the flag. Steel shipping case that housed his casket pictured in lower right corner.

The flag was held tightly for the entire time while the bugler played, and as the flyover took place. The honor guardsmen then proceeded to fold the flag in half, and they then folded it again. They were now ready to begin the process of making the final 13 folds on the flag that held 48 stars upon it. Very precise folds, and attention to every detail resulted in a flag that was perfectly folded.

The flag was then handed to Mr. Walker, who in turn presented it to Lieutenant Alba. Lieutenant Alba held the flag horizontally in front of himself as he walked slowly over to where Ernest and Viola were sitting. While kneeling, Lieutenant Alba held the flag with the long edge facing Mrs. Scott. He then said, "On behalf of the President of the United States, the United States Air Force, and a grateful nation, please accept this flag as a symbol of our appreciation for Felix's honorable and faithful service." While clutching a handkerchief in her right hand, Viola proudly accepted the flag, and she brought it quickly to her chest. Lieutenant Alba then stood up, and he walked to where the honor guardsmen had congregated. Mr. Charles Miffleton, Post Commander of the San Saba Veterans of Foreign Wars, stepped forward to Felix's casket. He attached a magnetic pin to the top of the casket, and said, "Honoring your service and sacrifice, you took freedom to distant lands, and gave hope to a world oppressed. We will not forget. VFW welcomes you home, Felix Scott." Mr. Miffleton turned, and he walked back to his seat.

Reverend Anderson gave a final blessing, and he then walked directly to Felix's casket. He picked up the bouquet of yellow roses that had been sitting on top of the casket throughout the service. He moved towards the Scott family sitting nearby, and he handed the flowers to Johnnie Mae. She was a real go getter, and she felt honored to distribute a rose to each of her immediate family members. The crowd watched attentively as the casket was slowly lowered into the deep and dark hole. Ernest and Viola were the first ones to step up to the side of the grave. They bowed their heads and silently said their final goodbyes before simultaneously tossing their roses along with a handful of dirt into the hole. Felix's sisters, Aletha, Johnnie Mae, and Pauline, then followed. The rest of the family whom were given roses also took a few moments to say their individual goodbyes.

Several men with shovels began the laborious process of filling in the grave with the dirt that was piled up close by. As they made progress with filling in the hole, the Boy Scout troop was busy fetching cars for some of the elderly attendees. The scouts then proceeded to fold up the chairs, and they carried them down the small hill to the storage room at the church. Once the men had finished filling in the grave, many of Viola's friends and sisters helped to arrange the vast amount of flowers neatly upon the dirt mound. It was a beautiful sight to see, and it made Viola happy to have such attention to detail in the floral display. One final touch was made to the gravesite before the Scott family left for home. Ernest planted a small cedar tree on the left side of the tombstone, while Viola planted one on the right side. They made a promise to each other, and to Felix, that they'd visit his grave often so they could water the small trees. The trees would serve as a symbol, meaning that even in death, Felix would live on in their hearts. There were some folks who took pictures of the various stages of the service. Before the Scotts and their family members left the cemetery, they gathered together near the grave for a few final pictures.

Quite the pile of flowers atop Felix's grave following his burial at the Bend Cemetery.

Ernest and Viola Scott along with daughters Aletha and Johnnie Mae. Grandchildren Felix Wayne, Mary Jane, Nancy and Gayle. Burial 09 Jun. 1948 at Bend Cemetery, TX.

Ernest and Viola hugged or shook hands with nearly everyone who had attended. They thanked the members of the local VFW and the servicemen from San Angelo whom had helped with the service. They were physically tired and mentally drained as they headed towards their car for the ride home. They made sure to give special thanks to Lieutenant Alba. They hugged him, and reiterated how grateful they were for his time in escorting Felix's remains to San Saba. Ernest offered him a ride back to the train station, but Lieutenant Alba let him know that he was going to get a ride back with the VFW group. Ernest opened the passenger door to their Studebaker so that Viola could get seated. Viola held Felix's burial flag close to her chest as Ernest proceeded down the short cemetery road and headed home. Most of the family members headed back to their own homes following the service. Aletha and her husband, Steve, planned to return back to the Scott home for one more night. Aletha was a great cook, and she planned on fixing a few meals for her parents. Steve offered to help with the cleanup in the house and yard. When the group got back to the Scott home, Viola went straight to bed.

Aletha and Steve had two little daughters at the time. Mary Jane was nearly two, and Nancy was almost five months old. Aletha took her little girls out to the back yard so that they wouldn't be underfoot. She placed them on a patch of grass underneath the large oak tree in the Scott's back yard. Johnnie Mae and her family had decided to come over to assist with the cleanup, and they had planned to stay for supper. Felix Wayne and Gayle were also outside with their cousins. Ernest and Steve were keeping an eye on them as they cleaned up the outdoor mess that had been left over from the previous evening's supper. Aletha and Johnnie Mae got right to work by tidying up the small kitchen, and by washing all sorts of dishes and pans. They took turns glancing out of the kitchen window to ensure there was no mischief going on. The little girls seemed to be having a ball while they watched Felix Wayne climb the thick branches of the tree. They giggled every time he'd make monkey noises as he swung from a branch. Johnnie Mae noticed what was going on outside, and she said to Aletha, "It looks like Felix Wayne likes climbing trees just as much as Felix did." Aletha agreed, and replied, "Well, it'll have to be his tree now."

Steve assisted Ernest with the repositioning of all the living room furniture that had been displaced by the casket. When the chores were done, the men piled all of the children into a wooden wagon, and they brought them out to the front yard so that they could enjoy riding the new white wooden bouncy horse that Ernest had made for them. They had a grand old time bouncing up and down on that horse. Of course, Steve had to hold Nancy up on the horse so she too could enjoy the latest toy that Ernest had built for them. Their Pappy was pretty handy when it came to making fun toys for his grandchildren.

They were soon called inside to enjoy a fine enchilada supper, served with a fresh tossed salad and delicious homemade biscuits, that Aletha and Johnnie Mae had teamed up to make. There were a lot of smiles, and a feeling that life would go on with this family joining together. After supper, Johnnie Mae and her family headed home, and everyone else decided that it was time for bed. It had been a very long day.

Being that Viola had gone to bed early; she was the first to wake up on the morning of 10 Jun. 1948. She walked quietly across the wooden floors and out onto her front porch. Viola was careful to not let the wooden screen door slam shut. The sun was just starting to rise as she sat down in her rocking chair. The early morning hour was very peaceful, and it seemed to calm Viola as she sat and reflected on the events of the past few days. Most of her family and friends had returned to their normal lives, leaving Viola to figure out her new normal. She was glad to have the closure that came with burying Felix, but the reality had set in that she was now left without her only son. The raw emotions twirling within her head seemed to twist her spirit as she sat contemplating how she was going to move forward with her life. Viola still had so much to live for, being that she was a beloved wife, mother, and grandmother.

As Viola sat staring out towards South Live Oak Street, she saw a large bird fly onto the roof of her good friend Dixie's house. After a closer look, Viola could tell that this was no ordinary bird. Rather, it was a red-tailed hawk. The majestic and beautiful bird was motionless as is clutched onto the tin roof with its mighty talons. Viola could see that the hawk appeared to be looking directly at her. She was very excited to reciprocate by staring back. Viola had lived long enough to know about the folklore and symbolism that seeing a hawk brings. Legend has it that seeing a hawk will make you feel safe, and also be safe. Some folks even say that hawks are spirit animals that deliver messages from those living eternally.

Dixie happened to be out in her yard, and she noticed that Viola was sitting on her porch. She then proceeded out of her gate, and began to walk across the street to join Viola. As her gate slammed shut, the hawk became frightened and flew from the roof. The hawk ascended, circled back, and then flew directly over Viola's house. During the hawk's flight, a feather fell from its body and softly oscillated towards the ground. It landed on Viola's front lawn, and she quickly walked down her steps to retrieve it. Just as she picked the feather up, Dixie was standing right beside her. Dixie said, "That sure looks like a feather from a hawk." Viola replied that it was indeed from a hawk, and she began to share her experience in seeing the hawk on top of the roof. Dixie excitedly said, "Honey, you gonna be ok. Some people say that finding a feather from a hawk will help to heal your deep emotional wounds." Viola carefully placed the feather into the front pocket of her blouse, and they sauntered back towards her front porch.

The two women continued to sit out on the front porch, and they shared a pot of coffee. Viola then opened up to Dixie about how difficult it was for her to see Felix's bedroom day in and day out. Everything was just as Felix had left it before leaving for war. Viola took Dixie by the hand to lead her inside the house and into Felix's bedroom. His bed was neatly made, and his boots were placed on the floor by the door. There were various magazines and books stacked neatly upon his small wooden desk. His guns were displayed in a gun rack that was affixed to the wall. There was a shelf on both sides of the gun rack which held various knickknacks and pictures. The room was well kept, and Viola mentioned that she could still smell Felix's scent as she picked up his college sweater that was hanging on the back of his chair.

Dixie could see that Viola had a tear building near the corner of her eye. Viola sat down upon the bed, and said, "Dixie, would you be kind enough to help me with packing up all of Felix's things?" Dixie replied, "Honey, are you sure that is what you really want?" Viola nodded her head, and Dixie added, "Well, it would be my pleasure to help you with whatever you need." With that, the duo got right at it. Viola emptied the cedar chest that was positioned next to the bed, and all of the contents were neatly placed onto the floor. She then proceeded to organize, and repack the chest until it was filled to the hilt. Viola and Dixie worked very well together. All of Felix's personal belongings went into the cedar chest, and his military items fit perfectly into the footlocker that they had received from the Quartermaster General's office. The few things that Felix had from his time at Texas AMC all fit snuggly into his college suitcase. Finally, Viola reached her hands up to remove a frame from the wall, but this was no ordinary picture frame. This frame contained a magnificent display of about two dozen of the most prized arrowheads that Felix had collected while growing up.

Just like that, all of Felix's worldly possessions had all been packed and placed outside his bedroom door. Aletha popped into the bedroom to give her mother a hug, and she then expressed her favorable opinion that Viola had made the right decision to box up his things. Viola opened the bedroom window, and she called out to Ernest asking that he come inside. Ernest and Steve ventured quickly inside to see the neatly stacked items in the narrow hallway. Viola convinced Ernest that she needed to pack up Felix's belongings, and she then asked them to place all of the items into the attic of their home. Steve was strong, and he worked quickly with Ernest to get the heavy items into the attic where they'd remain for many years to come. Viola felt sorrowful to see that the room was now empty of Felix's things, but she seemed ready for brighter days ahead. She kept one large picture of Felix in his military dress uniform hanging prominently on her living room wall. In addition, there were plenty of family photos around the house that featured her only son.

Dixie went back home, and Viola went with Aletha into the kitchen. Aletha fixed a bountiful breakfast consisting of fresh fruit, biscuits with gravy, and, of course, bacon and eggs. After breakfast, Aletha and Steve prepared to head back to their home in San Antonio. Ernest picked up Mary Jane and Nancy, and gave them each a great big hug. Viola also hugged the children, and she kissed them goodbye on their foreheads. Aletha and Steve said their goodbyes, and hugs were shared all around. Ernest and Viola were certainly sad to see everyone leave. They stood on the edge of the driveway waving as Steve proceeded down South Live Oak Street with his family. Ernest grabbed Viola's hand, and he walked with her as they headed back inside their home. They were about to embark on the next chapter of their lives, and they were glad to have and love each other.

Later that afternoon, Ernest made his typical daily trip to the post office to retrieve their mail. It had piled up a bit since he hadn't had an opportunity to grab it with all of the family having been in town. After returning home, Ernest spread the mail out onto the kitchen table, and Viola promptly selected an envelope that had been sent by Emma Jo McDermott. Ernest poured her a cup of coffee as she sat down at the table to read the letter.

Dear Mrs. Scott, *June 7, 1948*

I received your letter in the post late last week, and I wanted to send my heartfelt condolences to you and your family. Thank you for thinking of me, and for inviting me to Felix's funeral.

I'm really sorry that I can't come to the service. When Felix left College Station that day, it broke my heart. When I heard that he had died, I genuinely felt as if part of me had died too. I truly believe that he was my soulmate, and I'm trying really hard to move on. I just don't think I could take the additional grief that seeing his casket and grave would bring me.

If those damn Japs hadn't bombed Pearl Harbor, surely my life, Felix's life, and y'all's life would've been very different about now. I haven't yet found anyone else that was as nice, and as kind as Felix. I sensed that Felix wanted to propose to me on several occasions, and, by golly, I undoubtedly wish that he had. I saw myself living there in San Saba, raising youngins, and having supper ready when Felix got home from his crop dusting. I know that he was your only son, but he was my only true love. I want you to know that Felix always raved about you and Mr. Scott, and, of course, his amazing sisters.

I don't know if y'all heard that Buzz was shot down while on a bombing mission over Leipzig, which is somewhere south of Berlin, in February of 1944. Witnesses that were on the mission with him say that his plane exploded, and his body was never recovered. From what we hear, Buzz was a highly successful pilot, and he never said no when he was given a mission to perform. Felix would've been so proud of him, and I'm very proud of both of them. They'll always be heroes to my sister and me, and we'll hold them close to our hearts for the rest of our lives. We all presume that he and his crew must've been killed in action. Betty Lou is still devastated by Buzz's death because he was due home for a break shortly after he went missing. They were engaged, and they had planned to get married had he come home. I often wonder what life could've been like for Felix and me, and for Buzz and Betty Lou as well.

I hope that y'all are slowly finding closure with Felix's death, and I'm so glad to hear that the government sent his body home to y'all. I'm sure that you'll find some comfort when you sit beside his grave, and think about all of the wonderful years you had with Felix. I'd give anything to hear him laugh, to hold his hand, or to see his smile, just one more time. Boy did I love him, and I'll always miss him.

With love,

Emma Jo

The hawk became a regular visitor to the Scott house, and both Ernest and Viola felt that Felix was watching over them. Seeing the hawk provided them with a sense of peace and reassurance that Felix would always be there looking down from above. Life had indeed continued on for Ernest and Viola, and keeping busy helped them cope from day to day. Ernest continued to make his daily trip to the San Saba Post Office each weekday during his lunch break. It had been more than eight months since Felix's funeral, so Ernest was certainly not expecting anything from the Office of The Quartermaster General's office in Washington D.C. when he opened his P. O. Box on 30 Mar. 1949. Needless to say, he was eager to see what the correspondence could possibly be. He opened the envelope to find a simple letter, along with an application for a headstone or marker. Ernest was mystified as to why the government would be offering these options so long after Felix's burial. Did they not figure that a family would have a tombstone for their loved one at the time of the funeral? The paperwork intrigued him, so he went directly home to show the information to Viola.

Viola sat down at the kitchen table, and she carefully reviewed the documents. She turned to Ernest, and said, "Well, I reckon if they want to provide us with a granite marker at no cost, what do we have to lose? We already have a fine tombstone for Felix, but it says right here that we can get a flat one to add to his gravesite." With that, Viola got right to work with completing the forms. She giggled a bit, and found it rather amusing that one of the documents needed to be signed by the caretaker of the Bend Cemetery. Viola figured that it would be rather easy to get that signature, since the caretaker was none other than her very own father, W. J. Millican. She hopped into the car and drove out to the River Bend farm to visit with her father. He too thought that it was funny that he was the one to authorize the placement of the additional marker in the Scott family plot. Pa didn't hesitate to approve the paperwork, and he and Viola headed over to the cemetery to visit the graves of both Ma and Felix before she headed home.

Ernest dropped the paperwork off at the post office on 1 Apr. 1949. The Scotts figured that the Quartermaster General's office must've received the forms since they got another letter on 21 Apr. 1949. There was a receipt of sorts in the envelope that confirmed that an order was ready to be placed for the flat granite marker with Felix's pertinent information on it. After a careful review, the Scotts realized that the government had misspelled Felix's first name. They made the correction on the paperwork, and returned the document as directed. A few weeks later, Ernest once again found a letter from the Quartermaster General's office in his P. O. Box. This time, it was a letter confirming that the marker had shipped, and it would be arriving by train at the San Saba freight station in the coming weeks.

Mr. Ron Sloan, from the Santa Fe Railroad, was glad that Ernest answered the phone when he called him on the morning of 27 May 1949. He let Ernest know that a heavy box had arrived for him, and he asked that he come down forthwith to pick it up. Figuring that the heavy item was the granite marker, Ernest thought it would be fitting to take Felix's 1941 Chevy truck down to the train station to pick it up. His inkling was correct, and Mr. Sloan gladly helped him load the wooden crate into the back of the pickup. Upon returning home, Ernest grabbed a crowbar, and he proceeded to pry the lid off the crate. Viola thought that they had done a fine job with the marker, and Ernest was equally pleased with the finished product.

Felix's second grave marker at the Bend Cemetery, compliments of the United States of America.

Viola did what she did best, and she notified everyone in the family that Felix's new marker had finally arrived. She invited all the family members who could possibly attend to help them mark the special occasion. The Scotts thought that it would be a grand idea to place the new marker into the ground a few days later on Felix's birthday, 30 May 1949. More than five years after his death, there was now another marker adorning Felix's gravesite. The family watered the small cedar trees, and they placed fresh flowers around his tombstone. Before heading home, everyone sang "Happy Birthday" to Felix. They wanted Felix to know that they were still thinking about him every day.

Unfortunately, the Scotts would be back at the Bend Cemetery to bury W. J. Millican just a few weeks later. He passed away on 11 Jun.

1949, and Viola was once again grieving the loss of a loved one. She was overcome with sadness, as anyone would imagine, but she took some comfort knowing that her mother and father were there looking after Felix and Chauncey. Furthermore, Viola found solace knowing that Felix had more company within the confines of the cemetery. Viola looked up into the sky, and she figured that the three men were fishing off the edge of a cloud overlooking the Colorado River, while Ma was certainly cheering them on.

CHAPTER 4

The Auction

It was 20 Jun. 2018, and a day that Mack Sorrenson had been looking forward to for many weeks. A father and son road trip, a treasure picking quest, and a time to catch up with family out in Richland Springs, Texas.

Mack was 17 years old, and he had just finished his junior year at Mustang High School located in Mustang, Oklahoma. He was eager to get out on the road with his dad, Sam, in their brand new Chevy Silverado pick-up truck. This year, Mack was going to help with the drive as they made the five and a half hour journey south down I-44. Sam was a teacher at the local junior high school, and he was surely glad to have the summer off. Mack had a part-time job, but he was able to get time off for this special trip, and he too, was glad to be out of school for the summer. Their journey was to be a two week adventure which would end upon their arrival back home on 4 Jul. 2018. The duo arrived in Richland Springs on Wednesday afternoon 20 Jun. at the home of Sam's Brother Bruce.

After an afternoon of visiting, the family sat down for a delicious supper consisting of chicken fried steak, homemade biscuits, squash, and watermelon. Apple pie, pecan pie, and chocolate cake made for a wonderful dessert. After supper, Mack and Sam sat down on the living room sofa. They were eager to tear through the local newspaper to see what estate sales were being held in the nearby communities for the upcoming weekend. The public announcement section was right there at the top of page three. They noticed that a large estate auction was going to take place on Saturday morning 23 Jun. in the nearby town of San Saba. The announcement mentioned that the auction was being held at a multi-generational ranch house, complete with a barn, sheds, and storage containers. Mack had never been to San Saba, and Sam thought that it would be worth the 20 minute drive over there.

With a location in mind, and a plan set for Saturday morning, they had found the nearest ATM to get some cash on that Friday. Every good picker knows that cash on the barrel is best. Sam took out $500, and so did Mack. Mack had been saving money from each of his paychecks by working at his hometown Dairy Queen. With cash in their pockets, and clear directions to the auction site, the fellas decided to turn in for the night.

Bruce's wife, Sue Ann, was an excellent cook, and Mack and Sam awoke early to the smell of freshly cooked bacon, eggs, hashbrowns, and a pot of hot coffee. The roosters were crowing, and the farm was in full swing at 6 a.m. that morning. After breakfast, Bruce asked Mack if he wanted to help feed the hogs. Having never seen anything quite like this, he jumped at the opportunity. Tossing buckets of corn, soybeans, barley wheat, and food scraps into the pen was quite a sight.

The auction was to start at 9 a.m. sharp, so the boys took quick showers and got dressed. The pair left around 7:30 a.m., and they headed southeast over to San Saba, trying to ensure that they'd be on-time for registration. Mack was drawn to the old town vibe that San Saba provided. As they cruised through town on U.S. Highway 190, he could tell that this town had been around for a while. The courthouse appeared to be a historic landmark with many stores nearby. They even passed by a jail reminiscent of the wild, wild, west days.

As Sam continued driving, Mack did some research on his phone, and he found out that it was the oldest operating jailhouse in the nation at that time. It didn't take very long to get through the small town. Once they got past the east end of town, they turned right onto Road 400.

There are many dirt roads in Texas, and Mack and Sam certainly had found themselves on a winding and rocky one. With all of the cars heading down the road towards the auction site, it looked like a great dust storm had rolled into town. They finally arrived at the old Jacobsen ranch, which was about a mile down the road on the left. The main house looked like a modest ranch style home consisting of 3-4 bedrooms. They were now able to see the large barn, sheds, and shipping containers spread around the property. After parking, the men headed to a shade tent designated as the place to register for the auction. They completed the paperwork, and Sam was issued a paddle with their bidding number of 413. The time was 8:15 a.m., and they had about 45 minutes to look around the vast property before the start of the auction.

The usual things that one might expect at a place like this were omnipresent. Mack and Sam entered the barn from the south side. As the men looked to the left and to the right, they noticed quite a few road signs, gasoline signs, and even store signs from shops that had been long gone in San Saba. On the north wall of the barn, there were rows of vintage cross cut saws, pitch forks, thrashers, axes, and a host of other farm related equipment. Mack could tell that the east side of the barn was dedicated to a vintage car and auto parts collection. There were dozens of hubcaps, car grills, vintage tires, headlamps and rows of Texas license plates from many different decades. On the remaining wall, there were bridles, neck yolks, wagon wheels, and a great deal of blacksmith tools. Mack was simply in awe of the immense offerings hanging on the wall, and things dangling from the rafters and joists above them. Sam figured that it must have taken decades to amass the quantity of goods found thus far.

After leaving the barn, they ventured out to a trio of shipping containers. The heavy steel doors were open on each one so that the attendees could easily take a few steps inside to get a general idea of what was up for auction. Each container had a general mix of home furnishings. There were vintage dining room chairs, tables, bed frames, dressers, pie cabinets, gun cabinets, and rocking chairs. These items were very eclectic and definitely painted an image of the Texas lifestyle from early 1900 to the mid 1950's. Mack and Sam weren't interested in the big and bulky furniture items, so they moved on to the sheds located out behind the house.

The sheds were pretty well built. They had a wooden exterior with a tin roof. The items inside the sheds appeared to be well protected from the harsh Texas elements. Each unit had solid wood doors that seemed to close up nice and tight. Boxes and boxes of dishes, ceramics, ornate colored glassware, and cast iron pans filled upon the first shed. With time running short before the start of the auction, the fellas quickly began to look through the other sheds. There was a step ladder at shed number two, which was needed to peer over an assortment of odd ball items packed inside antique wooden boxes.

Inside shed number three, there was a wooden crate marked as lot #0922. The top of the crate was open, and the contents quickly captured Mack's eye. He could see a vintage metal suitcase, a military footlocker, and a cedar chest, all stacked one on top of the other. This collection of items was certainly going to be at the top of Mack's watch list, once the bidding was set to begin.

Folks began to gather around the barn since it was now a few minutes to 9 a.m. A voice came over a portable public address system, and the person identified herself as Kelly Spinelli. She welcomed everyone to the auction, and she asked the crowd to gather inside of the barn so that the auction could begin on time. Mack and Sam overheard some of the other folks talking about how Ms. Spinelli had a reputation all over Central Texas. They said her voice was as loud as a firecracker, and folks were amazed at just how fast she could talk.

Ms. Spinelli opened up the bidding by saying, "Today on the auction block we have almost 1000 items, which are among some of the finest things collected in these here parts in the last 100 years." She swung her gavel up in the air, and then said, "Alright, the auction is on, and let's get 'er done." As Mack and Sam nestled into some folding chairs that were neatly aligned in rows, they were intrigued by Kelly's voice as it crackled through the speakers. Her Texas drawl was reminiscent of a person who had grown up and lived in Texas their whole life. Sam reached over to Mack, and said, "This gal is amazing! How is she able to speak so darn quickly?"

Kelly then proclaimed that the first item up for sale would be a vintage Seeburg Wall-O-Matic juke box. According to the information provided, the item was purported to have come from the Laird corner drug store, which had its heyday during the 1940s and 1950s there in San Saba. Out came, "What ya want to give for it? Would you give $20, would you give $30, now a hundred dollar bill, hundred and a half? I have two, would you give two and a quarter? Two and a quarter again, no? Alright, sold for two hundred dollars to the gentleman in the yellow shirt."

The order in which things were being auctioned off seemed very methodical. Everything was well organized, with many items grouped together in lots. The auction moved right along, just like clockwork. Watching the paddles going up and down, and seeing bidders out bidding others was fascinating to Mack. The cadence in which Kelly ran the auction was exhilarating. A great deal of the bulky items found inside of the barn were gone within the first hour. By the end of the second hour, the barn auction was in full swing. Lot after lot went to the highest bidder. Shortly after 11:30 a.m., the auction in the main barn was complete. Kelly asked everyone who was interested in the items within the sheds to move to the new staging area that had been set up outside. After sitting through two hours of bidding on the items found in sheds one and two, the moment that Mack and Sam had been waiting for had finally arrived.

Sam reached over to Mack, and said, "They are about to open bidding on lot #0921, and the one you want is coming up next." Mack felt like a youngster on Christmas morning, just waiting for the opportunity to open his presents. In this case, he was hell bent on winning lot number #0922. Mack was certainly disappointed when the staff at the registration desk had told him that he couldn't participate in the bidding directly, since he wasn't yet 18 years old. However, he was glad that he was allowed to watch, and he could root for his father along the way. It appeared that the crowd had begun to thin out a bit. Perhaps many had already spent their stash of cash, or maybe they just weren't interested in any of the remaining items. They liked their odds of being able to win their desired items.

Kelly finally announced, "Next on the block, we have lot #0922, which consists of the contents held within this wooden crate." Mack took one more glance at the pictures that he'd taken with his phone of the items inside the crate. He was certain that he wanted the lot, and he told his father to get his paddle ready. All of a sudden, Mack heard, "What do you want to give for it?" "Now a $100 bid, now $200, would ya give three?" As Sam raised his paddle high in the air, Kelly continued her rapid acknowledgement of the other bidders. She then said, "Three hundred, four, five hundred, would you give six hundred?" Once again, Sam quickly raised his paddle. Things were moving fast, and it seemed that Kelly never stopped to take a breath. Mack looked over at his father, and Sam nodded as if to affirm the continuance with the bidding. Kelly continued the bidding with, "Seven hundred, would you give eight, eight now, would you give nine?" Sam raised his paddle to acknowledge the $900 bid. Kelly quickly went on with, "Nine hundred, would ya give ten, nine would you give ten? We have $900, last call." It seemed like an eternity, but it was like music to Mack's ears when the gavel finally landed loudly on the block. Kelly finished the bidding on the lot with, "Sold to the gentleman in the black shirt. Say, is that Ferris Bueller on your shirt?" Sam yelled out, "Yes ma'am, it sure is. Thank you." Mack began to feel a sense of relief and excitement after they were named the winner of lot #0922. He was now very eager to see what was actually inside the crate.

Having won the lot, an attendant came by and handed Sam a sheet of paper. It provided instructions on how to pay for the lot, and how to take possession of the items. The registration tent had now become the cashier tent. Running low on cash, and not being interested in anything else, the fellas headed over to the tent to settle up their bill. Mack and Sam each pulled out a stack of twenty dollar bills. Sam uttered, "Cash on the barrel is best, right, son?" Mack nodded affirmatively, and he gently pushed the stack of cash forward towards the young woman serving as the cashier.

After Mack was given the receipt, he and Sam walked to the truck, and then drove over to the designated loading area. As Sam was backing up into the assigned space, a big gentleman by the name of Kyle, was patiently sitting on his forklift, and waiting to deliver the large wooden crate onto the back of Sam's truck. The forklift's blades were already balancing the crate, and, after Mack let the truck's tailgate down, Kyle carefully placed the crate onto the bed of the truck. Being prepared was always a motto for Sam, so of course, he had plenty of straps and rope to accommodate a crate of this size. With the crate securely fastened to the truck, the fellas felt that it was time to go and grab something to eat. Mack thought that it would be entirely cool to stop at the local Dairy Queen there in San Saba before heading back to Richland Springs.

Mack was rather quiet on the ride back to his Uncle Bruce's house. He was anxious to find out what was inside the crate, and he just couldn't stop thinking about all of the possibilities. Would there be any contents inside of the suitcase, the footlocker, or the cedar chest? Could it be possible that they might be empty? That thought hadn't yet crossed Mack's mind until that very moment. He figured that it would be highly unlikely that there wouldn't be anything of value inside. Mack was certain that some special things had to be inside for someone to take the time and money to crate and store these things for so many years.

As Sam barreled down the highway back to his brother's house, Mack was texting his Uncle Bruce to let him know they were coming back with a large crate. Being that the lid to the crate had been nailed shut at the end of the auction, Mack asked his uncle if he had a crowbar or hammer to help them deal with that situation upon their arrival. As Sam turned down the gravel road leading to Bruce and Sue Ann's ranch, Mack asked his dad to watch out for potholes so that whatever was in the crate wouldn't get broken before they even had a chance to see it.

CHAPTER 5

Discovering Felix

Bruce was waiting outside with a crowbar and a hammer as Mack and Sam pulled up. Sue Ann came out of the front door with a pitcher of iced tea for everyone to enjoy before they dug into their find. The group relaxed on the front porch for a bit as Sam explained what had led them to getting the crate that sat in the back of his truck. Mack just couldn't contain himself any longer, so he set his glass down and headed for the back of his father's Silverado.

Sam could clearly see the anxiety pulsating through his son's body, so he got out of his rocker, and he proceeded to let the truck's tailgate down. Mack quickly jumped up into the bed of the truck and his Uncle Bruce was right behind him. Bruce had some serious crowbar skills, and, with tools in hand, and in no time flat, the crate was opened. After tossing the lid off the side of the truck, there was an aroma that can only be described as "old," emanating from inside the crate. Mack felt like someone had opened a bottle with a genie inside. His wish to find a treasure had finally come true, and the reality of the moment was exhilarating to him.

The suitcase was smack on top, and it was the first thing to come out of the crate. Mack grabbed the handle, and he then quickly released his grip after he noticed the delicate, paper laced metal bar that had probably once been covered in leather. He noticed a big T on the top center of the suitcase, and it had orange, yellow, and brown lines running vertically down the middle of the case. "Texas Aggies" was featured inside of the middle section of the "T" emblem. The suitcase was made of metal, and the outside had an olive drab color scheme covering the majority of the case. There were numerous metal rivets holding everything together all across the case. The clasp on the right side was broken, but the main locking mechanism on the center of the case was operable. The left side clasp was functional, and it was closed in place. The suitcase was dented throughout, and it surely had seen better days.

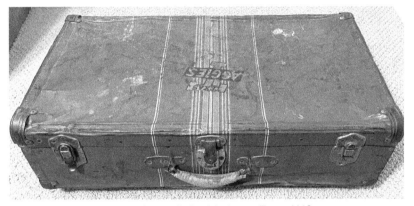

Felix's suitcase during his time at Texas AMC.

Mack began to think that the suitcase had probably belonged to a college student at one point. It measured 25" long x 13" wide, and it was 7" deep. The suitcase certainly had a great deal of character, and Mack was intrigued. He grabbed the suitcase using both of his hands, and he gently handed it down to his father who was waiting beside the truck. After setting it down on the ground, Sam lifted the top to reveal a beautiful cloth interior lined with wood all around the inner perimeter. The contents of the suitcase started to reveal hints about its previous owner. A maroon and white sweater made of wool was the first thing that Sam pulled out. As Mack looked down from the truck bed, a pennant for the Agricultural and Mechanical College of Texas followed. Next, there was a photo of a young man outfitted in what looked like a military uniform. The picture was well protected within an 8" x 10" wooden frame, and it featured a brass nameplate on the front. The nameplate showed "Felix E. Scott, senior class of '42." Mack blurted out, "Do you think that he could be the original owner of these things?" Sam replied, "That's a great possibility, son, but let's keep digging."

The final things to come out of the suitcase were pieces of what appeared to be a military uniform of some kind. The jacket was green with a leather shoulder strap affixed to the front, and it looked a bit different than the typical styles that they'd seen before. There were large brass buttons down the front, and it had smaller ones on the pockets. On the upper collars, there was a metal pin with the letters "AMC" on each side. Just below the AMC pins, there was a crossed rifle pin affixed to the lapels. Beneath the coat, there was a pair of unique cavalry style trousers that had a very interesting look to them. The trousers had unusually large, flared areas around the thighs, which tapered into a much narrower area around the knees. There was an extra piece of white material sewn onto both sides of the trousers from around the top of each boot to above the knees. There was also a pair of white gloves, a white collared shirt, and a black tie.

A round tin can with small holes in it was found inside the suitcase. Sam looked up at Mack, and he told him that those were mothballs used to keep the clothes free of moths, which were known to be pesky, cloth eating insects. Sam handed the jacket up to Mack, and he then rubbed his thumb over one of the AMC pins. Mack turned to his Uncle Bruce, and asked, "What do you suppose this symbolizes?" Bruce, being a lifelong Texan replied, "Those AMC pins are from the Agricultural and Mechanical College of Texas, which is located over in College Station. The school is now known as Texas A&M, and it served a as a huge military prep school before and after World War

II." Sue Ann then chimed in by saying, "Yes, it's still a school with a cadet program, and it's located about three hours east of us." Mack was amazed at what he'd found in the suitcase, and he hadn't yet opened the other two items. He now had the name of Felix E. Scott, but who was Felix E. Scott? Could he have been a Marine, a pilot, a father, or someone's husband? Mack was about to find out more as the footlocker was the next piece to be opened.

With the suitcase now safely out of the way, there was more room to remove the sides of the crate, which made it easier to access the footlocker and cedar chest. The well faded wooden footlocker had a military green shade to it, and Mack felt that it really showed its age. The stenciling on the top was somewhat faded, and a few of the letters were rather hard to read. The footlocker measured 33.5" long by 16.5" wide by 13" deep, and it had one latch on the front of it. There were no handles on the heavy footlocker, but it was easy to lift due to the thin wooden strips that ran along the outside edges on both ends. The footlocker was built well, and it had plenty of nails holding it all together. There was a vintage padlock keeping the contents locked safely inside. Since there was no sign of a key, Bruce returned from the garage with a pair of bolt cutters, and he quickly took care of the lock. The hinges screeched loudly as Mack slowly pried the lid open to see what was lurking inside.

The footlocker was well kept, and at a glance, the contents appeared very organized inside. There were military clothing items on the left side, and the right side had an assortment of other things. The interior was completely made of wood, and there were some stains here and there. Folded neatly was an olive drab coat with a sterling silver airman's wing pin located above the left pocket. There was a brass "U.S." pin located on both sides of the upper collars, and a colorful patch on the left shoulder. Each of the lapels had a pin that looked like a small propeller that was embedded within a pair of wings. Mack asked his Uncle Bruce, "What do you suppose those golden rectangular pins are on top of the shoulders?" Bruce replied, "Those pins indicate that this man was a second lieutenant." Similar to the school uniform, the coat had large buttons down the front and smaller buttons on the pockets. Sam blurted out, "Based on the look and presentation of this jacket, I'd say that this belonged to a pilot." Mack figured that Felix must've been in the Air Corps, most likely during WWII. He wondered what type of aircraft Felix would've flown, and which theater of operations would he have served in? Underneath the jacket was a pair of light colored trousers, a formal looking garrison cap, two tan shirts, and a pair of black dress shoes. All of these items were neatly pressed and folded as if they had just been placed into the footlocker. A rather heavy leather flight jacket came out next. The jacket smelled great, and it had that vintage look, so Mack knew that it had to be old. There was a large circular patch on the chest that had some sort of yellow tiger or cat with big teeth, claws, and a big red tongue protruding from its mouth. Mack lifted it up so that he could try it on, and it seemed to fit him pretty well. Considering its age, the jacket was in great shape, and the leather appeared to be mostly intact. Bruce said to Mack, "That flight jacket is worth some money. I'd bet that piece alone would be worth more than what you paid for the entire crate." Mack said, "Well, that would certainly be nice. I'm glad to know that this crate is not a bust. This sure seems like a time capsule of sorts, right?"

On the right side of the footlocker, there was a wooden box that was located underneath a small collection of miscellaneous things. On top of the box, there were several copies of *FLYING Aces* and *AIR FORCE* magazines, college football programs from a host of different Aggie games, a small stack of books, class yearbooks from Mesa Del

Rey and Luke Field, a class of '41 yearbook from Texas AMC, a folded Japanese flag, a type 30 Japanese Arisaka bayonet complete with scabbard, and also a journal. Sam told Mack that it was common for soldiers to bring souvenirs home from the war. Servicemen would either keep the items, trade them, send them home to family and friends, or they would even play cards, and use the items for wagering purposes. Mack thought that these items were extremely cool, and he was now very interested in the history of these items. He briefly thumbed through the journal, thinking that it might shed some light on the items within the footlocker.

The small wooden box didn't have a lock on it, but the lid fit snugly to protect the contents held inside. It was truly as if Mack was going back in time as he lifted the lid to the box. Mack's eyes lit up as he looked down into the box to see a fine collection of things that probably hadn't seen the light of day for quite some time. He grabbed a cloth bag, imagining that it would be filled with coins. It was rather heavy, and when he dumped the contents out onto the lid, marbles of all kinds, colors, and sizes spilled out. The next group of items to come out was a collection of about a dozen letters addressed to Felix E. Scott from a variety of people. The envelopes were neatly grouped together and bound with a shoe string. A 5" x 7" framed picture caught Mack's attention, and he lifted it out of the box for a further look. The writing on the back showed October 1943, and it had the photographer's information on it there in San Saba, Texas. Mack stared at the picture thinking that these folks must be his family, sisters, parents, spouse, or maybe even a girlfriend. Mack was determined to find out.

Tucked into the frame of the family picture, and on top of the glass, was a picture of a soldier that looked different than Felix. The picture was in the lower left corner of the frame, and it looked like it had been purposely placed there. His uniform looked noticeably different from Felix's. His garrison cap wasn't fancy, but it had some sort of pin just off the front center. There were two medals pinned to his uniform above the left pocket. The soldier looked sharp, and the uniform had no other marks to distinguish a rank. Mack couldn't really tell, but perhaps, he was a private? Could he have been a Marine? On both sides of his upper collars, there was a pin that looked the same as the one on his cap. It had a globe in the center, an eagle on top, and an anchor at the bottom. Sam, being the history teacher, said, "I'm sure that he was a Marine because I know that that is the Marine Corps emblem that he is wearing on his uniform. The eagle represents the United States of America, the globe stands for the Marine's ability to defend America anywhere around the world, and the anchor symbolizes their long standing relationship with the folks from the U.S. Navy." Sure enough, scribbled on the back of the picture was the name, Chauncey White, U.S. Marine Corps Battery G, 3rd Battalion, 14th Marines Regiment, 4th Marine Division Fleet Marine Force, Pfc. Mack wondered, was this guy a friend, a classmate, or a cousin? He figured that he may find the answer within the journal or letters to help solve the mystery. With the cedar chest still looming, excitement was definitely building among the group.

Mack was elated to go through the remaining few things in the box. There were several loose patches, three handkerchiefs, ticket stubs from Kyle Field, a small handful of shiny 1943 steel pennies, a box of well-worn playing cards, a match book from Luke Field, and a really cool United States Army Air Forces (USAAF) identity bracelet. Felix E. Scott was inscribed onto the back of the bracelet which was made of sterling silver, and the USAAF wing emblem was featured prominently on the front. The final thing that Mack found inside the box was a small photo album. There were at least two dozen pictures, and with a cursory glance, Mack saw pictures of military training, and a man who looked like Felix having fun with other servicemen. There were several pictures of Felix posing in front of various planes, and possibly even a girlfriend or two. The album was most definitely a throwback to yesteryear, and Mack was on a mission to find out more.

Just as Mack was about to close the lid on the footlocker, he saw a very thin piece of paper stuck to one of the inside walls. After inspecting the document, Mack determined it to be a Flyer's Personal Equipment Record. Felix's name, grade, serial number, and signature were found on one side. On the reverse side, there was a checklist of 17 specific clothing items and pieces of equipment that had been issued to him. The list included issuance of his B-4 bag, a pair of flying glasses and goggles, a leather flying helmet and jacket for summer and winter, an oxygen mask, a parachute, shoes, trousers, a life vest, a winter vest, gloves, and a sweater. Mack noticed that the grade listed Felix as an aviation cadet, so Sam's conclusion was that these things were issued to him very early on in his aviation training. The form was rather forthright by stating, "This equipment is issued to you for the Duration. It must be CONSERVED—it is critical. You are personally responsible for its care." Mack found the checklist to be a very intriguing last minute find, and he could picture Felix with his arms full of all of this equipment.

After having gone through every inch of the footlocker, Bruce and Mack lifted the lid of the cedar chest to reveal its bountiful contents. The chest measured 50" long by 22" wide by 18" deep, and it appeared to have been made by a real craftsman. There was a beautiful mahogany inlay in the shape of Texas found on top of the lid, and it was remarkably done. The initials F. E. S. were emblazoned onto the front of the cedar chest. The items were well organized and protected from breakage. There were so many things in the cedar chest, and it was very heavy. Therefore, a decision was made to unpack it right there in the back of the truck, and then offload the chest once it was empty.

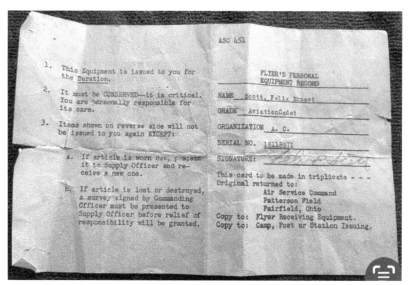

Felix's Personal Equipment Record that was found in his footlocker.

Right smack on top of the things in the cedar chest was a large red, white, and blue quilt that featured a bright yellow biplane in the center. This was a durable quilt made with quality materials, and it had to have been crafted by a very talented person. Sue Ann got up from her chair, and said, "Land sakes, let's see what y'all got there." Each of them took a corner of the fabulous quilt, and they held it tight to see just how exquisite a piece this was. At the very bottom of the lower right hand corner, there was a white patch with the name Viola Abigail Scott in blue stitching. Sue Ann then stated that Viola Abigail Scott was probably the person who had made the quilt. Mack was determined to find out if she was Felix's wife, mother, or grandmother.

As a gun enthusiast, Mack certainly noticed the two rifles, which had been placed underneath the quilt. He reached into the chest, and he pulled out a Daisy air rifle, which was confirmed to be a BB gun. The other gun was a .22 caliber Remington long rifle, and it didn't seem as if any ammunition was present. Mack turned to his dad, and asked him if he thought that Felix might've used the rifles as a young man. Sam replied, "Well, I reckon, those are sure some mighty fine rifles, and they're in top notch condition." There was a vintage bamboo fly fishing rod sitting right next to the .22 long rifle. Mack figured that all of these items were surely an integral part of Felix's childhood.

The next thing that Mack pulled out of the cedar chest was a photo album that was larger than the one that they'd found in the footlocker. As Mack glanced through the album, it seemed that he was seeing pictures that showed Felix as a baby up until the time that he left for duty in the war. A large envelope was tucked into the back of the photo album. Sam peeked into it, and then began to pull out the contents that had been placed neatly inside. Out came Felix's birth certificate, his high school diploma, and the telegram from the War Department, notifying Felix's parents of his death.

Everyone was saddened to read the telegram, as they had just learned that Felix had been killed during the war. The Western Union telegram read, *"The Secretary of War asks that I assure you of his deep sympathy in the loss of your son, 2nd Lt. Felix E. Scott. Report received states he was killed 13 Apr. 1944 in India in a plane crash. Letter to follow. Signed by Robert Dunlop, acting Adjutant General."* The telegram was dated 16 Apr. 1944, and it had been generated out of Washington D.C. There were several different clippings from the local San Saba newspapers, and Sam found some correspondence from the War Department included within the envelope as well. Mack began to wonder about the plane crash. How did this happen, and how did he die? Was he a fighter pilot or a bomber pilot? Was it an accident or was he shot down in combat? These were all good questions, and Mack assured himself that he'd find out more.

A shadow box with a United States burial flag folded neatly inside was the next thing that Mack pulled out of the cedar chest. There was also a funeral program dated 9 Jun. 1948 taped to the back of the shadow box. Sam said to Mack, "I bet you that that flag was placed upon Felix's casket at his funeral." Mack nodded his head in agreement, and he then asked, "Why do you think this funeral program is dated in June of 1948 when he was killed in April of 1944? Why would they have had the funeral so many years after he died, and well after the war had ended?" Another great question for Mack to find an answer to.

A patriotic piece of Felix in his college uniform. Someone had written his name underneath "Our Hero."

Beneath the flag, there was a stack of pictures and other framed items. The first piece was rather heart rendering, and probably hung in someone's living room. It appeared to be a little bigger than a standard 5" x 7" size. The frame was made of pine, and the matting was very unique. It had two American flags in a crossed fashion at the top with a blue border all around the perimeter. There were five white stars at the bottom along with an image of a ship and tank. Right square in the middle, there was a picture of Felix in his Texas AMC uniform with the words, "OUR HERO," beneath the picture.

The second item was encased in a dark brown wooden frame that measured 14" by 16", and it housed a letter from President Franklin D. Roosevelt regarding Felix's death. After looking at the letter, Sam figured that the president's signature was probably not real. However, the content and the presentation of the letter was still fabulous. The frame was well worn, and it had lost much of its original paint, making it rather rustic looking now. The presidential seal was located at the top of the document, and beneath that, it read, "*In grateful memory of Second Lieutenant Felix E. Scott, A. S. N. 0-756719, who died in the service of his country in the Asiatic Area, April 13, 1944. He stands in the unbroken line of patriots who have dared to die that freedom might live, and grow, and increase its blessings. Freedom lives, and through it, he lives in a way that humbles the undertakings of most men.*" Signed Franklin D. Roosevelt, President of the United States of America. The piece had some water damage in the upper left corner, but it wasn't torn. It was simply remarkable that the item had survived so many years later. In the lower left corner, someone had placed a graduation announcement. At the top of the announcement, there was a symbol that had a pair of wings with a propeller in the middle. Mack recognized that symbol, as he had seen it on Felix's uniform. The card read, "*The Commandant and staff of the Army Air Forces Pilot*

School (advanced—single engine) Luke Field, Phoenix, Arizona invite you to attend the graduation exercises of class 43-I to be held on the concert green at 9:00 a.m., October 1, 1943." In the lower left corner of the announcement, it read, "P*resent this card to the guard at the gate for admission."* Mack turned to his dad, and said, "If you needed to have this card to get in, I wonder if anyone got to go and watch Felix graduate?" Sam replied, "Golly, who really knows, but that would've been sad if his family couldn't have made it there to celebrate with him."

A memorial letter sent to the Scott family from President Roosevelt.

The third item in the stack was an artistic piece nestled within a very eclectic red, white, and blue frame, which measured a whopping 18" by 16". The piece seemed to be hand crafted upon some sort of fabric that could've been made of silk. At the top, it read, "To Polly and Ted," with "Felix" underneath that. In the middle, there was a very ornate rendering of a pilot's pair of wings, and it said, "U.S. Air Force in India 1944." Mack recalled that one of the pictures in the album had the name Polly on the back, so he figured that this piece must've been sent from India to a very special person back home. Sam then said to Mack, "This piece is dated in 1944, and that's the year and place that Felix died. It must've been very nice for Polly to have received something so special, only to become entirely sad by losing him so soon after receiving it."

The fourth piece was probably the most poignant. The frame measured 12" by 15", and it was made with a light colored wood border that featured an ornate inlay of a darker wood along the inner perimeter. This was a fabulous color photo of Felix smiling and enjoying life in what looked like a tropical paradise of some sort. In the picture, Felix appears to be wearing the very same dress coat complete with pins, tan slacks, cap, and black shoes that were found in the footlocker, which made this piece very special. Mack figured that this picture was more than likely taken at a training base or while on deployment. Although nothing was written on the picture, Mack could tell that this item had meant quite a bit to someone. When looking at the glass at an angle, he could see a thumbprint on the left and right sides. This would seem to indicate that someone had held it directly in front of them. Additionally, there appeared to be a few water drop marks on the glass. Mack began to wonder if someone had cried over the picture while holding it in their lap.

A handcrafted gift made in India from Felix to his sister Pauline and her husband Ted.

The final framed item wasn't a picture, but rather a marvelous collection of arrowheads of all different sizes and shapes. They were individually sewn onto a cardboard backing, and then secured within a dark black frame. Sam then reached into the chest, and he pulled out a kite made of cloth and light weight wooden pieces. It had a colorful tail, but there was no string found in the chest. Mack imagined that Felix would've probably spent a great deal of time flying it, while dreaming that he'd also fly one day. There were two small balsa wood planes still in their original boxes. Mack figured that they were something that Felix just never got around to opening. Next, Sam grabbed a quart sized blue mason jar that was heavy and full of marbles. The zinc lid was screwed on tight, and all of the colors in the marbles were marvelous to look at. Sam then said to Mack, "This boy sure liked his marbles." The jar of marbles was sitting on top of a small stack of American Boy magazines, and the one on top was dated April of 1931. This particular issue was entirely amazing, as it portrayed a man in a pilot's flight suit, looking upwards towards the sky with planes flying overhead. Mack felt that the magazine must've been a very inspirational piece to Felix as a boy, and perhaps it fueled his desire to want to become a pilot himself.

There were just a few things left in the cedar chest. Mack reached in, and he grabbed a small square cardboard box with no distinct markings on it. He proceeded to open the box to find an item inside that was wrapped securely with pages of an old newspaper. Mack was certainly curious as he carefully pulled the item out of the box. He was in awe as he held the vintage airplane that was attached to a pedestal. The item appeared to be made of brass or bronze, and it measured about six inches tall. It was missing one blade of the three blade propeller. The markings on the bottom showed that it was made by a company called "Trophy Craft" out of Hollywood, CA. There was a captivating inscription on the side that made Mack a bit sad as he read it, "Mother and Dad, Felix, May 9, 1943." Mack thought to himself that Felix must've purchased this item as a gift to his parents, but the date on it was throwing him off a bit. The graduation announcement stated that he graduated from Advanced Flight school in October of 1943. So, what would he have been doing in May of 1943? Where was he living at that time, and could he have been training in California? Mack was bound and determined to find out.

A gift to "Mother and Dad" from Felix.

Mack found two toy planes that were made of iron on the floor of the cedar chest. They were pretty small, each one measuring about four inches long. It appeared that some paint had worn off, but one was red and the other blue. Both of the planes had black rubber wheels. Mack turned to his dad, and said, "There's no plastic on these toys, eh?" Similar to the letters found in the footlocker, there was a small stack of 12-15 letters from Felix addressed to his parents, and one or two addressed to his sisters. They were gently wrapped with a piece of brown twine, and tied with a bow. Mack thumbed through the letters to find that they had been sent from CA, AZ, FL, and India. For a small town boy from Texas, it seemed that Felix had been to some faraway places.

The final thing found inside of the cedar chest was a leather bound certificate holder. Mack opened it, and it read, "*In Memory of Felix Ernest Scott who has given his life in the service of our country in the second World War. His Alma Mater, the Agricultural and Mechanical College of Texas, has inscribed his name on the permanent honor roll of the college. Given at College Station, on the twentieth day of May, 1944. Signed by F. C. Bolton, President of the Agricultural and Mechanical college of Texas.*"

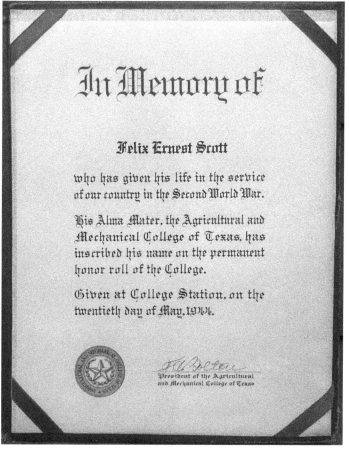

Memorial certificate from the Agricultural and Mechanical College of Texas to honor Felix.

With the cedar chest now empty, Mack and Sam pushed it towards the tailgate. Bruce joined in to assist them in getting it safely to the ground. The experience of opening all of those things, and discovering so much about Felix was emotional, educational, inspirational, and even a bit exhausting. It had been a long day, but it sure was a memorable one to say the least. As the boys had been unpacking the crate and all of its goodies, Sue Ann had been taking the items into the den inside their home. She had placed everything neatly on the floor. When Mack walked into the room while carrying the cedar chest with Sam, he was quite amazed with the haul that was laid out in front of him. Mack sat down on the floor before supper to take a closer look at the photo albums, and at Felix's personal effects. He hadn't seen Felix's flight log come out of the crate, but after picking it up off of the floor, he found it to be fascinating, since it described all of the planes that he had flown, and where he had flown them.

All during supper, Mack kept wondering how he had become the one to come into possession of these items. Did Felix not have any family members in the area anymore? Did he have children or grandchildren who might want these treasures? Mack was thinking of ways to find the answers to these questions. He wondered what other of Felix's belongings might be out there somewhere, just waiting to be found. Mack figured that with a little research, and a lot of luck, who knows what he may come up with. With his cellphone in hand, and by relaxing on the couch after supper, Mack took to the internet to see what he could find. On his favorite search engine, he typed in Felix E. Scott, San Saba, Texas, and he had several results pop up.

The first thing that Mack clicked on provided Felix's serial number, basic information on where he was from, and where he had died. It also provided an acronym that his death was labeled as "DNB", which meant that he had died non battle. Mack knew that Felix had died, but died non battle? This was a bit of a twist that he needed to dive deeper into. The next thing that he saw was from a genealogy website. Mack didn't have a membership to the site, so he moved on to the next result. The third result provided the name of some website that locates graves from around the United States. Mack clicked on it, and two pictures came up displaying two different tombstones. Mack showed the screen to his dad, and said, "Now why do you suppose he has two grave markers? Could one be located in India, and maybe one here in Texas?" The website did say that Felix was buried in Bend, Texas. Bruce heard what the fellas were talking about, and said, "Bend is a very small town near San Saba." Mack then said to his dad, "We need to go out to Bend and pay our respects to Felix." Sam seemed to be on board with that idea.

Wanting to know more about Felix and his hometown of San Saba, Mack did a new search for upcoming events and activities going on there. He was hoping that just maybe there would be some locals who might have known Felix's family, and who could still be living in or around San Saba. Mack noticed that one of the search results was for an ice cream social being held the following day after the 10:00 Sunday service at the San Saba Methodist Church. Mack and Sam were Christians, so they decided they'd make the drive back to San Saba to see if they could attend the service. They also hoped that they'd be invited to the ice cream social afterwards.

Mack woke up to a beautiful Sunday morning, and after a wonderful breakfast cooked by Sue Ann, Mack and Sam headed over to San Saba. They arrived at the church at about 9:30 a.m. There were plenty of cars in the parking lot, but it wasn't quite full. They got out of their truck, and began to walk the grounds, making their way towards the front of the church. They took great pleasure in admiring all of the beautiful old trees that were around the church. The church looked quite old, and it looked to be made of marble, or some kind of stone. While standing near the front steps of the church, Mack glanced over to his left, and he noticed Rogan Field. It had all the markings of a typical high school football stadium, and after a quick search of the internet, he confirmed that it indeed belonged to the San Saba Armadillos. The year of 1935, which was prominently featured on the arched entry way, seemed to coincide with Felix's high school days. As he peaked through the chain link gate, Mack imagined Felix running down the field scoring touchdowns while the crowd cheered him on.

While milling around in front of the church, Mack and Sam were approached by a well-dressed lady, who seemed to have a whole lot of spunk. "Good morning, my name is Natalie. I'd like to welcome y'all to our church. Are you fellas from around here?" Sam replied, "No ma'am, we're just visiting family in Richland Springs. We're hoping that it would be alright with y'all if we attend today's service?" Natalie replied, "Well, I'm the pastor's wife, and we'd be very pleased to have you join us today." Natalie then turned towards the front door of the church, and she waved to a tall man that was wearing a preacher's robe. The man waved back to Natalie, and he quickly walked up to her and the fellas. Natalie said, "Mack and Sam, this is my husband, Reverend Quinn Alden, pastor of our church." "Nice to meet you folks," said Reverend Alden. He then went on to say, "We're very glad to have you with us today, so please join us inside for services as we are fixing to begin soon." Natalie added, "We're having an ice cream social and fundraiser right afterwards, and I'd like for y'all to join us if you have time?" These words were music to Mack's ears. He hadn't been there but ten minutes, and he'd already met two nice people. Mack had also been invited to the social, where he'd be able to network, and put some feelers out regarding Felix. Sam said, "Thank you very much for the offer, and we'd be honored to join you folks today."

With that, Mack and Sam proceeded to walk up the church steps in order to go inside. After finding an empty pew inside the beautiful old sanctuary, they noticed the smell of old polished wood, and they admired the magnificent stained glass windows as the sun shined down upon the congregation. As the other parishioners found their seats, Reverend Alden welcomed everyone to the service. He took a moment to introduce Mack and Sam as special guests. Mack and Sam stood up to acknowledge the nice gesture, and then sat back down into the wooden pew. Reverend Alden was a jovial gentleman, and he gave an uplifting sermon to the large congregation. At the conclusion of the service, Reverend Alden proclaimed, "Everyone is now welcome to join us on the back lawn for some refreshments, cold drinks, and, of course, some ice cream." As Mack and Sam walked back towards the entrance of the church, they ran into Natalie again. Mack was no longer feeling shy or rushed, so, as they were walking, he explained why they had come to town, and that they were looking for any information about Felix or his family. He briefly told her that he'd just come into possession of many of Felix's things, and that he was eager to learn more about him. Natalie said, "That sounds like a mighty fine thing you're doing, and I have the perfect group that I'd like to introduce y'all to."

Natalie led the fellas out to a round table that had a beautiful floral centerpiece on it. The table was located underneath a large oak tree just a bit away from the other tables. There were oak trees everywhere, and they provided a terrific shade canopy, which served as a welcome respite to the Texas heat. Natalie then said, "Now I want y'all to know that this isn't an official club or anything, but we all call 'em the six matrons. In church, they sit with their families, but for social events, the six of them generally sit together right here." The trio made it to the table, and Natalie said in her perky southern voice,

"Now Mack and Sam, I'd like to introduce y'all to Maude, Michelle, Minnie, Mabel, Marissa, and Mary. These fine ladies here know all about the comings and goings in San Saba. They don't call it gossip, but they rather liken it to just being in the know. I hope that they can help y'all with your search." As Natalie walked away, the fellas shook hands with all of the matrons. The ladies asked Mack and Sam to grab a few chairs, and they said that the men were welcome to join them at their table.

Michelle inquisitively asked, "Now Mack, what brings you to San Saba, and how may we help you?" Mack explained that they were at the auction out at the old Jacobsen place, and he ended up with a crate full of things that had belonged to Felix E. Scott. He shared with them that he'd found a suitcase, a footlocker, and a cedar chest along with an awesome array of things inside. Sam then shared that Felix had been a pilot, and that he'd been killed in 1944 during WWII. Mack followed with, "I feel blessed to have come into contact with these things, and we're looking to see if any of his relatives might still be alive?" Mabel excitedly spoke up, and said, "Now, I do declare that I've seen Felix's grave out at the Bend Cemetery. I have kin buried there, and I remember his grave because of his handsome picture on his tombstone. If I recall, his family lived in the San Saba area for quite a long time, and I'm pretty certain that they even attended this church." Mack replied, "That is amazing. Would you happen to know if his family still lives around here? My dad and I are going to visit the Bend Cemetery later today."

The other ladies at the table were softly speaking among themselves when Minnie spoke up, and said, "I have a friend named Ruvonne, who lives over in Buchanan Dam, and I'm fairly confident that Felix just might've been her uncle. I'm fixing to call her right now, and I'll ask her." Minnie placed a call to Ruvonne, and then she gave her a synopsis of what was going on in the conversation. Ruvonne was astonished, since Felix had been dead for over 74 years, and it wasn't every day that someone was asking about him. Ruvonne then confirmed to Minnie that she indeed had referred to him as Uncle Felix.

The fellas could hear Ruvonne loud and clear coming out of Minnie's phone. Ruvonne then asked Minnie to give the phone to Mack or Sam so she could speak with them. Mack took the phone, since he was the closest to Minnie, and then said, "Howdy," into the receiver. Ruvonne, in her sweet and charming voice, said, "Well, I'll be. I understand y'all came into contact with a whole bunch of stuff that had once belonged to my Uncle Felix?" Mack acknowledged in the affirmative that indeed they had bid on a crate, and he briefly described some of the things that they'd found. Mack could tell that Ruvonne was a warm and generous person, since she proceeded to invite them out for a visit at her place. Mack asked if they could pay her a visit the following day? Ruvonne thought the idea was splendid, and Mack typed her phone number and address into his phone. He thanked her very much for the invite, and he ended the call with Ruvonne. Mack then kindly handed the phone back to Minnie. Mack looked rather dumbfounded, and he was in disbelief as to what had just happened. It was as if things kept clicking, one by one, and it was both a little overwhelming, yet exhilarating. After having further conversation with the matrons of San Saba, Sam stood up, and Mack followed suit. They thanked the ladies for their time and information. Marissa responded by saying, "Y'all are just the cutest things. Now, if you boys need anything else while you're here in San Saba, you just let me know, ya hear?" Mack and Sam shook hands with all of the matrons, and then headed over to the table where the ice cream was being served. After getting a cup of delicious homemade ice cream,

Mack dropped a $20 bill into the donation jar. He was very glad that they'd decided to attend the service and social.

Mack convinced his father that it was still a great day to go and visit the Bend cemetery. He plugged the information into his phone, and it was a rather quick 25 minute drive that began on U.S. Highway 190 East. As the fellas rolled into the very small town, it was now well past noon. They were hungry, and they just happened to see a sign near a general store that read, "Mouthwatering burgers served here." That sounded perfect to the guys, so Sam parked the truck. Mack and Sam proceeded across the parking lot to where the burgers were being served out of a food truck. The fellas promptly proceeded to order cheeseburgers and fries. They then found a nice place to sit, eat, and relax for a bit at the picnic tables that were located next to the food truck. Without a doubt, Mack said, "That was the best tasting burger I've had in a long time."

After Mack dumped the burger wrappers into the trash barrel, he asked a man who was eating lunch nearby if he could give him an idea as to where the Bend Cemetery was. "You betcha," the gentleman replied. "It's just a short walk from here. Simply go across the road to where that monument is. Then, walk down the road over yonder, and it will be on your left." "Much obliged," said Mack as he headed into the general store. He grabbed a bottle of ice cold Big Red soda from the cooler, and he then slapped a $2 bill onto the counter. He told the young gentleman working there to keep the change.

Mack exited through the swinging screen door, and he proceeded to walk across the street with his father. They stopped at the monument for a moment, and Mack was amazed at what he saw inscribed upon it. Felix's name, along with Chauncey's name, were both listed on the stone memorial. Sam noticed that Saipan had been misspelled under Chauncey's section, but he thought that it was a very nice tribute to the fallen soldiers. Mack suddenly realized that Felix and Chauncey must've been related, or they at least knew each other well. It was pure dumb luck that Mack had stumbled upon the memorial for the men, and he was thrilled to have seen it. Mack and Sam then continued down the road until they reached the Bend Cemetery.

A memorial for local soldiers killed in action. Located in Bend, Texas.

They walked past the Bend Methodist Church, and up the small dirt hill until they reached the cemetery. There were plenty of birds chirping and singing as if they were welcoming the men to the property. Mack and Sam walked through the chain link gate to find the tombstones grouped towards the center of the cemetery. At first glance, Mack figured that this cemetery had been around for a long time. After walking across the freshly mowed grass, he confirmed his intuition by noticing the dates on the tombstones. It didn't take long before Mack stumbled upon a large plot containing Felix's grave. He noticed that there were two tree stumps cut close to the ground, one on either side of Felix's tombstone. There were other graves located in the plot with Felix. Mack presumed that they were possibly the graves of his parents, and perhaps his sister, Pauline, along with her husband. Mack stood stoically there at the foot of Felix's grave markers, staring at the picture that was located at the center of his tombstone. The tombstone was in remarkable condition considering its age.

Felix's tombstone located in the Bend Cemetery. Mack placed Felix's pilot wings on top of the marker before taking the picture.

Sam had remembered seeing a picture of the family surrounding Felix's grave at the time of his burial. He said to Mack, "Being here is so surreal. That must've been a very difficult time for the Scotts. They were probably not expecting that their son would be the first to be interred within the family plot." Mack then walked over to his left, and he noticed that the tombstone for Chauncey White was located nearby. He was glad that Felix and Chauncey would spend eternity together. Mack and Sam paid their final respects, and then began walking back to their truck. Mack was clearly just getting started with learning more about the life of Felix E Scott.

After a long day of attending Sunday service in San Saba, and having made a trip to the Bend Cemetery, the boys were ready to head back to Richland Springs. Mack and Sam arrived at Bruce and Sue Ann's ranch about an hour or so before supper. They had plenty to share about discovering Ruvonne as a point of contact, and for being able to see Felix's gravesite in person. It was quite an extraordinary day to say the least. Mack let them know that he and his father would be headed to Buchanan Dam early the next morning to meet with Ruvonne in person. She was a living relative of Felix, and he knew that they just had to meet her in person. Bruce said, "That sounds mighty fine. I reckon Buchanan Dam is about an hour away from here. Y'all will take 190 east, then 16 south, and then finally 29 east. That will get you to the wonderful Buchanan Lake, and to the city of Buchanan Dam."

After supper, Mack went into the den to take a closer look at some of Felix's belongings. He stood over the collection, gazing at the items that were laid out neatly on the floor before him. Mack was thinking about the items that Ruvonne might be interested in seeing. With that in mind, he first picked up the journal, and then grabbed the larger photo album. Mack felt that these items were two of the most personal things that Felix had, and they'd be something for Ruvonne to enjoy and reminisce about. Mack turned out the light in the den, and he then headed down the hall to his room in order to peruse the items a bit further before bed. He popped his head into the living room to remind his father of the 10:00 a.m. visit with Ruvonne the next morning. Sam suggested that they leave at 9:00 a.m. Mack nodded, and he continued to his room for the rest of the evening. He ended up falling asleep while reading in the journal. After waking up the next morning, Mack told his father that he'd had some of the best dreams that he could ever remember from the night before.

Mack was anxious, yet focused on thinking about questions that he'd want to ask Ruvonne. After a light breakfast, he proceeded to the front porch swing. Mack sat down, and he thought about what was about to play out over the next few hours. Being outside in the fresh air, and enjoying the tranquility of the peaceful Texas ranch, seemed to ease Mack's nerves. After Sam came out of the heavy screen door, he and Mack got into their pickup and headed for Buchanan Dam.

The fellas turned onto Texas State Highway 261, and they proceeded north. Ruvonne had told Mack that their home was just south of Jeckers Cove. Buchanan Lake was very beautiful, and the water looked clean. As they neared Ruvonne's home, Mack thought that the area looked like a nice place for people to live there in Texas. He saw boaters out on the lake fishing, a few water skiers, and some other people just enjoying a midsummers day. They turned off the highway, and then proceeded down a street into Ruvonne's neighborhood. It didn't take long for Mack to spot her single level house. There were many pecan trees spread throughout her yard, which provided a great deal of shade on the property. From the street, it looked like her house backed right up to the lake. Sam said, "Ruvonne and her husband's names are right there on the rock façade above the arched entryway."

The number on the house also looked correct, so they pulled into the driveway and parked.

They got out of the truck, and then Mack grabbed his backpack that held Felix's journal and photo album. They headed up the front walkway to find a woman standing behind the glass screen door. As Mack and Sam got closer, Ruvonne opened the door, and said, "How are y'all doing today? You must be Mack and Sam?" Mack replied, "Yes, I'm Mack, and this is my father, Sam." Mack reached out to shake her hand, and Ruvonne, being a friendly Texan, said, "Ah, just give me a hug. Y'all are welcome here, like family." She hugged Sam too, and then the three of them entered her home. Ruvonne then said, "My husband Harold is out back, and I reckon he'll be in here in a few minutes."

Ruvonne proceeded to lead them to her family room. Mack was amazed with all of the vintage items that were creatively displayed. The eclectic decor really showed her Texas roots, and the love for her family. Her couch wasn't new, but it looked like it would be very comfortable. There were plenty of pictures of her family hung on the walls. She had an incredible collection of antique tables, furniture, and knickknacks spread throughout her lovely home. There was a rather large rustic looking wall clock hanging above her fireplace. Sam said to Ruvonne, "That is an awesome clock you have there." Ruvonne replied, "Thank you, it belonged to my Aunt Viola and Uncle Ernest Scott, whom were Felix's parents. The story goes that Viola got it at a tag sale that took place after some sort of fire in the coffee shop at the old courthouse that was located there in San Saba. I think she paid $5.00 for it back in the 1950s, and it had purportedly hung in the courthouse dating back to the days of Sam Houston."

As the fellas made their way across the family room to the couch, Mack said, "That's a really cool radio sitting on that table." Ruvonne replied, "That too belonged to Viola and Ernest, and I've had it longer than I can remember. My aunties, cousins, and I would listen to music, dance around it, and even listen to news about world events. There were many times that I remember everyone being glued to it during WWII." When Mack heard that the radio had been inside Felix's home, he stared at it in awe, imagining Felix turning its knobs for fun as a child. He gently placed his hand on the side of the radio, while thinking of all the things that would've come through that speaker hidden behind the brown mesh screen. Sam, being the history teacher and all, then said, "President Roosevelt's speech to declare war upon Japan, and General Macarthur's speech to end WWII, probably emanated out of it." Ruvonne replied, "I reckon. It was a very central part of our lives back then, and a treasure, still to this day." Ruvonne invited them to sit down on the couch. She asked if they'd like some iced tea, or perhaps some Jim Beam with Coca Cola. Mack and Sam settled on the iced tea. Ruvonne returned from the kitchen with a large pitcher, glasses, and a spread of spiced pecans on a serving tray.

Everyone heard the back door slam shut, and then Harold appeared in the family room. After exchanging pleasantries, Harold sat down next to Ruvonne in his easy chair. Ruvonne then said, "So, tell us a little bit more about y'all. Where are you from, and what brought you folks out here to this part of Texas?" Mack replied, "We're from Mustang, Oklahoma, and we came to Texas for a little vacation, and to visit with my aunt and uncle over in Richland Springs." Ruvonne then said, "I understand you fellas bought some of my Uncle Felix's things at an auction on Saturday?" Mack replied, "Yes ma'am." He began to explain that they had purchased a large wooden crate at the estate sale of Mr. Jacobsen over in San Saba, which contained the suitcase, the footlocker, and the cedar chest inside. Ruvonne then said, "Well, I'll be damned. This is just so amazing, and it brings back a great deal of memories for me. I was just a little girl, maybe about six or seven when Felix passed. I really don't remember too much about him, although there was this one time when he was home on leave, and he placed his big military hat on my little head. I probably looked real silly, but we all had our family pictures made that day."

Mack then asked, "So, Felix was your uncle?" Ruvonne replied, "Well honey, it's a bit of a story. My mother and daddy were killed in a tragic car wreck when I was thirteen years old. My daddy's name was Rufus, and my mother's name was Veo. One of my mother's sisters was named Viola, and Felix was Viola's son. Technically, we were first cousins, but I've always thought of him as Uncle Felix for a couple of reasons. First, Felix was quite a bit older than me, and the second reason is also sort of complicated. After mother and daddy passed, I went to live with my cousin, Pauline Burnham, and her husband, Ted, there in San Saba, until I got married. Since Pauline was Felix's sister, I just have always thought of him more like an uncle than as a cousin." Mack replied, "That is some amazing information, and I'm so sad to hear about your mom and dad." Ruvonne then replied, "Pauline and Ted took me in as their daughter, and they raised me very well. I really appreciated them for all that they did for me."

Mack reached into his backpack, and he pulled out the photo album and journal. He then said, "Speaking of pictures, I reckon I saw that picture that you were describing of you in the hat with the rest of your family." Mack quickly thumbed through the pages in search of that specific picture. Suddenly, his hand stopped, and he flipped the album around so that Ruvonne could see it. She replied, "Yes indeed. That's the one, and it has been some time now since I've seen it. What a fine bunch we were, eh? Those are my aunties, cousins, grandparents, Felix and me."

Mack could tell that looking at the album brought happiness to Ruvonne, and perhaps made her a bit sad at the same time. Harold must've felt the same way too, as he said, "Now Ruvonne, why don't you just relax right there, and look through that album and journal? I'll take the boys out back, and show them around for a bit." Mack and Sam seemed excited to see the back of the property, and the lake as well. Ruvonne agreed, and she said, "I'm going to enjoy going through this album, so y'all just go on outside, and let me be for a bit." With that said, Harold and the fellas exited the door which led to the garage. They then hopped into Harold's all-terrain vehicle that was parked inside. Harold proceeded to drive them down to the lake's edge by zipping and zagging around the enormous pecan trees. Mack and Sam could hear occasional pecan nuts and shells getting crushed under the tires of the cart as they sped along.

The back of the house had a fine covered patio, and it was fully decorated with flags hung for the 4th of July holiday. The grass was well manicured and freshly cut. The lake was a bit choppy, as there was a good breeze blowing. It was rather sensational to see the sun rays beating down upon the lake. The men continued around the southern tip of Jecker's cove, and they were having such a wonderful time. Sam said to Harold, "Y'all are really lucky to live here in such a fabulous place like this." Harold replied, "Thanks, it's home, and we love it here. This is definitely not the big city life, but rather a really nice small town where we know our neighbors, and feel safe."

Being that it was now about noon, and they'd been gone for about an hour or so, the group decided to head back to the house. As the men approached the back of the house, they saw Ruvonne sitting in a rocker on the patio. She appeared to be flipping through the journal. When Harold stopped the vehicle at the back patio, Ruvonne got up out of that rocker, and said, "Now y'all must stay, and have dinner with us, ya hear?" Sam replied, "That's so kind of you, but we certainly don't want to intrude." Harold then said, "It's our pleasure, and we have some real nice steaks, which came from a friend who owns a nearby ranch. Ruvonne makes the best mashed potatoes and biscuits that you've ever had." Ruvonne then chimed in with, "It's settled then. We'll have pecan pie for dessert, and I won't take no for an answer."

Mack and Sam accepted the gracious offer, and they stood out on the patio with Harold as he grilled the steaks. Ruvonne popped her head out of the door, and said that all the fixings would be ready in about five minutes. Harold then turned off the grill, and he placed the steaks upon a platter before leading everyone into the dining room. Mack said, "You have such a marvelous view of the lake from here. This dinner looks great, and we're very glad to be here." As they were eating, Mack finally asked Ruvonne the question that he'd been pondering for the last few days, "How do you suppose all of Felix's stuff ended up in a crate out at the Jacobsen ranch?" Ruvonne replied, "I was thinking about that while y'all were out with Harold. Now Viola nearly lost her mind when Felix died, and she had a broken heart for the rest of her life. She'd be happy at times, and also sad at times. She may have boxed up all of his things after his death. They could've been stored out in Ernest's shop, which was right there on their property. His things were probably too painful for her to look at, but I do remember she had some of his pictures on the wall. Ernest owned and operated a tire and tube repair shop, and it had rafters above the shop floor. My guess is that the items y'all got were stored high up there, and were protected from the critters and the elements."

Ruvonne continued with, "Aunt Viola died in 1962, and Uncle Ernest died in 1966. After Ernest passed, Felix's sisters, Aletha, Pauline, and Johnnie Mae took what they wanted before the house and the shop were sold. Furthermore, Pauline may have taken Felix's things out of Ernest's shop and placed them in Ted's machine shop, where he built his pecan shakers and pecan pickers. He too, had rafters high above the concrete floors, and those items very well could've been there until Ted died in 1998. Pauline sold off his shop and all of its contents after his death. She may not have realized, or may have forgotten that those things were stored there. There also may have been some of Felix's things in Viola and Ernest's attic. Viola also had a cedar chest that at one time held some of Felix's things."

Mack and Sam listened attentively as Ruvonne continued sharing her story with, "Old man Jacobsen was well known in those parts for junking, and for buying up lots of stuff at estate sales, and barn auctions. He was really good at it. I'd bet he bought those things a ways back at one of those type of auctions, and he then didn't know what to do with the items. Those things probably sat in the crate for many years, perhaps decades. Those items that y'all got aren't worth a ton of money, but they have a great deal of sentimental and historical value. Felix had no wife or kids, and all of his sisters are long gone now." Mack said, "I want you to know that that is such an amazing amount of great information. I bet you're right, Mr. Jacobsen probably bought the stuff from the sale of Ted's shop, and he just never got around to dealing with it. Apparently, he didn't try very hard to find any of Felix's kinfolk."

Everyone began to finish up with dinner, and Mack offered to take the dishes to the kitchen. Ruvonne said, "Now you fellas just go sit down, and relax for a spell. I'll join y'all in a few minutes." Mack and Sam went back to the family room. They sat down on the couch, and Harold followed right behind them as he proceeded to his chair. Mack had a surprise waiting for Ruvonne, and he felt that she'd really appreciate it. Before arriving at Ruvonne's, Mack took time to snap high quality photos of all the pictures in the photo album. Each picture was held securely to a page with these little white corner pieces that were glued to the pages in the album. When Ruvonne came back to her easy chair, Mack said, "That sure was a delicious meal, and now I have a little treat for you. I'd like for you to have the photo album since it makes sense to me that it should belong to a member of Felix's family. I'd also be willing to give you some of the other items too, if you'd like them." Ruvonne, with a light tear in her eye, said, "That's mighty nice of you Mack, and I'll gladly accept the photo album. However, I do declare that I just don't have room for any more stuff. Harold and I will be moving up to South Dakota soon to be near our children, and we just can't take a lot with us. I'll cherish these photos very much for the rest of my life."

Ruvonne then looked at Mack, and asked with a slight grin on her face, "Did Harold show you what's in the garage out back?" Mack replied, "No ma'am, not yet." Ruvonne stood up and grabbed Harold by the hand, and said, "Well, follow me young man, ya hear?" Mack and Sam followed, and they proceeded through the back door, and onto the patio. They made their way across the lawn to a white two car garage with a very stylish wooden door. Ruvonne then said, "Now, before I open this door, I must tell you a little story. Felix loved planes, trains, and his automobiles. He was so proud of his very first car. I've been told that he saved and saved money from his jobs, and purchased a gently used, 1937 Ford coupe shortly after he turned 18. The car was fast and stylish. Having a hot rod in San Saba certainly would've made Felix popular among his friends and with the local girls in town. Although the car was great, it was just not as versatile as a truck. The clean lines, bountiful chrome trim, and the simplistic design is what attracted Felix to his Chevy truck." Mack chimed in with, "I reckon you're right, and I believe there are pictures in that album of him with those vehicles that you're talking about." Ruvonne then said, "Yes, you are correct, and I saw them too as I was looking through the album. I, however, have something better than pictures." Ruvonne was smiling as she opened the garage door.

Mack could hardly believe what he was seeing. He was now standing in front of a 1937 Ford coupe and a 1941 Chevy truck. "Holy shit," screamed Mack. He apologized for his choice of words, and then said, "These cars are so awesome." Ruvonne began to explain, "After Felix died, his cars were kept in a garage made of stone with a tin roof, which was located next to Ernest's shop. When Ernest died, Pauline kept the cars in a garage that was located behind her house. After Pauline's death, I couldn't deal with the thought of parting with them, so we built a garage like hers, and here we are. Harold and I used to take them out on occasion to classic car shows, and to a parade here and there." Harold said, "They're both in great shape, but they've been sitting here now for quite some time. I don't keep any gas in them, since we don't drive them much anymore." Ruvonne then said, 'I mentioned that we're going to be moving, and we'll need to downsize. I'm afraid it's now time to part with these beauties." Mack said, "Are you sure that you really want to part with them?" Ruvonne replied, "Yes, and I want to give you the first opportunity to purchase one. Which one would you choose, assuming that you're even interested in buying one?" Mack could hardly believe what he was hearing. He suddenly felt as if he was Daniel LaRusso from the Karate Kid movie. In the film, Mr. Miyagi gave Daniel a similar proposition to choose from an assortment of cars. Mack was almost speechless, and he could hardly contain his emotions as he walked into the garage for a closer look.

Mack stepped up to the '37 Ford, and he ran his finger slowly across the hood. He then continued up the windshield, over the roof, and back down the rear window. The rather thick layer of dust clouded the color, but it looked like it could be the original maroon paint underneath. Mack thought that the ornate hood ornament was kind of cool and unique, and the chrome hub caps certainly made an impression. He then opened the door, and the interior was very clean. It certainly had a well-aged, vintage smell permeating from within. The door was heavy as he slammed it shut, and he said out loud, "They sure don't make cars with this much steel on 'em anymore, right?" Harold laughed and nodded in agreement.

After being thoroughly impressed with the Ford, Mack then turned to the '41 Chevy light-duty pickup. This truck had style written all over it. The chrome grill and front fender looked so sharp, and the chrome continued down the side of the engine to the doors. Harold then said, "It has a six-cylinder engine with a three speed manual transmission." Everything about the truck looked original, and the bed had a wooden floor that was a bit worn. However, the truck was still in great shape for its age. The truck also had chrome hubcaps on the wheels, which were similar to those on the Ford. Harold opened the driver's side door, and Mack then climbed in. Ruvonne then opened the passenger side door, and joined Mack upon the rather stiff bench seat. The cab was small, but comfy and roomy enough for a few people. Ruvonne asked, "Do you like her?" Mack replied, "Do I ever! This is fantastic, and probably the coolest truck that I've ever been in." Mack noticed a tan cowboy hat sitting upon the dashboard, and he turned his head to Ruvonne to ask about it. Ruvonne replied, "That there hat belonged to Felix. Word has it that he had driven himself and his parents to the train station in this truck for the last time, when he left for war in late 1943. The story goes on to say that Felix left the hat right there. He then asked his mother, Viola, to keep it and the truck safe until he returned one day."

Mack felt sad after hearing the story about the hat. Felix's parents must've been devastated to look at it and the truck after his tragic passing. Mack felt that the Scotts must've kept both of his cars with the hope that his death was just a mistake, and that he'd one day return to San Saba on the train just like he said he would. Mack asked Ruvonne, "Does the hat go with the truck?" She replied, "Yes, Mack, for a fine young man like you. Would you like to buy it?" Mack then asked, "How much are you asking for it?" Ruvonne replied, "How does $5,000 cash sound? I feel that you'd be a proud owner, and it feels right since you now have a great deal of his things." Mack replied, "That sounds like a bargain. Can I go ask my dad?" Ruvonne said, "You bet. Go on ahead, and ask him now." After exiting the truck, Mack walked out of the garage, and he then tugged on Sam's arm. They headed towards some shade under the nearest pecan tree, which happened to be right behind the garage. Mack told his dad about the hat, the offer to buy the truck, and the brief history that he had just learned about it. Sam was on board with the deal, as long as Mack was sure that he wanted to spend that much on a car. Mack said, "Dad, I've been saving, and the funny thing is, I have just a bit more than $5,000 left in the bank. You know that I've always wanted a truck. This truck is totally rad, and she's selling it for way less than its market value."

Mack raced back around the corner to where Ruvonne and Harold were talking, and said, "Ruvonne, you have yourself a deal." They shook hands, and Ruvonne congratulated Mack for making a fine decision to purchase the truck. Mack then said, "I think there is probably enough time left in the day to secure the funds to pay for the truck." Mack promptly got on the phone with his credit union, and he asked how he could get access to $5,000 cash, being that they were far away from their local branch. Mack was helped by a very friendly young man named Ryan. He guided him on how to get the cash from a local bank there in Buchanan Dam. Ryan quickly made the changes to the account, so that Mack's debit card would allow for the large withdrawal. He then provided Mack with the address for a local bank that could assist with the cash advance transaction, and he provided clear instructions on what to say to the teller. Ryan concluded with, "There are no fees for this type of transaction, and I hope that you enjoy your new truck. Congratulations."

Having finished the call with his credit union, Mack turned to Ruvonne, and he asked about where exactly in town this bank would be located. Ruvonne replied, "Oh honey, it's just down the road a few miles over on Ranch Road." Harold then said, "While y'all are gone, I'll get some gas in it, put air in the tires, and I'll get her washed up." Mack nodded that the plan sounded fine, and then he and his dad jumped into Sam's truck to head for the bank. Just like Ruvonne had said, the bank wasn't very far away. It didn't take long before the teller handed Mack fifty $100 bills simply by swiping his debit card, and by showing his id. Mack grabbed the stack of cash, and he proceeded to count the money one more time before putting it securely into his pocket.

Mack and Sam headed back over to Ruvonne's place, and as they came around the corner, the now shiny blue truck was parked prominently on their asphalt driveway. It appeared that Harold was nearly finished with drying the truck, and the chrome was certainly eye popping as the sun reflected off of it. As Sam pulled up next to the '41 Chevy, Ruvonne was standing in the shade underneath her carport. Mack said, "Good news, I've got the cash." Ruvonne quickly replied with, "That's terrific! Amazingly, I found the title to the truck." Mack removed the money from his pocket, and he then counted it out loud, as he laid each bill onto the tailgate of Ruvonne's pickup truck. Sam showed Mack where to check for Ruvonne's signature on the title, and suddenly, he was now the proud owner of this beautiful, blue beauty. Mack grabbed a towel, and he proceeded to help Harold with drying the rest of the chrome on the truck. Mack then said, "She cleaned up real nice I'd say." Harold then replied, "Yes sir. She's looks really good."

With the truck now dry and polished up, Ruvonne said, "Let's go inside for some iced tea, pecan pie, and ice cream." After relaxing and conversing for about an hour, it was time to head back to Richland Springs. Everyone got up and proceeded out of the front door to say their goodbyes. Mack and Sam then hugged both Ruvonne and Harold. They thanked them for the great stories, the information, the hospitality, and certainly for the opportunity to buy Felix's truck. Mack, having a curious nature about him, asked Ruvonne, "By the way, what are you going to do with the '37 Ford?" Ruvonne replied, "We'll most likely sell it for a great deal more than the truck, which will help us get settled in South Dakota. You got a real good deal Mack, and we're very happy to see you with the truck." Mack replied, "I'm so grateful that we got to meet y'all. I'll treasure this truck for as long as it stays running."

Sam started the engine on his truck, and Mack followed by climbing inside the '41 Chevy to do the same. It took him a few moments to figure out how to manually roll down the windows. Mack looked at the old radio with Chevrolet emblazoned across the front. It had a rotating knob on either side of it, but he wasn't quite sure how to operate it. Rather jokingly, he stuck his head out of the window, and said, "I bet I can't hook up my phone to this radio." Mack rotated the knobs around and around until he found a country music station. The music made Mack feel great that he was alive. In some peculiar way, he felt that Felix was watching, and that he was smiling down with happiness for Mack. Mack wondered to himself what the last song Felix would've heard crackling through the speakers on the truck.

Sam rolled down his window, and said to Mack, "We'll take it nice and slow, as we're in no hurry to get back to Richland Springs." Sam waved out of his window one last time before backing his truck up. Mack proceeded to find the reverse gear on his truck, and then, he too, backed out onto the street. Mack planned to follow his dad back to his Uncle Bruce's ranch. As they drove away, Mack looked into his rear view mirror to see Ruvonne and Harold hugging and waving to them. Mack stuck his hand out of the window, and he waved goodbye as he rounded the corner. He was feeling tremendous joy after such a wonderful day. Mack was very thankful, and he felt lucky to have received the information from Ruvonne in his quest to better understand more about Second Lieutenant Felix E. Scott.

CHAPTER 6

Growing Up

Driving that 1941 Chevy pickup truck from Buchanan Dam back to Richland Springs had to have been one of the coolest things that Mack had done in his young life. The difference between Mack's truck and Sam's truck was like night and day. There was no air conditioning, no cruise control, no USB ports, and no entertainment package. It did, however, have the cool factor. Mack received several thumbs up, as he cruised along the highway during the one hour trip back to his Uncle Bruce's house.

As the two trucks pulled onto the crushed granite driveway, Bruce and Sue Ann came out to admire Mack's newest treasure. Mack was so excited as he showed off his classic truck. Seeing it, driving it, all of it, was truly a throwback into a different time. Bruce thoroughly enjoyed sitting behind the wheel for a few moments, while Mack explained the story about the cowboy hat. The chrome was so shiny that Sue Ann could see her reflection bouncing back at her. Once they had seen enough of the truck, everyone but Mack headed into the house.

Mack told his dad that he wanted to take some time to just sit in the truck, and reflect on the events of the day. It had been such a whirlwind day; Mack hadn't had a chance to fully explore all that the truck had to offer. He looked over the entire dashboard, turned all of the knobs, and he even checked under the seat. Having spotted something small, Mack reached under the seat until his hand nearly touched the back of the cab. There on the floor, was a matchbook that had Santa Ana Army Air Base printed onto the cover. Mack really liked the design of the matchbook, and he thought that it was awesome that most of the matches were still untouched. As he rifled through the papers that were pulled from the glovebox, he found a picture of Felix and a young woman posing next to the truck. Looking at the picture made Mack feel sad, as Felix's eyes, and his wide smile were staring back at him. He wondered who the woman was, and what had become of her? He wondered what could've been if events had turned out differently for Felix. Mack sat stoically pondering the good times, and the last time that Felix would've been inside the truck.

As Mack sat on the driver's side of the cab, his left hand was firmly placed on the steering wheel. His right hand was clutching one of Felix's dog tags, which was hanging from the keyring. He gripped the tag tightly in the palm of his hand as he closed his eyes. Mack's mind began to run wild with what seemed to be glimpses of past events in Felix's life. It was as if Mack was somehow channeling Felix's spirit, and the visions just kept coming. Mack soon fell asleep after the visions began to present themselves. Suddenly, he was seeing events from Felix's childhood, young adulthood, and, of course, his military life. There was no particular order to the visions. Just as one would finish, another would come rolling in for Mack to see. Suddenly, a vision seemed to show a terrorizing experience, where Felix was spinning and flipping in the seat of a cockpit. Mentally seeing the plane make impact with the ground was quite shocking to Mack. He abruptly woke up, and he was startled further when he saw his dad standing by the door of the truck trying to get his attention. The experience was unlike anything that Mack had ever gone through before, and he wasn't quite ready to share the event with his dad just yet. Mack ensured that the truck was locked, and they headed into the house together.

Mack had a difficult time falling asleep that evening. He tossed and turned quite a lot, but he didn't experience any more visions. Mack was anxious, and, after eating breakfast the next morning, he felt that he needed to go back to San Saba once again. He explained to his dad that something was calling him back to San Saba, and he wanted to go by himself. Having just been to San Saba, and seeing for himself that it was a quiet community, Sam gave his blessing for the day trip. With that, Mack hopped into his old Chevy truck, and he headed back down the road towards San Saba. He took a backpack filled with pictures and paperwork that he'd found among the items that he'd bought at the auction. Mack really had no idea why he was being called back to San Saba, but he was willing to play along. Upon arriving in town, he pulled off the road, and he parked right in front of the San Saba County Historical Museum, which was located in the parking lot at Mill Pond Park.

After getting out of his truck, Mack peeked into the museum by looking through the glass doors. After noticing that the museum was closed, he began to walk around the main pond and waterfall located there at the park. He found a nice spot to sit on a block wall that was located just off to the left of the waterfall. The lush green foliage, colorful flowers, and the sound of the crashing water made for a peaceful place to ponder what he should do next. An elderly couple walked by, and they stopped on the pathway near the top of the waterfall. Mack said, "Hello," and he then asked them how long the park had been there. The gentleman replied that the spring fed pond had been around for a very long time, and improvements to the park had been evolving ever since the late 1880s. Mack thanked him for the information, and they continued on their walk.

Mack got to thinking about where Felix had grown up, and all of the places where he would've hung out with his family and friends. He pulled out some of the paperwork that he'd brought with him, and began looking for an address for Felix's childhood home. It turned out to be quite a job finding his address. All of the letters and military paperwork referenced the family post office box. Mack then began to look through the small pile of newspaper clippings, and he found an article that provided some details pertaining to Felix's funeral. The article didn't provide the complete address, but it gave South Live Oak Street as the street name for the family home.

Mack had no idea where in town South Live Oak Street was, but with his cellphone in hand, he was fixing to find out. He clicked on his favorite map app, and he entered the information that he had. Mack couldn't hardly believe what he saw when the search result loaded. South Live Oak Street was literally a few blocks away from the Mill Pond Park. Mack quickly gathered his things, and he ran to his truck. He pulled out of the parking lot directly onto East Commerce Street. After driving for about three blocks, Mack hung a left onto South Live Oak Street.

As he drove down the street, Mack could see that there was a mix of single family homes, and small to medium sized retail buildings. He continued driving down the street, not knowing which house had belonged to Felix and his family. Was it even still there, or had it been torn down? Mack had no idea, and even driving the nine or ten blocks down the street got him no closer to an answer. When South Live Oak Street ended, Mack turned around, and he headed back up the street. He pulled into the parking lot of the hardware store, which was located on the corner of South Live Oak Street and East Commerce Street. Mack took a moment to gather his thoughts, and he began to hatch out a plan. He remembered that he'd taken pictures of all the photos in the album that he'd given to Ruvonne. Mack began to glance through his photo roll, and he stopped at the photos featuring a home. With the pictures now firmly embedded in his mind, he ventured back down South Live Oak Street once more.

This time, Mack drove much slower, as if he himself was in some sort of parade. His head hung out of the window on occasion as he looked for just the right house. Once again, Mack made it to the end of the street, having not seen a match. He turned around, and he was hopeful, that with another pass, he might just hit the jackpot. His attitude had most definitely started to wane as he slowed down further at the intersection of South Live Oak Street and East Church Street. There happened to be an old man standing on the corner waiting for Mack to pass so that he could cross the street. The man looked like an average Texan, wearing his faded blue jeans, brown boots, and a light brown cowboy hat. Since the windows were already rolled down, Mack blurted out, "Hey old-timer, how ya doing today?" The man replied, "I'm doing all right. That sure is a mighty fine looking truck you've got there." Mack then said, "Thank you. Sir, do you mind if I ask you a question?" The old man replied, "Sure, I don't reckon I'll know the answer, but I'll do my best." With that, Mack backed the truck up a bit, and pulled onto the grassy shoulder just off the street.

Mack got out of his truck, and he briskly walked to the corner. He reached out to the man, and shook his hand. "My name is Mack, and it's very nice to meet you." The old man replied, "My name is Duncan. What brings you to these here parts?" Mack pulled out his phone from his back pocket, and he showed Duncan the pictures of the house that he was searching for. He further explained that he was looking for the home that had once belonged to Ernest and Viola Scott. Mack went on to mention that their son Felix, and their daughter Aletha, would've lived there as well, long ago.

As Duncan looked closely at the photos, Mack could tell that his mind was processing remembrances from yesteryear. Duncan then said, "I've lived here my whole life, and when I was a young boy, I remember the Scott Tire and Tube shop right over yonder. If I recall, Mr. Scott was a County Commissioner at one point, and he and his wife were very well-known and respected here in San Saba." Mack was visibly excited, to say the least, and he then said, "You say that the business was right over yonder?" Duncan pointed across the street, and said, "Yes, the house is no longer there, but it once stood where that gun store is located now. The tire repair shop was on the left side of the property, and the house was located just a short distance away." It was hot outside, and Mack could see that Duncan was sweating in the mid-morning sun. He shook Duncan's hand, while mentioning how thankful he was for the information that Duncan had provided.

As Duncan went on his way, Mack rolled up the windows and locked the truck. He left it where it was parked, and he proceeded to walk across the street. It didn't take very long before Mack found himself standing on what was purportedly Felix's former front yard. It was no longer much of a lawn per se, as the grass was sparse. There was now a gravel driveway in front of the business for customers to park. Mack walked up the ramp to the front door of the gun shop, only to find a closed sign hanging on it. He peeked inside, hoping to see someone, but he didn't notice any movement, and the lights were off. Mack turned around, and he jumped off the porch, clearing the steps facing the front door. He felt a little weird walking around the property, but since there were no cars or people around, he began to explore.

Mack walked around the corner of the gun shop that was nearest the former garage. He stood there for a few moments picturing

Ernest repairing tires, Felix riding around in his toy plane, and Viola tending to her girls. Based on the pictures, Mack was now standing directly in front of where the garage would've been. He bent down, and clenched his fist tightly, after grabbing a handful of dirt. Mack envisioned Felix's car and truck parked right where he was standing so many moons ago. He looked up into the live oak and pecan trees that were scattered around the property, imagining that Felix would've had a grand time climbing and swinging among the branches. Mack had seen what he felt that he needed to see, and after being at the place that Felix called home, he now possessed a feeling that would be hard for him to explain to anyone else. After walking back to his truck, he then drove the short distance to park for a few moments directly in front of the gun store. Mack took Felix's cowboy hat off the dashboard, and he raised it up and out of the window, and he then said, "Here's to you, Felix." Before driving away, he placed Felix's cowboy hat upon his head.

With all of the visions and images now beginning to race through his head once again, Mack felt that it would be best to return to Mill Pond Park to decompress. On his way to the park, Felix drove up South Live Oak Street a few blocks, and he stopped at the San Saba Courthouse. Mack was amazed at the architecture of the building that appeared to be made of bricks and stone. He figured that the building had to be at least 100 years old, and it was certainly a focal point in downtown San Saba. The town square around the courthouse was surrounded with an array of shops lined up across the street on all sides. Mack backed his truck into a shady parking spot right in front of the steps located on the back side of the courthouse. He got out of the truck with his backpack slung over his shoulder. After walking about halfway up the steps, Mack stopped to admire an engraved slogan at the top of the building, "FROM THE PEOPLE

TO THE PEOPLE." "SAN SABA" was also inscribed into the rock above the quotation. Close to the quotation, at the very top of the building, was a symbolic star that was set inside a circle on the marble facade. Mack was in awe of just how amazing the clock tower was, which was located high upon the center of the roof. He wondered to himself if the clock could be seen clearly from Felix's house just a few blocks away.

After deciding to walk around the entire exterior of the courthouse, Mack became intrigued on what he'd find on the inside of this magnificent structure. Since there didn't seem to be many people milling about, Mack opened the door, and, as the heavy wooden door closed behind him, he stood in a long hallway with offices on either side. There was a vintage tile floor, with dark wooden baseboards throughout. Significant amounts of wood trim adorned the walls, and there were plenty of old-fashioned doors complete with built in glass panels that provided entry into the various offices. This place was unlike anything Mack had ever seen before.

Mack took the steps up to the third floor, where he saw an amazing courtroom full of brilliant natural light. He traversed the beautiful courtroom by walking across the durable carpet runners that protected the lovely hard wooden floor. Very tall windows lined the entire wall located behind the judge's bench. Plenty of vintage wooden pews were present on the main floor of the courtroom. Mack noticed that the high ceiling appeared to be adorned with pressed metal tiles, and he was curious to see what he'd find in the balcony high above him. He inquisitively proceeded upstairs to the balcony, and he was thoroughly impressed with what he saw. There were several rows of stadium style wooden seats overlooking the courtroom floor below. Mack then walked back down to the second floor of the courthouse. Lacking real world experience, he had no idea what the courthouse offices were for. On his way towards the exit, Mack stopped at the office of the County Clerk. Feeling captivated by the experience thus far, he felt the need to make personal contact with someone who worked there.

Unsure exactly of what to do, say, or ask, Mack walked into the County Clerk's office, and he was greeted by a very friendly woman sitting behind a desk. Mack introduced himself, and he let her know how much he'd enjoyed seeing the courthouse. The woman stood up, and she approached the counter, and said, "Hi, I'm Shannon. What brings you to the courthouse today?" Mack explained, "I was driving over on South Live Oak Street, looking for a house that happens to be no longer there. I then saw this awesome place here on the way back to Mill Pond Park, and I just had to stop." Shannon replied, "Did you say that you were looking for a house? We keep records of the homes and property held by the citizens of San Saba here in my office. I'd be glad to help you?"

Mack felt that his day was just getting better and better, and he wasted no time in pulling out some paperwork from his backpack. He began to share some of it with Shannon, and he explained that he was looking for information on a property that was once owned by Ernest Scott and his family. Mack said, "I have an address, but I really don't know anything else about the property other than what the pictures show." Feeling confident that she could help, Shannon took the address from Mack and went back to her desk. Mack stood by the tall wooden counter, waiting patiently as she entered the information into her computer. Within moments, she said, "I got it. I was able to locate two properties here in San Saba that belonged to Ernest Scott."

The excitement on Mack's face was evident as Shannon returned to the counter. She had copies of two deeds that provided the dates that the properties were purchased, and the amounts that were paid for each of them. Shannon said, "We charge a $2.00 fee for each deed to cover the costs to print them." Mack quickly handed her two $2.00 bills, while continuing to express his gratitude. He picked up Felix's hat off of the counter, and tipped it in her direction as he placed it back upon his head. Mack was thrilled to no end when he heard that there was another property that Felix had once lived in. After exiting the courthouse, he decided to sit right down upon the steps to reflect on what had just happened.

Mack stared at the steps for a while, thinking that it was highly likely that Felix and his family had previously walked up these very same steps long ago. He could envision Felix's vehicles parked right where he was parked. Mack also figured that Felix, and his friends probably rode their bicycles up to the courthouse regularly to play. After pulling out Felix's journal, he began to thumb through the pages held inside of the old leather cover. The journal wasn't a complete life story, but more like a book full of life events and other memories. Felix had taken the time over the years to write down his favorite things to do in San Saba, and he jotted down some of the great memories spent with his family and friends. Mack kept flipping through page after page, becoming totally immersed into the life of Felix E. Scott. He was very much intrigued as he read the stories about animals, sports, hunting, schooling, working, farming, and relic hunting. Mack had been sitting there for more than an hour, and the courthouse steps were now completely covered in shade. As he continued through the last half of the journal, he found more stories pertaining to scouting, hiking, church socials, fishing, courting, and college life. Although Felix had died at a rather young age, it was evident to Mack that he'd lived an exciting life.

The magnificent courthouse located in San Saba, Texas.

After having spent more than two hours looking through the pages of Felix's journal, Mack's back had become sore from sitting for so long. He decided to return to his vehicle, and he climbed into the bed of the truck. Mack thought that it might help his back if he could lie down for a spell. He promptly placed his head upon his backpack, and he then pulled Felix's cowboy hat down over his face to provide a more relaxing experience.

Mack fell right to sleep with Felix's key ring and dog tag held firmly within the palm of his hand. Shortly thereafter, more visions of Felix's past began to dance around in Mack's head as he slept. The images were rather vivid, and they seemed to portray real life experiences. It was almost as if Mack was living in the moment with Felix as he grew up in and around San Saba. Mack abruptly woke from his nap when a large noisy truck that was loaded with watermelons and cantaloupes pulled up next to him. He looked at his watch, and realized that it was now way past dinner time. Mack grabbed his phone, and he texted his dad to let him know that he was fine, and that he couldn't wait to share all that he had learned about Felix. After texting his dad, Mack talked to the truck driver who had parked next to him, and Mack found out that he was a farmer from Llano who came to the San Saba Courthouse regularly during watermelon and cantaloupe season to sell his fruit. Mack talked to him for a few minutes, and then bought a couple of cantaloupes and a yellow watermelon.

Before leaving San Saba, Mack felt that he just had to go and look at the other property that Shannon had told him about. He plugged in the address on his phone, and lo and behold, it was just a short drive away. Mack headed back down South Live Oak Street, and he drove right on by the former Scott property that he'd just looked at. He made a left on East Annex Street, and then a right on South Bluffton Street. After making the final left turn that placed him onto Cedar Street, Mack was anxious to see the house. However, he looked to his left, and he didn't see a house. He was thinking, "Here we go again," since the former Scott home didn't appear to be there. Mack double checked the original map that Shannon had given him for the properties located in that tract. Sure enough, he was in the right place, and the house was supposed to be on his left.

Feeling pretty disappointed, Mack got out of his truck, and he began to walk around the vacant property. There were plenty of pecan and live oak trees, but they didn't appear to be 80-90 years old. Weeds and tall grass could be seen growing throughout the property that took up half the block. The property on Cedar Street was sandwiched between South Bluffton Street to the west and South Water Street to the east. Mack then noticed an interesting fact about South Water Street. At the time the Scotts owned the property, it was called Central Avenue. As Mack continued to walk around, he noticed a large dirt area in the middle of the property. He envisioned that this is where the house must've stood. Much to his dismay, there was nothing of the house left to see. As he walked to the back half of the property, Mack noticed dozens of thick pecan tree trunks hastily stacked in a pile. It made him rather sad to see the trunks lying there, knowing that, more than likely, they were probably the remnants of the trees that would've been growing on the property during Felix's heyday as a youngster. Having peaked the curiosity of the neighbor's barking dog, and with nothing really left to see, Mack returned back to his truck.

Overall, Mack was in a terrific mood, and he didn't even care that he had missed dinner. He felt excited, and inspired, as he traversed the hill country roads of Texas on his way back to Richland Springs. Everyone at Mack's Uncle Bruce's house was sitting on the front porch as he pulled up in his classic Chevy truck. Mack exited the truck, smiling from cheek to cheek. Sam asked, "How did your day go over in San Saba?" Bruce and Sue Ann were also eagerly awaiting his reply. Mack enthusiastically replied, "I had a terrific time, and I saw some of the coolest things. Let's go inside, and I'll fill you in on all of the details that I learned about Felix today."

After everyone had found a seat in the den, Sue Ann brought in a pitcher of iced tea, and she placed it upon the coffee table. Mack began to explain that he'd been to the Mill Pond Park, the courthouse, and he'd even visited both of the properties that Felix had lived at. Sam seemed awestruck as he said, "Son, how in the world did you figure out where Felix had lived?" Mack was excited to share the details pertaining to the chance encounter with Duncan. He also recapped the experience that he had with Shannon at the courthouse. After reaching into his backpack, and pulling out a small bag, Mack then said, "Look, I even grabbed some dirt from one of the driveways." He eagerly shared the pictures on his phone that he'd taken at both of the properties. Mack then began to explain all that he'd learned and seen while in San Saba. For the first time, he even shared the fact that realistic visions, and images were appearing randomly in his head. Mack pulled out a notepad that he'd been using to gather his thoughts, and stated, "Are y'all ready to hear the details regarding the life story of Felix E. Scott?" Everyone affirmed that they were ready to listen, and so Mack began.

Ernest and Viola Scott were married on 13 Apr. 1913 on the porch at the home of her parents W. J. (also known as Bill) and Polly Ann Millican (often called Annie by her friends) in the small community of Bend, Texas. To the Scotts and their extended family, everyone referred to W.J. as Pa, and Polly Ann was lovingly known as Ma. The Millicans owned a large plot of land, upwards of 500 acres or so. Their property was named the River Bend farm for its proximity to the natural bend in the Colorado River at Cherokee Creek. The property was quiet and very peaceful, and only accessible by car via a long country road. There were large pecan and oak trees located fairly close to each part of the house that provided an abundance of shade. Their home sat on a prime piece of fertile land right between the two waterways, and it was very close to where Cherokee Creek forms. With an abundant supply of fresh water, the Millicans operated one of the finest pecan groves in all of Texas at the time. They had hundreds, if not thousands of pecan trees, featuring many different varieties of pecans. There was a seemingly endless line of pecan trees along the banks of the Colorado River.

Ernest and Viola were just starting out. They didn't have much money at that time, and so they decided to live with Viola's parents. Ernest was a hard worker, and he did many things to earn money.

He worked tirelessly in order to save and build for their future. The young couple planned to be property owners of their own one day. Although living with his in-laws wasn't an ideal situation for Ernest, the Millican house was large enough for everyone to be comfortable. After all, Viola and her five sisters had grown up in that house, and had done just fine. Viola convinced Ernest that they could make it work.

W. J. and Ernest were quite adept at hunting and fishing, so there was always plenty of meat and fish to go around. Polly Ann and Viola worked well together in the garden, and they were experts at canning homegrown fruits and vegetables. The Millicans had a root cellar that was located just off the back porch, and it was built with tree trunks and rocks. The shelves were generally stocked full of glass Mason jars that contained quite a variety of fruits and vegetables, grown right there on the farm. A variety of pork and beef was also stored after it had been smoked or salted. A large henhouse proved to be a valuable source for fresh eggs, and delicious chicken dinners. Life on the farm was hard work, but it was most certainly a fine place to raise a family.

Ernest and Viola were blessed with their first child, Johnnie Mae, on 09 Sep. 1914. They became happy parents to another sweet little girl, Pauline, on 03 Jul. 1917. The Scotts were now ready to go out on their own, and, shortly after Pauline was born, they moved to San Saba. They rented a small place on the west end of town. It wasn't a grand place, but they made do, and they were happy. Felix was the next addition to the growing Scott family, and he was born on 30 May 1920, at the River Bend farm. Viola had been comfortable with her mother and sisters assisting her in the delivery of her first three children. The Scott family grew one last time, when Aletha Veo was born on 26 Oct. 1922.

Felix wishing that he could fly at an early age with his sisters Johnnie Mae and Pauline.

Some folks say that the decade of the 1920s was known as the roaring twenties. For Ernest Scott, things were most definitely looking up for him and his family. He was the sole proprietor of "Scott's Tire Service," and his shop specialized in rubber vulcanization, shoe repairing, and anything to do with repairing tires. During the roaring twenties, many folks took advantage of the bull market pertaining to stock trading. The Scotts didn't get caught up in buying stock in other companies. Instead, Ernest was focused on investing in himself and his family. His first tire shop was a success because Ernest had earned a reputation of someone who could fix just about anything. If he couldn't fix it, he would just simply make a new one, somehow, some way.

Ernest's father, John J. Scott, and his father-in-law, W. J. Millican had always told him to invest in land. W. J. had an excellent reputation in town and at his local bank. As such, he was able to assist Ernest and Viola with the purchase of their first home in San Saba. The property encompassed about one half of a block, and it was rather close to downtown. W. J. was the co-signer on the note, but the Scott family was now on their way to prosperity. They moved into the house on Cedar Street shortly after the deal closed on 14 Sep. 1925. There weren't too many houses built in the neighborhood at that time, but there were plenty of friendly people living there.

Ernest Scott and family. Circa 1925 in San Saba, Texas.

Times were changing with so many new things and technologies coming to the marketplace. Even at a young age, Felix demonstrated that he had a strong work ethic by helping out around the River Bend farm, and by assisting Ernest with cleaning up around the tire shop. Felix sure knew how to handle the farm equipment, and he worked well around the cows, pigs, horses, goats, and chickens. Like his father, Felix was good with his hands. He also had a keen eye, and he was a quick thinker. Ernest and Felix made a great team, a real father and son duo. Spending time with his grandparents out at Bend provided for a solid upbringing, and a fine start at boyhood.

As a youngster, Felix could tell that a great deal of the residents of San Saba County lived on a ranch or farm. For those who didn't, they surely knew someone who did. He got the sense that many of his family members had been in the area for generations. Felix thought that it was wonderful for his family to enjoy the country way of life, but he was longing for something much different for his future. When Felix was nearly seven years old, he first shared his dream of becoming a pilot with his father. One day, Felix said to his father, "Do I have to be a farmer when I'm all grown up? I want to see the world. Maybe I'll even be famous someday."

Ernest could tell that young Felix was very impressionable, and he certainly admired his ambition. When Felix wasn't working, playing, or going to school, he'd spend countless hours looking at books and magazines that featured the most important events and stories of the Great War, also known as WWI. Felix was fascinated by the pictures of the pilots and their planes, much more than the actual words themselves. Ernest felt that Felix probably spent too much time with his nose buried in his comic books and magazines. However, he allowed it as long as Felix got his chores and schoolwork done first.

Felix enjoyed spending time after supper in the living room with his folks. Viola loved reading books, while Ernest enjoyed the weekly newspaper. Felix would often sit on his father's lap as Ernest flipped through the pages of *The San Saba News*. When the newspaper came out during the fourth week of May in 1927, Felix was very excited to hear Ernest read all of the details about Charles Lindbergh, and his flight across the Atlantic Ocean. Even though he was young, Felix seemed to grasp the magnitude of the historic event. Mr. Lindbergh had piloted his plane, "The Spirit of St. Louis," from New York to Paris, France. He had become the first person to complete the transatlantic flight while piloting the plane all by himself. It had taken

Mr. Lindbergh nearly 34 hours to complete the solo nonstop flight. There in the paper, was a picture of Mr. Lindbergh right next to his plane when he landed in France on 21 May 1927. Ernest then said, "It says right here in the article that Mr. Lindbergh couldn't take his cat Patsy on the journey with him, so he took his Felix the Cat doll instead." Felix got a real good chuckle from that, and he was fascinated by the story. He could tell that Charles Lindbergh had made a name for himself, and Felix went to bed that evening dreaming of what it might be like to be famous. Ernest carefully cut the picture from the newspaper, and he hung it on the wall in Felix's bedroom.

Ernest was very supportive of Felix's dreams. To further foster Felix's aspiration to fly, Ernest built him a kid-sized plane. Ernest had worked on the plane here and there over at W. J.'s barn, so that it would be a complete surprise to Felix for his birthday on 30 May 1927. The plane was smaller than an actual military plane, but it was still about the size of a small car. The plane's body (fuselage) was enlarged to resemble the shape of a pecan, and it had long wings protruding from both sides. There was a realistic wooden tail, and the plane even had a wooden propeller complete with two blades that actually spun. With Ernest being in the tire business, there were, of course, real rubber tires.

It was the summer of 1927, and Felix spent a great deal of time out at the River Bend farm piloting and cruising around the property in his plane. Ernest and W. J. spent countless hours pulling Felix's plane with the assistance of a tractor. They dodged around the oak and pecan trees, and there was plenty of dust kicked up in the process. Felix was thrilled with his plane, and he had a ball imagining what it would be like to actually be a real aviator. Felix jumped up and down, and he ran around the yard screaming with joy when Ernest told him that he was going to be a part of the San Saba street parade held on 10 Nov. 1927.

On the day prior to the parade, the Scott family adorned the wings of the plane with bright colored cloth and ribbons for Felix's special "flight" through town. Viola had found some chalk, and she wrote "Spirit of San Saba" on both sides of the plane, paying tribute to Mr. Lindbergh's "Spirit of St. Louis." Felix was so excited that he went to bed wearing his leather jacket, leather flight cap, and he had his pilot goggles dangling around his neck. On the big day of the parade, Felix was dressed to the hilt in his flight outfit. As many as 5,000 folks from far and wide were in town to attend the parade and related festivities. Most people who were there that day would say that Felix was the highlight of the parade, and some folks talked about it for years afterwards. There were many other floats, but they, nor the San Saba band could steal Felix's special moment. Young Felix may not have been flying across the Atlantic, but he had a ball "flying" through downtown San Saba.

Felix preparing for a parade in his "pecan plane." Prototype P01-A, circa 1927 at the River Bend farm.

The great stock market crash in October of 1929 was one of the factors that led to the Great Depression. Times were certainly hard, but Ernest Scott's family wasn't affected quite as much as so many other Americans were, mostly because they didn't possess any stock. Instead, Ernest and Viola were expanding their business ventures in San Saba at that time with the purchase of the Pennant filling station on 02 Jan. 1930. It was located on the southeast corner of the Courthouse Square, and a rather short drive from their home on Cedar Street. The filling station was in a prime location in the center of downtown, and the Scotts were glad that it was profitable. Felix was nearly ten years old at the time, and he was becoming ambitious in his own right. He worked regularly at the filling station, and he surely enjoyed all of the coins that piled up in his piggy bank.

Felix enjoyed living in San Saba as a youngster. There were plenty of things to do outside, and he thrived in that environment. Felix was friendly and outgoing, and he had an easy time making friends at school in San Saba. He made good marks at school, with reading and history being his favorite subjects. Growing up with his three sisters at home was exciting at times, but on occasion, it was also boring at times for Felix. He preferred hanging out with his boy cousins out at and around Bend. Felix had a particularly close bond with his first cousin, Chauncey White. He was a few years younger than Felix, and he lived at the River Bend farm with his grandparents, W. J. and Polly Ann Millican. Felix also developed close friendships with his pals Floyd, Tucker, and Frank there in San Saba.

During the school year, Felix was busy with his studies, yet he made time to help Ernest out in his shop. Felix learned how to handle many of the routine things in the tire shop, and he wasn't just a clean-up boy any longer. On weekends and during the summer, Felix became an adventurous, and sometimes even a mischievous young man. However, on Sundays, his manners returned just in time for Sunday school at the United Methodist Church in Bend. Felix spent a great deal of time hanging out at his favorite spots along the banks of the San Saba River. The river wasn't too far from the Scott home, and Felix and his pals would swim and splash around for hours in their cut-off jeans. Every now and then, on some of those hot summer days, there was even some skinny dipping as long as there were no girls around. Swimming was certainly Felix's favorite activity in San Saba County. He also enjoyed the countless hours spent swimming and playing in the Colorado River with Chauncey, over at the River Bend farm. Plunging into the chilly river water from a swing that was anchored to a large pecan tree, was by far the most fun that Felix had every summer.

Felix posing at a makeshift jail in San Saba, Texas.

Felix undoubtedly had connections for old tires, so he could be relied upon to bring a tire, and some rope to a new swimming hole that his friends or cousins would find. Hanging a tire from the local Beveridge Bridge for a dip into the San Saba River was certainly fun, until the local authorities showed up one day. There hadn't been any damage done, but the authorities just wanted to ensure that the boys were being safe, since cars would drive over the bridge from time to time. Felix and his friends would make so much noise, many folks may have wondered if they were really ok or not. There certainly wasn't much fishing going on for the fine citizens of San Saba with all of the splashing around. Cottonmouth snakes, also known as water moccasins, were seen on occasion, but they were never really ever an issue for Felix and his friends. Felix had a good head on his shoulders, and he was always looking out for the safety of his friends and family.

Felix received his first gun as a gift while celebrating his 10th birthday. Although it was just a BB gun, Felix thought he was so cool when handling it, and he felt grown up when shooting it. Once school let out in the summer of 1930, Viola took Felix and his sisters out to Bend to spend a month with Ma and Pa, who were very glad to have the youngins around the house. They spoiled them rotten and let them play and enjoy themselves as long as they didn't hurt one another or break anything along the way. There was one exception to the rule about breaking things around the River Bend farm. Felix, Chauncey, and the other cousins were allowed to shoot bottles and cans off of their grandfather's fence posts with Felix's new BB gun. Ma and Pa had been saving bottles of all colors, shapes, and sizes, so that the boys could hone their shooting skills that summer.

Spending time with his grandparents was always very special for Felix and the family. There would be regular get-togethers with the extended family, and, of course, with all of the cousins. Felix enjoyed having everyone together for the grand fish fries that were complete with hush puppies, potato wedges, beans, hand churned ice cream, pecan pie, and iced tea. Felix was always willing to lend a hand at churning butter for the homemade biscuits. After supper, many of the children would sneak into the house, thinking that nobody would notice, for pillow fights with some of Ma's beloved feather filled pillows. Ma would only get a little angry, if she was the one who had to clean up the mess, and then restitch some of the pillows afterwards.

Pa was so impressed with the shooting skills that Felix and Chauncey had displayed that summer; he ended up purchasing a brand new .22 caliber rifle for each of them. Since Chauncey was younger, Felix made sure that safety came first, and he was very mindful of the dangers. There were strict rules that the boys had to follow. Felix and Chauncey always had to shoot away from the house, and they needed to be sure that there wasn't anyone down range. Chauncey really looked up to and adored Felix. The boys were pretty much inseparable when Felix would visit his grandparents at Bend. With their new rifles, the boys would hunt squirrels in the pecan groves, and their grandfather would pay them five cents for every one that they bagged. They also hunted rattlesnakes that ventured too close to the house and barn.

During those summertime visits, Viola would assist her mother with fixing the most delicious chicken supper that a person could have. The boys would assist Pa with capturing, killing, and cleaning the chickens before turning them over to Viola and Ma for their part. The biscuits and cornbread were simply delicious. When staying at Bend on a Sunday, Felix could count on going to Sunday school and church with his sisters, Chauncey, and with some of his other cousins.

Felix frequently wore a long sleeve shirt with overalls when working and playing around the River Bend farm. On Sundays, however, he wore his best shirt, fine slacks, and he combed his hair nicely. Felix had quite a tan from being outside so much of the time. He certainly was a clean-cut, fine looking young man, and he looked mighty dapper at Sunday school.

The United Methodist Church in Bend was a small church, but a popular place for people in the community to congregate and worship together. W. J. was a proud member of the original building committee, and he played a crucial role in constructing the church. W. J., and his brother, Miles Millican, cleared the hillside of mesquite trees, rocks, and even prickly pear cacti, so that the building could be completed. W. J. and several of his fellow congregants hauled lumber from other nearby communities by wagon to the site when it was first built around 1911.

Long before the Scotts or Millicans lived at Bend or in San Saba, Native American tribes consisting of Comanche, Kickapoo, and Apache Indians, inhabited much of the area, and they called it home for centuries. Felix and Chauncey would frequently spend time scouring the riverbanks and surrounding areas for arrowheads, spear tips, stone knives, tomahawks, and any other Native American relics that they might stumble upon. Every tribe had a unique culture, and their own way of crafting and making stone tools and weapons. W. J. and Ernest were good relic hunters when they were young, and they proved to be a valuable resource for Felix and Chauncey as they went about their own treasure hunting adventures. They showed the boys where to look, and what to look out for. Stumbling upon fossils and animal skulls was always an epic bonus. The boys were in awe every time their grandfather would pull out some of his most special items that were found there in San Saba County. Felix sure enjoyed finding quality specimens, and he took a great deal of pride in his growing collection. Mr. Livingston owned a small general store there in San Saba, and he'd regularly buy high grade and unique pieces that the boys wanted to sell. The amount they made depended on the size, shape, and overall quality of each item.

Felix opened an account at the San Saba National Bank at an early age. At least once a month, he'd ride his bike from his home all the way down to the bank. The bank was located about one block west of the Courthouse Square, and the staff was always very welcoming to Felix each time he'd visit with a pocket full of change. They always went out of their way to show their support for Felix's thriftiness in savings vs. spending. Felix would have the biggest smile you had ever seen when the teller would record his new ledger balance in his personal passbook. He wanted to be successful like his father and grandfathers when he grew up. Felix was well on his way, since he was already an outstanding young citizen and a clever entrepreneur.

The Methodist Camp meeting is an annual tradition that dates back to 1858. Felix and his family looked forward to this outdoor gathering as a way to relax, and catch up with friends, family, and fellow parishioners. The meeting was held at the same location near Bend, each and every year. The camp meeting officially started on the Friday night before the third Sunday in August. The gathering could last for up to ten days, and many folks came from nearby communities to congregate spiritually, and to glean social enjoyment. Felix's extended family had camped on the same section of land at the campground for decades. Felix's great grandfather, W. W. Millican, and his family were among the original charter members for this gathering.

Ernest and Viola wouldn't camp for the entire length of the camp meeting. With four kids and two businesses, two or three nights was about all that they could manage. Over the years, Ernest had made each of his children a fishing pole, and the family surely enjoyed fishing together. He could regularly be seen climbing the elm and pecan trees near the creek at camp to retrieve the fishing lures that the kids had managed to cast into the trees.

Upon arriving at camp, Viola would deploy a large mosquito net to protect the family from many of the native insects. She was a wonderful cook around camp, and black coffee was almost always brewing on the camp fire. Viola regularly served bacon and eggs, sandwiches, and, of course, fresh fish caught in the nearby Cherokee Creek. She loved cooking with her cast iron skillet on the open fire. Viola would often boil a jar of molasses, and then Felix and his sisters would dip a piece of bread into the boiling molasses. Simply smelling all of the different things around camp was enough to make anyone hungry. Viola and Ernest made sure that their kids were always fed and well cared for.

The camp meeting of 1935 turned out to be a very special one for Felix. His two older sisters would visit the camp, but they usually wouldn't stay for very long. Essentially, with only two children to tend after at camp, Ernest and Viola were able to spend more time socializing with their extended family and members of their church. Felix was certainly old enough to do his own things around camp. He was thin, but strong and good looking. Felix was an outgoing person, yet he was somewhat shy around girls whom he didn't know. On that first Saturday at camp, Felix met a nice young lady named, Francine Waters, while wading in the creek with the other teenagers at camp. Francine had long auburn hair and beautiful brown eyes. Felix thought that she was a real doll, and he was quite smitten. Francine lived with her folks over in Lampassas, and she was at camp visiting her grandparents, who lived in Cherokee. It turns out that her parents were over in San Saba looking at properties to potentially purchase.

When Sunday rolled around, Felix was glad to hear the good news that Francine had shared with him. Her parents had agreed to purchase a place in San Saba, and her family would be moving in just before the start of the school year.

Felix had never been in a relationship with a girl, and he didn't really know what to do, how to act, or where he wanted it to go. Folks certainly married at a young age during that time, and he was definitely attracted to Francine. Felix had plenty of goals, and he didn't really have any intention of settling down anytime soon. However, after spending those few days hanging around Francine, he began to develop feelings for her, and he was hoping that she felt the same way about him. It was fair to say that Felix had been bitten by the love bug. He met Francine's parents at the camp supper that Sunday night. Francine's father, Thomas Waters, was a tall and well-built man. Felix was a bit intimidated when he introduced himself, and asked for permission to date Francine. Felix stood tall, and he answered all of the questions that Thomas grilled him with. Thomas seemed to like Felix and the answers that he gave to all of his questions. He'd heard that Felix was part of a well-respected family, and he liked his ambition. Thomas agreed that Felix and Francine could see each other, but there were a few rules. Realizing that Francine was a year younger than Felix, he'd allow them to hang out at school together. Outside of school, they could only hang out at each other's houses, or in a public setting when other adults were present. Felix and Francine were excited to begin this new chapter with one another.

As Felix began his sophomore year at San Saba High School, he continued to be a very busy young man. He'd recently achieved the level of Second Class in his local Boy Scout troop. Working his odd jobs all over town kept him in shape, but it also nearly wore him out at times. Felix certainly made time for Francine, and he was very excited to introduce her to all of his friends at school. The young couple hung out together regularly, and they had a fabulous time attending the school dances and church socials. Francine was very athletic, and she was pleased when she was selected to be part of the high school cheer squad.

Felix learned to drive at an early age out at the River Bend farm. Tractor racing around the farm was fun and exciting, but Felix yearned for a car of his own, and the independence that came with it. Felix was displeased that he couldn't legally drive in town because he wasn't 18 years old. However, being without a car didn't hinder Felix's ability to get around town. Everything in town was close enough to walk or ride his bike to. Felix's parents could be relied upon for a ride during times of inclement weather, and for trips out to Bend. San Saba was a small town, and it didn't take long to get to most places.

Felix had many friends in school, and as he got older, his adventures became a bit wilder. There are stories about Felix and his friends occasionally catching "free" rides aboard trains leaving San Saba. As a slow moving train left the station, it had to bank around a slight curve, which left some blind spots for the personnel on the train. There was an area next to the tracks that was thick with trees and bushes. The young men had carved out a terrific hiding spot among the overgrown vegetation. When the freight cars began creeping by, they sprung out of their hole, and quickly hopped aboard. Felix was fast, and probably the most athletic of his pals. He'd generally be the first one to climb aboard, and he'd then help pull his buddies up so that they wouldn't get hurt. The young men would enjoy the sun and the wind in their hair as they rode the rails. They typically didn't venture too far, and they were always sure to hop off before they reached the next station to avoid getting caught. Trains ran fairly regularly, so they had a similar process for the return trip home.

AJ Blanton was a regular visitor at the Scott home. Johnnie Mae met AJ during their time together at San Saba High School. AJ was handsome, muscular, and he had black curly hair. Johnnie Mae was tall, thin, funny, and she was a wonderful cook. AJ was about four years older than Felix, but they shared a passion for fast cars and airplanes. He felt like a big brother of sorts to Felix. They spent time together rebuilding car engines, and assembling sophisticated model airplanes. One day, Johnnie Mae accepted AJ's marriage proposal, and the wedding date was set for 13 Apr. 1937. This day was special in many ways, as Ernest and Viola would be celebrating their 24th wedding anniversary as well. Just like her parents, Johnnie Mae and AJ were married by her grandfather, W. J. Millican. W. J. wore many hats in San Saba County, and he also served as the Justice of the Peace. AJ and Johnnie Mae were in their early twenties when they got married, and the ceremony was held at the River Bend farm, which was home to some of the most scenic spots in all of Central Texas. AJ worked as a mechanic at Warren's garage, and Johnnie Mae owned Ketchum's Kitchen, which was a bustling cafe on the west side of the Courthouse Square. The cafe was best known for its fabulous BBQ, tamales, and delicious pies. A short time after getting married, Johnnie Mae persuaded AJ to use his culinary talents, and he became the cook there at Ketchum's Kitchen. They truly enjoyed spending every day together. AJ could play the trombone rather well, and he was a member of the San Saba town band. Johnnie Mae loved to listen to him play, and she'd often dance the night away with her friends and family, while listening to their concerts.

When Felix turned 17, his father gave him a Winchester hunting rifle as a present. With many years of practice, Felix had become a crack shot, and he could knock the bottle cap off of a soda bottle at a 50 yard distance. Felix liked to hunt with his friends, just about as much as he enjoyed hunting with his family. They'd hunt axis and white tail deer, sheep, wild hogs, bobcats, and on a rare occasion, even a mountain lion. Felix had a reputation of being able to catch some of the biggest fish in the San Saba area. He was the envy of many local residents when he reeled in a 62 pound yellow catfish out of the Colorado River. It would often be necessary for two people to hold up the pole laden with the days catch. Fresh fish was certainly a staple in Viola's kitchen, and in Ernest's fryer.

The summer of 1937 was a very exciting time for Felix. He'd visited the local car dealership countless times while growing up in San Saba, and he'd cruise through the lot on his bicycle at least once a week. When Felix first sat eyes on the sleek and stylish 1937 Ford Coupes lined up along the dealer's lot, he fell in love all over again. He wanted that car, and he felt that he needed that car. However, it was just not going to happen in 1937. Felix essentially had two main expenditures, Francine, and the collection plate at church. Felix had managed to stash away a nice little sum down at the San Saba National Bank, but he didn't have enough money for this car, just yet.

The variety of doing odd jobs for folks around town kept Felix plenty busy. He'd spend hours out in the Texas heat, cutting and stacking firewood. Felix was skilled with a saw, and he could cut cedar trees for fence posts as good as any older man in town. This kind of work was somewhat seasonal, and very labor intensive. Felix was certainly glad to have found a job at Mrs. Howard's bakery there in town. He'd now be provided with regular hours, and he had the added benefit of being inside, and out of the elements. In addition to the bakery job, Felix found ways to earn extra money by helping out at his grandfather's farm. He'd also provide his services at some of the farms and ranches that belonged to his family members, and to friends of the family as well. Ernest always told Felix that there was a job waiting for any man willing to work. Felix heeded his father's advice, and he proved himself to be a very hard worker. On occasion, Felix continued to sell some of the finest specimens from his personal collection of Native American stone and edged weapons to Mr. Livingston. Money was piling up in his account, and he still managed to do plenty of fun things with Francine and his friends that summer. Felix must've made an impression on Mr. Waters as well, since he decided that Felix and Francine could finally go on dates without a chaperone.

Felix first began to hear about Amelia Earhart a year or so after he received his pecan plane. Like Charles Lindbergh, Amelia had managed to catch the interest of young Felix. He'd read about a new record that she'd set, or another adventure that she'd taken while reading through his airplane magazines. When Amelia Earhart became the first woman to complete a solo transatlantic flight in May of 1932, Felix was certainly impressed. Although Amelia had missed her intended landing spot in France, she touched down safely in Northern Ireland to complete her record breaking journey. Of course, there were numerous awards and recognitions bestowed upon her, including the Distinguished Flying Cross, given to her by the United States Congress.

Early in 1936, Felix began to read about Amelia's plans for an around the world flight. Her journey was to be the longest ever attempted at around 29,000 miles, and she was hell-bent on becoming the first woman to complete such a mission. Felix felt that this would be an extraordinary and risky adventure, and he was highly interested in reading about the planning and preparation that would be needed for such a long flight. After a failed attempt in March of 1937, Amelia and her navigator set out on their around the world journey on 1 Jun. 1937 from Miami, Florida. Felix kept up with her progress in the weekly newspaper, and by the end of June of 1937, they had completed a little more than three quarters of the mission.

Felix was entirely sad to read about the fact that Amelia's plane has suddenly gone missing while she was en route to Howland Island, a tiny little island out in the middle of the Pacific Ocean. It was 2 Jul. 1937, and nobody had a clue as to what had happened to her. It seemed that she'd just vanished into thin air or into the depths of a very unforgiving ocean. Amelia was so close to completing the mission, since there was only a stop in Honolulu, and then on to the West Coast of the United States to complete her record-breaking journey.

Mixed accounts as to what had happened to Amelia and her navigator played out in the papers for weeks and months and even years afterward. Was it bad planning, poor navigational skills, problems with their equipment, lack of fuel, or perhaps, something even something more sinister? Felix figured that it had to have been very difficult to locate such a small island out in the vast Pacific Ocean. Had she crashed, and if so, where? Most folks speculated that she must've crashed into the sea, but some people felt that she just may have been off course, and that she could have landed on an island somewhere nearby. Could the Japanese have had anything to do with her disappearance? Had they somehow shot her down, or taken her captive? Felix was captivated by the mysterious ending to Amelia's journey, and he kept up with the story as best as he could as time went on. He'd been really rooting for her success, and he had a great deal of respect for Amelia as a pioneering female aviator. Felix hoped that one day, he too, would become a distinguished aviator.

Felix and Francine would spend a great deal of time together on Saturdays. She wasn't much into hunting or fishing, but rather she enjoyed swimming, splashing, exploring, and hiking. Felix was an aficionado of anything outdoors, so he naturally enjoyed doing the things that she liked too. There would always be time during the weekend for a movie, and sometimes even a double feature at the Palace movie theater. Viola was always willing to fix, and pack, a nice lunch for Felix and Francine when they'd picnic. In between his leisure time, and a few shifts at the bakery each week, Felix also managed to attend meetings of the San Saba Chapter of Future Farmers of America with his father. Felix had his heart set on becoming a pilot, but he enjoyed the company at the meetings, and he figured a backup plan for his future wouldn't be a bad idea.

Although Felix didn't sit on his father's lap anymore while Ernest read the paper, he still enjoyed hearing the happenings that were going on around the world. Over the years, they had followed the subsequent events after Japan took over the Chinese province of Manchuria back in 1931. By the end of the summer in 1937, Japan had controlled large sections within China, and their aggressions were beginning to cause concern across the world. Felix and Ernest had many conversations as to what could or should be done about the conflict taking place on the other side of the world.

When September of 1937 rolled around, Felix found himself as a senior at San Saba High School. Francine continued as a member of the cheer team, and she was finally able to convince Felix to join the football team. Felix wasn't the biggest or the tallest person on the team, but he was tough and quick. He wore number 10 for the San Saba Armadillos, and Francine certainly enjoyed cheering for her Felix from the sidelines. Felix played mostly as a halfback, but he competed as a wide receiver on occasion. Having a rather small football team necessitated flexibility among all of the players, and Felix enjoyed helping out wherever he was needed. Felix was glad to have finished the summer that had been full of football practices in the sweltering Texas heat. He was eager to give up the countless hours of sprints and repetitive drills. Felix was going to miss the strength and physical conditioning exercises though, as he enjoyed getting bigger and stronger. The memories of the after practice gatherings at the San Saba River near his home would be treasured forever. Francine would regularly be waiting along the banks of the chilly water with ice cold soda pop, and cookies for Felix and his buddies. Felix had developed great friendships with most of his teammates, but he enjoyed hanging out with Jack, Charles, and Bobby Joe the most. The tight knit team went on to win the regional football championship for the '37–'38 season.

Playing football on Rogan Field was thrilling, but it was also a bit eerie at the same time for Felix. He remembered back to early 1935 when their new football field was still a full-fledged cemetery. The cemetery was created on land owned by the Rogan family in the years after San Saba was first settled. It housed many of San Saba's earliest residents, including some soldiers who had served in the Civil War. Felix and his friends knew to stay clear of the area since it had become unsafe and unsightly. It was an eyesore in the community, and the Rogan family had grown tired of dealing with the matter. Therefore, they decided to donate the land to the city in an effort to clean up, and to make better use of the property. In June of 1935, work began to transfer those who were interred there to other cemeteries in San Saba County. However, Felix recalled times when he and his friends would watch the construction as it took place. He thought that it was very strange that the crews evidently didn't relocate all of the decedents who were buried within the cemetery. As the crews prepared the ground for the new stadium and football field, some of the tombstones were allegedly bulldozed over, and the human remains apparently were left in their graves. The top layer of the ground was tilled, and the new grass field was planted so that football games could begin there in the fall of 1936.

Felix seemed to have known why some areas of the football field were greener than others. Now and then, Felix and his teammates would have unexplainable things happen to them during practice or games. If an Armadillo or visiting player unexpectedly tripped while running down the field, Felix figured it was just one of the "residents" who had reached up and grabbed the player by the ankle. All in all, Felix loved playing football in front of his loving family in the stands.

Felix was an average student throughout his high school career. He'd rather be working, playing, romancing, or even sleeping, than doing homework. Felix loved to read; he just didn't like to read textbooks. He spent countless hours reading on his front porch. Felix didn't like all of the writing in his English classes, and he had a rather hard time with arithmetic. In the spring of 1938, Felix began the process to finalize his admission to Texas AMC. There was no thought given to attending a faraway school, since he wanted to remain fairly close to home, and to Francine. Felix chose Texas AMC mostly for its cadet program, which he figured would help him in the event that he'd ever be selected to become a pilot in the Air Corps. He felt that he was moving one step closer to achieving his boyhood dream of becoming a pilot, and he was excited about what the college experience would bring. College Station was located about three hours to the east of San Saba, and it would be ideal for him to be able to return home for birthdays, holidays, and school breaks. Francine was as smart as a whip, and she achieved A's in every subject. However, since she was just a junior, her college planning would have to wait just a bit.

Felix was excited to flip the calendar to May of 1938. With Francine's tutoring assistance, Felix was able to pass all of his final exams, and he ended up with mostly B's and C's during his high school tenure. He was now anxiously counting down the days until graduation. Felix ensured that all of his extended family knew the date for this high school graduation ceremony. He invited nearly everyone whom he could think of, as he was very proud that he was going to be the first in his family to attend college. When Felix woke up on 30 May 1938, the celebration wasn't going to be limited to just a graduation ceremony. This special day just so happened to be Felix's 18th birthday as well. There were streamers hung along the walls of the Scott home, and some even dangled from the kitchen ceiling. Viola had made a bountiful breakfast complete with eggs, toast with jelly, potatoes, bacon, and fresh strawberries. Felix couldn't help but notice the small, wrapped present on the kitchen table. He sat at the table pondering what could be inside the little box. Felix noticed that the tag had his name on it, but when he tried to touch it, Viola told him that he'd have to wait until he was given permission to open it at his birthday party being held later that day.

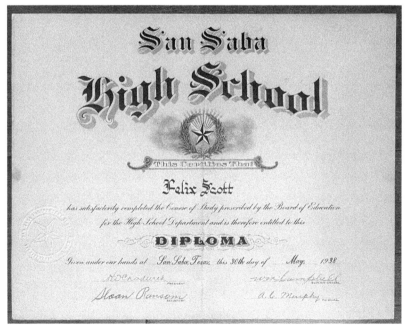

Felix graduated from High School on his 18th birthday!

Felix's aunts, uncles, grandparents, sisters, cousins, and several friends started showing up around 12:00 p.m. at the Scott home. This was to be a grand dinner party to celebrate his birthday, graduation, and to commemorate Memorial Day, which also fell on this eventful day. Viola was busy preparing summer squash, cornbread, and fried chicken. Pauline brought a huge pot of gumbo, while Johnnie Mae brought many dozens of fresh biscuits. Aletha helped out by cutting several watermelons into small square pieces, and she also prepared the garden fresh tomatoes, radishes, and onions onto Viola's finest serving trays. Most of the menfolk had gathered around Ernest outside, while he prepared his fryer for the large bucket of catfish fillets waiting to be fried nearby. Ma and Pa Millican brought pecan, cherry, and apple pies, and also a large rectangular shaped chocolate cake, which Felix just loved to no end. Everyone raved about how delicious the pies and cake looked as they sat out on the dessert table. There was plenty of room in the backyard for all of the guests to sit at a table in one of the three neatly arranged rows.

There was a joyous applause among those in attendance when Ernest yelled out, "The catfish and chicken is ready. Let's eat, y'all!" The womenfolk who were inside brought out all of the serving trays of food and placed them on the tables in the center row. W. J. asked that everyone bow their heads, and he then proceeded to give the blessing. He concluded by thanking God for the glorious day and family celebration. It didn't take long for the food to disappear into the mouths of the hungry guests. After everyone had finished their dinner, it was time for the desserts, and Felix and his friends ensured that there was nothing left over. While folks were finishing up their desserts, Viola and her sisters quickly cleaned up the platters, and they brought the dishes into the kitchen. It wasn't long before Viola came back outside with the little wrapped box, which she placed on the table with the other gifts. Viola proclaimed, "It's now time to open presents, so everyone gather round."

There was a large stack of birthday and graduation cards waiting for Felix as he approached the table full of gifts. While opening his birthday cards, Felix could hear the sound of a car revving its engine up and down the streets directly next to their home. Felix looked up, and said to Bobby Joe, "Doesn't that car sound marvelous?" Felix received a very nice gift from his maternal grandparents, and he'd already amassed a nice little stack of cash. When he had finished with all of his cards and presents, Ernest and Viola nodded that it was time for him to open the wrapped box. As Felix picked up the box, everyone could hear the sound of a horn honking from the front yard. Felix said, "What on earth is going on out there?" The sound was repetitive, but not all that annoying, and it seemed to cease as Felix tore open the gift wrap on his present.

Felix lifted the lid off the box to reveal a $20.00 bill. The bill was rolled up with something tucked inside, and it was bound with two rubber bands. Felix removed the rubber bands, and a key dropped upon the table for all to see. At this point, the noise from the horn picked up again, and it had most definitely drawn the attention of Felix and his guests. Ernest suggested that Felix go out front to see what all the ruckus was about. As Felix entered the front yard, his jaw dropped when he noticed the 1937 Ford Deluxe Coupe that he'd been eyeing for quite some time. Mr. Oleson, the sales manager over at the used car dealership, was standing next to the beautiful maroon hot rod. Felix turned to his father, and asked, "What is this all about?" With a grin, Ernest replied, "Well, what do you think the key is for?"

Felix dashed over to the driver's side door, and he asked Mr. Oleson about the vehicle parked on the front lawn with its motor humming powerfully along. Mr. Oleson said, "Your father mentioned that you'd been saving for a car, and he knew that you were really into this little gem. Come on down to the dealership tomorrow with your money because your father said that he'd co-sign on a loan with you for the difference." Felix then said, "This is mine? Is it really mine?" Ernest stepped towards the car, and said, "Son, we're very proud of how hard you work and save. We wanted to help get you something that you'll truly enjoy." With that, Mr. Oleson left with one of his salesmen in a different car. Felix quickly grabbed Francine's hand, and he opened the passenger door to assist her into the front seat. Felix shouted, "I'm gonna take her out for a short spin." Knowing that Felix didn't yet have a driver's license, Viola called out, "Now y'all be careful, ya hear?"

Felix and his 1937 Ford Coupe.

Felix and Francine retuned home unscathed about ten minutes later. He was grinning from ear to ear as he exited the car with the keys held high in the air. It was obvious that Felix was on cloud nine, and he was so happy with his new ride. He knew that the loan and paperwork down at the bank would be a mere formality, and he'd be obtaining his driver's license in the coming days. Felix's friends began to head home, as they had graduation parties of their own to attend, yet his special day continued to roll along. While visiting with all of his family members still at the party, Felix hatched an idea in which he would lead the family in a caravan of sorts over to the high school for the graduation ceremony. Surprising to Felix, Ernest and Viola were on board with the idea.

With the graduation ceremony starting at 8:15 p.m. that evening, Felix had been instructed to arrive at the high school by 7:30 p.m. Right about 7:15 p.m., Felix backed his Ford Coupe out onto Cedar Street, and he then parked it at the corner of South Bluffton Avenue. Ernest pulled up behind him in his Studebaker, and Pa Millican followed in his Oldsmobile. One by one, the other family members followed suit in their Buicks, Pontiacs, and Chevrolets. The line of cars stretched around the corner, and out onto Central Avenue. Once Felix was satisfied with the look of his caravan, everyone began the short trek over to the high school. Felix made quite a splash as he entered the school parking lot in his shiny hot rod. While the family members parked their vehicles, Felix made his way to the back side of the gymnasium for a class picture. Francine joined Felix's family members as they found seats on the wooden bleachers inside the gymnasium. Promptly at 8:15 p.m., the girls led the procession of graduates, with the boys following close behind. The 64 graduates looked well dressed, and happy to be there.

Felix acknowledged his family sitting in the stands as he made his way to his assigned seat. After the invocation, the Principal, Mr. Murphy, stood up at the podium to address the crowd. After presenting his opening remarks, he said, "We have a graduate among us who is celebrating another very special event today. Our very own Felix Scott turned 18 years old today." He then directed Felix to stand, and he asked that the crowd join together in singing "*Happy Birthday*" to him.

Felix smiled as he stood proudly, yet he was blushing the whole time. He felt special to be recognized that way, and he waved to the crowd to acknowledge the nice gesture before sitting back down. Felix's mind had drifted elsewhere during the valedictorian's speech and comments to the class. However, he snapped back to attention as they began to call the names for the presentation of the diplomas. It was really no surprise that the loudest applause by far came from the section where Felix's family and guests were seated. As Felix walked out of the gymnasium for the last time, he stopped for a few moments to reflect on all of the fun times that had been spent there. Then, the realization suddenly hit him, he was now a man in charge of his own destiny.

Felix and Ernest were at the front door of the San Saba National Bank a few minutes before 9:00 a.m. the morning after the graduation. The bank staff welcomed them into the lobby, and they congratulated Felix on his graduation. With his passbook in hand, Felix made his way to the teller window to find that the ledger balance in his savings account showed $395.26. Felix asked for a cashier's check to be payable to the dealership for $390.00. With the check and cash in hand from his party, Felix was prepared to make a down payment of $450.00 towards the purchase of his car. That was a rather sizable amount of money for a young man of his age. The money that Felix had saved from many of the past holidays, birthdays, and all of his hard work was definitely paying benefits now.

After securing the loan, Felix and Ernest left the bank, and they drove directly to the dealership in the '37 Ford in order to meet up with Mr. Oleson. He was prepared for the Scotts, and he was very impressed that Felix had saved that amount of money. Ernest and Felix signed the required paperwork for the purchase of the car, and just like that, it was officially a done deal. Felix had a little extra giddy up in his step as he returned to the car. The next stop was the Texas Department of Public Safety. Felix was a good driver, and he had always been very perceptive when riding in cars with others. Luckily, he had no problems obtaining his driver's license, and he was thrilled that he could now drive on his own. They then left for home to drop Ernest off, and then Felix was on his way to pick up Francine. They went for a drive out to his Pa Millican's ranch in Bend to hang out with Chauncey. Felix was eager to show his grandparents his new driver's license. They planned on celebrating by spending the afternoon plunging into the chilly Colorado River from one of W. J.'s many tire swings. Ma and Pa enjoyed watching the fun from the shade as they sat underneath a large pecan tree. Felix was thankful for his newfound independence, and he loved driving his car. After dropping Francine off at her house, he raced home to wash all the country road dust off of his new hot rod.

Felix planned to spend his last summer at home before starting college doing the things he loved doing the most. He stayed plenty busy working at the bakery and with his side hustles. Felix really enjoyed helping his father around the tire repair shop, and when he wasn't working, he enjoyed hanging out with Francine and his other friends. He spent an untold number of hours fishing for white bass and catfish on the San Saba and Colorado Rivers. When he wasn't fishing at one of his favorite places, Felix could be found hanging out at the local swimming hole. He really enjoyed the tranquility of sitting on the rocks alongside of the San Saba River with Francine, while they discussed what the future might hold for them. Felix had really grown to love Francine dearly, but he felt terrible that she wasn't going to be able to go off to school with him. This matter weighed upon him heavily, and he tried to keep his true feelings and concerns bottled up inside him. Francine could tell that something was bothering him, yet she couldn't seem to get Felix to open up about his thoughts.

The morning of 19 Jul. 1938, started out like any other Tuesday. Felix was up before dawn, and he finished his shift at Mrs. Howard's bakery around noon. After work, he picked up Francine at her home, and they headed to the San Saba River to hang out, and picnic with friends. There was very little sun breaking through the clouds, but it was warm enough for them to enjoy their time in the water. The intermittent drizzle made it difficult to leave the food out on the picnic tables. However, the hungry teenagers managed to gravitate towards the food that had been placed inside several of the nearby vehicles. Suddenly, the group was no longer worried just about the food, they were becoming concerned with the severity of the rain storm that was developing around them. Lightning was seen, thunder was heard, and the dark clouds were consistently rolling in over the hilltops.

The rain was coming down so hard at times, Felix and his pals could hardly see one another. Upon realizing that things were getting increasingly worse, Felix grabbed Francine's hand, and they ran towards the car together. As he was getting inside his car, Felix yelled out to his pals, "Y'all drive safe, and take your time getting home." It should've been just a few minutes' drive over to Francine's house on West Lewis Street, but it ended up taking over fifteen minutes due to the lack of visibility. There were giant puddles everywhere, debris of all types had already found its way onto the roads, and there were plenty of cars carrying folks just trying to get home. Finally, Felix pulled up in front of Francine's home. Since the rain was coming down so hard, Felix felt that nobody from inside the house would be able to see inside of his car. Felix and Francine talked for a few minutes, and they were in awe of what was happening around them. Felix reached over, and took a moment to share a lovely kiss with Francine. The deteriorating situation that was evolving outside was making Felix very anxious as the ominous storm continued to pound San Saba.

He felt the need to give Francine one more goodbye kiss, and then he quickly escorted her to the front door. With water pouring off the tin roof from the tumultuous downpour, Felix and Francine hugged, and said their goodbyes.

Felix sprinted back to his car, and he began the not so ordinary trip home. He just couldn't help himself with the temptation of hitting the puddles at a high rate of speed. Felix enjoyed watching the giant spray of water that was propelled high into the air as a result. He nearly lost control of his vehicle a few times, but he was lucky that he didn't cause a wreck, or sustain any damage to his car. As he neared his home, he didn't see any people moving about the streets in his neighborhood. Felix finally arrived home safely, and he parked his car. He then ran towards the front door to see his mother standing there on the porch. Viola was quite relieved to see Felix standing before her as she had been worried about his whereabouts. She then said, "Land sakes son, you're soaking wet. What were you doing messing around outside during a storm like this?" Felix said, "Ma, it's just a little ol' rainstorm, typical for this time of year, eh?" Little did Felix or anyone else know that there was nothing typical about the advancing storm, and the havoc it was about to create upon most of the community.

The rain kept falling hour after hour, and day after day. Several days into the storm of the century, there were downed telephone and telegraph lines. Communication with neighbors, friends, and relatives had become nearly impossible. Ernest wouldn't allow Felix to drive anywhere, but he was able to walk, or ride his bike around the neighborhood, and into town. Felix and his pal Jack decided to walk into town on Friday morning to survey the havoc caused by the unrelenting storm. They quickly found a much different looking San Saba than what they'd seen just a few days before.

Wanting to see the damage that had been done by the flooding, the boys first went to the area around Mill Creek. They noticed that San Saba's main water pumping station, which was located there at Mill Creek, was inoperable and underwater. That explained why there was no running water at the Scott home, and Felix feared that many of the residents and businesses would be without water as well. Felix really wanted to check on Francine, since he hadn't heard from, nor had he seen her since he had dropped her off on Tuesday. He was able to convince Jack to join him in the trek over towards her house. Traveling through the streets of downtown was rather perilous at times with the incessant rain still coming down. After trudging up North 3rd Street, the boys noticed that Rogan Field was now a soggy mess. They were able to make it into an open field just across the railroad tracks before the flood water had become too much to handle. It had taken nearly an hour to reach Francine's neighborhood due to the detours, uprooted trees, downed power lines, and road closures. Felix was quite dismayed that he couldn't reach Francine's house, and it saddened him to see that her house was now halfway under water, and parts of it appeared to have broken apart, and washed away. Felix and Jack couldn't see anybody milling around, and most of the homes in that area appeared to be uninhabitable. The same fate had fallen to many of the homes in other nearby neighborhoods. The San Saba River had risen so much that it plowed right through the San Saba City Cemetery and beyond. Francine's house was only a few blocks west of the cemetery, and it stood little chance against the raging water, which was surging uncontrollably in nearly every direction possible.

Feeling dejected, helpless, and downright sad, Felix and Jack headed back towards their neighborhood. They decided to cruise by the courthouse on the way home to see what might be happening there. As they neared the Courthouse Square, Felix noticed a Red

Cross banner hanging from the brick and sandstone facade of the building. There were several military style trucks with the Red Cross logo emblazoned upon them parked out front along Wallace Street. Unlike Francine's neighborhood, there were a great deal of people congregating in groups around the courthouse steps. Folks could be seen coming and going through the heavy courthouse doors. Felix was curious, and he wanted to get an idea of what was going on inside. Jack decided to peel off for home as Felix walked up the steps, and entered the courthouse.

There was lots of commotion emanating from within the long hallways as Felix made his way through the second floor of the courthouse. He recognized some of the folks meandering about, but there were plenty of people whom he didn't know. When Felix reached the third floor, he was surprised to see Francine's father, Mr. Waters, coming out of the court room. It had been temporarily converted to provide assistance benefits to those affected by the flood damage. Troubled by the situation, Felix asked, "Hello Mr. Waters. Is Francine here with you?" Thomas replied, "Yes, she is. Unfortunately, we lost nearly everything with the flooding, and my family is staying down the hall until the storm moves on." Felix replied, "I'm so sorry to hear that. I was out by your place about an hour ago, and I saw the destruction and devastation to your neighborhood." Felix walked with Thomas down the hall and around the corner to find Francine, her mother, and her two sisters resting inside a room occupied by many other people.

Clearly, the storm didn't appear to be over, but the torrential rain had shifted to a light sprinkle for just a bit. Felix asked Thomas if he and Francine could go for a walk around the Courthouse Square. Thomas agreed, so Francine grabbed her umbrella. As they walked, Francine explained how they'd watched the floodwaters inch closer and closer to their home. Having just one car and Thomas's work truck, it was quite hard for them to decide what to take with them as they evacuated the neighborhood. Thomas had stripped down his work truck to make room for some of their worldly possessions. Being a mechanic, and with his shop located on the back side of their property, his ability to make a living had now been thwarted. Francine explained that her father was so sad and depressed that he was now contemplating moving the family out of San Saba.

Felix was somberly listening to Francine's account of the unfortunate set of events bestowed upon their family. Felix then asked, "When will he make the decision on whether y'all will move or not?" Francine replied, "I reckon soon, but I'm not really sure. The folks with the Red Cross provided us with some money for food, gas, clothing, and so on. Daddy says that most of the things in his shop were lost due to the flood." Felix then said, "That's terrible. Where are y'all going to stay when this damn storm finally stops?" Francine replied, "We're going to stay over at the home of Gretchen O'Grady. She is one of mother's friends, and she lives at a nice place out past the east end of town, away from all of this mess." Felix could tell that Francine was sad and exhausted. Suddenly, the rain started falling heavily once again, so Felix assisted Francine up the slippery courthouse steps. Before leaving Francine with her family, he hugged and kissed her goodbye. As Felix left the courthouse, he saw quite a few men with their heads miserably buried into their knees, and he heard the woeful cries of women and children.

The rain continued to fall, quite heavily at times throughout the weekend. The businesses in town were all closed up; thus Felix couldn't work at the bakery. Felix was tired of being cooped up inside, just watching the rain continually pour off the roof. Luckily for the Scott family, the high water levels didn't approach their home.

Ernest's shop was able to weather the storm for the most part, but the shop's roof wasn't as sound as it could be, and there were some puddles here and there.

When Felix woke up on Monday, 25 Jul. 1938, it was barely raining. He went outside to sit on the front porch, and waited for Mother Nature's next move. It was just before noon, and the sun was finally visible behind the cover of the large gray clouds. By late afternoon, the clouds had finally moved on, and the sun was once again shining all over San Saba. Felix was now feeling less anxious about the storm, but he still felt helpless regarding the situation with Francine and her family. Since the streets were beginning to dry out in his neighborhood, Felix hopped in his car, and drove the short distance to the courthouse to check on Francine. He ran up the steps, and sprinted down the hallway to the place he had last seen Francine and her family. Felix was quite distressed when he opened the door to see that she was no longer there. He asked a Red Cross volunteer who was working in the room about the status of the Waters family. As she checked her paperwork, Felix, having a sharp memory and all, mentioned that they might be out at the Gretchen O'Grady residence. The woman replied, "Ah yes, here it is. You're correct about them staying over at their home." She wrote down the address, and Felix then hightailed it out of the door and to his car. He peeled out of the parking lot, and began to make the arduous trek across town to check on Francine and her family to see how they were doing.

The main drag through town was quite a sight. Felix knew that there was sure to be devastating losses throughout San Saba, along with many displaced people. He quickly began to see the broader scope of the damage. Tree trunks were everywhere, animal carcasses were beginning to decay on the streets, and shopkeepers could be seen sweeping and shoveling the sidewalks around their businesses.

For the most part, Felix ended up making pretty good time getting to the O'Grady home, and he noticed Francine's father's work truck parked out front. He casually walked up to the door, and just before he could knock, Francine opened the door. She was very excited and glad to see Felix. They quickly embraced and shared a kiss, and at that point, she really didn't care if anyone happened to notice. They found the front porch swing to be a fine place to sit, and catch up on the events of the last few days.

Francine reached out and grabbed Felix's hand, and she began to provide him with an update to her family's situation. She started off by saying, "Mother and Daddy traveled to Amarillo. Daddy's brother lives there, and he owns some business property. He told Daddy that he'd let him set up a new shop without worrying about paying any rent." Felix started to feel a little uncomfortable since he didn't like the sound of where the conversation was heading. Francine continued, "They'll be back before this weekend, and if they like what they saw, then I guess we'll be moving there. With school starting soon, they want us to be there when the new school year begins." The realization that his girl was more than likely going to be moving away hit him right in the chest. Felix, with tears building in his eyes, said, "Y'all are just gonna leave? Just like that? Can't your father just rebuild here with help from all of the community donations, and money from the Red Cross? Couldn't you go and live with your grandparents for a while?" Francine was crying noticeably at this point, and said, "Daddy feels that he can get back on his feet quicker there. I'm going to miss out on my senior year at San Saba High School, I'm gonna miss this little town, and I'm certainly gonna miss my Felix."

Felix suddenly felt as if his head was spinning around and around as he tried to digest this discouraging news. He sat stoically as the many different scenarios raced through his head. How far was it from

College Station to Amarillo? What did Francine really mean when she said, "Miss my Felix?" Felix wondered if he could find a way to make their relationship work being so far away from one another. After a few moments of silence, Felix emphatically asked, "Have you given up on us?" By now, Francine was feeling terrible, and she was quite devastated about the situation she found herself in. She then leaned her head into Felix's shoulder and squeezed his hand a little tighter. Francine wholeheartedly replied, "Babe, I know that you want to fulfill your dreams of becoming a pilot. That adventure will probably take you all over the world. I want to start a family after graduation, and I know you aren't quite ready to settle down and all." The scenarios were once again racing through Felix's mind. Should he give up on Texas AMC? Should he put off his dream of becoming a pilot? Should he move to Amarillo to find work and then marry Francine, or should he stay the course, and continue down the path to realize his boyhood dream?

Felix really didn't know what to say regarding the two completely different directions this relationship was heading for. The conversation with Francine had made Felix's stomach churn, and he felt miserable. He had never faced a hardship during his relationship with Francine, so Felix figured that it would be best for him to leave in order to clear his head, and reflect on what to do next. He stood up from the swing, and he helped Francine up as well. Felix then said, "I love you with all my heart. I just need to take some time to think about this new reality in our relationship. Mrs. Howard, down at the bakery, asked me to come in, and help get the shop cleaned up so that she can re-open." Francine reached out to hug Felix tightly, since she understood the crossroads at which they were at. Francine then said, "You go on and do your work. Come back and see me this Saturday, and we'll go do something fun together." Felix agreed, and he felt that this would give him time to think about how he wanted to approach the most difficult decision that he'd ever faced in his young life. He and Francine embraced, and shared a nice goodbye kiss. As Felix slowly drove away, he turned his head so that he could wave to Francine as she stood on the porch.

Felix reported to the bakery first thing on Tuesday morning. The building was in decent shape overall, but muddy water had found its way under the front door, and there was surely a leak or two in the roof. By the end of Thursday's shift, they had removed all of the mud, mopped the floor, repaired the roof, washed all of the windows, and cleaned the display cases. Mrs. Howard gave Felix a little cash bonus before he headed home since she was so pleased with all of his hard work. Felix stopped by the family's filling station to find that Ernest had reopened to customers earlier that day. He then walked over to Johnnie Mae's cafe, and he was glad to hear that she was going to reopen the following morning for breakfast. For the most part, the businesses in the Courthouse Square had fared pretty well, and the Scotts were just glad that no one in the family had been injured during the flood. However, since the telephone lines were still being repaired all over San Saba County, Felix wondered how Ma and Pa and all the other relatives out at Bend had fared during the storm. After supper that evening, Felix asked his father about making a trip out to Bend to check on his grandparents. Viola thought that it was a splendid idea, and Ernest agreed to take the day off so that he could ride along with Felix out to Bend.

Felix woke up early on that Friday morning so that he and Ernest could begin their journey over to the River Bend farm. Ernest was a realist, and he wasn't sure if they'd be able to reach their kin at Bend. Ernest figured that the Millicans would be alright since W. J. was quite adept at handling most things that were thrown at him.

He realized that the trip to Bend was important to Felix, and he was willing to ride along. On a good day, the dirt road to Bend had its problems, and Ernest worried about the several low water crossings that they were going to have to deal with. As Felix raced down the muddy dirt road from San Saba, Ernest held on for dear life. There was plenty of debris, tree branches, and rocks strewn about on the road, but Felix skillfully maneuvered around the obstacles. Felix was having a ball navigating his roadster through the sloshy terrain. However, their journey came to an abrupt halt when they determined that they wouldn't be able to make it across their first river crossing. The water had swelled so much, they couldn't even get close to the path that would take them to the other side.

Begrudgingly, Ernest told Felix that they'd need to go back. Felix understood since he didn't want to get stuck in the mud, or even worse, get washed down the river due to the swift moving currents. Felix then said, "Man, it looks like that storm really washed the rocks and moved some dirt. I bet we wouldn't have to look too hard to find some nice arrowheads." Ernest had had many years of experience hunting arrowheads, and he agreed that it would be a good time to go exploring. With that, they turned around, and proceeded to their favorite spot along the San Saba River just outside of town.

They spent nearly the whole day traversing and digging along the ravaged river banks. The fast moving flood water had certainly moved layers of rock and sediment, and as a result, there were suddenly newly exposed places for them to look. They made sure to check all of the known places along the river that the Native Americans had once made camp at. Ernest ended up finding some outstanding pieces, but Felix found some extraordinary pieces. Felix had sharp eyesight, and he was quite a natural when it came to relic hunting. It was as if Felix had a sense about him, which allowed him to envision exactly where the tribes had once lived, played, and hunted. Ernest and Felix continued to search high and low until they filled their lunch pail full of arrowheads. Felix really enjoyed the fresh air from being outside that day, and the quality time spent with his father. However, Felix had been preoccupied throughout the day thinking about what exactly he was going to say to Francine when he'd see her the following morning. It weighed upon him emotionally, which somewhat dampened an otherwise splendid day.

As the Scotts rolled back into San Saba, and headed down Wallace Street, Felix suddenly recalled the time that he had participated in the parade while piloting his homemade plane. Felix was certain that the event had sealed the deal for him to want to continue on the journey to becoming a pilot. He was a hard worker, but he always felt that his father was the hardest working man in town. Felix really looked up to his father, and was inspired by his seemingly endless work ethic. This was confirmed when Ernest offered to wash all of the mud off of Felix's hot rod as it got dark, just so that it would look nice for his date with Francine the following morning. As Felix sat down for supper with his parents and Aletha, he shared his thoughts and feelings regarding Francine. Everyone listened attentively, and they provided support and advice. Felix went to bed that Friday night certain in his decision on what to do and say, but he was afraid that Francine's pretty smile, charm, and persuasive personality, might sway him.

Before Felix left home that Saturday morning, Viola had prepared some sandwiches, cornbread, and fresh chocolate chip cookies for his picnic dinner with Francine. She even pressed his light colored pants and colorful striped shirt. Viola stopped Felix on the way out of the front door to check that his hair was neatly combed, and she gave her approval after giving him a good look over. Viola then said, "Go with your heart, son. God will be there with you, and He'll be there to guide you." Felix loaded the picnic basket, fishing poles, and a nice little watermelon into his car. The local market had finally reopened from the flood, so he also stopped by to pick up some ice and soda pop.

Chauncey (left) and Felix (right) in Bend, Texas.

Felix had tried calling over to the O'Grady home several times that Friday night. He couldn't get through, and the operator told him that some of the telephone poles and cables that were damaged during the flood were still being repaired. Felix figured that it would be safe enough to arrive at the O'Grady home around 10:00 a.m. for his date with Francine. The roads were finally clear enough, and Felix made the drive over there rather quickly and safely. As he pulled up in front of the home, Felix didn't see either of the cars belonging to

Francine's family. He figured that her parents may still be away in Amarillo, and someone may have borrowed her father's work truck. Felix gathered his thoughts, set his mind straight, and he then proceeded towards the front door.

This time, Felix knocked, and Mrs. O'Grady opened the door. Felix said, "Good morning, ma'am, is Francine here?" She replied, "You must be Felix. Land sakes! I must agree with Francine that you're a fine looking young man." Felix was beginning to blush a bit when he asked again, "Thank you, ma'am, I'd like to see Francine." Mrs. O'Grady quickly replied, "I'm so sorry, Felix, Francine left for Amarillo with her family yesterday morning. She figured that you'd be coming by, and she left this for you." Mrs. O'Grady then handed Felix a small gift wrapped box, which was tied with a bow made of blue ribbon. Suddenly, Felix was left stunned, dumbfounded, and he was downright in shock. He reluctantly accepted the box, and he asked Mrs. O'Grady if he could sit down on the porch swing to open it. She replied, "Well yes, Felix. You just sit right there, and take all the time that you need. If I can help you in any way, just let me know." And then, with that, she went inside her house.

Mrs. O'Grady shut the door, and the sound reverberated through Felix's head as he sat there trying to grasp what had just happened. With his hand resting on the spot where Francine had sat just a few days prior, Felix sat anxiously on the swing for a spell before unwrapping the box. Once he pulled off the lid, he saw Francine's favorite yellow headband. He immediately smelled the aroma of Lemon Verbena, which was Francine's perfume of choice. There was also a sealed envelope inside the box, and square on the back of it, there was an imprint of her lips in red lipstick. It was as if she had sealed it with a kiss. He delicately opened the envelope to reveal a letter which read:

My darling Felix,   *July 28, 1938*

I'm so sorry that I'm not here to go out with you on our special date. I feel so bad having to leave like this without getting an opportunity to give you a proper goodbye. I'm deeply saddened that Daddy wouldn't make time for me to see you again in person. Mother and Daddy arrived from Amarillo Wednesday evening. We collected the few remaining things that were salvageable over at the house on Thursday. I saw your car over at the bakery, and I didn't want to bother you there. We'll be up before dawn on Friday morning to load the cars, and we'll leave for Amarillo. Daddy is anxious to find a way to get back to work quickly, and he feels that a fresh start in a bigger town may be more rewarding. I tried calling you on Wednesday and Thursday evening, but there were still problems with the phone lines.

I'm so sorry babe. I already miss you. Knowing you, you probably have our favorite blanket in the car along with your fishing poles. I'm sure you probably also brought some of your ma's delicious sandwiches. Please say goodbye to your folks for me because they were always real nice to me. Daddy says that the church is much bigger there in Amarillo, and he tells me that I'll find a nice young man ready to start a family. I reckon he's wanting some grandkids sometime soon. I believe that it will be hard to find a finer man than you, Felix. However, in an odd sort of way, maybe all of this is a blessing in disguise. We had a good run, me and you. I really feel that we could've been happy together, and we could've had a terrific life together. I was always happy, and I felt safe when I was with you, Felix.

I don't want to be the one to hold you back, and keep you from chasing and fulfilling all of your dreams. I also believe that it is your destiny to become a pilot, Felix. You need to be set free, to fly high like the eagles. Daddy says school will be starting in a few weeks, and I know that you'll be off to college very soon. We would've been apart even if there hadn't been a flood. The main difference is that you would've come home from school on some weekends and holidays to visit your family. I could've seen you then. Now, I'll be more than 500 miles away from College Station.

I want you to remember the great times that we shared, as that is how I'll always remember you. I feel that I know you well enough to know what you would've told me about your wish for the direction of our relationship. I want you to have my headband, Felix. Remember all of the times that you ran your fingers through my hair? Keep it until you find a new girl someday, my love. I'll miss you, and I'll always hold a special place for you in my heart. Do great in school, become that ace pilot that you said you'd become, and be well, my Felix. I'll send you a letter after we get settled in and all, and I'd love to see you if you're ever in Amarillo.

I love you with all my heart.

Forever and always,

Francine.

With tears running down his face, Felix got up from the porch swing, feeling like he'd just been sucker punched. The day had started out with so much happiness and promise, and in a matter of just a few minutes, Felix was left broken hearted and despondent, being that he had no way to respond to the bad news. He returned to his car, unsure of what to do, or where to go. After losing his sweetheart, he unwillingly felt the real world pressures of being an adult for the first time.

Felix decided to go for a drive, hoping that it would relieve the sadness that had overcome him. His hot rod didn't have pretty hair and a great smile, but it had speed, and it was good looking in its own right. Felix derived a great deal of pleasure in driving his car. As he thundered down the road, Felix let his subconscious take over in deciding where to go. He figured that a quiet place would be nice, so that he could reflect on the happier times he had spent with Francine. Felix headed east from Mrs. O'Grady's place, and it didn't take long before he found himself at one of their favorite spots, Five Mile Hill.

The views of the entire valley were magnificent from Five Mile Hill, and Felix had spent many evenings there with Francine watching the sun set over San Saba. When he exited his car, he only saw a few deer and rabbits scurrying about, and he was hoping that he'd reached a place that would help assuage his sorrow. Felix grabbed the sandwiches and a few Cokes, and he began walking mindlessly around the area, in what felt like some sort of a trance. He slowly began to feel the calming effect that he was seeking at this most tranquil location. After sitting down in the shade, and leaning against the base of a tree, Felix ate the food that his mother had prepared. He sat there for more than an hour reminiscing about the last few years that he had shared with Francine. Feeling better about the situation, Felix then pivoted to begin the process of refocusing his goals, and he wondered what the next four years of college life would be like.

Felix returned to his car, and he pulled the headband from the box. As he held it in the palm of his hand, he realized that this situation wasn't Francine's fault, and neither one of them could've prevented the circumstances that led them down this path. Felix felt no ill will towards Francine, and he hoped that she'd find happiness over in Amarillo. He felt like a burst of energy had suddenly returned to his body, and he was beginning to come to grips with his new normal without Francine. With that, he hung the headband over his rear view mirror, and he promptly decided that he was going to begin calling his car "Elizabeth." Felix headed for home, and he even cracked an occasional smile along the way, thinking how silly it was to have given a nickname to his car. When he arrived home, Viola asked, "So, how did your big day go with Francine?" Felix replied, "Francine broke up with me, but I have Elizabeth now, and I'll be fine." Felix then walked into his room, and shut the door, leaving Viola with a perplexed look on her face.

By the following Saturday, the flooding had subsided enough that Felix decided to give it another try to reach his grandparents out at Bend. It was still a little hairy dealing with the muddy roads, and passing over the low river crossings, but when there's a will, there's a way, and Felix was certainly hell-bent on checking on his Ma and Pa Millican. Felix wasn't really all that concerned that his shiny hot rod was now a dirty mess. He was certainly relieved to find that his grandparents had indeed weathered the storm well. Felix listened attentively to his grandfather as he provided the harrowing details of how the rising flood waters from the Colorado River and from Cherokee Creek had affected them. He was glad to hear that his first cousin Chauncey had been able to check on all of the relatives around Bend while on horseback. Felix ended up spending the night there at the River Bend farm, and he relished every minute of the time he had spent there visiting with them.

When Felix retuned home, he found that the folks from the YMCA there on the campus at Texas AMC had sent him a copy of the student's handbook. There was a great deal of useful details about the school, and it described the many traditions that were revered there on campus. The book listed all of the events and activities that would be available on campus, and through the YMCA, during the upcoming school year. Felix was instructed to learn the information found between the covers of the book. One day, he sat around the kitchen table with Viola, trying to comprehend the "Aggie

Slanguage." Felix quickly learned that the cadets had nicknames for many of the common things found on, and around campus. Viola was entirely perplexed when Felix said, "I can't wait to have a bowl of worms sprinkled with dirt, and a side of sunshine, along with a glass of sky." Felix could tell that his mother was completely puzzled, so he said, "Ah mother, everyone knows that I meant I can't wait to have a bowl of spaghetti, sprinkled with black pepper, and a side of carrots, along with a glass of water. Viola then said, "Son, that all sounds very confusing to me, but I'm sure that you'll catch on right quick." After supper that evening, Felix practiced singing all of the school songs around the piano with his folks.

The last few weeks of August were a whirlwind for Felix. He felt excited knowing that he'd soon be heading off to college, but he also felt anxious that he'd be living in a different town. Although Texas AMC was an all-male college, he figured that there had to be some gorgeous Texas women somewhere in, or near, College Station. Felix felt a little weird attending the Methodist Camp meeting without Francine, but he went anyway because he knew that his folks would enjoy him being there for a few days. As he walked around the campground, the sound of the quick moving water in Cherokee Creek was quite soothing to his soul. Felix finally made it to the spot that he'd been searching for. On their one year anniversary as a couple in August of 1936, Felix had carved his and Francine's initials into the trunk of an old oak tree. It was a typical heart shape with F. S. and F. W. near the top. At that time, Francine also got Felix to carve "Forever and Always" into the middle of the heart. As his eyes focused on the heart, he remembered back to the day when they had promised each other that they'd regularly visit their special spot. Felix pressed his palm firmly onto the heart, and he then ran his index finger through the carvings. He stood there for several minutes, when an unexpected peacefulness began to surge through his body. At that moment, Felix knew that he was going to be fine moving forward without his first love.

Before heading off to College Station, Felix made it a point to hang out with all of his close friends and cousins. He went for drives around town in Elizabeth with Bobby Joe. He went swimming at his favorite spot on the San Saba River with Jack and Charles. He hunted hogs with Hilliard and Clovis. Felix searched all over San Saba County for Native American treasures with Dimmitt, Dardon, and, of course, his favorite cousin, Chauncey. He went to the movies at the Palace Theater with Nadaline and Helen. And just like that, the summer was over for Felix. He was now preparing to spread his wings, and to say goodbye to San Saba, at least for now. Felix felt glad to be part of such a wonderful family, and he felt blessed to have three wonderful sisters. He knew that everyone would be rooting for him while he was away at school, and he aimed to make them proud.

Mack concluded chronicling Felix's time spent growing up in San Saba upon reaching the last written page on his notepad. After sharing Felix's story for more than an hour, Mack reached over to get a refill from the pitcher of iced tea nearby. Sam proudly said, "You sure are the son of a history teacher. I think you did a wonderful job recounting the events of Felix's life with so many details." Bruce chimed in with, "It sounds like he had a lot of great times, and even a few challenges along the way." Sue Ann offered her support by saying, "I'm very proud of you, and quite impressed with your ability to paint such a clear picture of Felix's time growing up in San Saba. You learned so much in such a short amount of time." While sitting around the table at supper, Mack mentioned that he had some more information to share about Felix's time in college, and his journey to becoming a pilot in the United States Army Air Corps. The group seemed to be intrigued, and interested in learning more about Felix. As everyone enjoyed a fabulous dessert, Mack began to envision how he wanted to present the additional information about Felix the following morning.

CHAPTER 7

Fish Scott

Before Mack turned in for the night, he spent some time flipping through the pages of Felix's journal. He sat upright in bed reading all about Felix's time spent when he was away at college. Mack then moved on to his transition from college into the United States Army Air Corps. He studied all of the pictures, and he took excellent notes. Mack wanted to be prepared for his presentation to his Uncle Bruce, Aunt Sue Ann, and to his father the next morning. When Mack awoke, he promptly ventured into the kitchen to find a man sitting around the table having coffee with his Uncle Bruce. Mack cheerfully introduced himself to the man, and he found out that his name was Frank. He was a friend of his Uncle Bruce, and Frank was an Aggie alumnus who had also served in the United States Air Force. Frank was excited to hear about Mack's discovery, and he was also eager to be part of the discussion. After breakfast, the group headed back into the den and sat down. Mack pulled out his notepad along with Felix's journal, and he then promptly began his presentation.

The day was Saturday, 10 Sep. 1938, and it happened to be the last full day that Felix would spend in San Saba before heading off to the Agricultural and Mechanical College of Texas. The college was one of the most distinguished military cadet prep schools in all of the United States, and even the world at the time. Felix's family was very proud of him, and they felt that a potluck would be a great way to send him off to school. Viola mentioned to Ernest, "Our boy might not get any more home cooking until Thanksgiving!"

The party was held at the Scott residence, and there certainly was no shortage of food. Besides the fried catfish, there was an abundant supply of fried chicken, which was one of Felix's favorite dishes. Mashed potatoes, gumbo, pinto beans, hush puppies, summer squash, macaroni and cheese, watermelon, and, of course, fresh biscuits rounded out the meal. For dessert, there was plenty of pecan pie, chocolate cake, and homemade vanilla ice cream. Felix enjoyed spending the evening with his grandparents, aunts, uncles, cousins, sisters, and brother in-laws.

After church on Sunday, 11 Sep. 1938, Felix loaded up his 1937 Ford Coupe with a suitcase, a duffel bag, his favorite pillow, and a small wooden trunk. Ernest had built the custom made trunk to fit perfectly in the back seat of the car. Viola had made Felix a beautiful twin-sized quilt, which was red, white, and blue with a large Texas star right square in the middle. The suitcase had been purchased earlier that summer when Felix and his parents had visited the college for orientation. They insisted on purchasing the metal suitcase for him mainly because of the colorful Texas Aggies logo found on the lid. With his car all loaded up, Felix waived goodbye once again to his sisters, and he drove away. Ernest and Viola planned to follow him to College Station, where they had arranged to spend a couple of nights at the home of their good friends, Beth and Isaiah Morrison. Many of Felix's neighbors waived from their front porches as they drove up South Bluffton Avenue. As Felix made his way to the edge of town, he looked into his rear view mirror, and bid farewell to San Saba. Felix was excited, although perhaps a little anxious about starting his new chapter in life at Texas AMC over in College Station.

The Scott family headed southeast from San Saba, and they arrived at the Morrison home after more than a four hour drive. College Station was a small town located between the Brazos and the Navasota Rivers, and it had the same small hometown feel of San Saba. The Morrisons were excited to see Felix, as he had grown quite a bit since they had last seen him. The Morrisons were fabulous hosts, and they had prepared a wonderful supper for them shortly after they arrived. Felix needed to take placement exams in both English and math early the next morning. Therefore, after spending a little time catching up with the Morrisons over dessert, Felix proceeded to go to the bedroom where he'd stay for the night. He decided to review the study guides that Francine had made up for him, which had certainly helped to get him through high school. Not long after that, Felix was ready for a good night's sleep, since he had a full day planned for Monday, 12 Sep. 1938.

Felix wasn't exactly sure where he'd be able to park, and he couldn't remember the location of the building that he needed to get to. To avoid being late, Felix grabbed a banana and an apple from the Morrison's fruit bowl, and he ventured out the door. He only had to drive a short distance to reach the college, and he was quite relieved to find that there were plenty of folks holding signs directing people to the places that they needed to get to. It turned out that parking wasn't an issue, and Felix was on his way to the campus. Felix figured that he'd be done around 12:30 p.m., and he had asked his folks to wait for him until he arrived near the tall flag pole, which was located near the Sully Ross statue.

After the exams, Felix walked along a maze of concrete pathways. He then ventured around the Academic Building to find his parents waiting patiently by the statue. Felix felt like he had done well enough to pass the exams, and he told his parents that the results would be posted before 14 Sep., which happened to be the day that he'd register for his classes. Ernest asked, "Where can we go to get something to eat around here?" Felix replied, "I saw a sign that stated that food would be served for the cadets, and their families over at Sbisa Hall." With that, the Scotts walked around until they found the sign directing folks into Sbisa Hall. It was the biggest mess hall that any of them had ever seen, and it was very loud inside with everyone's lively conversations. The Scotts found plenty of good food being served at Sbisa Hall, and Felix enjoyed his first meal as an Aggie. He turned to his mother, and said, "This also happens to be the place where they hold many of the dances, and I cannot wait to do the Jitterbug with some of the finest ladies that College Station has to offer." Viola smirked a bit, and said, "Now Felix, I want you to have fun. Just be sure that you find a nice girl with good moral character, you hear?"

After their meal, they headed over to check out the YMCA building on campus. Before opening the door, Felix said, "Y'all just have to see what's inside of this place." Ernest and Viola were impressed with the pool and ping pong tables, the bowling alley, and even the barber shop. Felix knew that he'd be spending plenty of time in this building. Viola was glad to know that they had Bible study classes there, and she reminded Felix that he needed to find time to attend them. The YMCA, also known as the "Y," offered picture shows and live night-time entertainment on most weekends for the cadets.

The next stop was Kyle Field, which was home to the Fightin' Texas Aggie Band, and, of course to the highly successful football team. Felix was a bit sad that he wouldn't be part of the football team. However, he was eager to watch the upcoming football games that were to be held at Kyle Field, which was sure to be full of noisy and fired up fans. Ernest just couldn't believe how much bigger the stadium was over the one back home in San Saba. Felix was also excited to explore all of the other possibilities that the college had to offer. As the Scotts continued to walk throughout the sprawling campus, they noticed plenty of large two to three story buildings. In some ways, the large stone buildings resembled the San Saba Courthouse back home. The sizable green grass fields made for a picturesque view. Felix spotted the very large water tower on campus, and he reached over to his father, and said, "Don't you reckon it would be swell to climb that?" Ernest smiled, but Viola was clearly not amused.

After wrapping up their self-guided walking tour, the Scotts made their way along the broad walkway back toward the Academic Building. Felix had read that there was a memorial inside to honor the Aggies who had been killed during the Great War. Upon entering the Academic Building, they could see a tall flag adorned with many gold and maroon stars woven into the fabric. It looked magnificent as it hung downward from the railing high above in the rotunda. Felix felt proud, patriotic, and thankful for the service and sacrifice of the fallen students as he stood there marveling at its beauty.

Felix had parked his car on a different part of the campus, so Ernest offered to take him over to that parking lot. On the way, he showed his parents where Hart Hall was located. This was going to be Felix's new home for the next year, and he reminded them that they'd return the following morning for move in day. Things were beginning to get really exciting for Felix on 13 Sep. 1938. As he and his parents drove to the campus that morning, they noticed quite a bit of congestion on the college grounds. There were cars and pickup trucks everywhere, and plenty of folks were coming and going. Considering the craziness of the morning, Felix felt lucky not having to park more than a block away from Hart Hall. Since Felix was going to have two roommates, he was instructed to bring just the basics, and to leave the non-essential items at home. After checking in at the reception desk, the Scotts proceeded up the stairs to his second floor room. Felix and his parents were able to get all of his belongings to his room in just one trip.

Upon opening the door, Felix was thrilled to see bunk beds on one side of the room, and a twin bed on the other side. Having never slept on a bunk bed, he was quick to claim the top bunk as his own. While unpacking his things, Felix's new roommates arrived. Tyler was a tall and skinny young man, while Billy was stocky, and about the same height as Felix. The Scotts all concurred that the boys seemed to be fine fellows. Ernest and Viola were pleased with the room situation, so they decided to leave Felix with his new buddies.

Felix agreed to meet his parents back at the Sully Ross statue the following morning for registration day. He thoroughly enjoyed spending the rest of the afternoon with Tyler and Billy, and after a welcome meeting in the dorm, the young men all went to supper together in the dining hall. Later that evening, Felix and his roommates took turns quizzing each other on The Articles of the Cadet Corps and College Regulations manuals. They were instructed that a copy of each manual was to be kept in the room at all times. The fellas were informed that they could be tested on the contents found within the manuals by any upperclassman or senior officer at any time. Before going to bed, Felix made sure that he knew his general orders, the chain of command, and he became very familiar with the Code of The Corps of Cadets.

The next morning, Felix was too excited to eat breakfast, so he quickly combed his hair, and put on some clean clothes. There was no need to run, but Felix walked quickly towards the Sully Ross statue, so that he'd be there before his parents arrived. Plenty of folks were already milling about as Felix waited patiently for them to show up. The beginning of the new school year was purported to be a record year for the college, with more than 2,000 freshmen descending upon the campus. Felix had heard that the amount of incoming freshman nearly equalled the entire population of College Station at that time. Once Ernest and Viola arrived, they headed over to Guion Hall, where Felix would officially be welcomed as a new student by the college officials. They watched proudly as Felix walked between the large stone columns that were prominently featured on the front of the beautiful building. After leaving Guion Hall, the Scotts headed to the Administration Building where they found that the line of students had already wrapped around the building.

Felix had his course catalog in hand, and he'd already circled the classes that he wanted to enroll in. He had dreams of becoming a pilot one day, but he needed to have a backup plan in case that didn't work out. W. J. Millican, Felix's maternal grandfather, wanted to hand over the reins to the family pecan business one day. Felix knew that his cousins Hilliard, Dardon, Chauncey, and Dimmitt were sure to be worthy candidates, but he wanted to be well positioned to be considered for that role too. W. J. knew just about everything there was to know about the pecan business, but technologies and farming methods were always changing. Felix was excited and honored to begin this journey in order to learn the new tricks of the trade. He wanted to be successful, not just for his own sake, but he wanted to do well especially out of respect for his grandfather. Felix decided that he'd be majoring in horticulture, and he'd be taking many agricultural education classes along the way.

As the Scotts made progress in the line, they noticed some really inspirational signs that had been placed incrementally along the pathway. The rectangular signs were made of wood, and each one was painted with a blue background and featured a word in bold white letters. Some of the signs that they saw were "Pride," "Discipline,"

"Leadership," "Courage," "Loyalty," "Unselfishness," "Respect," "Precision," and "Honor." Viola asked what all of the signs symbolized, and Felix told her that these were the qualities that each new cadet would be expected to follow and adhere to in their daily life at the Agricultural and Mechanical College of Texas.

Felix finally made it to the front of the line, and he handed his paperwork to the pretty young lady sitting behind the table. After reviewing it for accuracy and eligibility, she confirmed that space was available for his class selections. The clerk then handed Felix some papers that validated that he was now officially enrolled for his first semester. She also handed him an itemized statement detailing the cost of his room and board, and the related school fees. Ernest reached into his billfold, and he paid the bill in full with cash. Being that Felix was a new cadet; he was then directed to wait in a different line in order to get his battalion assignment. While waiting in the new line, he reviewed his official schedule with Viola. She began to fill in the class times, and days of the week for his courses on a pocket-sized calendar that she had purchased for him. As a new Aggie, Felix would be taking Agricultural Resources 101, General Animal Husbandry, Animal Biology, General Inorganic Chemistry 101, English Composition, Infantry Military Science 101, and Physical Education 101. Felix finally made it through the second line where he was informed that he was going to be a first year private in the Infantry Regiment. He was assigned to "L" Company within the First Battalion.

It had been a very long morning, so Felix suggested that they go and grab some food over at Sbisa Hall for dinner. Before heading back to San Saba, Ernest and Viola walked with Felix over to the College Exchange store. Felix thoroughly enjoyed walking about the store picking out the various articles of clothing that would make up the different uniforms that he would wear during the year. For formal and special occasions, Felix selected a green jacket, several white shirts, slacks, a black tie, and a service cap to complete his "A" uniform, which the cadets called Alphas. To help differentiate a fish from sophomore cadets, a narrow white piece of tape was placed near the wrist on the left sleeve of the jacket, which was known as a "fish stripe." For everyday wear, Felix then chose some dark green trousers, several tan shirts, another black tie, a garrison cap, and even a Stetson campaign hat to make up his "B" uniform, which the cadets called Bravos. Next, he grabbed some coveralls, a few undershirts, and a belt to complete his military outfits. They continued to the next aisle, where he selected his official Texas AMC sweatpants, exercise shirts, socks, and sneakers. Near the front of the store, there was a table that provided him with the black cord needed for his campaign hat along with the appropriate patches and pins that were required for his clothing and dress uniform.

Felix then noticed a rack full of the most amazing brown boots that he'd ever seen. He proceeded to pick up a pair, and immediately began to try them on. Suddenly, a clerk approached Felix, and she asked him if he was a senior. By the look of the things in his cart, she could tell that he wasn't. The woman scolded him by saying, "Them boots is for seniors only. If you ain't a senior, then you just go on and put them right back where ya found 'em." As he placed them back upon the rack, Felix could only dream that one day he'd be lucky enough to wear a pair of these remarkable senior boots. After selecting a pair of ordinary dress shoes, Felix then moved to the other side of the store, where he selected the books and other supplies needed for his classes. Once again, Ernest reached into his billfold to pay the bill, and off they went. They happened to bump into Billy, Felix's new roommate, on the way out of the College Exchange store. He informed Billy that his folks were about to head home shortly, so Billy offered to take a picture of the Scott family with Ernest's camera.

Felix and his parents returned to Hart Hall with the bags of newly purchased goodies. Being an astute and savvy mother, Viola pulled a sewing needle and various spools of thread from her purse. She cheerfully sewed Felix's patches onto his shirts and clothing as per the instructions provided to them at the exchange. It was now getting rather late in the day, and his folks were eager to hit the road to get back to San Saba. Felix walked with them to their Studebaker, and he gave them each a big hug before they drove away. For the first time in his life, Felix was on his own, and he was able to make and live by his own decisions. He knew that his classes would be difficult, and the daily drills would be demanding, but Felix was ready for the challenge. He was also thrilled to forge new friendships, and he couldn't wait to enjoy his newfound freedom. However, was he really completely free? Essentially, Felix was swapping his parents for a Sergeant, a Lieutenant, and a Captain, all of whom who would certainly keep him focused, and push him to become a good student and a worthy cadet.

There were still several hours left in the day, so Felix decided to head back to the area near the Administration Building where he'd seen lots of people gathered around some tables. There were people sitting at the tables, and students were walking from one to another. Each of the tables had a sign that stated what type of club or organization was being represented. By the time Felix made it to the end of the row of tables, he had signed up for four different clubs. The Poultry and Egg Club, Heart O' Texas Mountaineer Club, Texas Horticultural Society Club, and the San Saba County Club were all on his list. Felix felt that the day had been a success, so he returned to his room to get ready for the evening meal.

After supper, Felix and his roommates made their way to the "Y" to attend their first yell session as Aggies. The yell sessions were typically held in front of the "Y," and this was a time where "yell" leaders would lead the cadets in chanting the school songs. These sessions were a great way to build school spirit and camaraderie. The cadets stood shoulder to shoulder practicing the new songs that they were supposed to have learned over the summer. The goal of the yell sessions was to prepare the cadets for further yelling at the football games. The freshmen were required to assemble up front near the yell leaders, while the upperclassmen congregated toward the back of the crowd. Felix had a splendid time raising hell with his fellow cadets, and he wondered if folks could hear them in the nearby town of Bryan.

Friday, 16 Sep. 1938 was the day that Felix began his journey in the classroom at Texas AMC. He was officially a freshman, but Felix and the other cadets of his class were now going to be known as "fish" for the duration of the school year. Felix would be referred to as "fish Scott," and he was on board with the extra duties that could be assigned to him as a fish. Before class had started, and as daylight began to replace the morning darkness, Felix and the rest of the cadets on his floor were assembled on the drill field. It was 0600 hours when Felix first heard the sound of the morning bugle, which was otherwise known as Reveille. Drill didn't officially begin until the colors had been raised. Calisthenics and a jog around the campus lawn was a sure fire way to wake Felix up, and propel him into his new daily routine. There would be no shortage of exercise for Felix as he walked to and from the Agricultural, Chemistry, and Science buildings. Traversing the grounds of the sprawling campus was certainly a change from his days at San Saba High School. Felix and his roommates would typically venture down near the "Y" to hear the early evening bugle call, which was known as Retreat. He felt proud and patriotic to watch the lowering of the flag.

"Fish Scott" at Texas AMC.

Felix made friends quickly, and his sociable demeanor helped him to avoid any conflicts. He enjoyed the clubs that he had joined, and he attended the meetings regularly. Some of the meetings were going to be held monthly, where others were held weekly. While growing up, Felix had observed his sister, Johnnie Mae, as she took care of the books at the River Bend farm. He too, had some financial experience of his own with his regular deposits at the San Saba National Bank. As such, Felix was elected treasurer of the Texas Horticultural Society Club, but he was most excited about his meetings with the San Saba County Club. This club was made up of cadets who came from, or who had lived in the communities of Bend, Cherokee, Richland Springs, or, of course, San Saba. He certainly knew the boys from San Saba and Bend, although he didn't know any of the fellas from

Cherokee or Richland Springs. Felix truly enjoyed hanging out with his new friends, and he liked sharing stories about their adventures all over San Saba County. Felix was named Sergeant at Arms for the club, and he was mostly responsible for keeping order during their meetings. He became known as "Sarge" during his involvement with the club, and it was a nickname that stuck with him during his time at Texas AMC.

It was 24 Sep. 1938, when Felix first stepped into the raucous confines of Kyle Field. As he and his roommates made their way towards the "fish" section, the band was playing, the crowd was already yelling, and everyone was standing. Felix had never seen anything quite like the excitement that was harnessed inside the stadium on that day. The Aggies squared off against the Javelinas from the Texas College of Arts and Industries. By the end of the game, Felix was amazed that everyone was still standing. The Aggies crushed their opponent in an impressive shutout victory. Felix felt that if this was going to be the norm moving forward, he was going to be in for a real treat during the football season. The following week was just as exciting, as the Aggies shut out Tulsa by nearly three touchdowns. Over the next several weeks, the Aggies faced some setbacks, and they were handed their first losses of the season. Win or lose, Felix was an Aggie through and through, and his support for the team was unwavering. He figured that he and his fellow cadets just needed to yell a lot louder to enable the team to provide more victories.

It didn't take long before Felix found out that the nearby town of Bryan was the place to be on a Friday or Saturday evening. There were restaurants and cute girls over in Bryan, and the downtown area seemed to provide a livelier nightlife experience than College Station could offer. The college had advised the cadets to avoid seeking employment during their freshman year unless a financial burden could be proven. Therefore, Felix didn't work, and he had quite a bit of free time on his hands. It would be fair to say that Felix enjoyed his clubs, social gatherings, and football more than studying. Hanging out with his friends at the "Y," or seeing a movie was much more enjoyable than hitting his science books. All of the fun and excitement had finally caught up with Felix, and he was rather disappointed in himself when he found out that he was failing his Biology and Chemistry classes halfway through the semester. He had no idea that the subject matter for his courses was going to be so difficult, but he assured himself that he could and would try harder. Luckily for Felix, there was a United Methodist church nearby where he sought advice and guidance from the pastor with the hope that he could turn things around before the upcoming holidays. He was afraid that his parents and grandparents would be disappointed in him.

The Aggies were suddenly having just a mediocre football season. It seemed that the high scoring games were now a thing of the past, and they continued to struggle to put points on the board. With the season winding down, Felix and his pals enjoyed riding the rails over to Austin for the final game of the year against the University of Texas that occurred on 24 Nov. 1938. The Aggies were squaring off against their formidable rivals, the Texas Longhorns. If there was one game to win for the year, the cadets felt that this was the one that they just had to have. The Longhorns hadn't won a game all year up to that point, and Felix and his pals felt the game would be a laugher. They were fully prepared to yell and scream in order to help their team secure a victory. In the end, it was a low scoring game, and the Aggies lost by just one point. This was no laughing matter to the Aggies and their fans, and it was most certainly a heartbreaking loss. The train ride back to College Station left everyone feeling shocked and dispirited.

Having sung hymns at church for nearly his whole life, Felix felt that he was a pretty good singer. Therefore, he didn't mind, and he rather enjoyed being part of a unit that was tasked with singing Christmas carols up and down Military Walk and near the dormitories. It was one of the rare occasions that doing something as a fish could be fun for the few weeks leading up to Christmas break. The cadets were dismissed for their winter break right after the noon drill on 17 Dec. 1938. Felix was eager to get home to relax, refresh, and regroup for the final exams that were looming at the end of the semester. He was also very excited to meet his baby nephew, Felix Wayne, who had just been born a month earlier. He was the son of his sister Johnnie Mae and her husband, AJ Blanton. Felix was proud to be an uncle, and having a nephew with the same first name as himself was marvelous. The Scott family was surely glad to have Felix home for the Christmas holiday, and, of course Viola had planned a fine meal to welcome him home. Ernest was tasked with providing the meat for the supper, and he was eager to taste the venison from the ten point buck that he had nabbed earlier that morning.

When Felix entered his room, he saw an unopened envelope addressed to him. Before leaving for school back in September, Felix had asked his mother to hold onto any letters that might arrive from Francine. He picked up the envelope, and he could smell a faint aroma of Lemon Verbena. It was sure to be a letter from Francine, and it was postmarked on 7 Sep. 1938. Felix hadn't noticed the envelope when he was home for Thanksgiving, as Viola had somehow managed to mistakenly place it underneath a stack of magazines on his desk. He was somewhat curious to see what would be inside the envelope, yet he was unsure if he really wanted to read about Francine's experiences in Amarillo. In reality, Felix felt that he didn't necessarily need to know what was inside since he was just not ready to revisit that sad day back in August. Therefore, he put the envelope back down on the desk, and went to the living room to join his father for some time on the piano before supper. After a wonderful meal, Felix hung out with his family in the living room as they danced and played some new sheet music on the piano.

Before bed that evening, Ernest was catching up with the local happenings and world events as he sat in his chair while reading the latest edition of *The San Saba News*. Details of Japan's ongoing aggressions, and their takeover of vast amounts of land in China, had made its way into this small town newspaper. Ernest and Felix were discussing Japan's continuing offensive, when Viola interjected with, "I pray every night that someone will kill Hirohito and all of the officers who are inflicting the pain and suffering on the Chinese people." Felix abruptly stood up, and said, "If I could learn to fly one of those brand new P-40s, I'd be all too happy to drop a 500 pound bomb on Hirohito's ass over in Tokyo."

Mrs. Howard, over at the bakery, provided an opportunity for Felix to work a few shifts, and he enjoyed earning the extra pocket money for his next semester in College Station. Felix certainly enjoyed the delicious Christmas supper with his family out at the River Bend farm. Catching up with his cousins, and visiting with all of his aunts, uncles, and grandparents was very gratifying. On New Year's Eve, he went with Jack and Bobby Joe to the Palace Theater to see a showing of *The Dawn Patrol*. He thoroughly enjoyed the movie, which featured several British pilots as they performed various missions during the Great War. However, Felix felt a bit emotional afterward because he realized that a great deal of pilots had been lost during the campaign due to the poor training that they'd received, and to their lack of effective equipment, that had ultimately led to their premature demise. Needless to say, he really enjoyed reminiscing and hanging out with his friends for the evening. After the New Year's day dinner at the Scott house, Felix was ready to go fishing. Chauncey, Dimmitt, and Clovis jumped into the car with Felix, and off they went to their favorite fishing hole on the San Saba River. He returned home just after sunset, and sat down with Aletha, Pauline, and Johnnie Mae for a game of Monopoly, which he'd just received for Christmas.

Technically, Felix was supposed to return to campus by 6:00 p.m. on 1 Jan. 1939. However, since it had gotten so late, he decided that he'd get up very early the next morning, and drive back to College Station. Felix planned to arrive back at the dorm before the morning roll call, so he climbed out of bed after having just a few hours of sleep. Ernest, Viola, and Aletha also woke up early to say goodbye to him. It was pitch dark outside, and there wasn't a sound to be heard in the entire neighborhood. Viola wasn't so pleased with his plan because she was fearful that he'd hit a deer or a wild boar on the dark country roads. Nevertheless, Felix loaded his suitcase and denim duffle bag into the back of his '37 Ford. Viola handed him a pail of freshly made biscuits and bacon wrapped in a cloth napkin. Felix gave everyone a big hug before getting into the front seat of his car. Ernest handed him a small stack of twenty dollar bills through the window, and said, "This ought to cover your next semester fees and supplies." Felix thanked him for the money, and just like that, he headed on down the road back to College Station.

Felix saw very few cars on the road that morning, and he was lucky that the wildlife had stayed off the road. By keeping his foot on the gas pedal, he ended up making good time. He quickly pulled into the parking lot near Hart Hall, and after grabbing his belongings, he hustled up the stairs to his room. Felix amazingly had just enough time to get changed, and he made it back downstairs on time for the morning formation. The last few weeks of his first semester flew by quickly. Final exams proved to be a challenge for Felix, and he wasn't all that happy with his marks. He was able to pass all of his classes except for Animal Biology and General Inorganic Chemistry.

On the morning of 6 Feb. 1939, Felix high-tailed it up Houston Street to the Administration Building where the line of cadets was growing by the minute. As he stood patiently in line, he reviewed his desired class schedule. Unfortunately for Felix, he was going to have to retake General Inorganic Chemistry and Animal Biology. After a brief discussion with the clerk at the scheduling desk, Felix walked away with the additional courses of Fundamentals of Crop Production, English 104, Agricultural Chemistry, Freshman Physical Education, and Infantry Military Science 102.

Anxiety was flowing through Felix's veins as he sat on a concrete bench located by the front steps of the Administration Building. He pondered how he was going to manage three science classes and one math class at the same time. Felix had really enjoyed his Military Science 101 class, where he learned about military courtesy, discipline, infantry drill formations, map reading, and marksmanship. Thus, he was excited to learn about the art of scouting, patrolling, and the basic fundamentals of combat tactics in his Infantry Military Science 102 class. Getting introduced to an automatic rifle was sure to be the highlight of the semester! Felix much preferred the practical and hands on military training, versus the theoretical and strategic ideologies of war.

And so the day had come, Felix began his first spring semester on 7 Feb. 1939. He had high hopes and lofty expectations for a much better academic performance this time around. Felix thrived with the regimented physical routine thrust upon him every day, but it didn't take long for him to once again fall behind on his studies. Good times seemed to regularly find him, and the excitement of college life proved to be distracting. There were plenty of dances held on campus, and Felix had heard that some others occasionally took place over in Bryan as well. Although there were no girls attending class on campus, Felix and his buddies had a groovy time driving around on weekends until they found a party flush with good looking girls. However, it seemed that the majority of the girls preferred socializing with the upperclassmen in their fancier uniforms. Nonetheless, Felix kept his head up, and he continued to smile, figuring that he had just not found the right party or girl yet. Felix stayed away from the alcohol for fear of getting into trouble if his commanding officer were to find him to be inebriated. Rather, it was candy, cookies, soft drinks, and smoking his pipe that Felix relished during his free time. He quickly learned that living with men was much different than living with his three sisters. Felix certainly enjoyed living in the dorm in College Station, and he was becoming very proficient in attending the social events found on and near campus.

Having a car was a blessing, but it was also somewhat of a curse as well for Felix. While there were many cadets who spent the weekends studying and catching up on their sleep, Felix was regularly asked to be the driver for short day trips, and weekend getaways. Those cadets who didn't have access to a car were left to the inconvenient and unreliable method of hitchhiking. Folks who lived in the area were very kind, and they would often stop to help an Aggie with a ride. Upperclassmen outranked the less senior students even out on the roadways of Brazos County. This meant that the "fish" would have to wait around until there were no more upperclassmen in need of a ride. Felix was popular because he could generally guarantee a pal a ride to a given place without them having to mess with hitchhiking, and the headaches of having to get in and out of several cars for hours on end.

The brunette and blonde haired girls from the Texas State College for Women (TSCW) were real lookers. Felix just couldn't believe how pretty they were as they exited the buses that had brought them to College Station from Denton, Texas. The girls from TSCW were regular guests to the balls and dances that were held on the campus there at Texas AMC. It was a Saturday night, and just a few days before Valentine's Day, when a large group of young ladies had come to campus for a dance. Felix and his roommates stood on the lawn as they watched the girls make their way to the YMCA to mingle with the upperclassmen who were waiting there for dates. Felix felt sort of sad that he didn't have a date or a girlfriend, so therefore he chose to return to his dorm with Tyler and Billy instead of attending the dance. Once back at Hart Hall, the young men enjoyed playing dominoes, backgammon, cribbage, and checkers up until lights out. Although Felix appeared to be having a grand time with his roommates, he suddenly realized that this would be the first Valentine's Day in several years without Francine. After the lights were turned out, he couldn't help but remember the fun times that were spent with Francine on previous Valentine's Days. As a result, he had a difficult time falling asleep, and he wondered if Francine was having similar thoughts about him.

Felix could generally be found at the YMCA when he wasn't in class or in his room. Sundays were an especially big hit for Felix and his pals when he was in town because it was the one day of the week that the "Y" offered free admission to the movies held on the premises. The movies were typically not the latest and greatest, so to speak, because they were generally several years old. Nevertheless, Felix and his buddies loved a good show, and they savored the snacks that were available at the snack bar. In late February of 1939, Felix saw the movie, *Sky Devils*, at the "Y." This film was a comedy that featured two guys on an epic adventure who end up in the Army Air Corps. Felix also enjoyed hanging around the Southern Pacific train depot which was close to campus. The depot reminded him of the one back home in San Saba, and he made it a point to be there at the train station at least once or twice a month as a train would come roaring in.

Felix thoroughly enjoyed reading every new edition of *The Battalion*. This was the Texas AMC newspaper, and it was typically published up to three times per week. Felix had a routine where after he'd grab a new paper, he'd head to his favorite bench located under a giant shade tree near the Academic Plaza. He happened to be reading the edition dated 19 May 1939, when an article caught his eye. It mentioned how the United States Congress had authorized a substantial purchase of new planes, and thus a need would be created for a large number of worthy pilots. The Army Air Corps was now looking for thousands of applicants each month, and it was estimated that they could be searching for qualified candidates for years to come. Potential candidates had to be unmarried, and over the age of 20, but younger than 27. A minimum of two years of college was required, or the applicant would need to pass a written test. All candidates who had met the basic qualifications were then placed on waiting lists. When a spot opened up at a government training school, the candidate would be notified, and he'd also be provided with transportation to the school. Felix was fascinated by this article since it rekindled his boyhood dream of becoming a pilot. However, he was unhappy that he didn't yet meet the qualifications to sign up for the program. Felix decided to return to his dorm to refocus his thoughts, and he ended up working on building his model airplane for a bit prior to the evening meal.

Felix had never spent his birthday away from home before, but that is how he spent his 19th birthday on 30 May 1939. His special day fell just as final exams were about to commence. Felix chalked it up to bad timing, and he figured that he'd celebrate with his family in just a few days when he returned home to San Saba. Receiving a bag of his mother's chocolate chip cookies and an assortment of candy bars in the mail certainly made him happy, and it brought a smile to his face on his birthday. Munching on the goodies surely helped get him through the last few days of the semester in College Station.

The day was 2 Jun. 1939, and it marked the end of the spring semester. Felix was excited to participate in his first "Final Review" before heading home for the summer. This was a really big deal for the seniors since their family members and friends would be present to watch the entire cadet corps march in formation on the drill field. Each unit of every class passed in front of the reviewing stand where the Commandant and his guests were seated. All of the cadets looked phenomenal as they made their way across the drill field with complete precision and synchronization. Felix was thrilled to have played a small role in the Final Review, and he was eager to be a senior one day so that he too could wear the coveted senior boots with spurs, and participate in the many events reserved exclusively for senior cadets. For now, obtaining an Aggie ring was just a dream, but Felix had heard that the annual Aggie ring dance and banquet was an event that he'd be sure not to miss. Felix could tell that this was a very special day for the seniors since it coincided with graduation later that day. He knew that he still had quite a journey to become a senior, although he was certain that the wait would be worth it.

Felix was able to obtain his final grades before leaving the campus for San Saba. He was fairly satisfied with three C's, and he was elated that he'd finally passed Animal Biology. However, Felix wasn't so happy that he'd once again failed General Inorganic

Chemistry. He'd also managed to fail his Agricultural Chemistry class, and he figured that this news was certainly going to dampen the excitement of being home once his mother found out. On the drive home, Felix tried to think of a convincing reason that he could provide for his failure with his chemistry classes. After all, he thought of himself as more of a farmer than that of a chemist. Of course, Ernest and Viola were glad to have Felix home for the summer. His mother had baked him a delicious chocolate birthday cake, and there were some presents waiting on the kitchen table. During supper that evening, Viola asked about how his final exams had gone, and about the grades that he'd received. Felix quickly reminded his parents that he'd had a difficult class schedule, and then he shared his marks with them. Viola encouragingly said, "Now son, you just keep doing the best that you can, and you'll get 'em next semester!" He was pleasantly surprised to hear Viola's response regarding his grades. Viola then told Felix that his Ma and Pa Millican were eager to catch up with him, and they too, wanted to hear about the semester. Felix was looking forward to seeing his grandparents and Chauncey, but he was afraid that his grandfather would be disappointed in him.

After supper, Felix went to his bedroom to unpack his bags and suitcase. As he placed his pocket change and billfold onto his dresser, Felix noticed that the envelope from Francine was still sitting in the same place as he had last left it. He picked up the envelope, which no longer smelled of Lemon Verbena, and sat down on the bed pondering whether he should open it or not. The effects of that miserable day back in late July had finally waned, and by now, Felix felt like he was finally fully at peace with losing Francine. He sliced the envelope open with his pocket knife, and began to read the letter folded neatly inside.

My darling Felix, *September 7, 1938*

I don't know when you'll be home to read this, but I wanted to let you know that we arrived safely in Amarillo. This town is much larger than San Saba, and you just wouldn't believe how many students are enrolled at my high school.

Daddy says that he'll be getting his shop up and running within a few months. We are staying with my Uncle Marcus for a spell until Mother and Daddy's new house is ready over at 2006 Jackson Street. It is a cute little house, and we hope to move in before Thanksgiving. To have my own room once again will certainly be a blessing.

My senior year will surely be different without you, Felix. I was lucky enough to make the cheer squad, but I'm sad that I won't have the opportunity to root for you. I hope that you're doing well, and are having a ball at Texas AMC. For all I know, you may have met one of those pretty college girls who came to campus.

If you come home for the holidays, and find yourself with nothing better to do, feel free to drive up to Amarillo. I'd love to see you, and catch up on things. Be well, my Felix, and keep chasing your dreams.

Forever and always,

Francine

Felix could feel the sincerity with Francine's letter, but now that nine months had passed, would she still be feeling the same way? After gently folding the letter, he placed it into his cedar chest with a collection of other letters that he held dear. It was now early Saturday morning, and Felix decided to make his way over to his grandparents' home at the River Bend farm. He planned on spending a week with them to catch up, fish, and hunt arrowheads with Chauncey at all of their favorite spots. Felix arrived just as Ma was fixing breakfast, and for some reason, the bacon, fresh eggs, and biscuits always tasted better at their house. After breakfast, Pa and Felix went for a horseback ride through the dry grass fields, and along the riverbanks. Pa was very interested in hearing about the people whom Felix had met, and the things that he had gotten involved with at school. Rather than having Pa ask about his grades, Felix prefaced the conversation by mentioning how difficult all of his science classes had been. Felix was honest and forthright with his grandfather when he went on to state that he'd failed several subjects. Much to his amazement, Pa wasn't critical of his bad marks, and instead, he said, "Felix, you're away at school for an adventure in both learning and life skills. Any sort of change in your normal routine, and being in a new environment, is sure to create a little havoc here and there. We're all very proud of you, and we know that you have plenty of years left to make a difference at the college." Pa suddenly stopped his horse, and said, "One day, this land and farm will belong to you and your cousins. My hope is that you'll learn many new things in school that will help you grow our business for generations to come. All I ask is that you give your best effort." Felix humbly replied, "I'm always inspired by your advice and wisdom. I know that I can do better, and I want to make you proud of me. I can only hope that one day, I'll be a successful man like yourself. I love you very much, and I appreciate the support that you've always given me." With that, the pair returned to the barn so that Felix could spend the rest of the day with Chauncey.

After a most enjoyable week out at Bend, it was time for Felix to return home to San Saba. Once again, Felix was able to pick up some shifts at the bakery. Mrs. Howard truly loved having him around, and she told him that there would always be a place for him there when he was home from school. Felix needed very little direction, and Mrs. Howard was quite impressed that he could still remember all of the steps needed to make the five different varieties of bread offered at the bakery. Having spent so much time around the American flag while at school, Felix felt even more proud and patriotic as he wrapped the orders for his customers in the red, white, and blue wrappers. The patrons there at the bakery always enjoyed Felix's service skills, and, of course, his smile.

When Felix wasn't working, there was always time for fishing, and fun around San Saba, and out at Bend. Flat Rock was another fabulous place for swimming, and a fine place to try and beat the Texas heat. Felix and his cousins loved fishing at Red Bluff, which was near the Colorado River Bridge. If their luck wasn't to be had there, they would head over to Devil's Holler. The bakery closed up early on 4 July, so Felix and a few of his pals, and his cousins—Chauncey, Dimmitt, Dardon, and Hilliard—took a hayride of sorts on a horse drawn wagon down to McAnnelly Springs. They had a terrific time shooting bottles and cans, and, of course, there was even some time spent searching for hidden treasures that may have been buried among the rocks and dirt. The afternoon was highlighted with a roaring campfire for their wiener roast, and the bottles of fresh pink lemonade, along with Viola's fresh chocolate chip cookies, all together certainly made for quite a refreshing treat.

The days of Felix's summer vacation were quickly winding down there in San Saba. Ever since reading Francine's letter, he'd been pondering if he should go to Amarillo or not. Felix still had Elizabeth, his sleek and stylish roadster, but over the last year, he realized that a car was just not the same as a pretty young woman in his arms. Seeing the other cadets with a girlfriend, or with a date to a dance, made

Felix wish that he could just pick up right where he had left off with Francine. He really wanted to know for certain if Francine had indeed moved on, and he needed closure one way or another. Felix figured that making the trip would be a long shot, since he had no way to know if Francine would even be home. He certainly didn't know her phone number, or whether or not she even had a phone. Anyhow, Felix decided to roll the dice, and hope for the best. He impulsively decided that he'd undertake the monotonous 6-7 hour drive to Amarillo to find out.

Well before the sun rose in San Saba, Felix was off to Amarillo. He'd packed an overnight bag just in case Mr. Waters would allow him to stay the night on the couch. He'd also purchased a dozen yellow roses, and he brought along a freshly baked pecan pie, courtesy of his mother Viola. With a long drive ahead of him, Felix had hoped to be there right about noon. His ideal plan was to meet up with Francine at her home, and then take her to dinner somewhere nearby, so that they could catch up with each other's lives. Felix made good time by cruising right on through Abilene as he continued his northbound journey towards the upper tip of Texas.

Just like Felix had planned, he arrived in Amarillo just before noon. Since the street for Francine's house wasn't on his map, he stopped at a local filling station to get a current map. With directions now in hand, and a course plotted out, Felix made the short trip across town over to Jackson Street. His Ford roadster hummed and purred ever so powerfully as he cruised up the street looking for Francine's house, first to his left, and then to his right. He saw 2000, 2002, 2005, 2007, and then finally, 2006 Jackson Street. There were no cars in the driveway, so Felix assumed Francine's parents were probably not home. He pulled up alongside the curb next to a relatively young oak tree, which was planted directly in front of the house.

Before turning the car off, Felix looked to his right, and he saw a young couple sitting on a swing that was hanging from the roof of the front porch. He could tell that the couple was clearly necking, but he couldn't yet tell if it was Francine or one of her younger sisters. The sound of Felix's car must've brought back memories for Francine, as she suddenly pulled away from the young man, and looked directly towards him. Francine made eye contact with Felix, and he could tell that she had suddenly become quite uncomfortable with the evolving situation. Feeling heartbroken and devastated once again, Felix hit the gas, leaving a trail of burnt rubber along with a cloud of smoke blowing down the street. As he raced up the street, he looked in his rearview mirror to see that Francine had popped out of the swing, and she was now standing on the sidewalk as the smoke quickly blew past her. Felix was certain that she must've seen her yellow headband hanging from his mirror as he drove away. With tears in his eyes, he headed for home, realizing that Francine had certainly moved on. This wasn't exactly the closure that Felix was looking for, but it was closure, nonetheless.

Felix kept up with the news in September of 1939 by reading every edition of *The San Saba News*. Japan was clashing with the Soviet Union, and Germany had invaded Poland. He was certain that there would be much discussion about these world events once he returned to campus. Felix had enjoyed his summer vacation at home, but the time had come for him to head back to College Station. He was eager to begin his sophomore year as a second year private, and he was glad that he was no longer a "fish." Felix topped off his tank, and he checked his tires over at the family filling station. He grabbed a Crunch bar, a soda pop, and just like that, Felix was once again leaving the comforts of home.

CHAPTER 8

Life as an Aggie

Felix returned to campus on 18 Sep. 1939 to find that the new dormitories were ready for move-in day. The brand new dorms were on the opposite end of campus from where he'd lived before. As he headed down Lubbock Street, there were plenty of signs, and folks were directing traffic rather effectively. However, Felix promptly ran into a problem when he learned that the new parking lot wasn't quite ready for cars. Therefore, he had to park several blocks away by the Petroleum Engineering Building. He somehow managed to lug his bags and suitcase over to the new housing community. Felix stopped at the desk where they were providing the dorm assignments, and he was in awe when he first saw the collection of twelve modern, four-story, brick and stone structures. After receiving his designated room location, Felix was on his way to dorm number five, which hadn't been given an actual name just yet. He also learned that he'd now be a second year private in the Infantry Regiment. Felix was assigned to "B" Company within the First Battalion. The grounds in the surrounding area weren't fully landscaped, and there were still many sidewalks and pathways yet to be built. With his key in hand, Felix made his way up to the third floor. He entered room number 326 to find only two beds versus three from the previous year. Everything was as clean as a whistle, and there was plenty of room for his belongings. Felix had nearly finished hanging all of his shirts when his new roommate, Charles Goldthwaite, walked in. Charles was from Abilene, and he came from a family of farmers. Felix could tell that their personalities and backgrounds were similar, and he figured that they'd get along nicely.

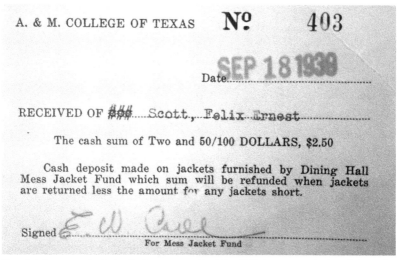

Receipt for mess jackets that were required for Felix's new part time job at the Dining Hall.

Trying to beat the crowd at the newly opened showers inside of dorm five, Felix woke up before the 6:00 a.m. Reveille on 21 Sep. 1939. He saw a sign posted on the door that said that there was no hot water, but he figured that it must've been left behind during all of the construction. When Felix turned the handle, a stream of ice cold water shot out, sending shockwaves throughout his system. Needless to say, he didn't spend much time in the shower that morning. Felix ran into his sergeant on the way to roll call, and he inquired about the hot water situation. He was told that the hot water delivery system wouldn't be functional until around Thanksgiving or so. Felix figured that, for the near future, there would be no more early morning showers for him. All in all, Felix was glad to be living in one of the new buildings, and he was just hoping that everything would be operational sooner than later.

Since it was once again time to register for classes, there wasn't going to be any company wide physical training held that morning. Felix knew the routine, and he showed up promptly at his assigned time. He walked away with his class list, which consisted of General Botany 101, Farm Machinery, English 203, American Government, Plant Propagation and Orcharding, Military Science 201, and a retake of General Inorganic Chemistry 101. Felix vowed that the third time would be the charm, since he certainly didn't want to be the guy that failed the same class three times in a row. As he was leaving the building, he overheard some administrators mentioning that the student enrollment was going to surpass the 6,000 cadet mark for the term.

Classes began early the next morning on 22 Sep. 1939. In early October of 1939, Felix heard a rumor about a class that was going to be offered on campus, which would provide ground instruction, and actual flight training. He really couldn't believe this until he started seeing articles about the class in *The Battalion*. Once he found out the necessary details, Felix promptly put his name down on the list so that he could be considered as a potential candidate for this new experience. Only fifty students would be allowed to enroll in this new class, and he realized that there would probably be way more students interested. There was a stringent selection process in order to pick the most capable and qualified cadets. Unfortunately for Felix, he was quickly eliminated from consideration, simply based on his sophomore status and his poor academic performance during his freshman year. Although he was very disappointed, he was thrilled that maybe one day, he'd make the cut for this exclusive opportunity to fulfill his dream of becoming a pilot.

Felix attended the United Methodist Church on campus regularly, and he was ecstatic to be invited to a social gathering that was to be held over at the First Methodist Church in Bryan on 15 Oct. 1939. His pastor had told him that there would be an abundance of food, and plenty of beautiful Christian women from their congregation at the social. This was music to Felix's ears, since those were two of his favorite things, besides his car and his family. On the day of the church social, and before driving over to the church in Bryan, Felix looked into the glove box to be sure that Francine's headband was still stowed completely out of view. The social was set to begin promptly at 12:30 p.m., and Felix figured that if he and his pal, Buzz Strickland, who was going with him, got there just after noon, they'd have first chance at meeting the ladies who'd be arriving. Buzz was a tall and good-looking young man from Round Rock, Texas. The boys had many things in common such as fast cars, good times, and good-looking women. Dressed in their neatly pressed cadet uniforms, Felix and Buzz arrived at the church just after noon.

After cruising through the parking lot, Felix strategically decided to park in the front row. His car was parked next to the path that led to the lawn, which was right beside the church. As they waited beside his freshly washed roadster, the boys got a few waves from several girls who were passing by, and also a few glares from some of the fellows who had also arrived. Felix thought that his heart might stop when he saw two gorgeous gals exit a vehicle driven by a man whom he presumed to be their father. As the girls strolled by, Felix and Buzz introduced themselves, and they kindly asked if they could accompany them to the awaiting tables located on the lawn. The girls seemed to fancy the fellas, and they agreed to walk with Felix and Buzz. They in turn provided the boys with their names of Emma Jo and Betty Lou McDermott. The girls said that they were twins, and Felix could only tell them apart from the different colored dresses that they wore. The young ladies were beautiful brunettes with the most wonderful smiles, and the most gorgeous legs that Felix had ever seen.

Each of the ladies in attendance brought a plate of their favorite baked treats for dessert. Felix immediately took a liking to Emma Jo and her snickerdoodles, while Buzz seemed to hit it off with Betty Lou and her pecan pralines. The afternoon was filled with a cake walk, and carnival type games of skill that included a beanbag toss. The boys also showed off their skills by throwing darts at balloons, and they also had the opportunity to throw balls at milk bottles. By getting to hang out with Emma Jo for the afternoon, Felix felt as if he had already won the grand prize. The boys mentioned that there was going to be a dance held on campus at the end of October, and they asked the twins if they'd like to be their guests. The girls looked at each other while nodding in agreement, and they promptly accepted the invitation. Felix got their address, and plans were finalized for him and Buzz to pick up the girls on 28 Oct. 1939 for the dance, which was to be held at Sbisa Hall.

Felix's social life was suddenly back in full swing. Things were going great for him and Emma Jo, so he invited her to attend the rodeo that was held on campus on 11 Nov. 1939. He had a great time explaining all of the different events to Emma Jo, and it brought back many fond memories of the rodeos he'd attended in and around San Saba County. The Aggies had begun the 1939 football season with an amazing 7-0 record, and it appeared that they were unstoppable. After enjoying the rodeo for most of the day, Felix was excited to take Emma Jo to see the Aggies square off against the Mustangs of Southern Methodist University. It turned out to be a low scoring game, with the Aggie defense reigning supreme to earn another nice win.

For most home football games, there was a dance held afterwards in Sbisa Hall. With such a fine looking young woman clutching onto his arm, Felix wasn't about to miss a chance to dance with his girl. Although it had been a long day with the rodeo and football game, the young couple figured that they had enough energy left to have an enjoyable evening at the dance. Felix was quite adept at swinging his feet as he danced the Lindy Hop, and Emma Jo had worked hard at showing him the proper form and etiquette of Waltz dancing. On the way back to her home that evening, Emma Jo asked Felix if he'd attend Sunday service with her the next morning at the First Methodist Church there in Bryan. He agreed to meet Emma Jo at the church that Sunday, and he committed to worshipping with her and her family as often as he could.

Felix really began to enjoy attending as many of the Aggie football games as possible. There was plenty of excitement generated from the large crowds of students, alumni, and fans who attended the out of town games. As such, on Saturday, 18 Nov. 1939, Felix and his pals caught the morning train to Houston, where they watched the Aggies defeat the Rice Owls. Felix loved watching movies just about as much as he loved football, and hanging out with Emma Jo. He therefore had no problem in putting his studies away for a bit so that he could attend the grand opening of the new Queen Theater over in Bryan with Emma Jo. Emma Jo's parents were friends with the owners of the theater, and they were very kind and generous to provide tickets for Emma Jo and Felix to attend the 8:00 p.m. showing of the comedy, *Fifth Avenue Girl*. Felix was thrilled to be there with Emma Jo, and he felt extra lucky that they were let inside the theater via a side door to avoid the large crowd of people waiting in line outside. It was truly a memorable evening filled with laughter and hand holding before Felix headed home for the Thanksgiving Day holiday. Thanksgiving

Day was originally supposed to be held on 30 Nov. 1939, and so the school had planned the activities accordingly. However, President Franklin Delano Roosevelt issued a proclamation changing Thanksgiving Day to 23 Nov. instead. He thought the move would help retailers by providing more shopping days between the new date and Christmas. The college still referred to the big football game that was to be held on 30 Nov. against the Texas Longhorns as the Thanksgiving game, even though it wasn't being played on Thanksgiving.

Upon returning to campus from his brief visit to San Saba for Thanksgiving, Felix was about to have the most exhilarating week yet while attending Texas AMC. He and Emma Jo attended the legendary Aggie Bonfire held on Wednesday, 29 Nov. 1939. The annual Bonfire was a way to celebrate the team, and to build school spirit for the big football game against the University of Texas. Some folks would even say that by adding logs to the fire, it helped provide the extra energy that the team would need in order to trounce the Longhorns. Felix felt that there must've been thousands of alumni, cadets, and guests in attendance. He was excited that he had a date with Emma Jo to the Bonfire dance that was held at the conclusion of the Bonfire celebration. The dance was once again held at Sbisa Hall, and it lasted into the early morning hours of Thursday.

Somehow, Felix had managed to miss viewing the annual Elephant Walk as a freshman. However, on the morning of 30 Nov. 1939, he was in for a real treat. The traditional Elephant Walk was typically held before the annual football game against the Aggie's archrival, the University of Texas. The Elephant Walk marked the end of the football season for games played at Kyle Field. The seniors had completed four long years of yelling and rooting for their beloved Aggies, and it was now time for them to move on, and to let the next class take the lead to continue with the unwavering support for the team. Thus, the

Elephant Walk paid tribute to the effort that the seniors had given in support of the Aggies during their time at Texas AMC, and it was a way to officially recognize them as they paraded through campus with the other cadets yelling in support of them. Felix and Charles picked out a great spot along Military Walk to watch the seniors stroll past them, one by one, with each man closely behind the other. Their formation resembled that of an elephant waving his trunk back and forth. The line of cadets twisted, turned, and wound its way from the YMCA to the old mess hall, and back.

The excitement continued that day when Felix and Charles found out that their dorm five was now going to be referred to as Gainer Hall. The official dedication ceremony was cancelled that afternoon due to the constant rain, which had resulted in extremely muddy conditions. After finding out that the evening football game was still going to be held, Felix and Buzz headed over to Bryan to pick up Emma Jo and Betty Lou. The couples were in for another exciting, yet long evening, since they planned on attending the postgame dance as well. The much anticipated football game resulted in another decisive victory for the Aggies as they blanked the Longhorns 20-0 at Kyle Field. It was a fantastic way to end the regular season with a perfect 10-0 record!

The festivities of the 1939 fall semester wound down with a Christmas celebration supper that was held at the new Duncan Mess Hall on the evening of 18 Dec. A delicious turkey dinner, along with all of the fixings was served for the cadet corps. Felix was excited to get home to San Saba for the winter recess, which officially began on 20 Dec. 1939. However, he was rather anxious knowing that final exams would be looming for him about a month after his return to campus from the Christmas break. Felix stopped at the Aggieland service station for a fill up before heading home, knowing that he was on the verge of potentially failing several classes once again.

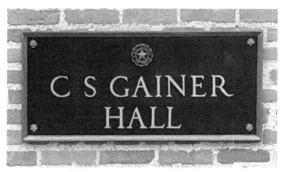
Felix's dormitory at Texas AMC.

Felix arrived home in San Saba with gifts stuffed inside of his bags so that nobody would notice them. He also brought his textbooks and notepads home, but he figured that there wasn't going to be much time spent studying. Felix surely enjoyed his Mother's home cooking, being around all of his family, and the break from the rigid daily routine that was essential and required in his daily college life at Texas AMC. The Scott family spent Christmas day over at Johnnie Mae's house. Felix Wayne was now a bit more than a year old, and Felix had quite a hard time getting near him, being that the baby's doting grandparents, and great-grandparents, were also in the room. Needless to say, it was exciting for Felix to spend some quality time with the newest member of the family.

It was New Year's Day in 1940, and the Scotts spent the day over at Pauline and Ted's place. Ted had been tasked with cooking the ham for the family supper, and Pauline was also hard at work in the kitchen when the Scott family arrived. Pauline received a new Philco clock radio for Christmas, and she was thrilled to spend the afternoon with Felix so that they could listen to the Aggies play in the Sugar Bowl game before supper was served that evening. Felix had considered traveling with some of his pals to Louisiana to watch the game in person, but he'd decided that he'd rather spend time with his family instead. Once Johnnie Mae and her family, along with the kin from Bend arrived, Felix gave everyone lessons on the proper way to yell before the game started at 1:15 p.m. The Aggies were matched up against the Tulane Green Wave at their stadium in New Orleans. The game was a nail-biter, and it was close to the very end. The Aggies won the game by just one point, and the victory culminated in an undefeated season. Felix was certainly happy with the win, and he felt that celebrating with his family was a fine way to begin the new year.

Before heading back to College Station, Felix made his way over to Harry's Boots, which was located across the street, and a block west of the San Saba Courthouse. He waited patiently by the heavy wooden doors, and he was very excited to get inside right when they opened for the day. Felix made his way around the entire store before selecting a fine wool coat and scarf as a late Christmas present for Emma Jo. Winter recess was over, and just like that, Felix was headed back to campus on 2 Jan. 1940. On the ride back to College Station, he thought that it was rather odd that his parents hadn't asked him about his grades while he was home, since he knew that the college had sent a status report to their home in early December. Felix felt a little awkward knowing that they knew he was doing poorly with some of his classes. He decided that he was just not going to worry about it, and he figured that his folks must've felt the same way.

Felix had left early enough in the day so that he could stop in Bryan to see Emma Jo. As Emma Jo opened the front door, she was surprised and rather impressed that Felix had brought a nicely wrapped box for her. Emma Jo really enjoyed her presents, and she felt that it was very thoughtful and kind of Felix. Her parents had begun to like Felix, and they insisted that he stay for supper. After a fine meal and some lively conversation, Felix took Emma Jo to see a show at the Queen Theater. Before he headed back to Gainer Hall, Felix was forthright with Emma Jo about his academic status. She was empathetic to his situation, and, thus, they mutually agreed to take a brief hiatus with their social lives so that Felix could spend some additional time studying, and preparing for his final exams. Felix then remembered back to his days with Francine, and how she had successfully helped him get through his high school classes. Emma Jo was certainly sweet and very cute, but she unfortunately didn't know how to help Felix with his science classes. It seemed to Felix that his hard work and effort had paid off to some degree when his end of the semester grades showed that he'd passed five of his classes, albeit barely so. However, he was upset with himself that he had somehow managed to fail his Military Science 201 and General Botany classes. Felix knew that he continued to struggle with his science courses, but he felt like he'd at least tried harder. Remembering back to what Pa had told him about giving it his best effort, Felix intended to buckle down, and he planned to be a more diligent student for the final semester of his sophomore year.

Registration day came again on 12 Feb. 1940, and Felix took care of his fees before leaving the Administration Building. Since he'd finally passed Inorganic Chemistry 101, he was now going to give Inorganic Chemistry 102 a shot. Additionally, Felix enrolled in Agricultural Economics, Dairying, English 210, Agricultural Math, and Military Science 202. Felix began the second semester of his sophomore year on 13 Feb. 1940. He was most excited about his Agricultural Economics class, because he saw himself more as a business owner than as a farmer. Felix felt that his grandfather had already bestowed a wealth of pecan information upon him, and he was now ready to learn how to take the family business to the next level in order to become even more successful. Felix learned about the new practice of crop-dusting that was beginning to become popular, and he felt that this was something that was right up his alley. He could totally envision himself in the cockpit of a plane spraying crops that belonged to his family, and to those all over San Saba County.

Felix and his roommate, Charles, made it a point to go see the Sugar Bowl trophy, which was being proudly displayed on campus. As Felix walked back-and-forth to Gainer Hall every day, he saw hundreds of new trees being planted. There were plenty of live oaks, elms, and willow oaks, but unfortunately, there were no pecan trees. Although Felix was disappointed that he was once again not chosen for the new flight training class, he was thrilled to learn that the new runway would be in close proximity to the school. Even though he wouldn't be flying the planes, he could still dream, and he surely would enjoy watching them take off and land.

Felix was very excited to resume social activities with Emma Jo, and February of 1940 was certainly shaping up to be much more enjoyable for him than the previous year had been. He didn't really see himself as a romantic kind of guy, but Felix was hoping for a very special Valentine's Day with Emma Jo. He picked up a box of assorted chocolates from a vendor at the YMCA, and he then stopped by Varner's Jewelry store to pick up a stylish wristwatch for Emma Jo. He made his final stop of the afternoon at Hrdlicka's Café to pick up some sandwiches and a few slices of Emma Jo's favorite chocolate cake. With the gifts loaded in his car, Felix then drove over to Bryan to pick up Emma Jo. The young couple had a magnificent evening as they watched the sunset at a scenic little spot along the Brazos River. Felix always acted like a gentleman by escorting Emma Jo to her front door when he'd bring her home.

On 24 Feb., Felix picked up his freshly laundered uniform at Campus Cleaners, which was located above the College Exchange store. He then returned to Gainer Hall for a warm shower before heading to Bryan to pick up Emma Jo. When her mother opened the front door, Felix could see Emma Jo looking remarkable, and standing there in the parlor in a gorgeous red dress with black nylon stockings and also black heels. Emma Jo's father quickly snapped a picture of the well-dressed couple before they headed out the door to the Sophomore Ball being held at Sbisa Hall at 9:00 p.m. that evening. The Aggieland Orchestra played an amazing selection of songs late into the night. Felix and Emma Jo skipped the after dance party at the Bryan Country Club so that he could keep his promise of having her home by 12:30 a.m.

On Saturday, 16 Mar. 1940, Felix saw the longest movie that he'd ever seen. He and Emma Jo went to see Clark Gable in *Gone With The Wind* at the Palace Theater there in Bryan. The movie was over three and a half hours long, but he surely enjoyed holding Emma Jo's hand the entire time. It was Felix's turn to pick the movie when they saw *Flying Deuces* at the Assembly Hall on 2 Apr. 1940. He was very excited to hear that the new Campus Theater was getting ready to open in May of 1940, and there was suddenly going to be plenty of places for a guy and his gal to see a movie. Felix and Emma Jo, along with Buzz and Betty Lou, hit the dance floor once again at the annual Infantry Ball, which was held on 5 Apr. 1940.

On 16 Apr. 1940, Felix was handed a flyer as he walked back to Gainer Hall. The flyer informed him that representatives from Barksdale Field in Louisiana would be on campus to answer questions about becoming a pilot in the United States Army Air Corps. The next morning, Felix visited the basement at the College Hospital to obtain information on what criteria the Army was using in their search for qualified candidates to enter the Air Corps cadet program. Felix didn't meet the qualifications to sign up, so he wasn't offered a physical exam that was being conducted on site. However, he found the session to be very helpful and informative because he now had a pretty good idea of what was required to become an aviator in the Army Air Corps. Adolf Hitler and his German Army continued to expand their stranglehold on much of the western part of Europe, and Japan continued to cause countless problems in the Pacific. To prepare for possible action against these aggressions, the United States Government was beginning to search for qualified applicants in order to ramp up the training programs that would churn out thousands of new pilots.

Just two weeks later, Felix found himself back at the College Hospital. This visit, however, wasn't for any informative purpose, but rather, he was admitted as a patient. The day was 30 Apr. 1940, and it started out like many other days in Aggieland. Felix would typically meet up with Buzz a few times a week for breakfast over at Duncan Hall. While conversing over scrambled eggs, toast, and fresh fruit, the boys hatched a plan to surprise their girls over in Bryan with supper and dessert later that evening. Buzz mentioned to Felix that it was his turn in the rotation to spray the blackberry orchard with pesticides, which was a requirement of his Plant Propagation and Orcharding class. Felix had just recently completed this course, and thus he was familiar with the procedures for spraying the orchard. This was the last class of the day for Buzz, so Felix offered to meet up with him that afternoon in order to give him a ride out to the field, which was just a short drive from campus. Upon their arrival, Felix offered to help Buzz prepare the pesticide mixtures and the tank sprayers, so that they could get to Bryan more quickly. The first objective was to spray all of the blackberry plants with a fungicide to keep the fungus away. After that, Buzz needed to spray the field with an insecticide to keep the bugs at bay.

Cadet Felix E. Scott, Texas AMC.

Buzz was rather quick to finish the first round of spraying, and Felix already had the next tank sprayer loaded with the prescribed mixture of water and the insecticide chemical. Shortly after Buzz began spraying the rows of blackberries, the tank sprayer on his back quit working. Felix could see that Buzz was struggling with the sprayer, so he headed over to assist him. Knowing that there was plenty of pressure in the tank, since he had just pumped it full of air, Felix began by checking the hose, the brass fittings, and the tank itself for any obvious signs of trouble. As Felix gave a slight tug on the hose, it suddenly broke loose from the tank, which resulted in a steady stream of insecticide spray right into his face and upper body. He screamed out in agony as he awkwardly stumbled backwards while trying to desperately wipe the chemical from his eyes. To prevent any further spray from reaching Felix, Buzz turned in the opposite direction, and he then tossed the sprayer away from his body. He could clearly see that Felix was writhing in pain, having taken a direct shot to the face with the high pressure spray.

Buzz knew that he needed to act quickly, so he hurriedly led Felix to the car. After grabbing the keys from Felix's pocket, he tore out of the parking lot, leaving a cloud of dust behind them. The college hospital was on the other end of campus, but Buzz made quick time in getting Felix there. As the nurses led them to a room, Buzz explained what had happened. Felix was still clearly in distress as he tried to explain where he was feeling the most pain. He described a burning sensation in his throat and nose, and he stated that his vision was severely blurred. The doctors repeatedly flushed his eyes, and treated him for the exposure to his throat and nose. It was apparent that Felix was still a mess, and thus he was admitted to the college hospital for further treatment and monitoring. Buzz felt horrible about the situation, so he made the difficult call to Felix's folks to let them know what had happened. Afterwards, he drove Felix's car out to Bryan to explain to Emma Jo and Betty Lou what had happened to Felix.

Ernest and Viola left San Saba for College Station early the next morning. They arrived at the college hospital to find Felix resting in his hospital bed. His eyes were bandaged, and his voice crackled as he responded to their greetings. Felix was glad that his parents had come to comfort him, and his folks were just glad that he was alive. When the doctor entered the room to check on Felix, Ernest and Viola asked him what they could reasonably expect for his recovery. Buzz had already given the medical personnel all of the details on the toxicity of the chemical involved. The doctor was honest with his reply by saying, "It will be a wait and see response at this point with the hope for a full recovery." The hospital staff was excellent at providing care to Felix, and they treated him with everything that they had in order to combat the chemical exposure.

Felix's folks stayed at the Aggieland Inn there on campus for three days until he was discharged from the hospital. Emma Jo came over to the hospital on the day that Felix was released, and Ernest and Viola were both very impressed with her friendliness, and her compassion for Felix's condition. His eyesight was still a bit blurry, and he continued to have some trouble speaking clearly. Ernest and Viola had originally planned to visit College Station for parents' weekend, which just so happened to fall on the upcoming Mother's Day weekend. Being that Mother's Day was now just a short one and a half weeks away; Felix convinced his parents to stay in San Saba to celebrate with his sisters rather than come back again so quickly. He shared the list of scheduled events that were planned for the parents' weekend, and they were certainly sad to hear that they'd miss the Full Review, which was to be held by the entire cadet corps on Mother's Day. Although Ernest and Viola were disappointed, they realized that Felix might not be well enough to march around the parade field anyways due to the unfortunate accident. They figured that there would be another year for them to come and see Felix get all decked out in his uniform in order to participate in a Full Review. For now, they were just hoping for him to recover quickly.

Before Ernest and Viola headed back to San Saba, Felix took them out to the drill field where they could at least see where he'd spent a great deal of time practicing for a Review. He pointed out the location on the drill field where they held the annual Bonfire event. Felix then took a few moments to lead his folks to the large granite marker that recognized the 52 former cadets who had been killed while serving during the Great War. In addition, the Scotts walked around the perimeter of the field and past the 52 live oak trees, that had been planted some 20 years earlier in memory of each fallen soldier. At the base of each tree, there was a small plaque memorializing the Aggie Serviceman with his name, class year, and some information pertaining to his death. Felix was proud to show the memorial to his folks, as he understood what it meant to serve, and die for your country. As they left the drill field together, Viola grabbed Felix gently by the arm, and said, "Son, I sure hope that I won't be standing beside a tree with your name next to it one day." Felix emphatically replied, "Mother, you don't need to worry about me. What would a country boy like me be doing fighting a war in some faraway land anyway?" Viola smiled, and she then placed her arm around Felix's waist as they headed to the car for her and Ernest's return trip to San Saba.

Felix was hoping that the last month of the semester would fly by pretty quickly. He knew that he'd be away from College Station for most of the summer, so he tried to squeeze in as many dates as he could with Emma Jo. Felix was still dealing with some lingering effects as a result of the accident, and he found his recovery from the chemical exposure to be arduous. His eyesight had finally returned to almost normal, however, he still some had reddish splotches on his face, and his voice continued to be a bit scratchy. Final exams were now just a week away, thus Felix tried to find some time to study. He didn't want his folks to think that he was a loafer, but with all that he had been through, Felix found it harder than ever to concentrate on his studies.

Classes ended on 7 Jun., and Felix was very proud to have received his first A. It hadn't come from a math or a chemistry class, but it came from his Military Science 202 class. Felix also passed three of his other classes, but unfortunately, he failed his Inorganic Chemistry 102 and Agricultural Math classes. All in all, he was glad to be feeling better, and he loved having Emma Jo in his life. Before leaving campus for the summer, Felix visited the Uniform Tailor Shop to get fitted for his Junior uniform. He then stopped by the Aggieland Barber Shop on the way out of town for a haircut. He enjoyed a fabulous dinner and dessert with Emma Jo over in Bryan before heading home to San Saba. Felix told Emma Jo that he was committed to making their relationship continue over the summer, and he let her know that they'd see each other at least once a month. With that, Felix gave Emma Jo a big hug and a kiss before getting into his car to head on down the road to San Saba.

Felix was glad to be back home, and he was undoubtedly pleased to sleep in his own comfortable bed. He surely enjoyed the love and support that being around his family provided. The redness on Felix's face was diminishing more and more with each passing day. He figured that his complexion would return to normal after a few weeks of fishing, swimming, and hanging out with his cousins out at the River Bend farm. Nobody had asked about his grades, and Felix was glad, since it was one less thing that he had to worry about. Felix did his best to write a letter to Emma Jo every other day, and he made plans to invite her out to San Saba shortly after her upcoming birthday on 3 Jul. 1940. Felix got such a kick out of the fact that Emma Jo's birthday fell on the same day as his sister, Pauline, and he was certain that the two of them would get along well. Felix sent Emma Jo some money for a train ticket, and he asked her to be on the afternoon train on Saturday, 6 Jul. 1940. He was very pleased to receive her letter accepting the invitation.

The redness on Felix's face had finally dissipated to the point that no one could tell that he'd ever had a problem. Therefore, as the month of June came to a close, he started working regular shifts once again at Mrs. Howard's bakery. Although Felix's voice was still a little raspy, his charming personality hadn't been lost in the accident. His customers offered him kindness, and they also provided him with words of encouragement, for which he appreciated. Emma Jo was indeed on the Saturday train, and Felix was waiting for her at the train station with a bouquet of freshly picked flowers from Viola's garden. He was very excited to show her around town, and he immediately took her down to Harry's Boots so that she could pick out a fine birthday present. Emma Jo selected an adorable beige sun hat with a pink bow that went exceptionally well with her beautiful brown hair. Felix's sisters, cousins, aunties, uncles, and grandparents were all looking forward to meeting Emma Jo. What better way to celebrate her arrival in San Saba? A fish fry, of course!

Felix was glad to see that plenty of his family members were able to attend the evening gathering at the Scott residence. Emma Jo got along fine with all of Felix's sisters, but after spending the evening socializing with Pauline, they both knew that they'd forever share their special day. Everyone enjoyed visiting with Felix, and they thought Emma Jo was a real doll. They were equally impressed with her singing skills when she jumped right in as some of the family members began playing their favorite musical instruments after supper. Before leaving school for the summer, Felix had gone to the College Exchange store to purchase the sheet music for "I'd Rather Be A Texas Aggie," written by a fellow Aggie cadet, Jack Littlejohn. Emma Jo was fascinated as she watched Ernest and Felix practice the song together on the piano. The song was pretty short, but Viola, Emma Jo, and, of course, Felix, gave their best vocal rendition of the lyrics. Before long, Emma Jo and Felix were swinging around the living room at the Scott house as the family's makeshift band played on. Emma Jo knew that Felix could dance, but she didn't know that he and his family were so musically inclined.

To avoid any perceived possibility of funny business, Viola insisted that Emma Jo sleep in Aletha's room, while Felix slept in his own room. Early the next morning, Felix drove Emma Jo out to the River Bend farm for a two night stay with Ma and Pa. She was very impressed with the size of their property as they drove up the winding dirt road towards the house. Emma Jo seemed to really enjoy the rural scenery that was blended with all of the beautiful oak and pecan trees in nearly every direction that she looked. After visiting for a spell, Ma gave Emma Jo a tour of their home. Felix then grabbed a few fishing rods, and he set out on horseback with Emma Jo through Pa's pecan orchard, en route to his most plentiful fishing hole. Call it beginners luck or not, but Emma Jo managed to snag a decent size yellow cat shortly after dropping her line into the Colorado River. After catching plenty of fish for supper, Felix convinced Emma Jo to try her skills on the tire swing. He was thoroughly impressed with the height that she reached before falling into the cool river water below. Emma Jo didn't break any bones, nor was she bitten by a water moccasin, and thus the afternoon was a complete success. Felix and Emma Jo had a wonderful and relaxing time along the riverbank.

Emma Jo had a private room all to herself during her stay at the Millican home. She felt welcomed as a guest, and she very much appreciated Polly Ann's thoughtfulness in having made her a homemade chocolate cake. After a wonderful visit with Ma and Pa, they drove back to San Saba on the morning of 9 Jul. 1940, to meet up with a few of Felix's high school friends at his favorite swimming hole on the San Saba River. Afterwards, Felix and Emma Jo stopped by Johnnie Mae's café for some delicious tamales, and a slice of her famous strawberry rhubarb pie. Felix then got Emma Jo to the train station in time for the afternoon train that would take her back home. He was sad to see her leave, but he needed time to finalize the plans for his next big adventure.

After Emma Jo returned home, Felix went right back to work at the bakery. Later that week, he pulled into his driveway after work to find Ernest on the front porch reading the newspaper. He sat down for a moment in the chair next to his father, and he inquisitively asked what was going on with the war in Europe. Ernest dolefully replied, "Well son, it looks like France was recently lost to the Nazis, and they are now attempting to occupy England." The Battle of Britain had just begun, and Felix liked reading all about the events and happenings that were taking place overseas. He was hoping that the Royal Air Force (RAF) would be successful in keeping the German Luftwaffe from taking control over the skies in the United Kingdom.

Felix worked full-time shifts every day until the morning of 16 Jul. 1940 when he and his good buddy, Billy Holmes, got a lift from Ernest to the outskirts of San Saba. He reluctantly left the young men on the side of the road with their suitcases, money in their pockets, and some wild ambition about hitchhiking to Mexico City and back. They planned for a three-week vacation, and they hoped to have some remarkable stories to share when they returned. Viola, on the other hand, was worried for their safety, and she wondered if they'd have enough money for the entire trip.

Felix and Billy caught their first ride to Llano, and from there, they picked up a new ride, which got them to San Antonio. The next morning, the boys finished off the bag of fresh biscuits that Viola had baked for them, and they were able to make their way down to McAllen, Texas. Just after dawn on 18 Jul., Felix and Billy were ready to cross over the border into Mexico. As they made their way further south, they found that the terrain was similar to that of Texas. The young men figured that it was going to take a few days, and many different rides in the back of rickety old pickup trucks to get to Mexico City. Felix and Billy met plenty of friendly people along the way, and language didn't seem to be that big of an issue. They were able to stay on course with their compass and map, and they were relieved to finally arrive safely in Mexico City.

Felix really enjoyed hunting ancient artifacts back in San Saba County, thus he was naturally very excited to see some of the biggest historical monuments in and around Mexico City. Their first stop was the Palacio Nacional, and then they moved on to wonder around Zocalo, which was the city center of Mexico City. By the end of the day, Felix had tried his very first churro, and he found it to be a delightful treat. He and Billy laughed that they could probably survive on tequila, tacos, tamales, and, of course, sopapillas during their stay in Mexico. For the most part, the young men stayed in cheap motels near the city center; however, there were several nights where they slept outside in public parks. They each purchased a thick Mexican blanket to keep warm, and they took turns keeping watch during the night to keep each other safe.

The walk to Chapultepec Park proved worthwhile, as it provided them with a spectacular view of the city below. Felix had been around many bulls while growing up in San Saba, but attending a bull fight in person one evening was a thrill on a whole new level. Being among the lively crowd with tens of thousands of screaming Mexican nationals was exhilarating. It was kind of like being at Kyle Field during a home football game, but different. Traversing the main canal of Xochimilco on a very small, but colorful boat was a very relaxing experience, and the Temples at Tlatelolco were also a big hit. Early one morning, Felix and Billy headed about two and a half hours southeast to the volcano at Iztaccihuatl. Luckily for the boys, they found someone who gave them a ride in the back of a truck. This was probably the best place for them, and it was much less embarrassing since they became carsick several times along the crazy winding road. Felix and Billy spent a few days in the area there, and they were both very pleased that they were able to complete the hike to the summit.

Felix and Billy wrapped up their weeklong stay in Mexico City by heading north to Teotihuacan. The multi-level climb up the steps belonging to the Pyramid of the Sun was demanding, but the views from atop the magnificent structure were amazing. The following morning, the boys traveled further north for most of the day in order to get to Tolantongo. Once they arrived, they found the hot springs to be very enjoyable, and the warm water provided much needed relaxation for their muscles. They spent the better part of the day exploring the caves, which were nestled among an abundance of lush green foliage. Felix and Billy spent the rest of the day playing in and climbing among the beautiful waterfalls.

After leaving Tolantongo, Felix and Billy headed east to the Gulf Coast. They stopped at many different coastal cities as they made their way north towards the southernmost tip of Texas. The boys were ready to bid farewell to the sights of Mexico as they crossed the border back into the United States. South Padre Island was the next stop for the boys, and after just a short time there, Felix believed that this had to be the most beautiful city in all of Texas. There were plenty of sandy beaches, and they really enjoyed swimming in the crystal blue water. While hanging around in town, Felix struck up a conversation with the captain of a commercial fishing vessel that was headed out into the Gulf of Mexico, and on to New Orleans. The captain admired what the boys had accomplished on their journey, and as a nice gesture, he offered them free passage to New Orleans. As they made their way through the Gulf of Mexico, Felix and Billy watched in awe as the fishermen caught some of the most lovely and biggest fish that they'd ever seen along the way.

Felix found New Orleans to be a bustling and exciting city, filled with people from all walks of life. Hearing the fabulous musicians everywhere they went left Felix longing to be back home with his own musically inclined family. The boys visited a variety of restaurants located in the French quarter, and they also dined at a few along Canal Street. Felix and Billy found the food to be exceptionally delicious, but they were ready to return to their own kitchen tables for some of their mother's home cooking. After spending another day meandering around the city, Felix and Billy caught the evening train bound for Houston.

After arriving in Houston early the next morning, and on a whim, Felix decided that he was going to surprise Emma Jo. He purchased his ticket to Bryan, while Billy planned to take a train back home to San Saba. It was time to say goodbye to Billy, and Felix asked him to stop by his house to let his folks know that he was safe, and that he'd return home in a few days after visiting with Emma Jo over in Bryan. Surprisingly, Felix still had some money left in his pocket, and he figured that it would be best if he had some clean clothes to wear upon his arrival at Emma Jo's. Thankfully, there were a few shops near the train station, and Felix was able to purchase a pair of trousers, and a couple of new shirts. Before boarding the train, he stopped at a barbershop where he got a cut and a shave. While getting his hair cut, Felix paid an ambitious young fella to shine up his boots.

Felix was excited to arrive in Bryan by train, since he'd only previously traveled in and out of the Southern Pacific Depot there in College Station. There had never been a need for Felix to hitchhike over to Emma Jo's home before, but he quickly found the bench where he needed to wait for a ride. Felix arrived on Emma Jo's front porch just after noon on 6 Aug. Emma Jo was quite surprised to see Felix standing there, and she promptly gave him a big hug. She then grabbed Felix by the hand and led him inside where she made him a ham and cheese sandwich with fresh lettuce and tomatoes from the garden. After a fine meal and a glass of lemonade, Felix and Emma Jo ventured outside to the back yard where they were promptly greeted by her adorable Labrador puppy named Amy. He had a fabulous time playing with the energetic little puppy, which made him eager to get back home to play with his own dog.

While sitting at her picnic table, Emma Jo listened attentively while Felix filled her ear with plenty of details and highlights from his trip to Mexico City. Felix then grabbed his bag, and he began pulling out a few gifts for Emma Jo. She was quite impressed with the nice assortment of seashells that he'd collected during his stay in South Padre Island. Felix also presented her with a silver necklace that was adorned with a precious dolphin charm. Finally, he gave her a little box that contained a bottle of her favorite perfume, Apple Blossom. Emma Jo liked her gifts very much, and she thought that Felix was very special to think of her while on his journey.

Right about supper time, Emma Jo's father, Cyrus McDermott, arrived home, and he was equally surprised to find Felix sitting on the sofa. Cyrus liked Felix, and he thought that he had a good head on his shoulders. Emma Jo then asked her father if Felix could stay with them for a few days. They were both pleasantly surprised to hear that Cyrus offered to allow Felix the opportunity to sleep on the sofa for three nights. Felix was glad to be able to finally rest his feet, and he very much enjoyed his time in Bryan with Emma Jo and her family. After a few movies, plenty of long walks with the puppy, and several trips to Canady's for ice cream sundaes, he wrapped up his stay with Emma Jo. On his way to work on the morning of 9 Aug., Cyrus gave Felix a lift to the train station for his trip back to San Saba.

Nobody was at the train station to greet Felix when he arrived back in San Saba later that day. He really wasn't all that surprised, since he hadn't let anyone know exactly when he was going to be home. Felix had hitchhiked all the way to Mexico City, so he figured that he could find the energy to make the relatively short walk home. While on the way, he stopped in at Ketchum's Kitchen to find his sister serving up food to her hungry customers. Johnnie Mae was very glad to see Felix walk through her door, and she thought that he might have actually lost some weight during his journey through Mexico. She figured that she could help put some meat back on his bones, and, therefore, she promptly brought him a large plate of beef tamales, and a few slices of apple pie. After sharing some details about his trip with Johnnie Mae, Felix continued his walk home to find his mother, and her sister, his Aunt Jessie, sitting out on the front porch. As Viola ran out to the street to give him a big hug, she yelled out, "Land sakes, my boy is finally home!" She then spun Felix around as she purposefully placed her hands on his face, arms, and upper torso to ensure that he had indeed returned home safely, and in one piece.

Early Saturday morning, Felix made his way out to see Ma, Pa, and Chauncey. They were all excited to see him, and they were eager to hear all about his adventures to Mexico City. After supper, Pa explained to Felix that he'd found him a job down at the Agricultural Adjustment Administration (AAA) office. Felix just couldn't say no to his grandfather, and he felt that it might be a great opportunity for the rest of the summer. Felix reported to the AAA office there in San Saba on Monday morning 12 Aug. 1940. He promptly introduced himself to the manager, Mr. Ben Ray, and he explained that his grandfather had said that there was a job opening. Mr. Ray confirmed that he was looking for a hard-working young man to fill the position. After conversing with Felix for about 10-15 minutes, Mr. Ray could tell that Felix was sharp, witty, and courteous. He figured that Felix would be a good fit for the job, and he offered him the position right there on the spot. Felix cheerfully accepted the job, and he told Mr. Ray that he'd be able to work full-time hours until he needed to leave for school. He scaled back his hours at the bakery, and he'd now be working there very early each weekday morning and on Saturdays. With two jobs, Felix was able to save some money, and stay busy for the duration of the summer.

During the last few weeks of his summer vacation, Felix made it a point to worship with his grandparents out at the Bend Methodist Church. He loved attending that church, and he had fond memories of his Sunday school days there. Felix attended church services with his parents at the San Saba Methodist Church on the Sunday before heading back to College Station. All of the family members from San Saba and Bend who could attend came for Sunday supper. There was quite a feast because everybody brought something delicious to share. The party lasted late into the evening with plenty of laughter, singing, music, dancing, and, of course, great food. The get-together was a big hit, and everyone had an opportunity to wish Felix good luck, and to say goodbye before he left to start his junior year at Texas AMC. Aletha undeniably enjoyed Felix's company when he was home, and she always cried when it was time for him to leave.

Felix left San Saba bright and early on Thursday, 19 Sep. 1940, and he headed for College Station to register for his next round of classes. By looking at the number of students in line, he could tell that the cadet population was once again going to be greater than the prior year. Before Felix registered for his classes, he had to stand in a different line at the registrar's office. He and his grandfather had had a long discussion over the summer about his progress at the college. Felix therefore had decided to switch his major to Agriculture, since he'd been around the farm his whole life. He knew the rest of the routine well enough, and he was able to get through the registration line at the Administration Building in just a few hours. Felix walked away with his classes consisting of General Botany, General Entomology, Commercial Vegetable Crops, Principles of Fruit Production, Geography of Horticultural Industries, and a retake of Agricultural Math and Infantry Military Science 201. As a junior, he remained the same rank as a second year private in the Infantry Regiment. Felix was now a member of "I" Company within the Third Battalion.

Felix made his way over to Gainer Hall, and he was very glad to find out that Charles would be his roommate once again. After unpacking their things, he and Charles made their way to the Uniform Tailor Shop to pick up their new junior uniforms. The uniform itself was pretty much the same, but new clothes to fit their growing bodies were certainly well received. Reserved for junior and senior cadets, Felix and Charles enjoyed their new solid brass belt buckles, which were much fancier than their previous brass framed buckles. In addition, the hat device, which screwed into the front of their campaign and service caps, was also different than before. The hat device was essentially an oversized brass pin, and the AMC letters that had been previously embedded within the banner above the eagle stack had now been replaced with individual cut-out letters. After affixing the shiny new devices to their service caps, the boys agreed that they were more stylish and noticeable. After the evening meal, Felix and Charles made their way to the area outside of the YMCA for what was sure to be the largest College Night on record. The first yell session of the year was exhilarating, and Felix sort of wondered if Emma Jo could hear all of the noise over in Bryan. He was a bit tired for the morning Reveille, but Felix was ready to officially start his classes on 20 Sep. 1940.

Texas AMC hat device for juniors and seniors. Photo is courtesy of the Sanders Corps of Cadets Center, Texas A&M University.

Keeping their room tidy and spotless was a high priority to remain on good terms with the First Sergeant. It was equally important to be dressed, and present, for Roll Call on the drill field at 0615 hours each morning. After hearing the 0630 hours bugle, Felix and his fellow cadets would perform their daily march to the Duncan Dining Hall for breakfast. Classes typically began around 0900 hours on weekdays, followed by an afternoon drill. As part of the requirements for his degree, Felix worked in the agricultural fields several days a week, before once again marching to supper. The variety of food was always appetizing to Felix, and the cadets typically finished in less than 30 minutes before marching back to their dormitories. After studying each evening, Felix would take some time to shine his shoes, and on occasion, his brass uniform pins as well. The cadets didn't have to go to bed right at 2230 hours when they heard the evening sounding of taps, but they were at least supposed to be in their dorm room.

Felix was hopeful that his beloved Aggies would repeat as Southwest Conference champions, and even as national champions once again in football. Since there was no football that first weekend back, Felix and Charles thought that it would be fun to enter the billiard tournament being held at the Aggie Amusement Club, which was located inside the College Inn Café. Fortunately, the food there was much better than their luck, as the boys didn't make it out of the first round. Dreamland, a fabulous ice cream sundae shop that was located nearby, helped the boys deal with getting bumped from the tournament. Felix was excited to learn that a new Piggly Wiggly had just opened in College Station, since he really enjoyed shopping at the one back home in San Saba. It was inside the Casey Burgess Building, and he and Charles stopped there for some snacks, and a few supplies on the way home from the tournament.

It was 27 Sep. 1940 when an alliance was formed by Germany, Japan, and Italy. The Tripartite Pact resulted in these countries coming together to be named the Axis powers of the Second World War. Realizing that the situation overseas was worsening by the day, officials from the United States Government arrived on campus in late September to assist those cadets aged 21 and older with registration for the draft. Felix wasn't yet 21, but he knew that many of his buddies, being cadets from a military prep school, felt obligated, yet proud, to register during the event. However, many of the cadets were unclear of what exactly they were registering for, since the United States wasn't yet directly involved in the hostility taking place on the other side of the world. Viola was certainly concerned when she got word of this draft registration, but she was very glad to hear that Felix wouldn't have to register until after his junior year was over. Felix could see the writing on the wall, and he figured that it was just a matter of time before the United States got dragged into the international conflicts.

Emma Jo was happy that Felix was back at the college, as she had really missed him. It had been a long, uneventful summer for her, and Emma Jo was looking forward to all of the upcoming activities to be held there on campus. They attended the first dance of the new school year on 28 Sep. 1940. Emma Jo loved to dance, and she thought that Felix looked really handsome in his dress uniform. Felix and Buzz loved swinging on the dance floor with their beautiful young ladies, and they knew that they were very lucky to be with them. After class one day, Felix convinced the manager at the Aggieland Bakery that he had some skills working in a bakery, and as a result, he was quickly hired to work some weekend shifts. The extra spending money sure came in handy with keeping Emma Jo happy and entertained.

Felix and Buzz got up very early on Saturday, 5 Oct., and they made their way over to Bryan to pick up Emma Jo and Betty Lou. They quickly returned to College Station to board the early morning train bound for San Antonio. The boys wore their formal dress uniforms, and the girls looked stunning in their maroon dresses and black high heels. Excitement was abound, as they watched the Aggies crush Tulsa at the Alamo Memorial Stadium. Everyone had a grand time riding the train back to College Station after the game, and the boys had their girls back home just after midnight.

The following weekend, the Aggies traveled to Southern California to play UCLA. That was a bit too far for Felix and his friends to travel, so on Saturday, Felix and Emma Jo decided to check out the new bowling alley that had just opened in Bryan. After a fun afternoon of bowling, they had a delicious dinner at the nearby Chicken Shanty. Having defeated UCLA, the football team arrived back in town on Tuesday, 15 Oct., and the players were met on campus with a victory march consisting of the entire cadet corps. Felix and Emma Jo got their dancing shoes out once again, when they attended the corps dance held at Sbisa Hall following the victory over TCU on 19 Oct. After working his Sunday morning shift at the Aggieland Bakery, Felix and Emma Jo saw the afternoon showing of *Dark Command,* a movie that featured John Wayne at the Campus Theater.

The Aggies left town to square off against Baylor on 26 Oct., and much of the corps traveled with the team to see the game. Felix and Charles decided not to travel to Waco, so they headed over to the YMCA to play billiards and listen to music. While at the "Y," Felix ran into his buddy Clancy. They began to talk about their classes, and Felix was very interested in learning about how Clancy was doing in the new flight training program offered on campus. He was only a month into the program, but he was already learning a great deal about aviation. Clancy described the amazing thrill that he had when he got to sit in the front seat of a PT-17 biplane while the instructor piloted the ship from the rear seat out to Valley Junction and back. Felix was very excited for Clancy, but he felt dejected, knowing once again that he was academically ineligible to register for the class. Clancy then mentioned to Felix that he thought that the company that was operating the aviation school had a few spots left for folks who were able to pay for the training without having to register through school. All of a sudden, Felix got to thinking about all of the possible ways that he could get himself into the training class. He could envision himself as the owner of a crop-dusting company serving all of San Saba County. There were plenty of crops that would need spraying, and Felix was eager to be the pilot doing the work. He imagined that his grandfather, W. J. Millican, might be willing to front him the money for the training, and perhaps, even be willing to help him down the road to cover the start-up costs for his new business venture after graduation. Felix abruptly snapped back to reality, figuring that his plate was already full with his classes, work, and, of course, Emma Jo.

Felix was excited to be headed to Denton for the junior class pre-corps trip on 8 Nov. Before leaving town, he and Buzz drove over to Bryan to have breakfast with Emma Jo and Betty Lou. The boys assured their ladies that they'd be gentlemen, and that they wouldn't dance with any of the girls at the Texas State College for Women (TSCW). The ladies of TSCW were hosting the Aggie junior class for the dinner and dance, and Felix and his pals were looking forward to a fun-filled evening. True to their word, Felix and Buzz stayed off the dance floor, but they may have moved their feet a just a bit while enjoying the fine food, drinks, and desserts.

Early the next morning, the boys left Denton, bound for Dallas to watch the game against Southern Methodist University (SMU). After crushing the SMU Mustangs, the Aggies ran their record to 7-0, and they sat atop the Southwest Conference. The boys were exhausted after a long couple of days, so Felix and Buzz boarded the 2330 hours train, headed back to College Station. Although they arrived very early on Sunday morning, the boys were glad to be back on campus. They were looking forward to the following weekend, when they'd attend the final home game of the year on 16 Nov. Felix and Buzz were delighted to be back with Emma Jo and Betty Lou for an afternoon of Aggie football. Felix's voice was a bit scratchy from the yell practice that was held the previous evening, but he still found a way to yell through the entire game against Rice. The young couples enjoyed watching the Aggies blank the Rice Owls at Kyle Field. It seemed as if everything was lining up perfectly for the Aggies to make a run at another National Championship.

Felix remembered back to his days as a fish when he was told that he and his buddies needed to gather large amounts of firewood for the annual lighting of the Aggie Bonfire. It was 26 Nov., and it was just two days before the big game against the Texas Longhorns over in Austin. Felix, Buzz, and the girls attended an unofficial yell practice at the "Y" before they headed over to join the large crowd that had gathered around the towering stack of wood. There was plenty of yelling going on as the cadets shouted out their ritualistic fight songs. Emma Jo and Betty Lou were quite impressed with the size of the Bonfire. Things continued to heat up that evening for the sweethearts, when they attended the traditional Bonfire dance, which was held over in Sbisa Hall.

Many Texans have a hard time deciding whether family or football comes first. Felix was certainly an Aggie through and through, and for him, the decision was easy. Thanksgiving supper in San Saba would just have to wait, since Felix chose to travel to Austin for the big game against the University of Texas. He, and a great deal of his fellow cadets boarded the train bound for Austin on Wednesday afternoon. They arrived about three hours later, and they were lucky to find a hotel that could accommodate up to six people to a room. Felix and his pals drew straws to determine who'd have the unfortunate honor of sleeping on the floor. Luckily for Felix, he got to sleep in a bed.

With their undefeated winning streak for the season on the line, the Aggies were ready to square off against the Longhorns on 28 Nov. This was the last regular season game of the year, and most folks expected that the score would be close. However, nobody could've figured what was about to happen between the lines on the field that afternoon. There were thousands of Aggies and fans in the stands. The cadets were all wearing their dress jackets, wool slacks, white shirts, along with their black ties. They definitely looked sharp, but the players were anything but sharp. The Aggies hadn't been shut out all season, but that swiftly changed. The football team couldn't even muster a field goal, and the Aggies lost in stunning fashion 0-7.

Shockingly, the winning streak was over, and so was their chance to repeat as National Champions. As the Aggies filed out of the stadium, their heads were down, the laughter had ceased, and their spirits were crushed. To some, it felt as if a good friend or a relative had died. Felix and his fellow cadets somberly boarded the buses that took them to the train station. Felix took the train to San Saba, and he arrived there around 2100 hours, with Ernest waiting there to greet him. By then, some of the shock of the devastating loss had waned. It was hard for Felix to be sad for too long around his folks and his sisters, since they were always so lively and uplifting whenever he was with them. By the end of their late supper, Felix's family had done a wonderful job in cheering him up just in time for dessert. He truly enjoyed hanging out with Chauncey, and the rest of his family, late into the evening. Before he knew it, the next few days had flown by there in San Saba, and it was time to take the train back to College Station on Sunday afternoon.

When the cadets returned to campus after the break, they were suddenly facing a serious problem with the flu. Nobody could really explain how it had happened, or how it had spread so quickly. Perhaps, it was the large crowd at the stadium in Austin, or maybe it was from nearly everyone being home for the Thanksgiving holiday. The unexpected situation had clearly disrupted the normal activities on campus, and it had even put a halt to Felix's plans with Emma Jo. The cadets were asked to rest, and to limit exposure to those off campus as much as possible. Essentially, they were being quarantined to some extent. Felix managed to visit Caldwell's Jewelry store for some early Christmas shopping. He purchased a pair of gold earrings with the most colorful opals that he'd ever seen for Emma Jo. Winter break began early on 14 Dec. because of the continuing flu outbreak. Felix stopped by Emma Jo's home on the way back to San Saba to present her with her Christmas gift. She in turn had a few gifts for him as well, and Emma Jo asked Felix to open his gifts as they sat out on the front porch together. Felix loved his new leather billfold, Medico pipe, and several cans of Prince Albert pipe tobacco.

Once again, Felix sure enjoyed being home for Christmas. He just couldn't wait to play Christmas music with his father on the piano, and to sing carols with his mother and sisters. Catching up with friends and family always meant a great deal to Felix. He worked a few shifts at Mrs. Howard's bakery to earn a little extra pocket money for some last minute Christmas presents. Felix was more than happy to trade the hectic day-to-day routine at school for the tranquil atmosphere of San Saba. He even managed to catch up on some of the required reading for his classes. Prior to leaving campus for the winter break, Felix didn't get a chance to pick up his Cotton Bowl ticket due to the school releasing everyone earlier than expected. He was hopeful that someone was still there on campus who'd be able to mail the tickets out to all the cadets who'd planned on attending the game. Felix was very thankful when his ticket arrived safely at the San Saba post office. Before he'd left College Station, he'd made plans to meet up with Buzz and Charles in Dallas for the big game. Felix was disappointed that he wouldn't be home to listen to the game on the radio with Pauline, but he just couldn't miss the chance to go in person. He spent New Year's Eve at home with his folks, and he was glad that Johnnie Mae, AJ, Felix Wayne, Aletha, Pauline, and Ted were able to join them to welcome in the new year.

It was before dawn on 1 Jan. 1941 when Felix left San Saba. After arriving in Dallas, he proceeded to the train station where he found Buzz and Charles waiting patiently out front. There were two other Aggies waiting on the bench with them who needed a ride to the stadium. Felix was always glad to assist a fellow Aggie in need, and thus, he offered them a ride too. The young men were certainly cramped inside of Felix's roadster, but luckily, they didn't have very far to go. They parked about half a mile from the stadium to avoid the congestion in the area. While walking towards the stadium, the group stopped at a restaurant for some delicious barbecue before the 1315 hours kickoff. With tickets in their hands, the group continued to the stadium. After passing through the turnstile, Felix purchased a colorful souvenir program for a quarter. Everyone found their seats, and they settled in for what was sure to be an exciting game. They enjoyed some ice-cold Coca-Cola's at half time while watching the Aggie band parade on the field. The New Year's Day game between the Aggies and the Fordham Rams was tightly contested until the very end. The Aggie defense proved strong by blocking both extra points that were attempted by the Rams kicker, and in the end, that had made the difference. When the whistle was blown, the Aggies were ahead by just one point, and they were crowned as the winner of the Cotton Bowl. This was the first Cotton Bowl victory for the Aggies, and it was sure to be a game that would be remembered for quite some time to come. Felix and his pals returned to College Station later that evening because classes were scheduled to resume the following day.

Everyone was glad that the flu outbreak had subsided, and things were mostly back to normal when the cadets returned to campus. With the semester winding down, Felix was determined to perform better academically than he had during the previous semesters. As such, he and Emma Jo decided that they'd go out on just two dates in January, and they'd resume their whirlwind romance right after he was finished with his final exams. On 4 Jan., the young couple enjoyed a fabulous supper, and an evening of dancing at Franklin's, which was a new restaurant that had opened just before the holidays over on Airport Road. Felix and his fellow cadets weren't thrilled about having to make up some of the classroom time that had been lost just before break. For the college to maintain its status as a preeminent institution, the cadets were required to attend Saturday afternoon class sessions on the 11th and 25th of January. On Saturday, 18 Jan., Felix and Emma Jo saw a matinee at the Campus Theater, and they spent the rest of the evening playing cards and a variety of board games at home with her family. Before heading back to his dorm, Emma Jo gave Felix a big hug with a kiss, and she wished him well on his finals. Their strategy had paid off, and Felix was thrilled that he'd passed all his classes for the first time!

Felix had finished the required two-year basic military training curriculum, and he hoped that he was finally on track towards a path to graduation. Unfortunately, he still didn't meet the scholastic requirements for the advanced military courses. However, Felix still had dreams and aspirations of becoming an aviator in the United States Army Air Corps, but he was unsure if that opportunity would ever materialize. He had previously shared his dreams of becoming a pilot with Francine, but he hadn't yet found the proper opportunity to share his vision with Emma Jo.

To accommodate the growing student population, the college decided to spread registration for the spring semester over a longer period of days than usual. There was some of the usual chaos, but the line was relatively short when Felix obtained his class schedule on the morning of 5 Feb. 1941. He certainly made sure that he paid all his fees, and he received the YMCA privilege card as well. When Felix began the spring semester on 11 Feb., he only had five classes: Agricultural Marketing, Principles of Fruit Production, Elementary Design and Construction, Poultry Production, and a retake of General Inorganic Chemistry 102. Although Felix wasn't taking any more Military Science classes, he was still required to participate in the daily drills, and the full-dress Reviews that were held periodically.

Felix was pleased that he could begin wearing his khaki slacks to start the spring semester. The college had decided to liven up the weekday breakfast and dinner trips to the mess hall. Felix was excited that he'd now be able to march to music for nearly all his meals. Under the new program, a small drum and bugle corps, complete with cymbals, would accompany the cadets as they marched in unison from the dorms to the mess hall. The larger and more complete band still provided the music for the evening Retreat and supper meals. As Felix was returning to his dorm after class on 10 Feb., he counted at least 10 planes flying in circles above the campus. While changing his clothes in preparation to visit the agricultural fields, he saw the contingent of planes drop out of the sky, one by one, to land at the College Station Airport. He was thoroughly impressed with the impromptu aerial show, and he was amazed at the tremendous sound that all the planes made together.

With the beginning of the new semester, Felix and Emma Jo were ready to commence their social activities once again. He figured that she'd be impressed when he got tickets to go see a performance by the Littlefield Ballet on the evening of 12 Feb. at Guion Hall. Felix wasn't really a fan of the performing arts, but he realized that he needed to occasionally step out of his comfort zone to keep his girl happy. Valentine's Day fell on a Friday in 1941; therefore Felix and Emma Jo were able to stay out late that evening. So, he hoped for a romantic evening by making plans for a nice supper, and then watching the sun set, and followed by a moonlit stroll on the banks of the Brazos River. Emma Jo thought Felix was just the sweetest thing for giving her a wonderful bouquet of flowers, some new records, and a box of delicious chocolates, all followed by a movie at the Queen Theater. They ended the evening sitting together on Emma Jo's front porch swing while gazing at the stars and sharing a passionate goodnight kiss.

President Walton of the Agricultural and Mechanical College of Texas had decided that the cadets would participate in a variety of exhibitions during National Defense Week for the very first time. Texas AMC was among the largest military colleges in the world at that time, and the cadets felt that it was important to show what the corps could offer the United States military if they were called to duty. Each of the various regiments on campus presented their specialized skill sets and areas of expertise. Felix enjoyed participating in the Infantry skills demonstration, where their tactics and weapons were on display for the large crowd in attendance. After proving his proficiency out on the shooting range, Felix especially liked charging with his rifle as he thrust the affixed bayonet into the "enemy" dummies that were stuffed with straw. The Aggie band played many patriotic songs over the three-day period, which culminated with a full-dress Review on 21 Feb. 1941. The entire cadet corps participated in the Review, which was purported to be the largest in the school's history. There was plenty of press coverage for the event, and Felix was hoping that his picture just might end up in the local paper back home. Felix really enjoyed the pageantry and all the marching in unison with his fellow cadets.

Felix was really digging his Design and Construction class, and he believed that he may have finally found his niche. Having the lighter class load provided him with the opportunity to be more involved with his campus clubs, which allowed him to forge deeper friendships with his battery mates. Felix and Emma Jo attended a mid-week viewing of *Pride and Prejudice* at the Campus Theater on 6 Mar. That weekend, he took Emma Jo to the Texas A & M grill, out by the north gate, to discuss their plans to attend the upcoming annual Texas Bluebonnet Festival. The festival was to be held over in Navasota, which was about 30 minutes from campus. They spent all day on Saturday, 29 Mar. enjoying everything the festival had to offer. There was plenty of live music, which even featured the Aggie band. The rodeo was certainly a thrill, and the fun-filled day was topped off by a parade complete with dozens of floats.

Felix returned to campus after having spent a few days with his folks back in San Saba for the spring recess. He and Emma Jo shook the dust off their dancing shoes to attend the Barnyard Frolic, which was held on Friday, 18 Apr. in the Agricultural Engineering Building. The couples were supposed to dress as a farmer and as a farmer's wife. Felix had no problem getting decked out in his cowboy boots, jeans, and his checkered shirt with snaps down the front. He even pulled his brown Stetson hat out of his wooden storage chest to complete the outfit. Emma Jo was able to pick out a blue and white checkered dress and some cute canvas shoes at the JC Penney's there in Bryan. Her hair was done up in pigtails and tied at the bottom with yellow ribbons. Felix and Emma Jo made for a cute couple, and they danced the night away as the Aggieland Orchestra played until very early Saturday morning.

The fun kept on coming the following Friday night when Felix and Emma Jo attended the Infantry Ball held in Sbisa Hall. He paid the extra money to receive the special favor being offered as a memento to commemorate the evening. It was a good-looking crossed rifle pin with the Texas AMC emblem placed prominently in the center. Felix gave the pin to Emma Jo that evening, and she said that she'd always cherish it. The cadet corps participated in a full-dress Review on 1 May to kick off the weekend of festivities for the first annual Agricultural Day held on campus. Felix and his fellow classmates had worked feverishly in the weeks leading up to this special weekend. The young men had built numerous exhibits, and he helped to set up many different displays. Felix had learned a great deal of woodworking skills from his father, and he was glad to see that the campus exhibits were a huge success. Good times were in full swing when Felix and Emma Jo attended the Cotton Ball on 2 May, and he enjoyed participating in the variety of sporting events that were held throughout the weekend.

The annual Mothers and Fathers appreciation weekend was always a hit on campus. Spirits were high as thousands of parents descended upon the sprawling grounds at Texas AMC. Felix was glad to have put the unfortunate event leading up to the prior year's celebration weekend behind him, and he was excited that his parents were coming for the visit. Hotels in Bryan and in College Station were at a premium, so Ernest and Viola once again stayed with their good friends, the Morrisons, on Friday and Saturday night. Ernest and Viola enjoyed seeing the campus again, and they even commented how the landscaping was really coming along around Gainer Hall. As they walked from the dorm to campus, Ernest jokingly said to Felix, "I still don't see any pecan trees round these parts."

On Sunday morning, 11 May, all the parents were treated to a spectacular Review by the cadet corps, which numbered around 6,500 strong. Each young man had a little extra kick in his step as they paraded in front of their proud mothers and fathers. After the Review, the fun and excitement continued over on the lawn in front of the Administration Building. Felix had made sure to secure meal tickets from his First Sergeant, and as such, he and his folks enjoyed a nice picnic on the grass. After a wonderful afternoon, Ernest and Viola headed home to San Saba for a fabulous Mother's Day lasagna supper that Aletha had spent much of the day preparing. Johnnie Mae and her family, along with Pauline and Ted, came over to finish off what had been a very pleasant day for Viola. Once his folks had left, Felix headed over to the Aeronautical Engineering Building to see the exhibits for Engineer's Day. He really enjoyed the short film about the history of aviation, and all their hands-on exhibits.

With just a few short weeks left in the semester, Felix was getting very close to wrapping up his third year as an Aggie. He remembered back to the first day that he had stepped inside the College Exchange store on campus when the lady had told him that the fancy boots were for seniors only. Well, the day that had been years in the making had finally arrived. Felix liked the staff, and the exceptional quality of goods that were provided at the Uniform Tailor Shop. Therefore, that is where he went to get fitted on 12 May 1941. Felix liked the finer things in life, so he just had to have a pair of the newly redesigned senior boots made by Lucchese. There were other brands of senior boots, but Felix preferred the durability and look of the Lucchese boots. Besides, it was a plus that they were made in San Antonio, Texas, which was just a few hours away from campus. There had been some recent talk on campus about eliminating the senior boot requirement for the upcoming semester, and Felix was very glad to hear that the idea hadn't gone anywhere. With his fitting done, and his order placed, Felix was ready to finish the year strong.

Felix pictured in his dress uniform with his Sam Browne belt across his chest.

The College Airport had recently been buzzing with what seemed to be a surge in activity. Planes out of Randolph Field, which was located near San Antonio, were regularly seen landing and taking off from there. A full Review of the cadet corps was held on campus on 22 May 1941, in honor of Jesse Easterwood. Felix was outfitted in his olive drab uniform, complete with his Sam Browne leather belt, as he paraded by some of Jesse's family and other important people. There was a ceremony held right after the noon meal over at the College Airport to officially announce that the airport would now be known as the Easterwood Airport. Jesse was a former Aggie, and, like Felix, he was a member of the Infantry during his time on campus. He had quite a distinguished naval service record as a pilot during the Great War, which earned him the Navy Cross for bravery. Felix agreed that it was fitting to name the airport after Lieutenant Easterwood, and he was saddened to learn that he had died tragically in an airplane crash shortly after the end of the Great War. Felix wasn't selected to participate in the ceremony that was held at the new Easterwood Airport, so instead, he walked over to the basement of the Administration Building to pick up his copy of the 1941 Longhorn. The yearbook was the biggest and most colorful school annual ever, and Felix thought that the magnificent eagle on the front cover was just fabulous.

Final exams were quickly approaching, so Felix and Emma Jo once again agreed to cut down on the social events that were to be held during the last few weeks of May. An exception to their agreement was made on Friday, 30 May 1941. It was Felix's 21st birthday, and he was ready to party. After classes were over for the day, Felix drove over to Bryan to get Emma Jo. They then headed to Franklin's for a fine supper, and an evening of dancing out on the terrace. Buzz and Betty Lou showed up, as did Charles and many of his friends from Gainer Hall. Felix enjoyed several shots of Canadian Club whiskey, and being the responsible fellow that he was, he ate much more than he drank to help ensure that he was able to get Emma Jo home safely. It was a fabulous birthday, but the upcoming week was going to be even more exciting.

The junior prom was held on 5 Jun., and it was an event that Felix and Emma Jo had been looking forward to for several weeks. Felix got a haircut that afternoon at the Aggieland Barbershop, and after getting dressed, he headed over to Wyatt's flower shop in Bryan to get a corsage for Emma Jo. Her fancy red dress was striking, and her hair and makeup made her look even more beautiful. Emma Jo thought Felix looked quite handsome in his uniform as he escorted her to his car. They arrived at Sbisa Hall around 2130 hours after dining over at the Texas A & M Grill. Emma Jo received permission from her father to be out later than usual, and they danced for hours to the music that was provided by Lou Breeze and his Orchestra. Felix presented Emma Jo with a heart shaped locket adorned with the Texas AMC seal, which was the favor that evening. The young couple was exhausted when the music finally stopped around 0200 hours.

The Final Review of the semester took place on 6 Jun. Felix hung around for the commencement later that evening since he wanted to congratulate and say goodbye to some of his senior friends. As he watched the graduates receive their diplomas, Felix imagined himself walking across the same stage one day. After the ceremony, he had plenty of time to bid farewell to his pals and pose for a few pictures. Afterwards, most of the graduates left with their families, so Felix returned to Gainer Hall for his final night as a junior.

While lying in bed, and staring at the ceiling, Felix reflected on the quandary that he found himself in. Recruiting officers from the flying cadet program had been visiting the campus more frequently over the last few months. Felix had heard that the criteria to join the program had become more relaxed to the point that he may now have been eligible to sign up. Having a chance to finally achieve his boyhood dream of flying was certainly appealing to Felix, but he realized that this war wasn't yet America's fight. He had a good thing going with Emma Jo, and the European and Pacific theaters of war seemed ever so far away from Texas. Before turning in for the night, Felix decided that he wouldn't pursue the flying cadet program for the time being, and he planned to return to campus in the fall. Felix wanted to finish what he had started at the college, and he surely didn't want his mother to worry needlessly about his safety.

Emma Jo knew that a great deal of foreign soldiers were dying in the overseas conflicts. Felix got the impression that even though Emma Jo was patriotic, she wasn't a fan of militaristic conquests, and she assuredly disliked the killing of all the innocent civilians. Emma Jo seemed to like her Felix as a potential farmer, and he was rather doubtful that she'd like or tolerate the potential fighter pilot version of Felix. The time had come to leave Gainer Hall for the summer, so Felix packed his bags and loaded up his car. He left early on Saturday morning, and headed to Bryan to hang out with Emma Jo for the weekend. Felix was certainly sad to leave Emma Jo there in Bryan, but he promised her that he'd return for her birthday.

The roads through the Texas hill country weren't congested, and Felix made good time by arriving in San Saba about an hour or so before dusk. As he rounded the corner, and drove down Central Avenue, Felix noticed smoke rising from one of the backyards up ahead. Upon pulling up along the front of his house, Felix could see that Ernest was out back stoking the fire in preparation for what he presumed would be an evening fish fry. He noticed that Pauline's car and his grandparents' Studebaker were both parked out front. Aletha saw Felix pull up, and she hurriedly ran out the front door to greet him.

Johnnie Mae and AJ, along with young Felix Wayne, arrived a short time later. Supper was delicious, and the iced tea and lemonade really quenched his thirst. Chocolate cake, apple pie, and juicy watermelon squares filled the dessert table. There was no doubt that Felix was glad to be home for the summer. However, he was frustrated with himself when he found out that he'd failed Inorganic Chemistry 102 AGAIN, but he was satisfied that he'd passed his other classes. It seemed that Felix and chemistry were just not meant to get along. He was excited to share with everyone that he achieved an "A" in his Design and Construction class.

Felix was eager to get right to work so that he could make as much money as possible during the summer. The next morning, he reported to the bakery at 0530 hours, hoping that Mrs. Howard could use his help. She was sure glad to see him, and he worked until 0830 hours. Mrs. Howard let Felix know that she'd love to have him for the summer, and that he could work Monday through Saturday mornings. After thanking her for the opportunity, he drove over to the AAA office to meet up with Mr. Ray to discuss his work schedule there. Mr. Ray was equally glad to see Felix, and he offered him the opportunity to work 40 hours a week, Monday through Friday.

Having a few of his afternoon meals each week over at Ketchum's Kitchen was certainly a treat for Felix. Johnnie Mae owned the joint, so Felix could always eat well for a great price. Although he loved the food, he really enjoyed spending time in the cafe talking with the old-timers from town. They'd talk about the weather, football, their crops, and even world events at times. On Monday, 23 Jun., Felix happened to be enjoying his meal there in the cafe, when he overheard a lively conversation taking place. Everyone knew that Red Shaken had served proudly as a pilot in the United States Army Air Corps. He wasn't all that happy after learning that the military had made some organizational changes on 20 Jun. 1941. Red thought that it was silly that his well revered Air Corps was now going to be referred to as the United States Army Air Forces. Felix was just an impartial observer, but he too was familiar with, and preferred the Air Corps name for the aviation arm of the Army. The Air Corps had been around since 1926, dating back to when Felix was just 6 years old. Red claimed that he'd read that the change was made to provide for a much stronger role for Army aviation as the United States inched closer to becoming involved in the conflicts around the world. However, at that moment, it was just a name change to Felix, and he figured that it really didn't affect him one way other another. As Felix finished his plate of tamales, he was glad to see that Red had calmed down before it was time for him to head back to work.

As the month of June was about to end, Felix had been too busy to read the newspapers that Johnnie Mae had been saving for him at the cafe. He happened to be in the cafe one afternoon when he overheard the Winston brothers talking about how Hitler had invaded Russia. They were telling anyone who'd listen that it was just a matter of time before Hitler showed up on America's doorstep. Felix didn't know whether Hitler, or even Hirohito, would really ever invade the United States. However, he found himself at the Registrar's office inside the San Saba County Courthouse on 1 Jul. 1941. It was a little surreal for Felix as he signed his name at the bottom of the draft registration form. He had no idea of what might become of his paperwork, and of course he was unsure if he'd ever be called to serve in Uncle Sam's Army. The one thing that he did know, was that he needed to get back to work.

Felix kept his promise to Emma Jo, and he arrived in Bryan on 3 Jul. to celebrate her birthday. The couch would once again be Felix's bed for the next several days. He spent the Fourth of July at the river, picnicking with Emma Jo and a whole lot of her extended family. The food and fireworks made for a terrific way to spend the day. Felix had a full day of activities planned for Emma Jo on Saturday, 5 Jul. After breakfast, he and Emma Jo headed downtown to check out the local shops. They ended up at the Deluxe Cafe for dinner, and Felix fed the jukebox until all of Emma Jo's favorite songs had been played. Upon leaving the cafe, they headed to the nearby community park for an afternoon of live music, outdoor dancing, and a barbecue supper. Felix fetched a blanket from his car, and he placed it on a nice open area of the grass so that they could gaze at the stars later that evening. He and Emma Jo were both exhausted from all the walking and dancing, so Felix held her hand as they proceeded to their blanket to relax.

One thing led to another, and, before long, the young couple were necking on that warm summer night. As Emma Jo slowly ran her fingers up and down Felix's neck, she suddenly felt something that she'd never felt before. Feeling puzzled by what she'd found, Emma Jo said, "Felix darling, what on earth is this lump in your neck?" Felix then placed his finger on the spot where Emma Jo had found the lump, and said, "Oh, don't fret about that. I'm sure that it's probably just a boil or a pimple." Emma Jo wasn't so sure since it was hard, and a little smaller than one of Felix's marbles. She could move the lump just a bit from side to side with her finger. Felix asked her to forget about it, and they returned to necking as the band played on. Before heading home, Felix finalized plans for Emma Jo to visit him in San Saba so that they could attend the upcoming church camp meeting in August. He left her some money for a train ticket, and gave her a big hug with a kiss before leaving town.

On the ride home, Felix became a bit preoccupied with the lump in his neck. Since the lump wasn't visible on the outside of his neck, he decided to carry on with his summer plans, and he didn't consider mentioning it to his folks. Felix was very glad to see Emma Jo when she arrived at the San Saba train station on 20 Aug. 1941. After a long hug and a kiss, he tossed her bags into the back seat of his car, and they then made the short drive over to Johnnie Mae's Cafe for dinner. Felix thoroughly enjoyed showing off Emma Jo, and Johnnie Mae was very glad to see her once again. Johnnie Mae thought that she was very down to earth, and she was happy that Felix had found such a lovely young lady. After a fabulous meal and some delicious chocolate cake, Felix drove past a few of his favorite places that Emma Jo hadn't seen the last time she had visited San Saba. The heat had become nearly unbearable, so Felix decided to finish off the tour with a stop at his favorite swimming hole. The cool river water provided immediate comfort, and all the wading and splashing made for a very relaxing afternoon. Felix made sure to get back home before supper, so that they could freshen up and change their clothes. Pauline and Ted came over for supper, and they too enjoyed visiting with Emma Jo.

Later that evening, Felix and Ernest began to load all their camping equipment into the back of the family truck. The Scott family certainly knew how to camp, and they were sure to be fully prepared for the four-day Methodist Church Camp meeting. It was Thursday, 21 Aug., when Ernest led the family procession out of San Saba heading towards the campground. Felix and Ernest made quick work of setting up their heavy canvas tent complete with mosquito netting hung near the entry. Emma Jo pitched in to assist Viola with setting up the food preparation table. The icebox, cast-iron skillets, and the crate of supplies were strategically placed to ensure a smooth operation. Viola placed a durable, checkered tablecloth upon the picnic table. Meanwhile, Emma Jo filled an empty soda can with some wildflowers that she'd found nearby. She then placed them on the table, which made for a very nice centerpiece.

Viola tasked Felix with catching fish for supper each night. So, each afternoon, he and Emma Jo made their way up the creek to his secret fishing hole. Felix had a wonderful time walking, talking, and exploring with Emma Jo as they made their way back to camp each day with their bucket full of fish. He made darn sure that they didn't go anywhere near the lover's tree adorned with the initials of him and Francine. Activity around camp ran as smoothly as a well-oiled machine. Viola and Aletha cooked up the family meals, and Pauline along with Johnnie Mae helped whenever they were in camp. Ernest gathered wood, and he kept the fire going. Everyone helped with the dishes, so they could get right back to relaxing.

On Saturday night, the Scott family made hand-cranked peach ice cream. Each family in camp tried to make a different flavor, or they had some other special dessert to share. It was all very delicious, and it seemed that everyone enjoyed tasting the different treats. Emma Jo really appreciated attending the daily prayer sessions, and she felt that the Reverend had made her time spent in camp the most spiritual experience of her life. Viola was completely amazed that Emma Jo could sing all the songs without needing a hymnal. During the Sunday morning service, Viola looked over at Felix while they were singing, and she even winked while nodding in her approval of Emma Jo's ability.

After breaking down camp on Sunday afternoon, Felix made sure that he got Emma Jo back to the train station on time for her trip back to Bryan. While waiting for the train to arrive, Felix held Emma Jo's hand as they sat together on a bench near the ticket window. She had quite a smile on her face as she thanked Felix for a wonderful weekend. Emma Jo then said, "I can see why you love this little town. Your family, and the others are all just so friendly." A thought had suddenly crossed Felix's mind to get down on one knee to ask Emma

Jo to marry him, but he chose not to act upon the impulse. Felix and Emma Jo shared a nice kiss, and after a long hug, they said their goodbyes. Before she boarded the train, he reminded her that he'd be back in College Station in just a short two and a half weeks. As he drove home alone, Felix wondered if he'd later regret his decision regarding proposing to Emma Jo.

The final few weeks of the summer flew by, and just like that, Felix was back in College Station for his senior year as an Aggie. It was 11 Sep. 1941, when Felix found himself registering for classes once again. His slate of classes included: Introduction to Soils, Agricultural Chemistry, Public Speaking, Genetics, Fruits and Vegetable products, and Systematic Pomology. The semester hadn't even started, but Felix quickly became dismayed when he realized that even with six classes on his schedule, he most likely wouldn't have enough units to graduate on time with the rest of his class. Felix knew that his family would be thrilled to watch him graduate, and he was willing to give it a go and hope for the best.

With his assignment card in hand, Felix found out that he'd remain as part of the Infantry Regiment, and he'd continue to be part of "I" Company within the Third Battalion. He was still assigned to Gainer Hall, but this time he was assigned to a room on the fourth floor. Felix had become such good friends with Buzz, and he was especially excited to find out that Buzz would be his "old lady" (roommate) for the coming year. Felix hung out in his "hole" (dorm room) until Buzz showed up with all his belongings. Once the room was tidy and everything put away, the fellas headed over to the Uniform Tailor Shop.

Felix was glad that all the pieces of his new senior uniform fit perfectly. The seniors, also known as "leather legs," referred to their wool breeches as "pinks" due to their pearl grey hue, and their jackets were known as "greens" since they were green. Felix was delighted to finally get his senior boots and spurs. The clerk had to assist him with getting the boots on his feet, since they were a bit snug. The soft leather boots smelled divine, and they fit like a glove. Felix figured that by wearing them every day, he'd break them in real soon. After pulling the spurs out of the box, he noticed that they were made in England. They were made of heavy steel with fancy chain links, and Felix worked diligently to affix them to his boots. Each spur fit snuggly above the heel of the boot, and they were secured tightly with a fine leather strap than ran across the instep.

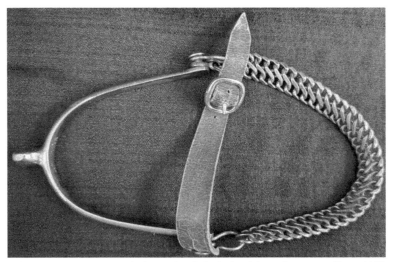

This is an actual spur that belonged to Felix during his senior year at Texas AMC.

As a senior, Felix knew that it was more important than ever to have a properly fitted uniform at all times. Everything needed to be kept clean and pressed regularly. His shoes and boots needed to be shined almost daily, and he was proud to finally sport the black and gold cord on his campaign hat that was reserved only for seniors. Now that the boys were outfitted in their new clothes along with their fancy boots with spurs, they headed over to College Night. Felix and

Buzz thought that they looked amazing in their senior uniforms as they made their way through the crowd gathered out front of the "Y." The crowd was very lively and pumped up as the yell leaders introduced a new song into the rotation, "The Twelfth Man."

Classes began on 12 Sep. 1941, which happened to fall on a Friday. With no football game scheduled that weekend, Felix and Buzz got all decked out in their fancy uniforms and headed to Bryan for the evening. Their double date started off with supper, and ended with a movie at the Queen Theater. The girls had a wonderful evening, and they thought Felix and Buzz looked rather dapper in their new senior uniforms. Before heading back to campus, Emma Jo and Betty Lou let the fellas know that their grandparents were visiting, so they'd have to find something else to do for the rest of the weekend. Felix and Buzz ended up hanging out at the "Y" for most of Sunday. While there, they had a friendly debate about which cigarettes were better. Buzz preferred Chesterfields, while Felix claimed that he liked Lucky Strikes. Felix actually preferred smoking his pipe over cigarettes since he thought it made him look more mature. The boys enjoyed playing many games of billiards and bowling on that Sunday afternoon. Before heading back to Gainer Hall, they stopped in at Casey's Confectionery for some ice cream sundaes, cigarettes, and smoking supplies. Felix picked up a few tins of Bond Street pipe tobacco, a product of Phillip Morris, a tobacco company first established in 1847. This was certainly his product of choice because Emma Jo didn't mind its fragrant aroma.

On the morning of 26 Sep., Felix combed his hair, and he made sure that his uniform was clean and pressed before heading out to have his senior picture taken. Later that evening, he and Buzz made their way over to the steps at Goodwin Hall, which was the new location for yell practice. Felix felt that it was a much better place to accommodate the growing cadet population, and the much-improved lighting made it easier to see one another. He also figured that the gravel gathering areas around Goodwin Hall would hold up much better during periods of inclement weather. This was very important to Felix, since he didn't want to get his new boots and shiny spurs all muddy.

Felix and Buzz were ecstatic to be able to finally sit in the coveted senior section at Kyle Field for the first football game of the year on 27 Sep. 1941. They found their seats in section 132, which was at the top of the stadium, just off the 50-yard line. With an all but certain victory in hand, Felix and Buzz left before the end of the fourth quarter to head over to Bryan to enjoy a nice supper at the New York Cafe with their girls. Emma Jo and Betty Lou were excited to be on their way to the first corps dance of the year in Sbisa Hall later that evening. Apparently, there was no shortage of offense when Felix found out that the Aggies had walloped the Sam Houston State Bearkats 54-0.

An Aggie ring is undoubtedly the most desirable and coveted item that any student at the college could ever want. Felix was thrilled to no end when he placed the order for his very own Aggie ring to represent that he was a member of the class of 1942. He filled out the order form after looking at the different sizes and color options. After the clerk obtained the proper size for his finger, Felix decided upon the biggest ring that they had. The old saying, "Everything is bigger in Texas," rang true for Felix that day. Many things, including Felix's new ring, suddenly cost more on 1 Oct. 1941, as a result of the new Federal Defense Tax. The new 10% tax even applied to train and movie tickets. The extra money cut into his budget, but he felt obliged to do his part to raise money for the United States Government.

Being that they were seniors, Felix and Buzz planned to attend as many football games as possible. Several games were going to be played in faraway states, so they were going to make every effort to go to the ones that were within a reasonable distance from College Station. The boys had picked up their tickets at the "Y" beforehand, and at 0530 hours on 4 Oct. 1941, they boarded the train bound for San Antonio. Upon arriving in San Antonio, they made their way over to the Gunter Hotel for yell practice. The local residents must've been impressed with the Aggies' appearance and their ability to yell loud enough to be heard many blocks away. The game was against the Texas A & I Javelinas, and Felix was certainly happy with another decisive blowout win. They returned to College Station by train very early Sunday morning, with plenty of time to go to church with Emma Jo and Betty Lou.

When Felix heard that the New York University (NYU) game was going to be played at Yankee Stadium, he considered traveling with the team to see it. He imagined himself parading through the streets of Times Square, and out to the Bronx. However, reality quickly set back in for Felix, since he knew that he didn't need any demerits for the unexcused absences. Besides, it was just too far away. Instead, he and Emma Jo attended the corps dance at Sbisa Hall on 10 Oct., which featured music by Red Nichols and his Orchestra. The following afternoon was game day, and Felix thought that it would be a perfect day for a picnic out on the college lawn. He and Buzz, along with the girls, stopped by the sandwich shop to grab food, smokes, and Cokes, before finding a shady area near the Academic Building.

The football game was broadcast over the campus loudspeaker system, and the sound quality wasn't all that bad. After another crushing victory, the group headed over to Creamland for some ice cream sundaes. Movies were no longer available at the Assembly Hall on campus, since the newly remodeled theater inside Guion Hall was now open for business. The girls were curious to see the theater, and the boys were especially eager to see the senior section, which was located in the first two rows of the balcony. The featured film was "*I Wanted Wings*," which was about three completely different recruits going through training in the Army Air Corps. Regarding the movies at Guion Hall, you had to see it or miss it, since the films didn't last very long there.

It was 15 Oct. when Felix sprinted over to the desk where they were handing out the Aggie rings that had just arrived from Jostens. He ripped opened the envelope, and let the ring drop into his left palm. Felix picked it up while admiring how shiny and heavy it was. A joyous sensation rushed through his entire body as he slid the ring onto his finger. There before him, was a beautifully engraved eagle right square on top with "A & M COLLEGE OF TEXAS" wrapped around the perimeter of the center circle. Near the bottom of the circle, it looked as if the eagle was clutching the number 42 with its talons. Felix was certainly one to follow Aggie traditions, so he made sure the 42 on the ring was pointing toward his body to signify that his time on campus wasn't yet over with. He was clearly looking forward to the Aggie ring ceremony and dance, which would be held just before graduation. Felix knew that Emma Jo would be there to turn the ring around, and he'd then be ready to make his mark on the world.

The first corps trip of the year came on Saturday, 18 Oct. After an exceptionally early breakfast, Felix and Buzz, along with most of their fellow cadets, made their way to Texas Christian University (TCU), over in Fort Worth, by train. Upon their arrival, Felix paraded through the streets with nearly his entire regiment on their way to the stadium. The Aggie offense had been limited to just 14 points, but they walked out of the stadium with another shutout against TCU. Everyone was in a good mood, and some were perhaps a little rambunctious, as they took the early morning special back to College

Station. Although feeling pretty tired, the boys received praise from Emma Jo and Betty Lou for making it home in time for church and a Sunday picnic.

The following weekend, Felix was very happy after watching his Aggies pound the Bears of Baylor at Kyle Field. The girls were sure glad to be back dancing with their boys in Sbisa Hall following the football game. Felix and Emma Jo spent Halloween evening watching *A Yank in the R.A.F.*, featuring Betty Grable at the Palace Theater. Before taking her home, they stopped at Hrdlickas's for a late supper and some lively entertainment.

Felix chose not to travel to Arkansas for the game on 1 Nov. against the Razorbacks. He had thoroughly enjoyed picnicking with Emma Jo while listening to the NYU game weeks before, and so he figured why not do it again? Felix had taken time to grab their favorite sandwiches, snacks, and drinks before driving over to Bryan to fetch Emma Jo. She thought that it was very sweet and thoughtful that Felix had planned such a special afternoon. After placing his blanket in a shady spot on the college lawn, they began to dig into the box of goodies just before the opening kickoff. It was a tough day for the offense on both sides, but the Aggies managed to pull out a win by just one touchdown.

The rodeo had rolled back into College Station, and Felix was especially eager to watch the bull riding, steer wrestling, and the calf roping events on 8 Nov. He and Emma Jo dressed up in their western wear for the events that were held on that Saturday afternoon. Felix thought Emma Jo looked really cute in her cowgirl outfit, and he could tell that she was having a good time taking it all in. He got her back home after dinner, so she could get cleaned up before the corps dance later that evening. Felix had brought his change of clothes, and he too was able to make himself look really sharp before heading back to campus. They made it to Kyle Field in time for the football game against SMU. After racking up yet another victory, they walked over to Sbisa Hall for a fabulous evening of dancing.

Felix was very excited to be going to Houston with most of his pals for the final corps trip of the year on the morning of 15 Nov. After congregating at the train station, Felix and his Infantry Regiment chanted the school fight songs as they marched their way through many of the streets in the downtown area before arriving at Rice Field. Felix and Buzz truly believed that it was their yelling ability that secured yet another win for the Aggies over the Rice Owls. The boys enjoyed the train ride home just about as much as the game itself. Cracking jokes, laughing, and storytelling was very relaxing, and it never got old.

The semester was flying by, and suddenly it was time for Thanksgiving break. The annual Thanksgiving meal was served to the cadet corps on 25 Nov., and the delicious supper consisted of turkey, rolls, dressing, green beans, and, of course, plenty of pumpkin pie. After class let out on 26 Nov., Felix and Buzz picked up the girls over in Bryan, and they returned to campus for the annual lighting of the Bonfire. The crowd was unquestionably bigger than ever before, and the pre-game yell practice was deafening to his ears. Emma Jo and Betty Lou thought the experience was exhilarating, and they were glad to be a part of it. As the Bonfire festivities wound down, the young couples made their way to Franklin's for supper, and just before 2100 hours, they attended the Bonfire dance held on campus.

Felix had watched several previous elephant walks, but this year was extra special, since he got to actively participate in it. There was no formal dress code, but the cadets were asked to at least wear their senior boots. It was about 1100 hours on 27 Nov., when Felix found himself at the flagpole with his hands on the shoulders of the man in front of him. There was a guy behind him, and so on. It appeared that most, if not all of the senior cadets were assembled to make up the wavy line. A couple of senior band members led the group as it wound its way down Military Walk to Legett Hall. The walk continued to wind past Guion Hall, before returning to the flagpole for dismissal. Felix had never laughed that much, or had so much fun. It was certainly a most memorable event for the seniors of Texas AMC.

The Aggies had already wrapped up another Southwest Conference Championship, even before the kickoff against the Texas Longhorns on 27 Nov. 1941 at Kyle Field. It had been almost a year to the day since the Aggies had lost their only game of the 1940 season to the Longhorns. The Aggie nation, made up of alumni and the current cadet corps, was eager to get payback for that devastating loss. The opening kickoff was at 1400 hours, and the Aggies were the consensus favorite to win. Felix figured that Pauline and Ted were surely listening to the game on the radio back home in San Saba before they'd be heading over to the Scott home for Thanksgiving Day supper. The Aggie offense struggled mightily throughout the game, and they couldn't even muster a single field goal. Maybe the players were too cocky, or felt too much pressure on their shoulders, or perhaps they were just not up for the challenge. Nobody could really figure out how it had happened, but the Aggies were blanked AGAIN! They were handed yet another loss to the Longhorns, which unfortunately ended their shot at a perfect season. The loss to the Longhorns was much more than a loss to Felix, since he realized that this was more than likely the last home game that he'd go to as a student while at Texas AMC. Felix reminisced about the last four Aggie football seasons as he drove home to San Saba after the game. It was late, but Viola had saved him a plate full of food from Thanksgiving supper. Before going to bed, Felix sat out in the living room until nearly midnight catching up with Aletha,

Pauline and Ted, and his folks. There was plenty of spirited conversation when discussing the events of the game with everyone.

Thanksgiving break was over, and Felix returned to campus on 1 Dec. 1941. While he'd been home, Felix discussed the state of world events with his father. The United States had stopped shipping oil to Japan during 1941, and the ongoing sanctions that had been placed upon the Japanese seemed to only escalate tensions between the two countries. Ernest read the paper regularly, and he was concerned about the breakdown in diplomatic negotiations with Japan as the month of November ended. Ernest and Viola were very glad that Felix was returning to college instead of reporting to an Army base in some godforsaken part of the world. They prayed every night for peace in the world, and for the safety of their family.

The final football game of the regular season was nowhere near College Station, or even Texas for that matter. The Aggies were set to face off against the Cougars of Washington State on 6 Dec. 1941. The weather was a bit too chilly to sit out on the college lawn for the radio broadcast, so Felix and Buzz opted to listen to the game while playing billiards and dominoes inside the "Y." The game was a nail-biter, but the Aggies defense stopped the Cougars at every turn, which resulted in a nice bounce back win for the team. Felix, and all other Americans went to bed normally that evening. When they awoke on 7 Dec. 1941, it was to be a day unlike any other. Their lives were about to be changed forever.

It was just after 1300 hours when Felix and his buddies noticed senior officers scurrying about uncharacteristically. They could tell that something was just not right, and their suspicions were quickly confirmed when a First Sergeant ran by and said that Pearl Harbor had been attacked. Felix just couldn't believe what he was hearing. He and Buzz ran to the "Y" in order to listen to the radio updates, and to get the latest details coming in from Hawaii. Apparently, the reports had suggested that Japan had preemptively bombed Pearl Harbor as a way to weaken or cripple the Pacific Fleet. The radio broadcaster presumed that Japan was trying to prevent the United States from interfering with its planned aggression in Asia, and in the Pacific as well. Reports kept coming in as Felix and the other cadets gathered around the radio with trepidation. Many of the young men around Felix were in shock, and thus, they were very quiet. However, others were already beginning to curse, and direct insults towards the Japanese nation.

The radio broadcaster emphatically stated that this had been a devastating blow to the men, women, and equipment there in Pearl Harbor. The Japanese had somehow pulled off the sneak attack, and they seemed successful in causing immense damage. Casualty reports kept changing from the hundreds, to perhaps thousands feared dead with many more wounded. Many ships and planes had been destroyed, damaged, or sunk. Felix and Buzz remained at the "Y" until the evening meal. They could hear most of the conversations around them while at supper, and they all seemed to center around what was going to happen next, and how this dastardly event might affect them.

It was around 1130 hours on the morning of 8 Dec, when Felix was informed that President Franklin Delano Roosevelt would be addressing the nation in front of Congress. The broadcast was played over the loudspeakers on campus, and the entire cadet corps listened attentively. The President provided a summary of the horrific events that took place the day before. It was also the first time that Felix had heard that Japan had attacked several other locations in various parts of the world on 7 and 8 Dec. Shortly after the President's speech, the United States Congress officially declared war on the empire of Japan.

The next morning, Felix read the statement from President Walton of the college, which was presented in the 9 Dec. edition of *The Battalion*. He essentially encouraged the student body to continue onward with their studies, but to be ready to serve if called upon. The consensus among Felix and his buddies was that they'd be willing to fight, when and if they were called to serve their country. Everyone was also in agreement that they'd be honored to follow in the footsteps of those who had fought before them, and to uphold the tradition of the "fighting Texan." After the events of Pearl Harbor, it seemed like the cadets on campus marched more forthrightly, shot a bit straighter, trained even harder, and yelled a lot louder.

World events were suddenly changing day by day, and sometimes, it seemed as if it were minute by minute. A few days after the United States had declared war on Japan, Germany and Italy in turn declared war on the United States. The United States could no longer remain on the sidelines of the war that was raging on in Europe, so, on that very same day of 11 Dec. 1941, the United States officially declared war on Germany. Alarmingly, Americans now had to worry about enemies off both the East and West Coasts of the United States. World War II was now officially in full swing, and Felix was uncertain of his path moving forward.

Despite the raging military conflicts around the world, the staff at Texas AMC made every effort to make day to day life go on as it normally would. However, it was clearly evident that things weren't anywhere near normal for the cadet corps on campus, but at least the daily routine of classes and drills continued on for Felix and his buddies. Felix was already having a difficult time with his studies before the attack on Pearl Harbor. After the United States entered into World War II, he had an even more challenging time with studying and concentrating, although he had certainly not lost his passion for watching movies. Feeling like they needed a diversion from the chaos unfolding around the world, Felix and Buzz made their way to Guion Hall on the evening of 11 Dec. to see *Devil Dogs of the Air*. The film featured a young man and his adventures as he made his way through the United States Marine Corps flying school. Although it was just a brief respite, the boys really did enjoy the movie. The evening ended on a somber note with a Silver Taps ceremony. A Silver Taps program was held on campus any time that an Aggie passed away while he was currently enrolled at the college. The solemn event was for a cadet who lived in Felix's dorm. Felix didn't know the young man very well, but he'd been killed in a car accident on the very same road that Felix would take on the way over to Bryan. Maybe it was just the timing, but to Felix, it was all a bit eerie.

Felix was very excited when "Keep 'em Flying" week kicked off on campus on 14 Dec. During the festivities, there were many presentations and discussions pertaining to the role of the United States Army Air Forces in the theaters of war around the world. Felix liked what he'd heard, and he began to seriously revisit his dream of becoming a military pilot. He felt that school and his venture of being a crop duster might just have to wait, as it seemed likely that Uncle Sam would be calling upon him to fulfill his patriotic duty in the near future. There was a time when Felix shared Emma Jo's sentiment about not wanting to fight the war that was tearing across Europe and in the Pacific. His opinion had promptly changed, though, after the heinous attack on Pearl Harbor. After the events of the week had ended, Felix drove to Bryan for an evening out with Emma Jo. Trying to improve his spirits, and maybe to even laugh a little, they saw the movie premiere of the comedy *Keep 'em Flying*, featuring Abbott and Costello.

After class on 19 Dec., Felix headed over to Emma Jo's for the night before heading back to San Saba for the Christmas recess.

While driving to her house, Felix tried to come up with an excuse to avoid spending the night. He really didn't feel much like celebrating with so many things going on in his life, and in the world, at that very moment. Felix was a bit nervous and pre-occupied with the possibility that he might be needed to go and fight in the war. He really didn't want to get drafted into an Infantry Division within the Army or Marine Corps. Felix wanted to be in control of his own destiny, and he knew that hand to hand fighting with knives, guns, and grenades would be frightening. Felix had heard that if he volunteered to join the military, he might have the ability to pick his desired branch of service. He envisioned himself going through flight training, and he also imagined what it would be like to be in the cockpit of a fighter plane for the USAAF. However, these visions were clouding his ability to live in the present, and then, there was the issue with his grades. There was no hiding his grades from his folks, since the registrar had already mailed the mid-semester report to his home. Felix had recently met with the school counselors, and the thought of academic probation perturbed him. He realized that he certainly wouldn't have enough credits to graduate with the rest of his class with another poor performance for the semester. Felix hadn't shared the whole picture with Emma Jo in regard to his grades. This situation embarrassed him immensely, and he felt that Emma Jo, and perhaps, even his family, would see him as a failure if he dropped out of school. Additionally, there was the lump in his neck, which continued to grow unabated. Needless to say, Felix's mind was filled with unpleasant thoughts, and he felt overwhelmed trying to deal with it all.

When Felix arrived at Emma Jo's, he presented her with her Christmas gift, but he didn't seem to care whether she opened it right then or not. While staying at their home, he was considerate and friendly; however, Emma Jo could tell that something was bothering him. Felix didn't show much affection towards Emma Jo while visiting, and she noticed that his attitude, and his overall demeanor, had changed. He was no longer her funny and happy-go-lucky Felix. He seemed to have taken on a new sense of bravado, and he kept saying that he was going to make those "Jap bastards" pay for what they'd done. Emma Jo knew that Felix was very much distracted by the state of the world's affairs. She felt sad and helpless that Felix had no idea what the future held for him, and she wondered how all of this might affect their relationship. Felix was glad to be on winter recess, but he was most eager to get back to San Saba to discuss the events that had happened over the last few weeks with his father. Therefore, early the next morning, Felix gave Emma Jo a big hug, and a kiss on the forehead, and then he headed home to San Saba.

As Felix drove through San Saba on the way to his home, he didn't notice anything different now that the country was at war. People were out walking around going about their business, and businesses were decorated for Christmas. When Felix pulled up into his driveway, Viola ran out of the front door to greet him with a great big ol' hug. Ernest had also come outside to welcome Felix home, and he helped him carry his bags inside the house. He didn't feel like working over the break, so he chose not to reach out to Mrs. Howard or Mr. Ray while home. Aletha arrived home on Christmas Eve from nursing school, and Felix was glad that the family could all be together for Christmas. Viola had fixed a fine Christmas supper, and the table was full of food that Johnnie Mae, Pauline, and his grandparents had brought. Nobody discussed the war during supper, since they knew that Viola wouldn't think that it was proper. Instead, the conversations at the table revolved around the family, school life, church, friends, and, of course, the successful pecan crops.

After supper, Felix, Ernest, AJ, Ted, Pa, Chauncey, and the rest of the menfolk all went out to the front porch to talk while the girls chatted in the living room. As Felix sat on the concrete steps, he lit his pipe, and Ted smoked a cigarette. Felix then asked the group if anyone thought that the Japanese or Germans would bring the war to the United States directly. The overall opinion among the men was that America would need to bring the fight to the enemy, rather than worry about the war being fought here in America. Everyone agreed that they felt safe in Texas, and Chauncey let it be known that he planned to join the Marines right after graduating from high school. To the surprise of some, Felix dropped a few hints that he might opt to pursue his passion to become a pilot in the USAAF. There was plenty of patriotism, love, respect, and support for one another on the porch that night. There was also a lot of fear and anxiety instilled into the parents and grandparents and siblings that evening.

New Year's Eve was spent out at the River Bend farm with Ma and Pa. Felix felt that the family celebration was somewhat subdued, and it just didn't seem as jovial as in years past. It was as if a big weight had been placed on the shoulders of many that were there. The gathering was just as large as usual, and there was plenty of room for anyone who wanted to stay overnight. Felix decided to spend the night in front of the fireplace on one of Ma's fabulous featherbeds that sat upon a large bear skin rug. While lying in their beds, he and Chauncey stayed up well into the early morning hours discussing among themselves their plans for future military service. After breakfast, Felix said his goodbyes, and he headed over to Pauline and Ted's place to listen with them on their radio to the Aggies in their return trip to the Cotton Bowl. Felix was somewhat sad that he wasn't going to be attending the game with Buzz, but smoking his pipe, drinking his whiskey, hanging out with his family, and eating all of the great food more than made up for not being there in person. Felix's beloved Aggies were facing off against the Crimson Tide of Alabama on New Year's day 1942. He could only imagine all of the cadets in the stadium yelling for the team over there in Dallas.

Pauline was a big fan, and she could be very loud and demonstrative after each Aggie touchdown. It seemed as if the game had gotten out of hand for the Aggies, being as that they were down by more than three touchdowns. However, the Aggie offense began to come alive late in the fourth quarter, and they rallied by scoring two touchdowns to make for an exciting finish. The Aggies fought hard until the very end, but it just wasn't enough, and they ultimately lost to Alabama by 8 points. Pauline was infuriated with the ridiculous amount of Aggie turnovers, and Felix felt that it was a disappointing end to the season. Nevertheless, Felix really enjoyed listening to the game with his sister and Ted, and he hoped that 1942 would be a great year.

Felix headed back to school on 4 Jan. 1942, ready to resume classes at Texas AMC the following morning. Aletha returned to her nursing dormitory in Temple as well, and the Scott household was rather quiet once again. Felix headed to Bryan on Sunday, 11 Jan. to meet up with Emma Jo in order to attend church with her and her family. He arrived early at the church so that he could have an opportunity to catch up on things with Emma Jo. She could tell that Felix was more relaxed, but she felt that he still seemed bothered by the mounting pressures weighing upon him. After church, Felix and Emma Jo went back to her place for a nice dinner. They listened to music, and they enjoyed sitting outside for a bit in order to discuss their plans for the following weekend. On Saturday, 17 Jan. Felix and Emma Jo saw the afternoon viewing of *Flying Blind* at Guion Hall. As they exited the building, he had a nagging feeling that this just might've been the last movie that he'd ever see on campus. They made their way over to

Hrdlicka's for supper, and for an evening of dancing. The food was terrific as usual, but the mood among the crowd was just not as lively as on previous occasions. After a while, Felix just didn't feel like dancing anymore. As they sat at their table, he and Emma Jo ended up talking for more than an hour while sharing a few drinks. Rather than struggling to continue the conversation, Felix ended up taking Emma Jo home. On the way back to College Station, he wondered if she'd even want to go out with him on another date. It seemed as though Felix's world was beginning to crumble all around him.

The powers that be at the college abruptly decided to cancel final exams, and they declared that 22 Jan. would be the last day of the term. A decision had also been made to move classroom instruction to a trimester schedule, which was to be effective on 26 Jan. 1942. The goal was to speed up the education process so that the college could graduate as many qualified cadets as possible before they might be called to duty. In order to come to grips with all of the changes going on in his life, Felix decided to take a walk around the campus on the morning of 22 Jan. He made his way past Kyle Field, the Administration Building, the Sully Ross statue, and he ended up in front of the Registrar's office. Outfitted in his senior boots, and wearing his Aggie ring, Felix looked sharp as he sat outside by himself on a concrete bench. He remained there for more than an hour pondering his options, and thinking about what he should do next. The extra burden of attending school while America was at war had become just too much to bear. Felix abruptly stood up, and he walked steadfastly into the office after deciding that it would be best for him to withdraw from school, rather than face the possibility of being kicked out.

Felix walked right up to the clerk and expressed his desire to withdraw from the college. The clerk then asked, "May I inquire as to why you are wanting to withdraw from school?" Felix emphatically replied, "There are many reasons, but I'm going to join the United States Army Air Forces so that I can become a pilot, and do my part to help win this goddamn war!" The clerk understood, and she mentioned to him that there had been many other cadets who had submitted their request to withdraw earlier that day as well. Felix dejectedly returned to Gainer Hall, and he made his way up to the fourth floor for the final time. Buzz happened to be in the room, and Felix began to explain what he'd just done. Buzz wasn't really all that surprised with his best friend's decision, and he was very supportive as they sat, talked, and packed up all of Felix's things. Before leaving the room, Felix looked out the window for one last time. They had a great view of the large quad that was surrounded by several of the other dormitories. Felix saw plenty of cadets normally going about their day, and he wondered what the rest of his day would entail. He said goodbye to the men on his floor, and then Buzz helped carry some of Felix's things out to the parking lot. After getting everything loaded into his car, Felix said so long to Buzz, while firmly shaking his hand. Felix then said, "You're such a great friend, and I hope our paths might cross again one day, ol' buddy." They vowed to stay in touch, and they wished each other good luck with whatever might come their way next.

Felix felt a little weird, but he was content with his decision as he headed to Bryan to see Emma Jo. As he pulled up in front of her home, he kind of wondered if he'd ever return to either city again. Emma Jo was quite surprised to see Felix standing on her porch when she answered the door. He asked her to grab her coat, so that they could go on a walk to talk about the important decision that he'd just made. As they walked up the street holding hands, Felix finally expressed his true feelings about wanting to become a pilot with the USAAF. He said, "Babe, I'm just not cut out to be a farmer. I've been dreaming about this day since I was a little boy. I firmly believe that it is my destiny, and my duty to serve our country. The time is right, and I'm ready to fight." Felix then expressed his sincere love for Emma Jo by looking directly into her eyes as he let her know how much he appreciated being with her during his time at the college. Felix began to cry as he recounted the fabulous dances, picnics, and countless dates that they'd been on together. He could see that Emma Jo was becoming more uncomfortable with the conversation when he mentioned that he planned to enlist as soon as possible.

Emma Jo sort of smiled when Felix mentioned that he believed that the Air Corps preferred unmarried men for those soldiers serving as pilots. Felix suddenly stopped walking, and said, "It isn't fair for you to have to wait around to see if and when I'll ever return from what could be a long war ahead. You'll make a fine wife to someone very special, and you'll be a terrific mother. Pilots live on the edge, and I don't want to worry about making you a widow if we were to get married down the road." For a moment, Emma Jo wondered what a future could've been like with Felix if it weren't for the war. She continued to cry as she listened to Felix carry on with expressing his preference for the war over her. Finally, they turned back towards her home making light conversation along the way. Felix could see that Emma Jo was disappointed when she heard that he'd dropped out of school. He knew that she had surely loved him and all that they'd done together there at Texas AMC. Upon returning to the porch, Felix gave Emma Jo a hug, and he placed a kiss directly on her forehead. After saying, "Goodbye, my dear," he turned around, and began walking slowly to his car with his head buried into his chest. He didn't look back as he heard Emma Jo crying louder as she ran into the house, slamming the door in the process. Felix felt terrible about what had just happened between him and Emma Jo. He'd been in

Emma Jo's shoes when Francine had sort of broken things off with him. Felix realized that it was certainly not any easier being the one leading the breakup conversation.

Felix was rather despondent on the drive back to San Saba. Tears freely ran down his face, which at times made it hard to see the road. All of the good times reverberated through his head as he recalled the wonderful experiences that he'd had during his three and a half years at the college. Felix truly believed that the friendships he'd forged would last a lifetime. It saddened him to think that many of his friends and fellow cadets would find their way into the war. Even worse, he knew that dozens, maybe even hundreds of them, would perish while serving. Although he was no longer a student, Felix knew that he'd be an Aggie for life. He also knew that he'd have a lot of explaining to do when he got home with all of his belongings.

When Felix pulled up in front of his house late that afternoon, he could see his mother sitting on the porch with a very puzzled look on her face. Viola could see that Felix's car was loaded to the hilt, so she spit out her snuff into the tin can beside her rocking chair, and headed down the steps. After getting out of his car, Felix gave her a big hug, and he asked that she come inside with him so that he could talk to her and Ernest about something very important to him. After sitting down at the kitchen table, Felix explained that he ended the semester by failing three of his classes, and he had barely passed two others. He had managed to get a B in Systematic Pomology, but in the end, it was just not enough. He told his parents that it would've taken him at least two to three more trimesters to gather enough units to graduate. Felix then slammed his fist onto the table, and he adamantly insisted that it was his time to fight, and that he didn't want to wait any longer. By the expressions on their faces, he could tell that they were disappointed that he hadn't finished his path to graduation.

Ernest and Viola surely had some concerns about Felix joining the military, but they most assuredly said that they'd be supportive of his decision. They also believed in Felix's ability, determination, and grit; and they, therefore, encouraged him to pursue his dream to become a fighter pilot.

Mack was still smiling when he reached the last page of his notes, and he was very glad to see that no one had fallen asleep. After the hours-long story telling session, he stood up to stretch, and he poured himself a glass of lemonade. Sue Ann looked sad as she said, "I think that it's just terrible that Felix and Emma Jo didn't end up getting married. To lose someone so dear, and to miss out on the remainder of his senior year at Texas AMC is just plain heart breaking." Uncle Bruce followed with, "I have a lot of respect for Felix, and I cannot imagine having to make such a difficult choice between love and country. I think that it's admirable and honorable that he chose to serve our country at such a young age." Sam also stood up, and he gave Mack a pat on his back. He then said, "I'm so proud of you and your storytelling skills. It was as if we were present in the moment as Felix made his way through his time at the Agricultural and Mechanical College of Texas. The knowledge and details that you were able to grab from his journal in such a short time is simply amazing." Frank got up off the couch, and said, "The images that you painted sure took me down memory lane. Many of the places and buildings that you mentioned are still there on campus. Felix had such a long life ahead of him, and had it not been for that damn war, he just might've been a successful crop duster over there in San Saba County."

CHAPTER 9

Sidelined in San Saba

Mack's Uncle Bruce could BBQ with the best of them, and the fine spread of hamburgers, hot dogs, and even a few sausage links, made for a delicious dinner. After everyone had finished their meal on the back patio, Sue Ann brought out some homemade sugar cookies and pecan brownies for dessert. In between bites of his cookie, Sam stated, "I cannot wait to hear about Felix's pilot training. That must've been such a difficult, yet rewarding and exciting time for him." With that, everyone took their plates to the kitchen, and they then returned to the den for Mack's final presentation covering the last two and a half years of Felix Scott's life. After pulling up some pictures on his phone, and having gathered his detailed notes, Mack began to speak.

    Viola had listened attentively to everything that Felix had to say regarding dropping out of school. She just couldn't believe it when Felix dropped the additional bombshell on them by mentioning that he'd also broken off his relationship with Emma Jo. Viola really adored Emma Jo, and she was very sad and disappointed that Felix had decided to let her go. After Felix had finished explaining all that had gone on in Bryan, and also in College Station, Viola was left completely dumbfounded, and perhaps, she was even in shock. In order to help her cope with the unsettling news, she took to the phone before supper to share the news with her daughters, sisters, and parents. Figuring that his mother would be on the phone for a spell, Felix headed out to the garage to find his father working on one of his many projects. He felt that this would be a much-welcomed diversion due to all of the dreadful things that had overwhelmed him throughout that day. Once outside, he couldn't help but notice the newly built pen containing two small hogs. He inquisitively asked his father, "Where did these guys come from?" Ernest jokingly replied, "Meet Curly and Shirley. I got 'em for a good price over at the livestock auction. I plan to use them as breeding hogs for our homegrown source of bacon, ham, and pork chops." Felix patted his father on the back, and said, "Sounds great, Pop."

Once Viola had finished with her phone calls, she summoned the men to supper. Felix momentarily retreated to his bedroom to change out of his college uniform for the final time. He was glum and dispirited as he hung his wool coat, laden with his Texas AMC paraphernalia, up in his closet. As he left his bedroom, he envisioned himself in a different, but similar uniform, emblazoned with the patches and pins of the United States Army Air Forces. Felix took a seat in the wooden chair located at his usual spot at the kitchen table. The casual supper conversation quickly became concerning when Viola asked, "Felix darling, what is that lump on your neck? Did you get stung by a bee?" Felix suddenly realized that he no longer had the collared shirt on that had prevented his parents from noticing the lump earlier that evening. He replied, "Oh, Mother, it's nothing. I first noticed it over the summer. The lump just recently became red, and it seems to have grown larger over the last few weeks." Viola was clearly concerned about the little bugaboo, so she immediately got up from her chair, and proceeded to the other side of the table. As Viola placed her finger on the lump, she then said, "Land sakes, son, let me get a good look at ya."

Ernest also looked at the lump on Felix's neck, and the consensus was that he should see a doctor right away. Viola took Felix to Dr. Frederick Farley's office early the next morning there in San Saba. Dr. Farley had been the family doctor for quite some time, and he was glad to see Felix. He took a few moments to catch up on the time that Felix had spent while he was away in College Station. Felix provided him with all of the details stemming from his poisoning accident while at Texas AMC. Dr. Farley then inspected the lump on Felix's neck. Felix could sense that the diagnosis was unsettling, and it was worrisome to his mother. Dr. Farley recommended that they visit a specialist in Houston for a further opinion. He told the Scotts that there had been new advances, and that there were improved options for treating matters like this there. Viola and Felix thanked Dr. Farley for his time, and they left with the phone number for Dr. Lundgren's office in Houston.

Felix was on the phone with Dr. Lundgren's office as soon as they got home. They happened to have an opening on Monday, 26 Jan. 1942, so he booked the appointment. Felix rode out to Bend on Sunday morning with his parents in order to attend church service with Ma and Pa. Viola figured that God would listen to a church full of folks praying for Felix's quick recovery. Right after the conclusion of the service, everyone headed to the River Bend farm for sandwiches and desserts. Ma prepared some extra sandwiches for Viola and Felix to take on their journey. After getting good luck wishes from everyone, Ernest drove them to the train station in San Saba so that they could make the afternoon train bound for Houston.

It had been a very long day for Felix and Viola. They were thankful that they'd been able to get an appointment to see a doctor in Houston so quickly, and were glad that they were able to check into a hotel near the doctor's office. The Scotts met with Dr. Lundgren on Monday morning as planned, and Viola felt that he wasn't only knowledgeable, but also capable of dealing with Felix's issue. After the exam, Dr. Lundgren suggested that the lump should be removed as soon as possible to prevent it from spreading. Felix was eager to get rid of the pesky lump so that he could get on with his plan to enlist in the Army Air Forces. Luckily, Felix was able to get a surgical appointment for the following morning, and therefore the Scotts didn't mind staying in Houston for an additional night. Viola prayed the entire time that it took for Dr. Lundgren to remove the lump. Afterwards, he met with Felix and Viola to discuss the details of the procedure, and, for the first time, Dr. Lundgren referred to the lump as a tumor. This language stunned Viola, and Felix was left wondering what would happen next. Dr. Lundgren advised them not to worry, since he believed that he was able to remove the entire tumor with no visible concerns that it had spread. The incision was relatively small, and Felix was glad to hear that it would heal up nicely. Dr. Lundgren told them to return home, and that he'd mail the results of the biopsy as soon as it came back from the lab.

It was a long two weeks before Dr. Lundgren's letter arrived. Felix ripped open the envelope with a great deal of anticipation, hoping for good news. Admittedly, there was some trepidation as he began to read the letter. Felix really didn't know what all of the medical mumbo-jumbo meant when he read that the tumor was benign, rather than malignant. The final paragraph of the letter seemed to calm his nerves when Dr. Lundgren mentioned, "I hope this good news finds you well, and I'd like to see you for a follow up appointment in three months."

Felix felt physically well, and he trusted Dr. Lundgren's prognosis that he'd recover relatively soon. He knew that he couldn't just waltz on down to the Aviation Cadet Examining Board office to volunteer for pilot training, since he knew that there would be a thorough physical. Felix was suddenly in a position where he had lots of time on his hands. Therefore, he ventured on down to the AAA office to meet up with Mr. Ray. Felix met with him for about half an hour as he took some time to explain that he'd left the college, the matter with the tumor, and his plan to enlist in the Army Air Forces at some point. Mr. Ray already knew that Felix was a hard worker, and he hired him on the spot. During his afternoon break, Felix drove over to Mrs. Howard's bakery, which was fairly close by. She was pleasantly surprised to see Felix, and he filled her in with all that was going on in his life. She told him that she had plenty of help on the weekends, but she could use him Monday through Friday with the same hours that he'd worked the previous summer. Felix gladly accepted the offer, and he thanked her for her time and generosity.

Felix realized the importance of remaining physically capable and strong to help ensure that he'd do well, if and when he ever made it to the Aviation Cadet Examining Board office. He continued with the daily physical training regimen that had become such a huge part of his life as an Aggie. Felix was an early riser, and he began each morning with a run while it was still dark outside. After running swiftly over to the courthouse, he'd then sprint up the steps to his left. After touching the thick wooden doors, Felix ran down the other set of steps towards home. He figured that he was doing well if he completed the nearly one mile run in six minutes or less. Felix was no longer satisfied with mediocrity, and he worked hard to achieve quicker times each week. He'd occasionally get chased by a neighborhood dog, which certainly helped him run a little faster. Felix repeated this run to the courthouse every evening after supper. On the return trip home, Felix would often stop at Johnnie Mae's cafe to pick up a bag of food scraps for Curly and Shirley.

Running sure helped with Felix's endurance and stamina, and he'd often do dozens of push-ups while on break at work. Although Felix was no longer a little boy, he certainly still enjoyed climbing trees. Nearly every evening before supper, Viola would look out her kitchen window to see Felix out back making his way up one of the pecan or live oak trees. Viola thought that he looked like a monkey, minus the tail, as he scurried about in the trees. He'd stop his climb at certain branches to perform a set of chin-ups. Before bed, he completed countless sit-ups on the living room floor while having a conversation with his folks. Felix felt good, both emotionally and physically.

Valentine's Day fell on a Saturday in 1942, and Felix found himself to be without a girlfriend. He remembered back to just one year prior, when things were swell with him and Emma Jo. Feeling a bit down, Felix figured that a trip to Bend to visit Ma and Pa would lift his spirits. He knew that Polly Ann's good cooking, and W. J.'s wisdom would brighten his day. Felix realized that he couldn't do much else to prepare himself to fly a plane, but he could continue to improve on his skills as a marksman. Felix could shoot well, and he knew that firing a rifle and a pistol would be part of any basic training program.

Felix was very glad to see Chauncey standing on the porch as he stepped out from his car. Chauncey was like the little brother that Felix never had, and they always enjoyed palling around together. He was also happy to see Ma and Pa again, and he certainly spent no time in filling them in about his physical training, work back in San Saba, and, of course, about his trip to Houston. During their conversation, Felix reminisced about the times that he and Chauncey had spent shooting squirrels and the caps off of bottles with their .22 caliber rifles. Pa was witty, and he could be a bit sarcastic when given an opportunity. He said, "Boy, the army ain't gonna teach you to shoot .22s." Felix laughed, and replied, "I've shot many different guns while at college, and I just need to keep my skills up by practicing." Chauncey continued to insist that he was going to join the Marines right after high school, so, he too, thought that shooting practice would be beneficial as well.

With that, Pa asked the young men to accompany him to one of the spare bedrooms. There in the closet, were cases upon cases of pistol and rifle ammunition stacked neatly. Pa then said, "Some things were really hard to come by during the last war. With all that has been going on in the world over the last few years, I decided that I needed to stock up, and that's what I did." Felix was amazed at the amount of ammunition, and he was equally impressed with the number of hunting rifles and pistols that were neatly arranged in the closet. Felix jokingly said, "Are you planning on defending all of San Saba County in the event that the Japs or Nazis attack us?" Pa then smiled, and said, "You boys can practice and shoot as much as you want. All that I ask is that you remember to make every shot count as if your life depended on it." Words of wisdom for sure. Felix and Chauncey spent the next several hours that day honing their skills, and they agreed that they'd do this every Saturday for the foreseeable future.

Felix was running into town one evening in early March when he ran into Mr. Livingston as he was coming out of his general store. It had been quite some time since Felix had been inside the store. After chitchatting for a bit, Mr. Livingston said, "I'm plum out of arrowheads, and I'm really low on my other Indian edged weapons." Felix nodded his head, and said, "It has been a spell since I've hunted any, although I still have a fair amount in my personal collection." Mr. Livingston asked, "Would you be interested in selling any of your items?" Felix knew that he had the upper hand since he had many things that Mr. Livingston wanted, and they agreed to meet the following evening after work. Felix paired his collection down to just two of the best arrowheads of each different style and tribe. He also kept the finest examples of the other weapons in his collection. Felix walked into the general store the following evening as planned, and he walked out with a nice wad of cash in his pocket.

It was St. Patrick's Day in 1942 when Felix happened to be driving by one of the local used car lots in town, and it happened that a royal blue Chevy pickup with red and white balloons attached to it caught his eye. He immediately slammed on the brakes, and made the quickest U-turn anyone in San Saba had ever seen. Felix thought that it was the most patriotic display he'd seen since he'd returned home from College Station. He also knew he'd fallen in love with the good-looking blue truck, and he was going to have to own this little gem.

Felix's sister, Johnnie Mae, and her husband, AJ, had purchased a 1941 Chevrolet truck when it had first become available. Felix envied their truck, and he vowed that he'd have one of his very own one day. He'd been working about 55 hours a week, and with the sale of his Native American items, Felix had amassed his own little pot of gold. He pulled out $200.00 from his pocket, and he asked the salesman to hold the truck until he could return with a check for the balance the following day. The salesman agreed to hold the truck until Felix returned, and before he left, Felix asked the salesman if he knew any history on the 1941 pickup. The salesman replied, "It belonged to an Army captain who was stationed over at Fort Hood. He bought it new last year, before we got ourselves into this war. The poor fella ended up taking a bullet last month while he was overseas, and his widow moved back here to live with her parents." Felix was sad to hear about the captain's death, but he was hoping that the truck would now be his to treasure for years to come. He felt that it was rather fitting that he'd end up with the truck, and he was eager to make his own memories in it.

Felix raced home, eager to tell everyone about his new purchase. Over supper, he provided all the details, and he then called Pa before going out for his evening run. In order to get the loan needed for the balance of the truck, Felix had hatched a plan for Ernest and Pa to meet him at the bank around 1600 hours the following day. Felix was so excited; he could hardly sleep. When he arrived at the AAA office, Felix asked Mr. Ray if he could leave a little early that day. It was evident that Felix was distracted by the events planned for that afternoon, so Mr. Ray agreed to let Felix leave early.

As planned, Ernest and Pa were waiting out front of the San Saba National Bank when Felix pulled up. It didn't take long before Felix found himself at Murphy Langdon's desk to discuss his need for the $600 loan. Mr. Langdon felt good with Felix's employment there in town, but he had some concerns when Felix mentioned that he planned to enter the service. Ernest and Pa had been listening attentively to the conversation, and Pa could sense that Mr. Langdon was on the fence regarding the loan approval. Pa suddenly pounded his fist on the desk, and said, "Come on Murph, my grandson is gonna go fight the Japs. He'll be making $75 a month during training as an aviation cadet, and he'll earn even more after receiving his wings. You know me, and I'll guarantee the loan if something were to happen to Felix." Mr. Langdon must've been convinced or scared, but either way, Felix walked out of the bank with the loan approval, and a check in hand. Felix quickly drove over to his house to drop off his Ford, and he then hopped into the back seat of Pa's Studebaker. The trio headed directly to the dealership, and it wasn't long before Felix made his way off the lot after Ernest and Pa had given their approvals, blessings, and even a few high fives.

It was now early April in 1942, and Felix was glad that his incision had healed up well. He'd made arrangements with his employers to take 13 Apr. off, so that he could drive to Houston to enlist in the Army Air Forces at the Aviation Cadet Examining Board office. Felix was hoping that he'd meet the qualifications, and pass any physical that they'd perform. He could totally see himself heading down the highway to Houston in his shiny pickup, but more importantly, he could feel his path to becoming a pilot inching closer towards reality. Felix figured that his life was about to change, but he was certainly not prepared to deal with what was to come his way on 11 Apr. 1942.

After waking up on that Saturday morning, Felix was making preparations for his visit to see Chauncey over in Bend. As he was showering, he unwittingly felt a lump on the upper part of his neck, right underneath the jawbone. The previous lump was on the same side, but about two inches lower. It sure felt eerily similar, and Felix was worried. He then walked out into the kitchen, visibly shaken by his discovery. Felix asked Viola to take a look at it, and she started to cry. Coincidentally, Felix had his three month check up with Dr. Lundgren prescheduled for 20 Apr. He vowed that he'd do his best to deal with this lump as soon as possible, so he reached out to Dr. Lundgren via the telephone on 13 Apr. to explain what he'd discovered. The appointment was promptly changed from a checkup to a surgical appointment in order for the lump to be removed expeditiously. Felix took the setback in stride, and he intended to remain positive.

Felix arrived early at Dr. Lundgren's office on 20 Apr. so that the lump could be examined. Dr. Lundgren suggested that the mass be removed before it got much bigger, and shortly thereafter, Felix was wheeled into the operating room. A small incision was made just under the jawline, and Dr. Lundgren got right to work on the pesky lump. The amazing surgical talent of Dr. Lundgren was evident when he explained to Felix that there would be just a small, and hardly noticeable scar. Felix was always thinking ahead, and he had a plan in the event that he was to be asked about the scars on his neck. Assuming that he was to ever have his aviation cadet physical, he was prepared to say that he'd obtained the scars by hitting a branch during a fall while climbing a tree. With the tumor successfully removed, Felix headed back to San Saba the following day to wait the two weeks for the pathology results to arrive. Driving his '41 Chevy down the highway with the windows down and the radio blaring loudly, helped keep his mind focused on something other than the tumor.

Although Felix wasn't yet involved in the war, he did his best to keep up to date with the major events as they unfolded. Feeling like he needed to get out of the house, Felix walked down to Johnnie Mae's cafe on 22 Apr. to read the latest details in the newspapers that she'd set aside for him. Felix and many other Americans were captivated by the stories pertaining to the reports from Doolittle's Raid on the Japanese homeland, which had happened just a few days earlier on 18 Apr. Lieutenant Colonel James Doolittle had led a group of 16 B-25 Mitchell bombers consisting of men from several different squadrons. The men had headed for Tokyo after launching their mission from an aircraft carrier, the USS Hornet, in the Pacific Ocean. From what Felix read, there wasn't a great deal of damage inflicted upon Japan, but the event certainly seemed to boost morale among many United States servicemen. Felix felt great that the United States had proven that it could attack the Japanese at their core, just as they'd attacked Pearl Harbor. He had a grand time discussing this event with the locals that were in the cafe that day, and many felt that the tides were beginning to turn in our favor. Felix couldn't believe that all but one of the B-25 bombers had been forced to ditch, or had crash landed in China after the raid. Unfortunately, some of the airmen involved were killed during the crash landings, and a few were executed after being captured by the Japanese. Felix knew that flying planes during war was risky and dangerous, but he remained eager to get into the fight. He just hoped that he could get trained quickly enough to participate in the war before it was over.

Although the matter with a second tumor had caused Felix yet another unplanned delay, he was very glad to get the news that his latest tumor was benign, just as the prior one had been. He felt blessed and lucky to be alive, and Viola was very thankful that her prayers had been answered. After reading the good news in Dr. Lundgren's letter, Felix proceeded directly to his mother's calendar that hung on the wall near the kitchen sink. Based on Dr. Lundgren's comments, Felix figured that he'd fully heal within two months. Therefore, as he circled the date on the calendar, he exuberantly proclaimed to his parents that he'd be off to the Aviation Cadet Examining Board in Houston on 1 Jul. Just as Felix put the pen back into the drawer, Viola chimed in with, "Boy, you better remember that date in your head, because, come July, that calendar may very well be in one of the many boxes of things being moved to our new house." Felix replied, "Yes Mother, I'll keep it fresh in my head. When I set a goal, I intend to make it happen." In the meantime, Felix continued training, working, and praying for a speedy recovery.

With all that had been going on, Felix hadn't really given too much thought to his parents' decision to downsize their home. Being that Aletha was away at nursing school, and with Felix planning to go off to war, Ernest and Viola figured that they could make do with a smaller place. However, there were three main things that would be required of their new place. It had to have at least three bedrooms, a garage/shop for Ernest, and it had to be closer to the Courthouse Square there in downtown San Saba. Weeks of searching, waiting, and a little luck had culminated with the Scotts securing their new property at 403 South Live Oak St. It was just a stone's throw to the courthouse, it had a garage that could be enlarged, and it met Viola's requirement with the three bedrooms. Ernest liked that they'd be closer to their filling station, and he also figured that the new location would be able to attract more customers to his vulcanization shop. It seemed like a win-win for everybody when they closed the deal on 23 May 1942.

It was fair to say that Felix had quite a bit on his plate with work, and training nearly every day of the week, except for Sunday. Sundays were the Lord's day, and it was a time to relax, and hang out with his family and friends. It seemed that everyone in the family had become so busy all of a sudden. Felix was glad that his parents hadn't forgotten his 22nd birthday when it rolled around on 30 May. After the birthday celebration, Felix found time to help his parents pack, and prepare to move to the Live Oak location. Luckily for the Scotts, they didn't have to be out of their current home by a certain date. They still owned the house outright, so this afforded them the necessary time to make a smooth transition. It seemed like there was an endless list of things to do between the two properties. Felix planned to spend a few weekends helping his father enlarge the new garage to make room for Ernest's growing tire repair shop.

Felix was less than a month away from his planned trip to the Aviation Cadet Examining Board in Houston when he heard the news about the Battle of Midway. He had no idea where this place was, but he was eager to learn more about the details. As its name suggests, Midway is an area out in the middle of the Pacific Ocean, somewhere between the West Coast of the United States and Japan. Felix found time to make his way down to Johnnie Mae's cafe every day over the course of the four-day long campaign stretching from 4 Jun. through 7 Jun. 1942. He'd hoped that someone had left a newspaper from one of the larger communities in the area so that he could read as many details of the events going on at Midway as possible. Felix was fascinated with the accounts from the battle, and he was glad that America was continuing to exact revenge for Japan's attack on Pearl Harbor. Johnnie Mae assured him that she'd continue to save any paper that she saw. Although it was mostly a naval battle, Felix wondered how well he would've done as a pilot during the fight. Admittedly, he had his reservations about the thought of taking off from and landing on an aircraft carrier in the middle of an ocean. Felix figured that he'd prefer the safety of a runway on land in order to take the fight to the Japanese or to the Germans.

With dozens, if not hundreds of planes in the air at once, Felix believed that it must've been an epic battle in the sky. In fact, the Battle of Midway was a lopsided victory for the United States, with many more Japanese soldiers getting killed than Americans. He could only imagine what the American pilots had gone through in order to secure the victory. Felix figured that it must've taken tremendous skill, courage, and bravery to inflict the thousands of Japanese fatalities, and the complete destruction of many Japanese ships. He realized that there had to have been a lot of fear as well, but by the end of the battle, the heroism of our servicemen seemed to have placed the balance of sea power back into the hands of the United States Navy.

There was plenty of work to be done on 20 Jun. when the Scott family completed the final few trips to the South Live Oak property. Felix was able to put his new truck to good use in order to move the animals to their new home. He had worked hard to move and expand the hog pen. Curly and Shirley were getting much bigger, and they seemed to like their new surroundings. Next came the chickens. Felix had built some wooden crates, which made transporting them rather simple. He added a new baby chick enclosure to the henhouse, and all the chickens seemed to acclimate quickly. Finally, Felix moved their dog, Daisy, and the cat, Inky, to the new house in the back seat of his Ford roadster.

Before saying goodbye to her former house, Viola asked Felix to dig up two of her prized fig trees so that she could feature them proudly next to her new garden. Ma and Pa stopped by later that evening to bring a delicious catfish supper for the worn-out Scott family. They also brought hush puppies, baked beans, vegetables, and fresh biscuits. Aletha had come home from school to help Viola set up her new kitchen. Pauline and Johnnie Mae, along with their family members, pitched in to help where needed as well. Johnnie Mae brought several cherry and apple pies, and everyone had a fun evening during the first family fish fry at the home on South Live Oak Street. Pa liked how everything had come together, but he thought the property was a bit short on the pecan tree count. Therefore, he returned the following day with three pecan trees that were about six feet tall. Pa figured that the trees would grow quickly, and they'd complement the existing mulberry and live oak trees found on the property. All in all, Felix and his folks were glad to be settled in, and they were glad to be together.

CHAPTER 10

Pre-flight at SAAAB

When Felix went to bed on 30 Jun. 1942, he was hoping that his life was about to become much more exciting. He hardly slept a wink as he tossed and turned all night, wondering if he'd even be accepted into the Army Air Forces. Would he be able to handle the grueling training program, or would he wash out and be sent to serve in a different role? Would he end up fighting in the Pacific, Europe, or elsewhere? Would he turn out to become a legendary pilot or an ordinary one? These were all good questions, and he hoped that the answers would be revealed sooner than later.

It had been more than six arduous months since the attack on Pearl Harbor, and Felix finally felt healthy enough to take a chance with the first step in becoming a pilot. He didn't want to be late, and he figured that he could get to Houston faster if he drove his '37 Ford. Felix arrived at the Aviation Cadet Examining Board office on the morning of 1 Jul. 1942, and he wasn't really expecting to find the great deal of men already standing in a line outside the building. However, America was at war, and men of all ages were feeling patriotic by offering their services to the United States Army Air Forces, and to the other branches of service. Felix believed that there were probably millions of young men, just like himself, trying to get one of the coveted training slots.

While at Texas AMC, Felix had heard that if a man volunteered to join the military, he could have the opportunity to select the branch of service that he most desired to enter. If it were left up to fate, he knew that he could be drafted into the Navy, Army, or the Marines. As he progressed through the line, Felix made small talk with the men around him. During the conversations, Felix learned that the government had recently dropped the ban on married applicants for pilot positions back in January of 1942. After a few hours, he finally managed to get through the long line. Felix really didn't know exactly what was going to happen next, but he was as ready as could be expected. He could see men in uniforms directing the applicants to a room that resembled a classroom complete with tables and chairs. Felix then heard an announcement that their mental capabilities were about to be put to the test by taking the two-hour Aviation Cadet Qualifying Exam.

Felix felt pretty good after completing the exam, and although he was feeling hungry, he was whisked off into another line for a complete physical. He was certainly feeling anxious as he got closer to the front of the line. Luckily for Felix, he didn't have any birth defects, disabilities, vision problems, or motion issues. With a great sense of relief, he finished up his day after finding out that he had passed the physical exam at the Aviation Cadet Examining Board office. He was told to go home, and to wait for a letter that would provide him with directions as to what to do next. Felix was a very friendly and easy going fellow, so he asked a few of the guys whom he had met there if they wanted to go and grab a bite to eat. Several men took him up on the offer, and they had a nice supper at a nearby Mexican food restaurant. They each discussed their individual plans and desires to serve their country. It was nearly dark by the time the men left the restaurant, so Felix figured it was time to head home to San Saba.

Upon returning home, Ernest and Viola were very interested to know how everything had gone at the Aviation Cadet Examining Board office. After providing them with all the details, Felix planned to return to his normal daily routine of work and physical training. However, there was one new addition to his daily schedule. Every evening when Felix would get home from work, he'd ask his mother and father if any mail had arrived from the United States Government. The weeks slowly passed by, and Felix was beginning to wonder if the government had forgotten about him. Could the letter that he had been expecting been lost in the mail? Needless to say, Felix was thrilled to find that a letter had finally arrived from the United States Government when he arrived home from work on 10 Aug. 1942. Felix ripped open the envelope while standing at the kitchen table, and he was very excited to read that he'd been accepted into the United States Army Air Forces. However, the letter didn't indicate the role in which he'd serve, but it did say that further details would follow after his enlistment. Felix was glad that he'd been given the date and time to report at the enlistment center. Being completely overjoyed, he hugged his mother, and gave a high five to his father. Felix just had to share the details, so he called Ma and Pa, and he also spoke with Chauncey about the good news.

Felix was once again off to Houston on 19 Aug. 1942. However, this time, he was heading directly to the enlistment center, and he was ecstatic to be officially sworn into the United States military. After spending several hours there, Felix was categorized as an aviation student, and he was once again told to go home to wait for the letter that would call him to active duty. Before leaving, the men were advised that it might take a few months before their orders arrived. At that point, Felix would then be directed to report to one of the large Army Air Forces training centers located around the country. There were record numbers of pilots graduating every month, and with a substantial amount of men trying to enter the system, the backlog was real. Felix accepted that he'd need to be patient, and he knew how to follow orders. Therefore, he returned home to San Saba to await the letter that would set the stage for his path to becoming a pilot. There were plenty of hurdles yet to come, and he knew that he'd probably need a good deal of luck along the way as well. Ernest and Viola were very proud of Felix. She took comfort in her Bible, and she prayed every night for Felix's well-being and safety as his military career was about to commence.

The end of summer had arrived, and Felix was beginning to become impatient as he waited for his orders. Weeks turned into months with still no word on when or where his training would be held. Felix was glad to spend the extra time in San Saba so that he could celebrate the birthdays of his father, his grandmother, Johnnie Mae, and his little sister, Aletha. It was a typical morning for Ernest Scott on 4 Dec. 1942 when he made his usual trip to the post office to check for mail in their P. O. Box. As Ernest rifled through the small stack of mail, he abruptly stopped when he saw an official looking envelope addressed to Felix. He had a good feeling that this was the letter that Felix had been anxiously waiting for. Therefore, Ernest jumped into his car, and he drove immediately to the AAA office where Felix was working.

Felix was certainly surprised to see his father walk through the office door. Enthusiasm was bubbling from Felix's pores when he saw that his father was holding an envelope high in the air. Ernest quickly handed the envelope to him, and Felix feverishly tore it open. He carefully began to read every line, and he promptly confirmed that the letter was indeed the orders that he'd been waiting for. With a huge grin on his face, Felix then said, "It looks like I'm going to California for my Pre-Flight training. It says right here that I need to report on 21 Dec. 1942." Ernest gave Felix a big hug, and Mr. Ray followed with a pat on the back along with a handshake. Felix then asked Mr. Ray, "May I leave early? I just gotta go tell my grandparents about this." Mr. Ray was glad to oblige, and after Felix thanked his father for bringing the letter by, he sprinted out the door. Ernest followed by walking out the door to his car, and he was immediately met with a giant dust cloud that had been created by four squealing truck tires as Felix tore out of the parking lot. Ernest was excited for Felix, and he headed home to share the news with Viola.

Ma and Pa were sitting on their front porch enjoying a cup of coffee when they noticed a vehicle traveling up the dirt road towards their home at a high rate of speed. They could clearly see the trail of dirt that had been kicked up into the air as the vehicle moved quickly around the bends in the road. It took a few moments before they recognized that it was Felix's truck making its way up the final turn to their home. Felix had pulled up to the farmhouse so quickly, his truck nearly toppled over as it began to spin briefly before coming to a stop. He cautiously stepped out of his truck, looking around from side to side, hoping that he hadn't hit any cows, sheep, or dogs. Ma promptly asked, "Is something wrong? Are you alright? Why are you in such a hurry?" Felix ran towards the porch with his orders in hand, and he proceeded to show them what had arrived in the mail. They all went inside, and sat down at the kitchen table so that his grandparents could fully understand what was going on. Felix excitedly said, "I finally made it! I'm now one step closer to realizing my dream of becoming a pilot."

Pa was clearly happy for Felix when he asked, "Where are you going to be sent for training?" Felix replied, "I'll be headed for Santa Ana, California, in just a few weeks." Pa then pulled out his atlas to show Felix exactly where Santa Ana was located. He pointed to the area on the map, and said, "Your father and I have taken several trips to Los Angeles to meet with Mr. Killian. We helped him graft a great deal of pecan trees on his ranch, and in several other areas around the city of Los Angeles. It looks like Santa Ana is in Orange County, which is just south of Los Angeles." Felix asked, "Did y'all make your way down to that part of California?" Pa replied, "Yes, we drove down the coast for a bit before heading home. There were orange trees everywhere, and we had a ball throwing oranges into the ocean." Felix then said, "It sounds like y'all had an amazing time in California, and I'm hoping that I'll get some time to see some of it. I know that we'll be back over here on Monday to celebrate your birthday, but I just had to come by and tell y'all about my news. I think that it's just terrible that your special day has to be forever linked with the attack on Pearl Harbor. It's hard for me to believe that it has already been a year, and I still ain't in this fight. Well, I can't wait to get started with my training so that I can give those Japs some payback." Felix hung around for a while until he could share the good news with Chauncey, and on his way home, he stopped to update a few of his friends with all the details.

Having only a short time left in San Saba before he headed to California, Felix was dealing with a whirlwind of emotions. He likened it to the time that he'd left for college. There was so much to do, and so many people to see. Felix immediately gave his notice at the bakery and at the AAA office. That had made him rather sad, because Felix felt that he'd probably not work for either of his employers ever again. He was also quite dejected knowing that he was going to miss celebrating the Christmas and New Year's Day holidays with his family there in San Saba. Ma and Pa always seemed to find a way to brighten Felix's mood. As such, they offered to host the entire family over at the River Bend farm to celebrate Christmas early on 12 Dec. 1942.

Felix was glad to spend time celebrating with his aunts, his uncles, his sisters, his parents, his grandparents, and all of his cousins. As supper was wrapping up, Ernest asked everyone to raise their glasses in a toast to wish Felix a safe journey, and for the best of luck with his upcoming training. Felix appreciated all the kind words and support, but he felt sad knowing that he might not be able to come home for the holidays for many years to come. After all, there was a war raging in many areas all over the world.

The day was 16 Dec. 1942, and it was to be Felix's last full day in San Saba before heading west to California. He grabbed some of his friends, and he drove his cars all over town. Felix made sure that he hit all of his favorite hangouts, and he arrived back home with enough time to wash each of his cars before it got dark. There was some information in the paperwork that Felix had received as to what he could expect when he arrived at the Santa Ana Army Air Base (SAAAB). Aviation students and cadets were forbidden to bring their own cars, and the nationwide fuel rationing program sealed the deal for sure. Among a slew of other necessities, people were being asked to conserve, gasoline was being rationed, and adults were issued rationing coupons that would provide them with the ability to keep their cars running and the ability to purchase a certain quantity of gasoline. To some degree, it helped that the Scotts owned a filling station, but Felix was willing to play by all the rules by leaving his cars at home. Therefore, he begrudgingly backed his Ford, and then his Chevy, up against the wall next to his father's garage. There were a few tears in his eyes as he said goodbye to his cars by covering up "Elizabeth" and his truck with tarps. Ernest assured Felix that he'd keep the tires filled, and he'd keep 'em running. With months and months of training ahead of him, Felix suddenly realized that he just might be flying a plane before driving a car again.

Felix knew that the train ride to Orange County would take about two days including the connections and stops along the way. His orders stated that he was to report to SAAAB on 21 Dec. 1942. Therefore, Felix figured that he'd leave San Saba by train on the afternoon of 17 Dec. 1942. There were plenty of friends, family, and even local townspeople at the train station to say goodbye to Felix as he left for the West Coast. Felix looked at Pauline, and said, "Since the Aggies have done so poorly this season, it appears that there won't be a football game to listen to with you and Ted on New Year's Day." After giving lots of hugs and handshakes, Viola handed Felix a sack filled with sandwiches, fresh biscuits, pecans, chocolate bars, and several bottles of pop. Although he felt that it was rather exciting that he was beginning his journey, he also felt that it was a little depressing knowing that he had no idea when he'd be able to return home to San Saba. Everyone was waving as the train left the station, and Felix waved back until the train had disappeared from their view. Felix was eager, and ready to get on with his training, and he was keeping his fingers crossed that he'd be selected as a pilot.

After stowing his bags, Felix settled into his reclining seat nearby, and he was pleasantly surprised to find a 12" x 12" plush pillow in his knapsack. Viola must've sewn it together, and stuffed it into his bag before he'd left the house. Felix's final few days spent in San Saba had been emotionally draining on him. Not knowing what to expect during his upcoming training, and wondering if he'd "wash out" at any of the different levels, caused him a great deal of anxiety. While gazing out the window, Felix stayed awake for a few hours as the train chugged along. As the sun started to set, he began to eat some of the food from his bag. Felix had a hard time believing that he was finally embarking on the journey that he'd been dreaming about for years and years.

Felix found the red, white, and blue pillow to be very thoughtful and useful. It didn't take long for him to fall asleep, and when he woke up early the next morning, he found out that they'd entered New Mexico. Needing to stretch his legs, Felix began to explore all that the train had to offer. He found the meal car, and he was glad to have some hard-boiled eggs with bacon. Felix returned to his seat feeling energetic and amiable, and he then introduced himself to those sitting in the rows around him. He was very glad to meet two young men who were heading to the Santa Ana Army Air Base as well.

Skip was from El Paso, Texas, and Buster was from Alamogordo, New Mexico. They were both a bit younger than Felix, but they too, aspired to become pilots. The trio enjoyed each other's company by playing cards, telling jokes, and sharing their backgrounds with one another during the remainder of the train ride. After spending the day with Skip and Buster, Felix could tell that they were also willing to risk their lives in the defense of the United States.

It was Saturday afternoon, 19 Dec. 1942, when the train stopped at Union Station in Los Angeles, California. Felix and his new friends had two hours before their connection left for Santa Ana, California. He asked the conductor if there was any place where they could get something to eat. The man pointed, and he then told them to walk about five minutes until they reached Olvera Street. He said, "Look for the crowd of people, live music, and the extraordinary smell of authentic Mexican food." The men found Olvera Street to be a fabulous place, and after dinner and a churro, they headed back to Union Station to board the train bound for Santa Ana.

It was a fairly short ride from Los Angeles County to Orange County. Since Felix and his pals didn't have to report to their post until 21 Dec., they decided that they'd take a cab to a hotel that would be somewhere close to the base. The cab driver asked what had brought them to Santa Ana. Felix explained that they were from out of town, and that they were about to begin training at SAAAB on Monday. The driver thanked them for their service, and said, "I know a great little place down in Balboa. It's close to the beach, and the base is only about 20 minutes away by bus." Upon arriving at the hotel, the men liked what they saw, and they were very glad to settle into the last remaining available room at the Balboa Inn.

Felix, Buster, and Skip awoke early on 20 Dec. eager to hit the beach. The men walked by the hotel office where they noticed an assortment of fresh fruit that was available for the guests. Felix grabbed an orange to eat, and he placed another in his back pocket. They then headed to a nearby diner ready to enjoy a full breakfast. After a fabulous meal, the men walked to the Balboa Pier, which was just a block or so to the west. Felix had never been on a pier of this size, and he was amazed at the variety of fish being caught from the ocean below. There seemed to be a great deal of men in military uniforms looking for women, and plenty of good-looking girls looking for guys. Felix had come to town to become a pilot, and he wasn't really looking for a new relationship. However, that changed very quickly when he noticed a beautiful young lady sitting on a bench with two of her friends.

It took a few moments for Felix and his pals to muster up the courage to approach the lovely young ladies. Felix said, "Guys, I just have to meet the one with the jet-black hair," and with that, they headed towards the women sitting on the bench. Felix didn't see a wedding ring on her finger when he said, "Good morning, gals. What are your names, and what brings you fine ladies down to the beach today?" The gal that Felix was interested in replied, "My name is Elsie. My girlfriends and I came down here for the day hoping to find some cute military men." Felix was feeling a bit jittery while standing there, and Elsie appeared equally nervous as she wiggled her painted red toenails in the sand. After the men introduced themselves, Felix then said, "Well, it must be your lucky day. We're military men, and we'll be starting our training over at the Santa Ana Army Air Base tomorrow morning." He then began to wonder if Elsie would believe him or not, since they weren't wearing the uniform that so many of the other men walking around had on.

Buster and Skip seemed to hit it off with Elsie's friends, so Felix asked the ladies if they'd like to join them on a bike ride down to the Newport Beach Pier. The ladies looked at one another, and they collectively decided to take him up on the offer. Felix reached for Elsie's hand to assist her with getting off the bench, and he didn't let go of it until they reached the bike rental shop. The group split off into pairs as they began pedaling the ten minutes or so that was needed to get to the Newport Beach Pier. During the ride, Felix couldn't keep his eyes off of Elsie, and luckily for him, he avoided a few potential mishaps along the way. Elsie was a few inches shorter than Felix and had the most gorgeous complexion, along with painted fingernails to match her toes, and also a European accent that really intrigued him. Felix thought that she was just so beautiful, and he was amazed that even her eyes seemed to smile back at him whenever he would glance over at her. The slight breeze caused her white sundress to twist about, revealing her dazzling red bathing suit underneath.

The beautiful Orange County weather was certainly impressive to Felix, and the sun that was shining through a few of the scattered clouds made for a wonderful day. Felix's conversation with Elsie revealed that she was a receptionist, and she lived with her parents about an hour away in Bloomington, California. Felix explained that he was from San Saba, Texas, and he wasn't surprised that she had no idea where that was. When they arrived at the pier, Felix once again took hold of her hand. Elsie said, "You're so cute, and quite a gentleman. I bet you'll look even more handsome when sporting your new military uniform." Felix blushed a bit, and said, "Thank you ma'am. I sure could get used to this climate, the beach scene, and being with you."

Felix and Elsie walked to the end of the pier along with the other young couples. He then shared the story about when his father and grandfather had come to California, and how they had the opportunity to throw oranges into the ocean. Felix then pulled the orange from his back pocket, and he threw it far out into the pounding surf. Elsie seemed to like Felix's easy-going personality, and his throwing abilities. He and Elsie were having so much fun together, they didn't realize that they'd missed dinner. Elsie suggested that the group head over to the Balboa Fun Zone, which was close to the hotel on the eastern side of the peninsula. Before leaving the pier, Felix noticed that the men in uniforms were starting to clear out, and they were boarding some nearby buses. Elsie mentioned that the servicemen had to be back on the post for their Sunday afternoon parade. This really made Felix wonder what exactly was in store for him for the next three months. Upon arriving at the Fun Zone, everyone enjoyed some nachos, Hawaiian Punch, and ice cream. Afterwards, Felix was ready for some more fun and excitement. They rode the merry-go-round, Ferris Wheel, and he tested his skill at the carnival games until he won a cute, plush bear for Elsie.

There happened to be a boat rental place close to the Fun Zone. Felix declared that he was very proficient at piloting a boat, and he convinced the group to take a leisurely ride up and down the peninsula. After returning to the dock, everyone decided to get out of the sun for a bit by visiting the Balboa Photo shop. Elsie continued to be flirtatious with Felix, and he sure enjoyed posing for the fantastic pictures that were taken with her. After leaving with their photos, they headed to the Casino Café for an evening of dining and dancing. It had been quite some time since Felix had set foot on a dance floor. However, his legs quickly loosened up, and there were no signs of rust as he danced for hours with Elsie. Buster and Skip were equally enthralled with Elsie's friends. Felix had thoroughly enjoyed the day, and he seemed to be entirely smitten with Elsie. He could tell that the feelings must've been mutual when she leaned over to kiss him on the cheek.

Before the ladies headed home, Elsie wrote her address on the back of one of the photos that they'd taken. She then said, "Unless things have changed, you may be stuck on base for the first six weeks." Elsie then pushed her index finger into Felix's chest, and said, "Will I see you again?" Felix quickly replied, "Darling, you can bet on it!" He then reached for her fingers so that he could gently kiss the backside of her hand. After giving her a big hug, Felix committed to writing to her as often as he could, and Elsie said that she'd do the same once she had his post address. Elsie proceeded to stuff the picture into Felix's shirt pocket, and then he watched as they drove away. Felix began to wonder how Elsie knew so much about the base protocols and procedures. He then decided that he really didn't want to know. Felix had been in love before, but something about Elsie, and their special day, felt different. Viola had always told Felix that one day he'd cross paths with a kindred spirit. He believed in love at first sight, and he hoped for the best as he returned to the hotel with Buster and Skip.

Dawn broke over the Balboa Peninsula as Felix was out on the sandy beach doing push-ups and sit-ups. During a run along the coastline, he found a nearby park to get his chin-ups in. After an exhausting morning workout, Felix returned to the hotel for a quick shower, and to gather his belongings. Buster and Skip were ready to head to the base, and they were very impressed with Felix's commitment to his PT regimen. The men checked out of the hotel, and they were very lucky to be able to bum a ride off a guy who was heading towards the Newport Beach Pier. After thanking the man for the ride, Felix and his pals headed to the bus stop that he'd noticed the day before. Being unaware of the bus schedule, they wanted to be there plenty early. Before long, a bus arrived, and the driver confirmed that his route would take them up Newport Boulevard toward the base.

About 15 minutes later, Felix, Buster, and Skip exited the bus to find themselves standing in front of Gate No. 1. Felix figured that they were at the right place when he saw the words "Santa Ana Army Air Base" displayed in bold letters on a sign that featured a wooden propeller running vertically through the middle of it. The sign was prominently featured at the top of the center pole on a frame built with logs that were as thick as telephone poles. The gate doors appeared to be constructed with standard metal fencing material, and since they were already swung open, Felix and his pals proceeded towards the guard who was standing next to the hut, which was located near the bottom of the center pole. The guard coarsely asked, "What is your purpose here?" Felix seemed to be the logical choice to serve as the leader of their small group. Therefore, he replied, "We're here to serve our country, and also to learn how to fly airplanes. My name is Felix Ernest Scott, and we're reporting for duty, sir!" With a little smirk on his face, the guard then carefully checked their paperwork and credentials before letting them pass through. He directed the men to the reception center, which served as the staging area for the new cadets who'd already arrived earlier that morning. There were men in uniform moving about in every direction imaginable. From the look of things, Felix figured that there had to have been more men on the base than there were cadets back at the Agricultural and

Mechanical College of Texas. Felix glanced back at the front gate, and he then turned towards Skip, and said, "That gate reminds me of some of the ones back home in San Saba County, minus the cattle crossing guards of course." Skip chuckled, and said, "What on earth have we gotten ourselves into here? Felix confidently replied, "I reckon that we're about to find out."

It took nearly an hour for Felix to complete all the paperwork and questionnaires that he'd been given. Filling out the life insurance paperwork sort of made him cringe, but Felix realized the seriousness that war had brought, and he sincerely hoped that his family wouldn't ever need to claim the $10,000 benefit from the policy. Felix was told that the government would pay the life insurance premiums for the policy until he obtained his wings. Next, Felix had to fill in a few blanks on a form letter, which was then sent off to his parents to let them know that he'd arrived safely on base. The letter explained that he'd be quite busy as he made his way through the classification process to determine his role on an air crew. Felix was clearly hoping to become a pilot, but he knew that being classified as a bombardier, or as a navigator, could also be a possibility. The letter concluded with his squadron number and his post address there in Santa Ana, California. Felix was certain that his parents would appreciate the letter, and he also knew that his mother would share his post address with the rest of the family.

Things suddenly began to move rather quickly when the buses finally stopped arriving from the train station in Santa Ana. Felix found where his new squadron had gathered, and he promptly assembled into formation. The other squadrons had also gathered nearby as the base Commandant, Colonel W. A. Robertson, prepared to address the crowd of nearly 3900 men. Colonel Robertson began his speech with, "I'd like to officially welcome you all to the

Santa Ana Army Air Base, which we like to call SAAAB for short. For the duration of your training through the Advanced phase, you'll be under the command of the Army Air Forces West Coast Training Center (AAFWCTC). We have aviation students here from many different states, and, who knows, you might just run into a fella from a town near where you're from. Over the next few weeks, each of you will receive your classification, and then you'll begin your assigned training here at SAAAB." Colonel Robertson closed with, "We're going to give you the foundation for your training here in the Army Air Forces, and we need each of you to give 110% effort to help us build the finest, and most formidable air power in the world." Felix was crossing his fingers, and he planned to do his best, with the hope that he'd get chosen for the Pre-Flight training program, which would put him on the path to earning his wings.

Following their dismissal, the squadrons dispersed into many different directions to try and avoid congestion at the quartermaster's warehouse. Felix's squadron started off with a tour of the base to familiarize themselves with the location of the hospital, mess hall, theaters, post office, and the post exchange (PX). Being issued all sorts of clothing and shoes brought back fond memories from when Felix and his parents were selecting his clothing as an incoming freshman at Texas AMC. Unlike at the Agricultural and Mechanical College of Texas, Felix didn't need to break out his billfold, since there was no cost to receive his military issued clothing and personal hygiene items.

Boy was there a lot of clothing! Each man was given a duffel bag, and also a barracks bag, which would later be used for laundry purposes. Amazingly, the process was very orderly, and Felix moved quickly from station to station, filling his bags with the pieces of clothing that would make up the various uniform combinations needed at SAAAB.

Although different, the service and garrison cap that he received were strikingly familiar to the ones that he wore at Texas AMC. Felix was also issued a service coat, several pairs of woolen and cotton trousers, along with a tan belt. Additionally, he received a light brown tie, multiple cotton and wool shirts, and, of course, military issue boxer shorts. Next, he was given a pair of brown Oxford dress shoes, sandals, and even shower shoes. Finally, Felix received the required articles that were needed for his physical training, which consisted of a sweatshirt, sweatpants, T-shirts, overalls, gym trunks, socks, and gym shoes.

After all of the men in Felix's squadron had received their gear, they were directed to head towards their assigned quarters. Felix had his hands and arms full with his suitcase and the bags of clothing from the quartermaster's office. As the group marched onward, Felix noticed row upon row of two-story barracks buildings that were painted in an olive drab color scheme. The barracks were grouped together, which formed a large rectangular pattern towards the far end of the base. Felix had never seen anything like it, and he figured that there had to be at least 100 or more barracks buildings in total. Felix entered his barracks, and he quickly noticed that there were two rows of bunk beds located on the first floor. He presumed that there would be an equal number of bunks on the top floor, which meant that about 60 men or so would be living together in each building. Everything inside the building was in pristine condition, and it still smelled as if it were relatively new. There were two footlockers situated along the center aisleway near each set of bunk beds. Felix expeditiously found his assigned bunk, and he was eager to relax, even if it was for just a few minutes.

The men were quickly ordered to change out of their civilian clothes in preparation for their first supper at the mess hall. Felix was able to get everything put away neatly into his footlocker, and he was instructed on how to arrange his shoes in a particular order under the bed. He hung his shirts, trousers, and service coat on hangers, and he then placed them on a closet rod behind his bunk. Felix followed directions precisely, but he thought that it was sort of weird that even his clothes had to be arranged in a certain way. After getting the approval of their squadron's commanding officer, Felix and his squadron mates marched to the mess hall together, and he was rather impressed with the atmosphere that he found inside. He wouldn't compare the mess hall to a fancy restaurant, but it was clean, orderly, and he liked the quality of the food.

Conversations were allowed among the men while they were eating. However, they were told to be respectful, and to talk quietly during their meal. After the meal, Felix followed the other aviation students by stacking his tray at the end of the table along the aisleway. He dropped his utensils into a large cup, and then, the men of his squadron marched out of the mess hall back to the barracks. The sound of taps marked the end of a long day. The bugle call was reminiscent of his time in College Station, and Felix was very glad that he was now one day closer to getting his wings. Before bed, the men practiced and practiced the proper military way on how to make their bunk at the start of each day. The blanket needed to be pulled tight across the bed, and then tucked firmly underneath the mattress. Some of the men were clearly frustrated with this seemingly mundane task. Lucky for them, Felix was an old pro, and he was glad to assist many of his new friends.

Military discipline began immediately, and Felix's superiors demanded courtesy, along with adherence to the base regulations. Focus, attention, and precision was also expected of each man. Felix's second day began at sunrise with Reveille, followed by the raising of the colors. The aviation students were told to expect a full day of classes geared towards orientation and expectations for behavior while on the post. Before breakfast, Felix and the men had their first introduction to close order drills, which was very helpful to the newbies, since they had no idea how to properly march or parade for their superiors. With the countless Reviews held at Texas AMC, Felix didn't break a sweat in performing the morning maneuvers. Many of his peers admired him as he moved perfectly in unison with the commands given to them. After the morning meal, each squadron took a trip to the post office. Since only government issued clothing was to be worn on base, everyone was required to box up their civilian clothes, and any other unnecessary personal items for shipment back to their homes. Felix wondered what his parents would think when his box of clothing and personal belongings arrived back home in San Saba without him.

An afternoon class convened so that the men could be given their General Orders, which outlined the specific rules and requirements for when a soldier might be needed to perform sentry duty. They were told to memorize all of the General Orders by the end of their first week. There was also a discussion pertaining to all of the Articles of War, which basically set forth the broad list of military laws concerning the personal behavior of United States soldiers. Although most of the Articles of War governed the conduct of officers, it was important for every soldier to understand the laws that they'd be required to abide by. After learning the importance of military confidentiality, the men were told that there was to be no gambling or consumption of alcoholic beverages while on base. Felix planned to conduct himself in a proper manner each day, and he figured that with good judgment, and some common sense, he'd get to the next stage of training.

A picture taken of Felix E. Scott after classification day at Santa Ana Army Air Base in California.

The instructors also reviewed the process to sign in and out when leaving or returning to the base. Felix thought that it was a bit odd when he found out that hitchhiking was forbidden near the base. The men were told that they'd be allowed to leave the base by car with a weekend pass if they were picked up by a family member or friend. They were also advised that the bus and Pacific Electric trolley car schedules would be posted on the bulletin boards across the base. Felix realized that Elsie had been correct, and there was certainly some grumbling among the men, when they learned that there would be no weekend passes given during their first six weeks at SAAAB. At sunset, there was the customary sounding of Retreat, followed by the lowering of the United States flag. After a long day of lectures, discussions, and drill practice, Felix and his squadron marched back to their barracks. Upon their arrival, they were given a schedule that provided them with rotational assignments for dusting, mopping, and sweeping duties inside their quarters. "Pulling a detail" wasn't exactly fun, but Felix knew that it was just a part of ordinary military life. When Felix heard the sounding of taps ringing throughout the base at 2100 hours, he knew that his day was nearly over. The men were told that they should use a few minutes before bed to shine their shoes and the brass pins for their uniforms.

Lights out at 2200 hours meant that it was time for some quiet time, and reflection on the events of the day. As Felix looked around the barracks while lying in his bunk, he wondered which of the men would make the cut to become pilots. Over the next two weeks, he was about to find out who'd move on, and who'd wash out. Up to that point, there had already been plenty of classroom instruction and physical training sessions together, but the men really hadn't been given much time to socialize with each other. Having been around the other aviation students in his barracks for just a few days, Felix already knew that he wanted to become friends with the fellow located just two bunks over from him. While wrapping up a long day there in the barracks, everyone always seemed to be laughing around Ray Simon. Felix could tell that there was never a dull moment for those who were hanging around Ray. Felix just wished that his bunk was a little closer to Ray so that he could hear more of his stories, and be a part of the fun.

The next morning, Felix and the other men in his class were given a great deal of paperwork to begin the classification process. He was asked to officially designate his preference for a position on an air crew. Knowing full well that there were no guarantees, and he could be assigned as a bombardier or a navigator, Felix selected pilot as his primary choice. When asked why he wanted to become a pilot, Felix wrote about how he'd received his pecan shaped airplane at an early age. He was very clear that this was something that he'd dreamed about for a long time. Felix wanted the staff at SAAAB to know that he believed flying airplanes was his destiny.

Over the course of the next few days, Felix began the mental testing phase of the classification process. There were many written aptitude tests with paper and a pencil. In addition, Felix was verbally tested on his ability to concentrate, and he was continuously grilled with questions to assess his mental focus and alertness. The examiners were also trying to determine his knowledge regarding the basic principles of mechanics, as well as his ability to interpret maps, charts, and graphs. The mental testing period concluded with sessions involving general knowledge, reading speed, comprehension, good judgment, and decision-making skills. Felix was mentally drained at the conclusion of the first stage of testing, but he figured that as long as he was able to continue on with his testing, he must've been doing well enough. Before turning in for the night, Felix figured that he'd unwind by writing a letter to Elsie.

Dear Elsie, *Dec 24, 1942*

I've settled in nicely here at the post. We are kept busy with plenty of paperwork, testing, and, of course, physical training. You just wouldn't believe how many men are here on base. It's like a city all of its own.

I'm still marveled with our chance encounter in Balboa last weekend. Holding your hand, and being together with you for the day was the best thing that has happened to me in the last year. Seeing the reflection of the setting sun in your beautiful brown eyes still has my heart racing.

There's something very special about you, Miss Elsie! You're so gorgeous and genuine, and I cannot recall ever meeting someone as spunky as you. Unfortunately, you were right that we cannot leave the base for another five weeks or so.

I know that this won't arrive until after Christmas, but I hope that you had a wonderful time celebrating with your family. I wish you a happy new year, and I know that 1943 will be amazing with you in my life. We hear that we'll be kept busy here on base during the holidays, and they say that the food and desserts are supposed to be better than the usual offerings.

I'll write as frequently as I can, and I long to have you in my arms again real soon. You'll find my address information on the front of the envelope, and I hope that you'll write back often.

All my best,

Felix

Felix donned his tan-colored trousers and long sleeve shirt for his first Sunday afternoon parade on 27 Dec. 1942. He neatly tucked in his tie about halfway down his shirt, and his garrison cap was placed properly on top of his head. The weather cooperated by providing a light breeze with partly cloudy skies for the late afternoon parade. As Felix marched side-by-side with his squadron past the review stand, he recalled the numerous times that he'd paraded on the manicured lawn during his time in College Station. Later that evening, Felix met up with Skip to see *Yankee Doodle Dandy* during his first visit to one of the post movie theaters. Upon his return to the barracks, Felix felt really lucky to find that a few men had already washed out within their first week, and he was able to move to the bunk right next to Ray. Felix could tell that Ray was strong, and he knew that he wouldn't stand a chance in an arm-wrestling challenge against him. Ray was a little younger, about two inches taller, and, just like Felix, he came from a small town. Felix just couldn't believe how small Ray's hometown of Napoleon, North Dakota, was when Ray told him that it probably didn't even have 1,000 people living in it.

It was time for Felix to begin the physical testing portion of the classification process. Over the course of several days, his dexterity was evaluated with interactions involving a variety of mechanical gadgets. Felix was measured on how skillfully and quickly he navigated each test using his fingers and hands. He was also tested on his hand eye coordination abilities. As Felix and Ray moved along through the classification process, they both realized that they had a lot in common. They figured that the military would provide them with the opportunity to travel the United States, and even the world. Both Felix and Ray aspired to become pilots, and they had a magnificent time dreaming of who'd fly the biggest or fastest plane in the Army Air forces. Felix hailed from a family of successful business owners, and Ray's father was the prominent town doctor back home in Napoleon. They shared stories of growing up, having to make do with what they had. They both used amazing ingenuity while learning to build some of the things that were needed around their homes. Felix quickly realized that Ray was smart as a whip, and he appreciated Ray being there to help him with his studies. It didn't take long for the pair to become best buds.

Although the men weren't told how well they were doing on the hand eye coordination tests, there was clearly some back and forth bragging about who'd done better. Even when the classroom quizzes and tests were hard, Ray could always find a way to see something positive in the situation. Felix very much appreciated Ray's kindness and his upbeat attitude, which helped to keep him motivated to succeed. Ray would often finish with his coursework first, which provided him with the time to draw some amazing caricatures featuring Felix, and the amazing Felix the Cat. Ray got a real kick out of the uncanny likeness to their names, and the sketches would typically feature an aerial themed rendering of something comical. They both knew that they were in for a long haul ahead, but they figured that together, they'd make for a good team.

The next step in the classification process was to meet with a staff psychologist. Felix was always quick on his feet, and he felt confident that he'd do well throughout the conversation. He knew that he was going to be asked a broad range of questions in order to determine if he had the proper temperament to be a member of an air crew. The doctor began the conversation by trying to see how well Felix reacted to stress, pressure situations, and sudden changes in the environment. He then became a bit uncomfortable when discussing his sexual preferences and desires with the doctor. The doctor seemed satisfied with the answers that he provided since Felix couldn't stop talking about how he'd dated Emma Jo during college, and now Elsie there in Orange County. Felix was attentive and open with the psychologist as the conversation concluded with a discussion about his background, aversions, and fears. Word quickly got around that the comprehensive testing program was tough, and nobody felt that the process was a cakewalk. Felix felt that he'd done his best by trying to limit mistakes, and all he could do now was hope for a positive outcome. After another successful round of testing, he was most definitely happy that he wasn't one of the unlucky ones who were sent packing to find another role within the military.

Felix was feeling a bit nervous about the final part of the classification process. Would they somehow find out about his lumps, and would they notice his scars? The time had come for Felix to meet with the flight surgeon staff for a physical that was to be more thorough than the initial one that he'd been given when he first entered the service. The process was very rigorous, and it lasted for the better part of two days. The dental examination went well, being that Felix got to keep all of the teeth in his mouth. There were many different vision tests to determine if he was colorblind, or if he had any depth perception issues. Felix figured that he possessed keen eyesight, evidenced by his skill at shooting marbles, and by plinking bottle caps off of Coke bottles back home in San Saba County. His blood pressure and pulse rate were tested while under stress, and as well as with no stress. Felix was then inoculated against smallpox, typhoid, and tetanus. He certainly hoped that he wouldn't have to see another needle for quite some time, but he knew that vaccinations were important, and that they'd be given at regular intervals to keep everyone safe. The final day of medical testing concluded with blood and urine samples along with a chest x-ray. Felix finally breathed a sigh of relief when Major Pawlowski handed him his immunization and medical record cards. He was then told that he'd passed the physical, and that he'd need to take the cards with him from base to base.

It was New Year's Eve, and Felix was glad to have been given a little breather from the exhausting testing process. After receiving his partial month's pay, Felix visited the PX for some supplies, stationery, and a few gifts to send back home. He was getting weekly haircuts at the post barbershop, and he embraced the weekly routine of dealing with the laundry service that was offered on base. Felix really loved the wonderful weather in Orange County. The sunny breezy days with comfortable temperatures and low humidity made for a perfect training environment. As his second full week on base was about to come to a close, Felix was finally able to collect his incoming mail. Felix loved the letters that he'd received from his kinfolk and friends back home, and he was beyond thrilled to see that a letter had arrived from Elsie as well. After reading through all his mail, he took a few moments to get a letter off to his folks.

Dear folks   *Dec 31, 1942*

I really enjoyed the train ride out here to California, and that little pillow sure came in handy. I'm sure that you were surprised to see all my stuff arrive back home there in San Saba. Don't y'all worry though, we have plenty of good clothes to wear around here. I met some nice fellas on the trip, and they're also training here at the base. The California weather is unbelievable, and I've already been to the beach. I had a ball throwing an orange into the ocean just like Pa and Pop did years ago.

Life on the base is going really well. There are so many men training here, but apparently there are NO planes on this base. Ugh! We've learned that there are four stages of training, and it may take up to nine months to earn my wings. They call this Pre-flight training, which would be similar to my year as a fish at Texas AMC. If I successfully make it out of here, I'll move on to Primary training, which would be equivalent to my sophomore year at school. We'd finally get to fly a plane during the Primary stage. After Primary, I'd move on to Basic training, where I'd learn to fly a more powerful plane. The final stage of training would be like my senior year, and they call it Advanced training. The planes there are even more powerful, and the maneuvers demand a great deal of skill. That is where I'll earn my wings if I successfully navigate this lengthy process. Don't worry, Mother, you've always said that God will be my copilot. Unlike my senior year at Texas AMC, I plan to finish what I've started here in Santa Ana. I really hope that this war won't be over before I complete all of my training. Well, on second thought, maybe that wouldn't be such a bad thing after all.

They're keeping us well fed, and I've managed to keep up with all of the physical training thus far. It was rather weird being away from y'all at Christmas, but they kept us so busy, I reckon that I lost track of the days. I'm sure that everyone there had a great time, and I hope that y'all have a terrific new year.

Orson Welles was here on the base the other day to entertain us with some of his buddies from Hollywood. They really made us laugh, but I sure would like to see Ginger Rogers, Betty Grable, or Bette Davis make the next trip down here.

I've met some really swell guys here on base, and we should find out any day now who was selected for pilot training. Keep your fingers crossed, and please say a prayer or two for me. I shall write back once I find out, assuming that I don't wash out for some reason or another.

Let everyone know that I miss them since it might be a good while before I get to come home.

Love y'all,

Felix

In addition to the classification process, there was daily physical training and plenty of calisthenics. All of Felix's hard work back home in San Saba had really paid off. The running, sit-ups, pull-ups, push-ups, leg lifts, and sprints were now seemingly unchallenging to him. A friendly rivalry had developed between Felix and Ray, and, at times, it was hard to determine who was the most athletic man in their barracks. Although the drills were difficult for many, Felix was determined to excel in this area. He thoroughly enjoyed the obstacle course, and he had a great deal of fun playing basketball, volleyball, baseball, and throwing horseshoes with his pals. Felix had never played tennis before, but with a few pointers from Ray, they certainly became a tough team to beat when playing doubles on the tennis court. The instructors told the class that their time at SAAAB would probably be the most demanding of all the physical training drills along their training path. If that were true, Felix felt pretty good about his chances moving forward.

Felix anxiously awaited classification day as the New Year's Day celebration began on 1 Jan. 1943. Over the course of that weekend, the staff met with each of the new aviation students at the personnel office. Felix was rather nervous as he walked into the room where he found two superior officers seated at a table. After saluting, and confirming his name, Felix was handed a card with his name on it. He was elated beyond belief, when he saw the word pilot next to his name on the card. Following a brief discussion pertaining to their decision, Felix stood up as tall as he could to salute the officers, all while trying to contain his enthusiasm. Finally, he signed a certificate of acceptance to officially begin his Pre-flight pilot training. When Felix returned to the barracks later that afternoon, he was glad to find out that Ray had also been selected for pilot training. Although not everyone in the barracks had been chosen for pilot training, each man had been selected for a program based on their individual strengths. It didn't matter if you were selected as a pilot, a bombardier, or as a navigator, everyone knew that they would each play a vital role in the success of an air crew during the war. However, it was fair to say that Felix was thrilled that Ray would be moving on with him as they began their journey to become pilots.

Felix and the other men were each issued an Aviation Cadet Regulations Handbook, and they were ordered to read it thoroughly. There were plenty of extra copies available in the barracks, so it was clearly evident that the men were to adhere to the regulations. Felix was certain that he'd meet this requirement without any difficulty since he was very familiar with a similar book during his time at Texas AMC. He felt that his college experience would surely help him get off to a good start, and he was ready to make a lasting impression on his commanding officers. Felix had already been issued an identification card, a mess card, a commissary card, but he felt really official when he was issued his SAAAB name badge. Felix had never had a name badge for any of his previous jobs, and he wore it proudly.

Felix began his pilot training at SAAAB on 4 Jan. 1943. He was now officially designated as an aviation cadet, and a member of class 43–I, which would remain his class number throughout his training. Felix remained part of the 3rd Air Force, but he was given a new squadron number, and he was assigned to live in new quarters with the other cadets who were training to become pilots there at SAAAB. He received several aviation cadet pins, which were to be placed on the lapels of his service coat and shirts, and a larger one was to go on the front of his service cap. As he affixed the pins to his coat and cap, he realized that they were very similar to the SAAAB sign located on the front entrance gate that he'd walked through on day one. Felix was given a copy of the Military Training Aid Manual For Aviation Cadets, along with a stack of other radio, airplane, and pilot manuals. The thought of having to read all of the books was very daunting to Felix, and his mind suddenly drifted back to his days at Texas AMC. Felix quickly snapped out of that momentary lapse of weakness, and he assured himself that he was entirely capable of learning this material. He sure was glad to see that there were no chemistry books in the stack.

The results of the classification testing weren't revealed to the men, but Felix realized that he must've done well enough on those silly mechanical tests. It was too early to know if the aviation cadets would be piloting a bomber, a cargo plane, or a fighter plane. However, Felix figured that his 5' 8½" frame would probably have something to do with the decision that would affect his future assignment. Being rather short and thin made him a perfect candidate to become a fighter pilot due to the limited space in the cockpit. Either way, Felix was happy that he was one step closer to realizing his dream of flying a plane. Felix and his new squadron mates marched to class daily with precision, and they taught each other new cadences to make the daily journey more enjoyable. Near the end of his first full week of training, Felix happened to run into Buster and Skip over at the mess hall. Buster had been assigned to the navigator training program, and Skip had been chosen for the bombardier training program. They knew that it would be quite a long shot for them to be assigned to the same air crew one day, but they had a blast imagining the possibility over some delicious chocolate cake.

Time on the pistol and rifle ranges was quite enjoyable to Felix. He'd been around guns for much of his life, and this was just another area for him to excel at. All the practice back at Pa's ranch had clearly come in handy as Felix fired many rounds from a .45 caliber pistol and from an M3 submachine gun. Felix also spent time firing an M1 carbine rifle as well. Seeing the damage that was inflicted by a .50 caliber round fired from a Browning machine gun never got old. Felix was proud of his skills, and he had no trouble qualifying at each of the ranges. The Army's motto of "kill or be killed" really made him realize that his life was truly on the line, and that there were no do-overs in actual combat. Felix's instructors and commanding officers seemed to be very pleased with his appearance, his uniform presentation, the tidiness of his bunk, his marching skills, his firearms proficiency, and his physical training abilities. Everything up to that point had felt like second nature to Felix, and he was certainly glad that he was making a good impression and doing well in the program.

Before his nine-week training class was over, Felix would be required to take many classes, including Aerodynamics for Pilots, Trigonometry, Practical Air Navigation, Physics, Aerial Photography, Chemical Warfare, Meteorology for Pilots, and Cryptography. The courses were to be taught by both civilian and military instructors, and each class would run for about 50 minutes. The men were set to learn all about the specific duties of the ground, air, and naval forces of the United States. Felix was looking forward to the domestic and allied aircraft recognition class since he'd built many model airplanes over the years. The instructors planned to use pictures, films, and models in order to help the cadets differentiate between cargo planes, bombers, and fighters of the United States and British forces. The identification of German, Italian, and Japanese planes would come during the next phases of his training. An introduction to chart and map reading, along with a discussion on weather patterns was also on the docket. Finally, the aviation cadets would be studying the design and function of many different aircraft engines.

The men were told that the class sessions would typically last for a few weeks before a different subject was introduced. Felix was excited with the course pertaining to the Theory and Principles of Flight. Although he was bummed that he wouldn't be flying a plane while at SAAAB, he was eager to learn everything necessary about the mechanics of how to fly a plane. Felix began to learn about aerodynamics, and the principles of physics that would allow him to get a plane off the ground. He studied Newton's laws pertaining to inertia, force, action, and reaction. Felix found the concepts of acceleration, gravity, mass, air pressure, velocity, vectors, and energy to all be a bit overwhelming, but fascinating at the same time. The cadets then studied the composition of air, and how it's related to flying a plane.

They dove into topics involving gases, air density, weight, altitude, humidity, air speed, and ground speed.

Just when Felix thought that he'd learned all there was to know about the science behind flying a plane, there came the discussion about drag, lift, and thrust. He had no idea that there was this much science involved with flying a plane. He also learned what speed, force, and pressure could do to the human body. Felix found the discussion pertaining to how an airplane was built to be rather tedious, since he already knew what the fuselage, the propeller, and the control stick were. However, he paid much closer attention to learn what the ailerons, the rudder, the flaps, and the elevators could do. The learning just kept coming with a presentation regarding yaw, pitch, and roll, and there was a discussion where the cadets learned the difference between a lateral, a longitudinal, and a vertical axis. The instructors discussed the importance in knowing the advantages and disadvantages of headwinds and tailwinds. Felix learned that a plane would fly faster with a tailwind since both the wind and plane are moving in the same direction. Although the speed of an aircraft will be reduced when flying into a headwind, he learned that it would be best to take off and land into one. Conversely, Felix was instructed to avoid taking off with or landing with a tailwind whenever possible.

The cadets were told that they may be flying in and out of airfields that didn't have a control tower in the coming months. Therefore, they were advised to always pay attention to the windsock that would be located near the runway. A windsock is a conical looking tube, made of durable material that is attached to a tall pole. It is a very helpful tool for a pilot to determine the direction of the wind, and the approximate wind speed when landing or taking off. Felix knew that math would finally come into play at some point, and he figured that there would be plenty of formulas and equations to learn. Some of them would surely be rather complex, but he was hoping that most wouldn't be. There were certainly some restless nights for Felix as he wondered how he was going to remember all of this material.

At the end of his first full week of class, Felix found a few minutes to write a letter to his parents back home in San Saba.

Dear folks,　　　　　　　　　　　　　　*January 9, 1943*

Your thoughts and prayers have thankfully paid off, and I'm very excited to let y'all know that I was selected to receive further training as a pilot. What a blessing! They told us that they were going to mail a form letter to y'all that would provide all the pertinent details.

We've already had long days inside of the classroom, but I'm enjoying every bit thus far. We'll be learning much more over the next couple of months here at SAAAB.

Mother, I'd like to wish you a very happy birthday. I sent a separate gift along with a card, and I really hope it arrives by your special day.

I've met a great friend here at SAAAB. His name is Ray Simon, and hanging out with him reminds me a great deal of being back home with Chauncey. We're having a terrific time palling around the base together.

Don't y'all worry about me. I'm certainly feeling well, and I have a healthy appetite! Please keep me in your thoughts, and be sure to say hello to everyone for me.

　　　　　　　　　　　　　　　　　　　　　　Love y'all,

　　　　　　　　　　　　　　　　　　　　　　Felix

Felix had already received a few letters from Elsie since his arrival at SAAAB, and he excitedly replied to each one. He was glad to let her know that he'd be hanging around in Orange County for the next few months due to him being selected for pilot training. Elsie seemed to be really into Felix, and he was certainly thrilled to see where the relationship might go. Felix had never been in a relationship where he had to get to know someone mostly through the mail. Nevertheless, he felt a real connection to Elsie, and he certainly hoped that a bona fide relationship was blossoming.

Generally speaking, there was very little downtime for Felix while on base. He was diligent about his studies, and he knew that he had to do well in order to move on to the next stage of training. On occasion, Felix would spend time in the service club there on base when he was in need of a respite from his demanding coursework. The club reminded him of the many days that he'd spent at the YMCA while on campus back at Texas AMC. The comfortable lounge was a great place to meet new people, write letters, listen to music, play board games, and play ping-pong. There were regular performances held at the service club that featured live cadet follies, which Felix and the other men on base found to be very entertaining. Felix made it a point to go to the service club every Friday night to read the newest addition of *The Cadet*, which was the name of the base newspaper.

The weeks were flying by rather quickly for Felix. He'd finally received his dog tags, and he was getting used to the clanking noises they produced during his strenuous exercise routines. Felix really enjoyed all of the different subjects and classes being taught on base. Having to learn the proper way to handle and adjust a gas mask was a bit unsettling to Felix. However, he realized the importance of being able to rapidly deploy the mask to his face in the event of a chemical attack. Felix had heard about Morse code before arriving at SAAAB, but now, he was excited to find out that he was going to have an opportunity to learn, and practice it. In order to pass this portion of the training, he needed to be able to decipher a minimum of eight words per minute by sound, and at least five words per minute by the blinking light. Felix seemed to have more trouble with the sounds generated by Morse code than with the light, but with lots of daily practice, he determined that he was actually pretty good at both. Some of the cadets weren't so happy to learn that Morse code was going to be taught the entire time while they were stationed at SAAAB. Additionally, the men were told to expect that Morse code lessons would be part of their curriculum throughout the entire course of their training program.

As January was about to come to a close, Felix continued to send letters to Elsie several times a week. He was thrilled to receive one from Elsie in which she agreed to pick him up for a date on 30 Jan. 1943. Felix had just received his first full paycheck of $75.00, plus an additional $1.00 per day for a ration allowance. He sent some money to his father back home for his truck loan, but he had plenty leftover to show Elsie a great time down in Newport Beach. With the six-week confinement to base restriction having been lifted, Felix was pleasantly surprised to see Elsie pull up in front of Gate No. 1 in her Oldsmobile at 1530 hours that Saturday afternoon. Felix had always enjoyed driving his Ford roadster for all of his previous dates back in Texas, but he quickly realized that he needed to adapt to his new environment. Naturally, he felt a bit weird as he climbed into the passenger seat of Elsie's car. However, after a nice hug, and a kiss on the cheek, Felix felt completely at ease. He was just glad to see Elsie once again as they headed to the Balboa Pavilion.

After collecting shells with Elsie while walking along the beautiful sandy shoreline, Felix figured that it would be entirely appropriate to have supper at Guss's Seashell Café as the sun began to set. He hadn't eaten much seafood since his brief trip to New Orleans, but with the shortage of beef in the United States, Felix felt it necessary to expand his horizons by trying new things. Before heading back to Elsie's car, the young couple stopped at an ice cream stand for a sweet treat. Felix hoped that he hadn't bored Elsie too much as he continued to let her know about all that had been going on at the base. He felt that their conversations throughout the afternoon had gone well, and both of them laughed nearly the entire evening. Elsie let Felix know that she'd enjoyed their date, and she offered to come back to Orange County the following morning. Felix just couldn't believe that he was going to have another opportunity to hang out with such a beautiful woman.

Elsie once again pulled up in front of Gate No. 1 on the morning of 31 Jan. 1943. Felix knew that he had to be back on base by 1500 hours, so he was eager to get going. He wanted to experience the thrill of driving along the California Coastline, so Felix asked Elsie if he could drive her car as they headed south on Pacific Coast Highway to Laguna Beach. Elsie agreed to let Felix drive, and with the windows rolled down, she could tell that he was thoroughly enjoying himself as the cool ocean breeze ripped through the cabin of her car. They stopped at a local deli to pick up some sandwiches, and he filled her cooler with bottles of ice cold Conco Grape punch along with a slew of Coca-Colas.

After finding a place to park near Broadway Street, Felix rented some reclining chairs and a large beach umbrella from a nearby hotel. They enjoyed the early afternoon breeze while relaxing and talking on the beach. Afterwards, they spent some time shopping at the wonderful eclectic shops in the downtown area. While standing on the sidewalk, the young couple stared through the window of a fine jewelry store. Felix could tell that Elsie's eyes had become fixated on a gold ankle bracelet adorned with colorful gemstones. After going inside for a closer look, Elsie was elated when Felix impulsively decided to purchase it. After affixing the bracelet to Elsie's ankle, he thought that her legs looked even more gorgeous. Felix was thankful that she was able to get him back to the base on time. Before Elsie headed home, Felix asked her if she and her two friends would like to join him, Buster, and Skip at the Balboa USO club the following Saturday night. The idea sounded appealing to Elsie, and she said that she'd get a letter off to him to confirm within a few days. Felix then reached over towards Elsie to share a pleasant kiss before heading back onto the post.

February of 1943 turned out to be an exciting time for Felix, both on, and off the base. A new theater opened on 1 Feb. 1943, which made it the third, and largest one yet on base. Tickets were a hot commodity, and Felix wasn't lucky enough to attend on opening night. However, he saw *Air Force* a few days later in the spacious new theater with Ray and Skip. There were several other films that Felix viewed in the classroom during February. The United States Department of War produced a film series titled *Why We Fight,* and all United States servicemen were required to watch the movies. Felix was unsure of what to expect when he viewed the first installment in the series, *Prelude To War*. This film discussed the planned conquests of Hitler, Mussolini, and Hirohito. It also provided a scenario where both coasts of the United States were subject to an invasion from the Axis powers. Next, he saw the second installment in the series, *The Nazis Strike*. This film discussed Hitler's complete disregard for treaties, agreements, and non-aggression pacts as he continued his path towards world conquest. Felix and his classmates saw just how formidable the German Luftwaffe could be with their long-range bombers, fighter planes, and dive bombers. A few days later, Felix watched the third installment in the series, *Divide And Conquer*. This film focused on how Hitler's German armies took control of Austria, Czechoslovakia, Poland, Denmark, Norway, Luxembourg, Holland, Belgium, and finally France. The film also showed how Hitler's broken promises and savagery resulted in the utter destruction of entire cities, which resulted in countless civilian deaths, and even more refugees. These films confirmed Felix's beliefs that there were some very cruel and evil people within the leadership of the Axis powers. He felt adamant that he had made the correct decision to sign up and fight. The Axis powers were clearly a real threat, and for the people of the world to be free again, Felix knew that the war machines of Germany, Japan, and Italy needed to be stopped square in their tracks. There was quite a discussion that evening in the mess hall as to which man would stack up best against the enemy fighters in the battlefield of the sky. Once again, Felix was itching to get into the fight, and he was a little bothered that he couldn't do anything to speed up the course of his training.

Felix and his pals were very glad to see Elsie and her gals pull up in front of the USO club at 4th and Main, over in Santa Ana, on 6 Feb. 1943. The party began around 2000 hours that Saturday night, and it lasted long into the evening. Everyone had a terrific time with the live music, great food, and plenty of dancing. Plans were made for the group to meet up at the club every Saturday night for the rest of February. Felix was very glad to hear that Elsie agreed to return once again to Orange County the following morning to spend more time with him. After pulling up in front of Gate No. 1, Elsie tossed the keys to her car to Felix, and they were off to enjoy a fabulous brunch at the USO club in Newport Beach. There were plenty of surfboards available, and Elsie was quite entertained as she watched Felix try to learn how to surf. Before heading back to the base, the young couple enjoyed some ice-cold soda pop as they walked out to the end of the Newport Beach Pier. Felix truly didn't want the day to end, and he sure enjoyed holding Elsie's hand as they made their way to her car. On the way back to the base, Felix was trying to muster up enough courage to ask Elsie if she'd want to join him for an extra special date the following weekend. With his left hand on the steering wheel, Felix reached out for Elsie's hand. While still a few blocks away from the base, Felix looked over at Elsie's adorable smiling face, and said, "I've had the most remarkable time with you over the last two weeks. It seems like we've known each other so much longer than we actually have. Next weekend happens to be Valentine's Day weekend, and I have something very special planned for the two of us. Would you mind packing an overnight bag when you come to town next Saturday?" Elsie didn't seem to need any time to ponder the thought. As she clutched his right hand, Elsie then winked, and smiled at Felix as she accepted his invitation.

Dear folks, *February 9, 1943*

How's everything coming along? Everything's swell here, couldn't be better. Found out today that I'll be here for about another four weeks or so.

That medical deal along the line has really dealt me misery. If it hadn't been for that recurrent growth, I could've already had my wings.

Incidentally, if I ever get my wings, and <u>when</u> I get my wings, we're going to have a new member in our family. Her name is Elsie Jerina, a little Czechoslovakian girl, who's really a peach. You'd have to see her, and be with her, to find out what I'm talking about. Texas has never produced anyone like her before.

Now don't go getting worried because it's a long time off, and I've got a date to keep with Uncle Sam first. Just breaking it to you kind of gentle like, so that you can start getting used to the idea.

Talk about a rugged athletic instructor, we really have one. That's the way I like it though; the tougher they are on us, the better off we are. No sissies in this man's Air Corps. Write to me because I sure like to hear from home.

Love y'all,

Felix

The plans to continue partying at the USO had been put on hold for the weekend, and Felix let Buster and Skip know that they'd need to make their own plans with Elsie's friends. Once again, Felix stood outside Gate No. 1, but on 13 Feb. 1943, he was holding a lovely bouquet of flowers, a box of chocolates, and another box that was wrapped in fancy red paper. When Elsie pulled up, she was very excited to see Felix with his pile of goodies. He presented her with the flowers and chocolate, but he told her that she'd have to wait until later that night to open her other present. This time, Felix served as the navigator while Elsie followed his directions as they headed towards the beautiful Orange County Coastline.

Elsie finally came to a stop in the parking lot right between the Balboa Pier and the Balboa Inn. She was ecstatic when Felix pointed towards one of the rooms with a direct view of the ocean and said that they'd be staying there. After collecting their belongings, Elsie grabbed his hand, and they hurriedly made their way to the front desk in the lobby. She became even more elated when Felix prepaid for the next three Saturday nights as well. Elsie thought Felix looked very handsome in his "pinks and greens" with his service cap fitted properly atop his head. Just like at Texas AMC, the cadets at SAAAB referred to their uniform in this fashion, since their khaki pants seemed to have a hint of pink to them, and they wore a green service coat.

Felix and Elsie's fabulous evening began with a long walk that included a stop to watch the sunset at the end of the Balboa Pier. Next, they enjoyed a spectacular supper at a nearby Italian restaurant, and afterwards, they returned to the hotel room where Felix presented Elsie with the rest of her present. She tore the paper off the box to reveal an opulent pearl necklace. He placed the magnificent necklace around her neck and closed the clasp. Felix just couldn't believe how beautiful Elsie looked wearing it, and before long, she wasn't wearing anything else but the necklace. One thing led to another, and just like that, Felix and Elsie shared a passionate evening as the waves crashed mightily just outside of their balcony, capping the end to a wonderful day.

The work in the classroom was going well for Felix as graduation day quickly approached, and he was glad to find time for some more fun and excitement on base. The evening of 19 Feb. 1943 was quite a night to remember, since it was Commander Robertson's birthday, and it was time to celebrate the one-year anniversary of the Santa Ana Army Air Base. The celebration included live music, and, of course, plenty of cake. After the Sunday afternoon parade on 21 Feb. 1943, Felix and Ray saw *Reveille with Beverly* at the new theater on base. There was tremendous excitement on base when word spread that the Yankee great, Joe DiMaggio, would be joining their ranks on 24 Feb. 1943. Initially, it was unclear to the men what his role would be exactly, but everyone sure hoped that he was going to be part of the baseball team there on the base. Felix happened to be in the right place, and at the right time, on Sunday, 28 Feb. He was relaxing and writing letters in the service club, when Joe walked in and began passing out some autographed pictures of himself. Felix was beside himself after meeting, and shaking hands with one of the most well-known Yankees at the time. He felt that he was very lucky to have snagged one of the few autographed pictures, and it quickly became featured inside his footlocker next to Elsie's and his family's pictures. Later that day, Felix made it a point to watch Joe hit some balls during practice on the baseball field. Watching Joe hit the balls with such power, Felix wondered if some of them might have cleared the base, and landed into the Pacific Ocean.

Felix was always excited to get mail from home, and he was quite intrigued to find that the envelope he'd received on 1 Mar. was a little larger than usual. After eagerly tearing it open, he was pleasantly surprised to find a delightful postcard from Buzz along with several other letters from home. Felix had kept in touch with Buzz ever since he'd left College Station, and he'd last heard from Buzz in December of 1942, just before heading to SAAAB. At that time, he knew that Buzz was about to start his Advanced training as a B-17 bomber pilot. Felix thought that the front of the postcard was hilarious, and he couldn't wait to read the back. After flipping it over, he was rather disappointed to see that it was nearly blank. However, knowing that Buzz had quite a sense of humor, there was a smiley face with the words "see enclosed letter."

Howdy Felix,   *10 Feb. 1943*

I sure hope that this finds you well. I was over at the PX the other day, and when I saw this little postcard, I just knew that I had to send it off to you. I've got plenty to share, and I didn't think that it would all fit on the back, so I'm writing you this letter instead. Knowing you, you probably already have a beautiful blonde bombshell, and this is why the card is entirely appropriate.

I'm fixing to graduate from multi-engine Advanced training here in Sioux City, Iowa. I've been training in the AT-9, and in the last few weeks, they've had me up in the B-17. It's an amazing plane, Felix. You just cannot imagine the damage that I'm gonna do to those Nazi bastards if I get sent to the skies over Europe. I'm not exactly sure where I'm headed just yet, but as you probably know, it's classified.

Me and Betty Lou plan to get hitched when I get home from this wretched war. I'd love for you to be my best man, but dadgummit, Felix, it might be kind of awkward since Emma Jo will be there as the maid of honor. After we finish bombing the shit out of those squirrely little scoundrels, I hope that you'll invite me to San Saba so that we can catch some of those big fish you've always bragged about. I'll drop you a line when I get to where I'm going. Well, ol' buddy, I wish you luck with the rest of your training, and from what I hear, I'll need plenty of luck myself. Follow your dreams, and always watch your back out there, my friend.

All my best,

Buzz

A postcard sent to Felix before Buzz headed off to war.

Felix was still somewhat envious that Buzz had ended up graduating with their class there at Texas AMC in May of 1942. Furthermore, he was even a bit jealous that Buzz was on the doorstep of fighting in the war while he was just getting started with his own training. Nevertheless, Buzz was his best friend, and he was happy for him. Felix just wished that they could be piloting their missions together because he knew that they'd be a hell of a duo to reckon with.

As February was about to come to a close, Felix realized that his time at SAAAB was coming to an end. The fact that there were no planes at SAAAB remained a disappointment to Felix, but he was pleased that he was continuing to do well with his training. He figured that a trip into the altitude chamber would surely give him some idea of what flying a plane would be like. Felix was a bit apprehensive about the thought of having to spend nearly two hours inside the contraption that sort of resembled a submarine. The men were shown a film on what to expect, and they practiced the proper way of placing an oxygen mask on their face. Felix learned that his body would typically need supplemental oxygen at altitudes above 12,000 feet. He was undoubtedly concerned when he was told that a loss of consciousness, or even death, could occur at altitudes above 20,000 feet without supplemental oxygen. Felix had many takeaways from the training before they entered the altitude chamber. He learned that, as a pilot, he needed to continue to be physically fit, to avoid certain foods, and to not fly at higher altitudes with a head cold. A well-fitting oxygen mask would also be a key to survival at the higher altitudes.

Including the instructors, there were about a dozen men inside the chamber. Before the simulation began, the cadets were reminded that they might not realize that there is a problem as they reached the higher altitudes. However, they were told that there would likely be multiple effects upon their bodies including reduced vision, decreased hearing, and a plethora of other physical and emotional effects. The instructors didn't ask the men to put their oxygen masks on until they reached a simulated altitude of about 15,000 feet. The cadets gradually continued their climb to nearly 40,000 feet before making their slow descent within the altitude chamber. The instructors tested the men's cognitive abilities at different intervals during the experience, and Felix could tell that it was a rather wonky couple of hours for some. Felix felt bad for the fellow that passed out during his session, but he found the overall training to be enlightening and enjoyable. He was certainly glad that he didn't have any noticeable medical issues during the exercise, and he was glad to have exited the machine in one piece. Later that evening at supper, each of the cadets at Felix's table discussed their time within the altitude chamber. Felix was rather sad to learn that some of the cadets within his squadron didn't have the same positive outcome as himself. He realized that it must've been devastating for those cadets who had washed out at such a late date into the training since they had spent more than 200 hours in the classroom up to that point.

Felix spent every possible moment of his final weekend in Orange County with Elsie. Along with their friends, Felix and Elsie went to the dance party at the USO on that Saturday night, but they left early to spend another romantic evening at the hotel down in Balboa. After walking up and down the sandy beach under the moonlit sky, the young couple returned to the hotel room. Felix and Elsie cuddled up in bed for hours as they talked, laughed, and shared stories about their childhood. They remained in bed until it was nearly time to check out of the hotel the next morning. Felix was very happy that he'd be advancing to Primary training, but he was certainly miserable that he'd be seeing much less of Elsie. He really wondered where their relationship would go from there.

All of the laughs and giggles quickly turned into tears as Felix said goodbye to Elsie outside Gate No. 1 on that Sunday afternoon of 7 Mar. 1943. Elsie was proud of Felix's accomplishment, and she was glad that he'd be continuing on with his training. However, she was surely going to miss him, his smile, and their weekend trips at the beach. At that moment, Felix had no idea where he'd be heading to next since that information was classified until he actually arrived at his new post. Felix assured Elsie that he'd write to her as soon as he obtained his new post address. With that, Felix gave Elsie a big hug and a kiss before making his way through the throng of cadets trying to get back onto the base before the Sunday afternoon parade.

Felix was so pleased that he didn't fail any of his academic courses. Little did he know it at the time, but the Agricultural & Mechanical College of Texas had really prepared him with a solid educational foundation, and he'd learned that with proper study habits, he could do well at SAAAB. Just like that, the final few days of his Pre-flight training had flown by, and Felix officially graduated on 11 Mar. 1943. Felix was thankful that he was able to bid farewell, and wish good luck to most of his pals at supper that night. Later that evening, the men were bused to Santa Ana at different times, and they were told to get onto specific train cars. The aviation cadets of class 43-I were now being split up, and they were about to be sent off to more than a dozen different schools spread throughout Arizona and California. Felix was pretty bummed when he had to say goodbye to Ray, who boarded a different train en route to his own Primary training. When Felix's train would stop, he'd officially begin his Primary training, where he'd finally have an opportunity to fly a plane!

CHAPTER 11

Finally Flying

As dawn began to break on the morning of 12 Mar. 1943, the train continued to roar down the tracks. Felix looked out the window, and he saw plenty of agricultural fields, ranches, livestock, and wide-open swathes of land. In a weird sort of way, he briefly wondered if he were somehow back in Texas. Felix was glad that the train ride wasn't supposed to be nearly as long as the journey from San Saba to Orange County had been. However, he didn't expect that it would take about 13 hours to get from Santa Ana to his next post. Luckily, Felix and the men had been able to get some sleep in their seats, and in the aisleway aboard the train. A thick plume of smoke rose from the mighty locomotive as it slowly pulled into the train station in King City, California.

One by one, the cadets exited the train cars, outfitted in their tan slacks, their green service coat, and their service cap. Many of the men had their raincoat slung over one arm, with their bags in the other. Felix took a moment to take in a breath of fresh air, while noticing the rolling hills and mountains surrounding the King City area. The contingent of young cadets was met by friendly staff members, who were waiting near a very interesting looking transport vehicle. A modified pickup truck was hitched to three open air trailer cars, and each of the cars was adorned with colorful cloth roofs. Felix and the other cadets quickly hopped onboard for the short trip over to their new post, and it didn't take long before the men were waiting for the guard to open the front gate. Felix peered around the chap sitting next to him to see a more colorful gate than the one back at SAAAB. The gate featured crisscrossed metal beams throughout, and there was a large circular sign on each side of the gate. Each sign had "Mesa-Del-Rey" spelled along the top, and just beneath the name, there were four planes flying over a setting sun in the middle of the circle.

After passing through the front gate, there was a very tall flagpole located directly in front of a large building surrounded by manicured flowerbeds. The cadets exited their vehicle, and they were then led to an open area where some men in uniforms were waiting. Along the way, Felix noticed that the barracks were painted in different colors than what he'd seen at SAAAB. There were freshly cut lawns, green shrubs, and beautiful flowers throughout the grounds. Felix immediately felt that things around the post were much less formal than at SAAAB, and he could also see that it was a great deal smaller in size as well. After having had a pretty good look around the base, Felix thought that Mesa Del Rey reminded him in some ways to his stay on South Padre Island. The main difference, of course, was that he didn't see any sign of a beach nearby, and the United States wasn't at war at that time.

The new cadets gathered around a man in uniform who was now standing on a chair inside of a circle that had formed. Felix could tell that the man was more than likely the officer in charge, and everyone quickly became quiet when he began to speak. "Good morning, gentlemen. My name is Captain Dana Fuller, and I'm the Commanding Officer (CO) here at Mesa Del Rey. My staff and I would like to welcome you to our post, where you'll receive your Primary training over the next nine weeks. The foundation for your flying career will begin right here at Mesa Del Rey. Some of you may be wondering where we are exactly, and I'd like for you to know that we're about one hour and 15 minutes southeast of Monterey, and about one hour and 30 minutes north of Morrow Bay. As you can probably tell, this isn't an actual United States Army Air Forces base. Rather, this is a contract pilot school, operated by the Palo Alto Airport Inc. You'll find that civilians will be teaching you inside the classroom as well as in the air as your flight instructors. You men won't be "dodos" for too much longer. Before you know it, you'll be upperclassmen, and flying solo in one of the planes right over there." Felix and the other men yelled and clapped with excitement as Captain Fuller concluded his welcoming speech.

The group of cadets was quickly assigned to quarters, and as they made their way to the barracks, they passed the PX, the mess hall, and the classrooms that would be used for their ground school courses. Felix estimated that there were probably a tad more than 200 men that would be part of his 43-I class at Mesa Del Rey. He saw quite a few familiar faces, and he knew at least a few dozen of his fellow cadets. Upon entering the barracks, Felix could see that the room was configured much differently than what he'd lived in back at SAAAB. There were only six people to a room, which made for a more private bathroom experience. After sitting on the mattress that was housed within a wooden bed frame, Felix felt that it was actually pretty comfortable. Although the laid-back feeling seemed to be rather pervasive on the post, Felix and the men were still expected to keep their beds neat and tidy just like they'd done while at SAAAB. Additionally, the men were responsible for keeping everything clean within the room, including the nice blinds on the windows. Felix and the other cadets were told to expect personal inspections of their living quarters every Thursday.

Felix's first day at Mesa Del Rey wouldn't have been complete without a trip to the mess hall. The men marched to the mess hall together as a group, but they were allowed to leave after their meal, rather than having to leave all together at once. The atmosphere inside the mess hall was much more relaxed than at SAAAB, thereby allowing the men to have more lively conversations. Felix thought that the food selection was plentiful, and he felt that the taste was rather palatable. He ended the evening by writing a letter to Elsie, and with one to his folks as well. Felix let everyone know that he'd arrived safely in King City, and he provided them with his new mailing address.

Felix's second day on the post began early the next morning at 0530 hours. There was time for some calisthenics before Reveille, and then everyone headed to breakfast. There was plenty of excitement in the air as the men marched towards the quartermaster's building to draw their flight gear and other pilot supplies. The process was pretty similar to that at SAAAB, and the staff was very quick to handle the cadets at each station. First, Felix got his A-3 flyer's bag, which was a large bag capable of holding most of his equipment. He also received a B-4 bag, which was a more slimmed down version of the A-3 bag, but it was still more than adequate to hold his smaller items needed for a flight. Next, Felix was issued his winter and summer leather helmets, and also his B-6 jacket. He thought that he looked entirely cool in his thick Airman's jacket, which was made with sheepskin and sheep fur.

The seat style parachute harness was probably the biggest item that Felix received that day. It was worn on his back, so it didn't interfere with him collecting the additional pieces of his flight equipment. Felix continued down the line to receive a pair of A-6 flight boots, which were heavy boots made of rubber, leather, and they were lined with sheep's fur. There was a zipper down the front, along with two leather straps on each boot. Felix found some room in his bag for the next few items, which included a pair of A-5 sheepskin trousers, a C-2 vest, and a life vest. Before leaving the quartermaster's building, a supply officer provided Felix with his pilot's navigation kit, which included a D-4 time and distance computer, a flashlight with a red bulb and batteries included, a notepad, and several pencils. Finally, Felix was given a personal emergency kit for pilots, which included signal flares, basic field rations, matches, a compass, a pocketknife, and some first aid supplies.

Being that all of the cadets were together, folks from the King's Log yearbook staff were present to snap individual portraits of each cadet in their new flying duds. All of the gear that Felix received was recorded on a Flyer's Personal Equipment Record form. He was told to keep it with him as he moved from base to base. The staff made it clear to the cadets that the gear that was issued to them was for the duration of their time in the service. The men were also told that they were personally responsible for its care, and pieces would only be replaced if they became worn out.

After leaving the quartermaster's building, Felix and the men headed to an area adjacent to the flight line, where they were assigned to one of four different flights. Each flight had several flight instructors, and every flight was led by a senior flight instructor. There were five cadets assigned to each flight instructor, and Felix was assigned to flight three. Each cadet was then issued a Pilot Logbook, which was to be taken aboard the plane with them on each flight. The log would be used to record the date of the flight, whether it was a dual or solo flight, the type of plane flown, if it was a day or night flight, and the duration of the flight. Next, the men were given schedules for their individual flight instruction, and they were advised that they'd receive their flight training during a five-hour window, either in the morning, or the afternoon instead. When they weren't receiving flight training, the cadets would be required to attend ground school training sessions, which were to last about four to five hours per day.

F. E. SCOTT
San Saba, Texas

King's Log Yearbook photo, Class 43-I at Mesa Del Rey in King City, CA.

Captain T. G. Kelly, Director of Flight Training, stepped up to the podium to provide the cadets with an outline for their next nine weeks of training. During the first phase, each new pilot would ride along with their flight instructor to experience takeoffs and landings. The rookie pilots would also be shown how to perform straight and level turns, gliding turns, gentle spins, and how to recover from a stall. The second phase of training would provide Felix with the opportunity to fly solo for the first time. Additionally, he and the other pilots would learn how to perform pylon eights, chandelles, and lazy eights. The third phase was mostly about accuracy, and this is where Felix's precision in taking off and landing would be measured. He'd also learn how to take off and land on shorter runways. The final phase of his Primary training seemed to be the most appealing to Felix. This is where he'd perform mild acrobatics such as loops, climbs, dives, half rolls, slow rolls, snap rolls, spins, and he'd even learn how to complete an Immelmann turn. The concept of pilot life insurance was still relatively new to Felix, but he realized its importance when he found out that he'd be briefly inverted, in an open cockpit, during some of his maneuvers!

Felix with some of his fellow pilots featured in the King's Log yearbook at Mesa Del Rey. He is pictured in the bottom row, third from the right.

There was some grumbling among the cadets when they were told that they'd have at least one hour of physical activity each day. However, their fears subsided when the men saw the baseball field, basketball court, volleyball courts, and the large swimming pool. Of course, there would also be plenty of push-ups, leg lifts, rope climbs, and a great deal of running. Clearly, there were plenty of activities to keep a fella busy, and Felix figured that he'd enjoy the weight training program as well. However, he wasn't so sure that he wanted to get into the boxing ring due to the size of some of the other cadets on base. Having survived the physical training at SAAAB, Felix felt that this would be like recreation at a summer camp, and he knew that he wouldn't fail in this area.

As the cadets walked to the classrooms for their first session of ground school training on that Saturday afternoon, Felix stopped for just a moment to take it all in. There were planes flying all over the clear blue sky above him, and he marveled at the maneuvers that the more advanced pilots were completing. He was committed to giving everything that he had in order to do well at this level. Felix could hardly contain his excitement, but he knew that he too, would be in the air soon. Walking into the classroom didn't seem to bring too much anxiety to Felix. As the class got underway, the instructor appeared to be very likable, approachable, and easy-going. There might've been some edginess when the dozen or so textbooks and manuals were placed on the desk directly in front of him. Once again, momentary flashbacks raced through Felix's head dating back to his time at Texas AMC when he'd received a similar stack of chemistry, biology, and agricultural math books. Although Ray wasn't there to help Felix with his new courses, he reminded himself that he'd successfully made it through his Pre-flight training. Felix assured himself that with hard work and plenty of studying, he could comprehend the new material, being that he had a passion for what he was about to learn.

The cadets were each given a syllabus for what they'd be studying in ground school over the next nine weeks. The first five weeks of their Primary training would be devoted to topics mostly pertaining to navigation training. The rookie pilots would soon learn about the four different types of navigation that could be used while flying. The first type involved point-to-point navigation, and this is where a pilot would use landmarks and other ground objects to guide him during a flight. The second type centered around flying while using a compass. Felix was feeling pretty confident with the navigation discussion up to that point since he'd made it all the way to Mexico City and back while using his own compass. The third type of navigation involved "blind flying," which involved the use of onboard instruments exclusively during a flight. Felix figured that flying would be challenging enough, but to do it without being able to see outside of the cockpit, caused him some uneasiness to say the least. The final type of navigation that the cadets would learn about was celestial navigation. This is where Felix and the men would learn how to use the sun, the moon, and the stars as tools to guide them safely during a flight.

Before long, the cadets would quickly become adept at using maps and aeronautical charts to plot a course prior to each flight. Felix knew his way around San Saba County, and he could surely navigate the sprawling campus at Texas AMC. He could also read a map for city streets, but the thought of having to fly a plane over rugged terrain, mountains, rivers, and jungles using topographical maps and coordinates somewhat scared him, but the idea intrigued him at the same time. Felix figured that it was just like learning anything else, and it would be only a matter of time before he mastered this new skill set. The next two weeks would be spent reviewing relevant weather patterns. This would be the opportunity where the cadets would learn how flight can be affected by wind, speed, and other elements. Felix and a few of the other men got a real chuckle when the instructor mentioned the effects that frost and ice could have on a plane, the propeller, and the assortment of instruments that would be found within the cockpit. Having just come back from a drill out in the wonderful weather of King City, many of the cadets figured that they weren't going to have to deal with the cold for quite some time to come. However, they had the proper flight gear for when the time might come, and for the meantime, they were advised to stay hydrated, and to avoid strenuous exercise during the hottest part of the day.

The final two weeks of ground school training at Mesa Del Rey would be spent on the recognition of the aircraft and ships belonging to the Axis powers. Many of the cadets had heard about the German Messerschmitt and the Japanese Zero, but there were plenty of other

German, Italian, and Japanese fighters and bombers to learn about. Felix was unsure how he'd go about identifying an enemy aircraft under the cover of darkness during combat. Nevertheless, he figured that if another plane started shooting at him, he'd need to think of something real fast. Finally, the men would be spending time each day learning about aircraft engines, fuel systems, hydraulics, electrical and heating systems, and the mechanical operating system for the plane that they'd be flying. There would be plenty of hands-on training, lectures, and an assortment of films as part of the curriculum. It was very important to understand how a plane was powered, and put together in order to be able to fly it proficiently and safely.

Felix and the other four cadets within his flight group were excited that the time had come to meet up with their flight instructor, Randolph Shoemaker, at 0700 hours on Sunday, 14 Mar. 1943. It was as if Felix had walked through the gates of heaven as he stepped out onto the flight line for the first time. After making his way to the meeting area, he took a few minutes to look around at all of his surroundings. Felix stood there in amazement as he stared at all of the majestic Ryan PT-22s lined up wing to wing in uniform rows. Each plane had a unique number painted near the tail, and Felix estimated that there must've been close to one hundred planes on the flight line, with plenty of others flying above them. He noticed that some of the planes were nestled safely within concrete revetments, while others were being serviced within one of the few nearby hangers. Each cadet picked up a chair and moved it directly next to the plane that was sitting idly beside Randolph so that the meeting could begin. After getting to know a little bit about each of his new pilots, Randolph began the meeting with the basic characteristics and functionality of the PT-22. Felix felt that the plane's nickname, the Recruit, was appropriate since they were all rookie flyers. He knew that he needed to know the make-up of the Ryan PT-22, but he was anxious, and chomping at the bit to get into the cockpit.

The meeting was definitely going to be a hands-on experience, and each man was eagerly waiting his turn to sit in the backseat of the tandem, open-air cockpit. Randolph pointed out all the components of the plane, even including some of the mundane things like the propeller, the flaps, the rudder pedals, the stick, the throttle, and the various gauges. He then told the group that there would be more to learn about completing a thorough pre-flight check of the aircraft before each flight. Part of Felix's parachute assembly coupled as a seat cushion, and he wasn't about to let that get in the way as he prepared to hop into the cockpit. Felix was beyond thrilled as he climbed onto the wing walk and into the rear seat of the monoplane. The front seat was reserved for Randolph during the times that they'd fly together.

While smiling from cheek to cheek, Felix looked to his left, and then to his right, and he saw the United States Army Air Forces circle and star insignia painted onto the top of each wing. He had also noticed that US ARMY was spelled out underneath the wings with an additional star as well. He checked out the glass windshield located in front of his seat, and he figured that it would probably provide some protection from the wind and birds. Felix must've been dreaming for a few moments, as one of the other men had to repeatedly pat him on the shoulder to alert him that his turn in the cockpit was over. He then proceeded to walk around the plane, and he checked out the wheel that was located underneath each wing that comprised the front landing gear. After inspecting the much smaller wheel beneath the tail, Felix cautiously ran his fingers up and down both wooden blades of the propeller before moving safely away from it. He found that each blade was reinforced with metal at the end of the tips. Randolph closed the meeting by mentioning that the PT-22 had a 125 mph maximum speed, about a 200 mile range, and it could fly as high as 15,000 feet. Randolph then provided each cadet with a Pilot's Handbook of Flight Operating Instructions for the PT-22. He asked that each man read through the manual that evening, and the group was told to report back to the flight line at 0700 hours the following morning in order to begin their aerial training. Finally, Felix was only several hours away from being airborne!

It was 15 Mar. 1943, and to Felix, it must've felt like it was Christmas morning. He had hardly slept a wink, and he was restless nearly all of the previous evening. Felix momentarily recalled the many nights as a young man when he'd stay up late while reading airplane magazines underneath his sheets with a flashlight. After completing his required reading assignment, he had a pretty good idea in principle of what to do, and what not to do. Before heading to the flight line that morning, Felix stopped by the quartermaster's office. They had replenished their stock, and he was finally able to receive his goggles, sunglasses, and a flight suit that would fit him properly. The morning continued to go well for Felix when Randolph selected him to be the first one to join him for a spin in the Ryan Recruit. The other men assigned to Randolph were somewhat apprehensive as they took a seat on a bench waiting to get a turn of their own. They looked on attentively as Randolph walked around the plane with Felix to complete their pre-flight inspection.

Randolph stressed that safety was the primary objective for any pilot, and especially for a new pilot. He looked at Felix, and said, "If you always fly with safety in mind, there's a great chance that you'll be here tomorrow to fly another day." Before the engine could be started, it needed to be properly primed. After doing that, Randolph showed

Felix both ways to start the five-cylinder, 160 horsepower engine. He demonstrated how a crank lever could be turned repeatedly, or that the propeller could be turned by hand until it started up. Firing up the engine by hand turning the propeller seemed a little sketchy to Felix. He and the other cadets were glad when they were instructed to hand turn the propeller only if the crank option wasn't available for some reason.

In order to get to the runway safely, Felix needed to learn that there was a proper taxiing technique called "S"ing. There had been plenty of recent accidents on the parking ramp, and Randolph was focused on demonstrating the correct procedure for Felix. He told Felix not to rely solely on the ground personnel while taxiing, since that they might be inexperienced as well. Randolph advised Felix that his eyes needed to always be moving to the areas around and above him, and that he needed to look out for potential issues that might arise unexpectedly at any moment. Felix watched closely as Randolph skillfully maneuvered the Ryan PT-22 from side to side around the parking ramp while dodging obstructions, pilots, and the other planes. He reminded Felix to be aware of crosswinds that might adversely affect the process of "S"ing towards the runway. There wasn't much room for error on the ramp, and Randolph was very proficient with making the sharp turns from left to right as they made their way around the flight line. Due to the noise of the propellers that were whizzing nearby, Randolph had to practically yell the steps that he was taking within the cockpit. He said, "You need to use just the right amount of throttle and rudder, and be sure to use the brakes only as needed." Felix paid close attention to Randolph's instructions, and he was certain that he'd be able to get his plane to the runway by safely "S"ing when given an opportunity to do so.

Felix about to take flight in a Ryan PT-22 at Mesa Del Rey.

Felix double checked his safety belt, and just like that, they were up in the air. He took it all in as Randolph piloted the plane westward over the Salinas River, and across the mountainous Big Sur State Park until they could begin to see the Pacific Ocean. There were no headset radios in the PT-22 at that time, so Randolph did a lot of finger pointing to landmarks on the ground, and so on. However, to better describe a maneuver, or something more important, Randolph used a rather ingenious device. He talked into a funnel that was connected to Felix's helmet via a rubber hose. It wasn't perfect, but it worked well enough, and Felix did his best to talk back with this method of communication. As Randolph picked up speed in the PT-22, Felix found that the wind against his face was really something. Felix's goggles and leather helmet provided some protection from the wind, but there wasn't that much that could be done to make the experience any less noisy. His thick coat kept him warm for the most part as the chilly wind raced through the cockpit.

When Randolph touched down on the lone runway at Mesa Del Rey, Felix felt that his boyhood dream had finally become a reality. The experience was beyond exhilarating, and Felix had a smile that seemingly ran from ear to ear. Felix figured that the only thing that could top his first flight would be for him to be in control of the stick. He took a moment to ask Randolph about the crop dusting planes that he'd seen spraying chemicals over the agricultural fields beneath them. Randolph explained that the crop dusters in the King City area had a large A painted on the sides of the fuselage in order to make them more easily identifiable. Felix then let Randolph know that he envisioned himself doing the exact same thing back home in San Saba after the war was over. Randolph agreed that such a career would be a good fit, and he could tell that Felix was going to be a quick learner. As the other men took their turns in the plane with Randolph, Felix was able to write a letter to Elsie, and one to his folks back home. He let them know that he'd finally made it up into the air, and that they'd landed safely. Felix was very excited that he'd be performing solo flights within just a few weeks' time.

A crop duster that would've been seen in the skies above King City. Photo courtesy of the Jernigan Collection-King City, CA.

The main objective of the Primary training program was for the men to develop proficiency through repetition. Over the next couple of weeks, there would be many more flying sessions with Randolph. Meanwhile, in the classroom, the cadets would continue to view many different training films pertaining to takeoffs, landings, flying safety, and even acrobatics. The men learned that they needed to avoid sudden and jerky movements while piloting their plane. Instead, the young pilots were instructed to use gradual and controlled movements when using the throttle, the stick, and the rudder pedals. Randolph was very supportive as he continuously told his men that making errors was a normal part of learning how to fly. However, he expected that each of his cadets pay close attention to ensure that they were fully aware of all the steps needed to perform the basic maneuvers and acrobatics.

Felix seemed a little overwhelmed with all of the information that had been suddenly thrown at him. He realized that too much or not enough air speed when performing his acrobatics could be devastating. Felix also understood the importance of proper coordination when using the stick, the throttle, and the other surface controls together in order to correctly fly and perform his maneuvers. The ailerons and flaps that were found on the rear edge of the wings, along with the rudder and elevators that were found near the rear of the plane, were all very important pieces. Precise movements, exceptional timing, complete control, and creative acrobatics would certainly make Felix the ace pilot that he'd always dreamed of becoming. Randolph made it clear that each of his pilots needed to outwit and outthink the pilot of an enemy aircraft if they were to ever meet in battle.

Felix thoroughly enjoyed every flight with Randolph in the dual-controlled airplane. After Randolph would demonstrate a new maneuver while flying in the PT-22, he'd then let Felix take control of the aircraft from the rear seat to practice what he had just been shown. Randolph was prepared to take prompt action in the event that Felix made an error during the flight or while performing a maneuver. Day in and day out, Felix and Randolph had a blast practicing takeoffs, landings, spins, loops, and rolls until he could practically do them blindfolded. All of the practice and repeated drills was in preparation for Felix to make his first solo flight.

Felix watching members of Class 43-H flying above him while in formation at Mesa Del Rey. If you look closely, you'll notice the white strip of tape on his leather flying cap.

Getting paid at Mesa Del Rey was a much different process than what Felix had experienced back at SAAAB. The post staff provided transportation throughout the afternoon to get the cadets into downtown King City on 1 Apr. 1943. They were dropped off in front of the Bank of America location at the corner of 3rd Street and Broadway. The cadets had to stand in line at the teller windows to collect their money. When Felix finally made it to the front of the line, he asked for $25 in cash, and he requested that a money order be mailed to his home for the difference. It would've been nice if payday had fallen on a Friday night, but Felix and his pals were happy anyway. Felix was glad that he had some money in his pocket, and he was eager to perform his first supervised solo flight the following morning. Their tram driver provided the men with a brief tour through town as they made their way back to the base. Felix could certainly feel the small town vibe as he saw the theater, several hotels, a restaurant, a tavern, and he was very pleased to see the USO building on Vanderhurst Avenue. The men made plans to come back into King City on Saturday, 3 Apr. to further explore the town. They also wanted to have a night out to celebrate if all of their solo flights had gone well.

Up to that point, Felix felt that the training had been challenging, thorough, and mentally demanding. However, he figured that he'd proven himself to Randolph that he now possessed the skills to begin his solo flight training. Felix had achieved the minimum prerequisite of eight flying hours with Randolph, and he had logged more than the minimum of 25 landings in order to qualify for solo training. For everyone's safety, and for the purpose of having plenty of air space, Felix and Randolph flew over to one of the nearby auxiliary fields on Friday morning, 2 Apr. 1943. After landing on the dirt runway, Randolph made some adjustments before exiting the plane so that Felix could take full control from the rear seat. They reviewed the flight plan together, and Randolph instructed him as to which maneuvers were to be completed. Felix had already taken off more than a few dozen times with Randolph on board. Therefore, he managed to put the nervousness aside as he made his final preparations to take off.

Randolph proudly watched as Felix made his way around the PT-22 searching for anything that looked problematic. Felix then checked the fuel and other gauges to ensure that all of the fluids were where they needed to be. After Randolph gave Felix a high five, he reminded him that a landing wasn't complete until the wheels had fully stopped rolling. Randolph proceeded to crank start the propeller for Felix, and once Randolph gave him a thumbs up, Felix pushed steadily on the throttle until the Ryan PT-22 quickly made its way down the runway and into the air. Flying freely by himself through the clouds made him feel like he was on top of the world. To Felix, there was nothing mundane about being asked to fly a figure eight pattern over and over again. Randolph kept a watchful eye as Felix gracefully piloted his ship to about 5000 feet. Felix performed roll after roll, and he skillfully completed a few loops by making near perfect circles in the sky. After completing a successful landing, Felix found the whole experience to be enthralling, and he couldn't wait to do it again. Being that the other men that were assigned to Randolph needed their turns as well, Felix's first solo flight turned out to be about 45 minutes long. These were surely the best 45 minutes of his young life, and he'd certainly always remember what he'd accomplished that day.

Randolph was very pleased with Felix's performance, and after climbing up onto the wing walk, he gave him a congratulatory pat on the back. Felix then respectfully asked Randolph if he could remove the white strip of tape that had been placed down the center of his leather flying cap to signify his "dodo" status. Randolph looked him in the eye, and said, "You looked like a real pro out there Felix. You bet! Go ahead and peel that off as you definitely aren't a "dodo" anymore." The term "dodo" was a commonly used nickname among American pilots to signify that they had yet to make a solo flight.

Felix and Randolph quickly returned to Mesa Del Rey to find that the other cadets were waiting anxiously to see how he'd done. They could tell that the PT-22 was still in one piece, so they figured that he must've done fairly well. The men could see Felix's smile from where they sat on a wooden bench outside of the Flight Room. Felix was very excited to share the experience and his success with his pals. However, he remained humble, and he was very encouraging while he stood ready to yell for each of them as they took their turns. Everyone seemed to be in a good mood as each cadet proceeded to make their individual solo flight. Felix and the other men shared a lot of laughs, and they all joked with one another until the last man had returned to the flight line at Mesa Del Rey.

Randolph felt proud that each of his men had successfully completed their first supervised solo flight. Therefore, a celebratory trip into King City was in the cards for the men on Saturday afternoon 3 Apr. 1943. Felix was in need of a birthday card and a gift for Elsie's upcoming birthday on 15 Apr. Therefore, he and his pals walked up and down Broadway and the nearby side streets to see what the downtown area had to offer. Felix knew that San Saba was a rather small town, and King City seemed to be on par, or maybe even a bit smaller. He knew that Elsie loved horses, and he noticed that the local high school's mascot was a Mustang. As he passed by Bolton's Jewelry store, he happened to notice a fine selection of porcelain figurines displayed in the window. Felix stepped inside the store, and he picked up a beautiful piece featuring a Mustang standing high on its two hind legs. It was remarkably detailed, and he knew that he just had to purchase it for Elsie.

After having supper at the King City Grill, the men had a few drinks at the King Bean Tavern. From there, they went next door to the Hayloft to partake in a few games of bowling. Being that there was so much to do at the Hayloft, they didn't get a chance to make it to the USO that evening since the men needed to be back on the post before midnight. Felix had a great deal of fun that evening, and he enjoyed the brief break from the rigorous training program. It just so happened that it was Felix's turn in the rotation to assist with the evening security detail. He had certainly missed driving his vehicles back home, so he was thrilled to have the opportunity to patrol the grounds in the post pickup truck. Felix was a team player in many ways, and he would often volunteer to take a spot in the rotation for some of his fellow cadets.

Felix got Elsie's figurine into the mail plenty early, and he included a birthday card, along with a lengthy letter to catch her up on the happenings around the post. Felix let Elsie know that he was hoping to earn a four-day leave pass at the end of April. If everything worked out the way that he'd hoped, Felix planned to take the train down to visit Elsie and her folks for a few days. Everyone on base was excited that the pilots of class 43-H had graduated from their Primary training, and the next few weeks seemed to fly by rather quickly for the cadets. Felix was now an upperclassmen, and he was flying solo with regularity. There were still times that Randolph would tag along on a flight to demonstrate something new, or to rate his ability on maneuvers that had already been taught. Felix was certainly keeping up with the physical training by running all over the base, and there were plenty of men that couldn't keep up with him on the longer runs. The weather was generally nice and sunny in the King City area, and Felix got a big thrill seeing who could perform the best cannonballs into the refreshing pool on the post. It brought back many fond memories from home, when Felix used to jump off the rocks and boulders into the Colorado River.

As the month of April came to a close, it seemed that more cadets were continuing to wash out. Some of the young pilots either couldn't properly perform the more advanced maneuvers, or they repeatedly became airsick after flying, or they failed to do well in the classroom. Felix thought that it was sad to see them go, but he was assured that the Army would try to get the men trained in another role that better fit their strengths. He figured that as long as it wasn't him going home, then all was swell. Felix was doing so well at Mesa Del Rey; he earned the privilege to spend every Wednesday evening off post. He felt both lucky and honored, and he knew that several other cadets in his class had also received the special mid-week leave pass. Felix began to spend nearly every Wednesday and Saturday evening in King City with his pals. The USO building on Vanderhurst Avenue was a frequent stop for Felix and company. He loved showing off his skills at the pool table, and live bands and variety shows would be featured there nearly every Saturday night.

Cadets from Mesa Del Rey on payday inside the Bank of America branch. Photo courtesy of the Jernigan Collection-King City, CA.

Felix was certainly not planning on washing out anytime soon, and he indeed earned the coveted four-day leave pass. Therefore, he made his way to the Bank of America branch on the morning of 30 Apr. It was the last day of the month, and Felix found himself standing shoulder to shoulder with many of his fellow cadets looking to get some money for the weekend. Felix was glad to reload his stash of cash by asking the teller for $50.00, and, as usual, he sent the rest back home to his folks in San Saba. He then proceeded to the train station where he purchased his ticket that would take him back down to Southern California. Felix had several connections to deal with, but he managed to arrive in Riverside, California, on Friday evening. He had arranged for Elsie to meet him there at the train station, and Felix undoubtedly had no problem spotting Elsie as she looked absolutely gorgeous in her red dress and black high heels. He was pleased to see that she was wearing her gold ankle bracelet and pearl necklace as well.

The ride to Elsie's hometown of Bloomington was about 30 minutes away. Naturally, Felix was feeling a bit nervous about meeting her parents, and he remembered just how awkward it had been to sleep on the couch over at Emma Jo's home for the first time. Felix had no intention of sleeping on the couch when he hadn't seen his girlfriend in more than six weeks. The young couple soon arrived at a hotel near her home, and although it wasn't nearly as nice as the Balboa Inn, Felix wasn't really there for the amenities or scenery. Felix certainly thought Elsie looked beautiful in her outfit, but she looked even more remarkable once her dress hit the floor.

The food at Mesa Del Rey was really good, but Felix hadn't had breakfast at a restaurant for quite some time. After enjoying a terrific meal together, Elsie made the few minute drive over to her home. After a recent haircut and a fresh shave, Felix thought that he looked sharp in his tan slacks, his service cap, and in his service coat with all of the shiny brass pins on the front. Elsie thought that he looked very handsome as well as they walked into her home to meet her parents, John and Helen Jerina. At first, Felix had some difficulty with their thick Czechoslovakian accents, but he had worried for no reason. He quickly found them to be some of the nicest and most good-natured people that he'd met outside of his immediate family in quite some time. Felix noticed the mustang figurine sitting on top of Elsie's dresser, and she told him that she really loved it.

Felix felt comfortable in the Jerina home, and boy, could Helen cook! For dinner, she served roast duck with sauerkraut dumplings and homemade bread. There was really no comparison between the recreational activities found in Bloomington, and the variety of fun things that could be had along the pristine beaches of Orange County. Felix was content with hanging out there at the house for the weekend in order to get to know more about Elsie and her family. Like his own family, the Jerinas were musically inclined, and they seemed quite impressed that Felix could play the violin and piano. Helen seemed to really like Felix, and she insisted that they return for all of their meals while he was in town. Felix could tell that John was wise, and that he could see the very best in people. To Felix, John reminded him of his Pa Millican, and the two seemed to hit it off as well. However, Felix could tell that John was a little uncomfortable when he and Elsie left for the hotel that evening.

Elsie and Helen were in the kitchen preparing a wonderful Sunday supper, while Felix and John sat out on the back porch smoking their pipes. Felix had big plans for himself and Elsie, and as he and John conversed, he seriously debated whether he should ask John for permission to marry Elsie. After thinking about it for a short spell, Felix decided to stay the course, and to let things continue on as they had been. Besides, he figured that once he and his pals got their wings, it wouldn't take long for them to finish off the Axis powers by bombing them into oblivion. Felix looked forward to the day that he'd return to Bloomington to finish the conversation with Elsie's father. As the weekend wound down, Felix let Elsie know that he wanted her to come visit him in King City for his upcoming graduation. He also mentioned that he wanted her to accompany him to the class dance. Elsie eagerly accepted Felix's offer, and he left her with some money to purchase a round-trip train ticket. With their upcoming plans all set, it was time for Felix to head back to King City on that Monday morning. Felix said goodbye to Mr. and Mrs. Jerina, and he thanked them for a very relaxing weekend. He had thoroughly enjoyed spending time with Elsie, and Felix was ready to work hard during the final few weeks of his Primary training.

When Felix got back into King City, he stopped at the King City Mercantile Company to look for a Mother's Day gift. Unsure of exactly what to purchase, he happened to stumble upon an item that seemed appropriate for his mother. The item was similar to a trophy of sorts, and it featured an airplane sitting upon a pedestal. It appeared to be made of brass, and it was rather heavy. The clerk offered to engrave something on it for no additional charge. With that, he purchased the piece with the inscription of "Mother and Dad, Felix, May 9, 1943," which happened to be Mother's Day for that year. Before heading back to the post, Felix stopped at the El Camino Real Hotel to reserve a room for Elsie's upcoming trip. When he got back onto the post later that evening, Felix was able to mail a card, and the gift to his mother back home in San Saba.

There was still plenty of flying needed for Felix to meet the minimum requirements to graduate. Felix had a plan, and if he followed it closely, he figured that he'd end up exceeding all of the expectations.

Randolph expected each of his pilots to create an official flight plan before they could take off. Felix had become very methodical in his preparation for each flight, and he, along with the other cadets, spent a great deal of time in the Flight Room. He knew that he needed to have a specific destination in mind, a couple of alternate destinations in case of an emergency, his time of departure, and the estimated time of arrival. Additionally, Felix needed to have checkpoints along his planned route, he needed to designate his intended cruising altitude, and he needed to calculate his expected fuel consumption to ensure that he arrived safely. There was plenty of attention to detail as the cadets meticulously studied the latest weather charts as they plotted their courses. After a thorough review of the maps that hung on the wall, Felix always made sure to take note of the key landmarks to be on the lookout for along the way. Randolph continually stressed the importance of adhering to their individual flight plans. Felix knew that this was no time to be careless or disobedient, and there was certainly no need for showboating. The cadets were reminded not to buzz the locals, the nearby farmhouses, or buildings of any kind within the city limits. In addition, Randolph emphatically told the men who were assigned to him to not even think about flying under the town bridge.

Recklessness had caused crashes, and even death to some who had come to Mesa Del Rey before Felix. Accidents continued to be a problem at many training bases across the United States. As such, all of the men at Mesa Del Rey were once again cautioned that their safety belt needed to be fastened at all times to help ensure their safety before, during, and after a flight. Additionally, if the plane was equipped with shoulder straps, it was imperative that the straps be attached properly to the safety belt. The men were also reminded that their safety belt needed to go over their parachute harness, instead of through it, in the event that they might need to bail out. Before the men headed to their ground school classes that afternoon, Randolph took a moment to say, "Wearing your safety belt will more than likely keep you in the plane, and it'll help provide you with some protection in the event of an accident. I'll always do my best to double-check with each of you to ensure that your safely belt is fastened before we begin acrobatic maneuvers. I kindly ask that you do the same for me, and for any of your future instructors as well." Randolph knew that his pilots were nearing graduation, and he reminded them to be attentive to a few requirements when performing their acrobatic maneuvers. He said, "Whenever possible, avoid performing acrobatics over populated areas, and within a 10 mile radius of the base. Finally, I cannot stress how important it is to maintain a safe altitude, have plenty of visibility, and never perform acrobatics in unsafe weather conditions." Felix didn't want his folks to worry needlessly, and therefore, he planned to abide by the rules, and he intended to heed Randolph's warnings so that he might be able to safely move on to the next level of training. Felix knew that he was guilty in that he'd recently buzzed a herd of cows. Therefore, he figured that he ought to knock that silliness off, and that he needed to use better judgement from then on.

Since there was no radio on board the PT-22, Felix couldn't verbally communicate directly with the tower. Nevertheless, he had successfully acclimated to the rudimentary takeoff and landing procedure at Mesa Del Rey. The tower featured a green light that allowed the cadets to take off or land, and the red light was meant to hold on the runway, or to circle around for another landing attempt. Being that the pilots were unable to communicate with each other by radio, they needed to rely on their vision, and their familiarity with regular flying routes in order to be as safe as possible. There were a great deal of planes in the air at any given moment, and each pilot needed to be aware of the others around him at all times. Some foggy mornings along the way, and a few rainy days, had caused delays to several of Felix's assigned flight times. Luckily, there were many more sunny days than not in King City, and everyone realized that it was safer to fly under the best possible weather conditions.

For Felix, flying in formation with Randolph and his pals was even more amazing than flying by himself. Six ships flying together had to be just as awesome for someone on the ground to see as well. Randolph would typically be out front as the flight leader, with Felix and another man as his wingmen. The other three pilots in his flight typically filled in behind, and to their left and right, making up the shape of a triangle or something else. Randolph was very skillful in teaching his cadets some of the basic tricks pertaining to communicating with one another while flying in formation. For instance, when he needed to get the attention of his pilots, he'd repeatedly flutter the ailerons, or he'd rapidly move the tail from left to right. If he wanted the men to go into a different formation pattern, he would dip his wing to the left, or to the right, depending on which side of him he wanted them to be on. Echelon was a common type of formation practiced at Mesa Del Rey, and it consisted of the flight leader being out front with each man staggered diagonally behind him to his left or right. When Randolph decided that it was time to land, he would make a series of small dives before leading the flight back to the base. It took a lot of fortitude and practice, but the cadets were soon able to become very proficient at this new skill.

Felix's last few weeks at Mesa Del Rey were filled with repeating many of the maneuvers that he'd already learned. He was just completing them with more accuracy, confidence, precision, and speed. The bulk of ground school was now behind him, and he hoped that the remaining meteorology class would be easy. Felix was also required to spend some time in the mechanics' hangar to learn what was involved to keep the planes airworthy. He was really going to miss flying over the Santa Lucia Mountain Range and Pinnacles National Park. The forest below looked so green, and he sure got a kick out of flying over the peaks, and through its valleys. To avoid a potential disaster, Felix had to remember to account for the slow rate of climb in the PT-22 when cruising through the hilly canyons. He also flew over some rugged, and very unforgiving terrain.

Randolph had one last new trick to teach Felix, and he said that it was one of the best acrobatic maneuvers to change directions while flying. Some of the men were nervous about performing this maneuver, but Felix was open-minded, and he was willing to give it a go. The Immelmann turn was essentially a half loop with a twist. The scary part was that the pilot would be inverted for a moment until he performed a half roll to bring the plane back to right side up. When coming out of the loop, a pilot could become somewhat disoriented if he was looking into the sun, or if there was heavy cloud cover. Felix successfully practiced the Immelmann turn a few times with Randolph on board that day. He had feared the worst for no reason because he managed to complete several Immelmann turns during his next solo flight as well.

Felix wouldn't consider himself an outstanding pilot just yet, but he'd become rather proficient at flying over the last two months or so. He convincingly passed his final flight check with Randolph by recovering from an inverted spin. Slow rolls, stalls, loops, and spins were now handled with ease. Dives, high-speed descents, and even the Immelmann turn now appeared to be rather effortless for Felix. Training at Mesa Del Rey had come to an end, and Felix was proud to hear that he'd be moving on to Basic training. He had logged the minimum of 25 flying hours with Randolph, and he met the 40 hour requirement for solo flying. Additionally, he had successfully performed the minimum requirement of 175 landings. Although he may have been a bit surprised, Felix had even passed all of the final examinations for his ground school courses. Plenty of cadets from class 43-I had washed out along the way during their stay at Mesa Del Rey, but there were still about 180 men or so that would be moving on to Basic training. Felix was very proud of his accomplishment, and he hoped that Elsie and his folks felt the same way. Just like before, he had no clear idea where he was headed next. However, he did know that he needed to get himself to the King City train station to meet up with Elsie when she arrived on the evening of 20 May 1943. After waiting anxiously for her to step off the train, he gave her a big hug and a kiss. As the train began to leave the station, Felix grabbed her bag, and he let her know that he really liked the new perfume that she was wearing as they made the short walk over to the El Camino Real Hotel.

Felix had done so well with his training; he was granted permission to stay in town with Elsie for his last two nights in King City. Elsie was tired from the train ride, so they had supper at the hotel restaurant. Felix enjoyed a grilled salmon steak, browned with butter. Elsie had an avocado salad with a cup of homemade chili, and they both enjoyed some chocolate malted milkshakes for dessert. Afterwards, Felix grabbed her hand, and he led her up to the enemy aircraft spotting station that was located atop the rooftop of the hotel. Luckily for them, there were no inbound enemy planes that evening. However, there were plenty of kisses shared as they looked out at downtown King City and the Salinas Valley.

Felix was sure hoping that Friday, 21 May would turn out to be a fun-filled day. The afternoon graduation ceremony was certainly nice, but the speakers seemed to be rather long-winded. Thankfully, the airshow and flyover that followed at the end of the ceremony was even more exciting than Felix could've ever imagined. There was a legendary B-25 Mitchell bomber flying out front, with a flight of five spectacular P-39 Airacobra's flying top cover above the B-25. After the planes passed high above the crowd, which consisted of guests and townspeople, the P-39s circled back, and they performed an array of dazzling acrobatics. Just when Felix thought that the show was winding down, two P-51 Mustangs suddenly appeared, and they roared by just above the audience. The unbelievable moment happened to be Felix's first glance at an actual P-51, and the planes were so low, he believed that he could practically see one of the pilots smiling as he flew by. To Felix, the Mustang was a thing of beauty, and he thoroughly enjoyed watching the pilots perform their routine. The P-51 was one of the Army Air Force's newest fighter planes. It flew with such grace, and it seemed to have limitless raw power.

As the Mustangs began to disappear from view, Felix turned to Elsie, and said, "One day, I hope to be lucky enough to fly one of those little Mustangs." The underclassmen of class 43-J then paraded by as the band from Camp Roberts played on. At the conclusion of the festivities, Felix told Elsie, "When you pour your heart, mind, and soul into something, you can do well at almost anything." Indeed, Felix had done well thus far. The graduation, the celebration, and all of the pageantry was only a door prize of sorts to Felix, since he hadn't yet earned his wings. However, Felix's time at Mesa Del Rey proved that he could handle an airplane, and he was glad, knowing that he'd be moving on to the next phase.

Later that evening, Felix and Elsie attended the graduation party that was held in one of the airplane hangars on the post. The live music was quite entertaining, and there was plenty of good food and desserts. Many of the other pilots had their favorite ladies in their arms during the party, and Felix got plenty of thumbs up as he danced the night away with Elsie. Several cadets from the class of 43-I had convinced some of the local girls from town to show up to the dance and party. There were eight schools within the Army Air Force's West Coast Training Center that provided the Basic training course, and Felix didn't yet know who'd be moving on to the next base with him. Therefore, as the good times wound down for the evening, Felix made sure to say goodbye to all of his pals, and he took a few moments to exchange signatures inside their class yearbooks as well. The weather was very pleasant that evening, so Felix and Elsie decided to walk hand-in-hand back to the hotel. Before turning in for the night, Felix squeezed Elsie's hand, and looked into her eyes as he said, "I'm really hoping that I luck out, and that I get assigned to a base near Southern California so that I can spend a whole lot more time with you."

Felix found it hard to get out of bed with such a beautiful and wonderful woman lying next to him. Sadly, they said their goodbyes, and they shared a long kiss before he caught a ride back to the post. Felix got wind that they'd be taking buses to their next base, so he figured that his next stop had to be relatively close by. Elsie had some time to kill before her train headed back to Southern California later that morning. Therefore, she walked down the road a bit, away from the hotel. Elsie stopped underneath a large tree alongside the road that they'd walked along the previous evening. Meanwhile, Felix proceeded to board one of the Greyhound buses with his bags in tow. As his bus neared King City, some of the men near the front started whistling at the pretty girl they saw on the side of the road. Felix quickly noticed that the pretty girl wasn't just any girl, she was his girl! He managed to reach what he could of his upper body out the window to wave goodbye to her. Elsie blew him a kiss, and she waved as the bus rounded the corner and disappeared from sight.

While on campus at Texas AMC, Felix had been quite adept at "whipping out," which essentially was a process to meet new people with a howdy and a handshake. After glancing at the men who were seated all around him on the bus, Felix figured that he already knew most of them. He didn't think that he'd be meeting any other Aggies on the bus that morning, but he wanted to introduce himself to those whom he didn't know, nonetheless. Felix figured that this was a perfect opportunity to make some new friends while he waited for the bus to stop at his next base for Basic training.

Pilots generally have a good sense of direction, and Felix was no exception. He paid attention to the road signs as the buses headed south on US Route 101, and he became excited that he could be on his way back to Southern California. Being closer to Elsie ranked right up there with flying a bigger and more powerful plane. Felix's mood suddenly changed a bit when he noticed the bus turning onto California State Route 198 East. The winding road through the scenic hills reminded Felix of his time back home when he'd drive his '37 Ford through the Texas Hill Country. Felix had been on the road for just about two hours when the bus came to a stop at 27th Avenue along Route 198. He looked out the window to see several military police (mp) officers speaking with the bus driver at the guard house. Felix noticed an "Authorized Visitors Only" sign, and he could see a slew of military buildings ahead. Additionally, he saw a large rectangular sign that had the words "Lemoore Army Air Field" on it. He figured that they'd arrived at their new base since they were allowed to pass through the gate located on the south side of Route 198.

At first glance, the post seemed to be bigger than the base at Mesa Del Rey. Just beyond the gate, Felix noticed a slew of planes coming and going in the air, and he noticed what looked like a seemingly unquantifiable amount of planes on the parking ramp. After looking around at his new surroundings, he quickly realized that he was back on an actual Army base. Living the rather relaxed lifestyle at Mesa Del Rey was over, and Felix knew that he needed to promptly refocus his attention to proper military base protocols. It didn't take long before cadets started to arrive from other Primary bases as well. Felix estimated that about 300 aviation cadets had now been grouped together near the flag pole. The men were assembled in several rows, and they were standing shoulder to shoulder when the Commanding Officer, Colonel Donald B. Phillips, stepped up to a podium to address the men of class 43-I. Felix really enjoyed his speech, and he especially liked the fact that Colonel Phillips had spent a great deal of his service time within the state of Texas.

Major Thomas Netcher was the next officer to speak. He was the Director of Flying, and he took a few moments to set the expectations for their training over the next nine weeks. Major Netcher began by saying, "You men will have many long days spent between ground school and your flight time. Each of you will need a minimum of 75 hours of flight time in order to graduate before moving on to Advanced training. Safety is our number one priority here at Lemoore, and our mission is to make you an even better pilot than you are today. We aren't just training pilots here at this base, and most of you will probably notice the contingent of aircraft mechanics who are working hard while they are learning to keep your planes in tiptop shape. In addition, we are teaching men to become instructors for the Link trainer program. There are also men who are here to learn how to become a radio or control tower operator, along with a handful of folks who'll receive instruction to fill other support positions. Together, we will all keep 'em flying. You'll be taught and trained by skilled military instructors. They'll then rank each of you based on your coursework, flight capabilities, and overall conduct. There will be a heavy focus on flying with instruments, flying at night, and perhaps, even a flight in bad weather. We'll teach you how to push your plane harder than ever before, and you can bet that we'll even throw in a few new tricks as well. Finally, in ground school, you'll learn about radio navigation, air traffic regulations, wind drift, dead reckoning, how to properly file a flight plan, how to plan day and night cross-country flights, and much more." At the end of Major Netcher's speech, Felix was given a Basic Instrument Flying Manual and the latest edition of the Pilots' Information File. After thumbing through the books, he knew that there would be plenty of hard work ahead for him during his time at Lemoore.

Felix figured that he'd better be on the straight and narrow path during his time at Lemoore. He was resolved to stay away from the things that might get him into trouble, and he remained focused on moving on to the next level. Admittedly, Felix was a little wet behind the ears when it came to flying with instruments. However, he was up for the challenge, and he was committed to paying close attention during his ground school classes as well as in the cockpit. The cadets were then placed into squadrons of about 50 men. After gathering with their new squadrons, the cadets were further placed into a flight of four men, and they were assigned to a flight instructor.

A few moments later, a clean-cut man joined Felix's group. The slender young man then said, "Good afternoon, my name is First Lieutenant Jerry Houston, and I'll be your flight instructor during your time here at Lemoore." Although Jerry wasn't from Texas, Felix figured that with the name of Houston, they'd get along just fine. Roy, Eugene, and Arthur were the other men in his flight, and they each took a few moments to introduce themselves as well. Jerry then led the men on a tour of the base where they passed by the small theater, Cadet Day Room, flight line, Recreation Building, commissary, post exchange, post office, and the hospital before ending up at the barracks. Felix lost count somewhere along the way, but he figured that there might've been nearly 100 buildings of all sorts on the base. Before leaving the men in his flight, Jerry ordered them to meet up on the flight line at 0800 hours the following morning.

The barracks looked similar in style from the outside to those found at SAAAB, but there were a few differences. These barracks were painted white versus olive drab, and there were four men to a room versus the open style arrangements back at SAAAB. The men quickly realized that they'd been assigned to their room alphabetically, and Felix suggested that they flip a coin to decide who'd get the two top bunks. Felix was elated to have won the rights to a top bunk, and the men got right to work at putting their things away. There were desks for studying, a footlocker for each man's personal things, and a closet for their other clothing items. After learning that smoking was permitted within the dorm room, Felix's roommates were glad that they'd be able to smoke their cigarettes. Felix was also pretty happy knowing that he'd have the opportunity to enjoy his pipe while in the room studying at night. After everyone had finished settling into their room, the men reported to the mess hall for supper. Surprisingly, they found the atmosphere to be relaxing, and the taste and overall quality of the food was excellent.

Felix and his roommates were up early on Sunday, 23 May 1943. There was the raising of the colors, some early exercise, and, of course, some chow. The men wanted to make a great impression upon Jerry, so they arrived early for their meeting that was scheduled at 0800 hours. With several minutes to spare, the cadets decided to wander around the flight line. By Felix's rough multiplication skills, he figured that there had to be at least 200 planes sitting upon the expansive concrete ramp. Many of the planes were lined up wing to wing, and they were positioned in neat uniform rows. Because the area was so large, they really had to hustle to get back over to their meeting place.

Luckily for the men, they made it back in time, and Jerry seemed pleased to get off on a good start. He let the men know that the base was about a year and a half old, which Felix had already figured out since everything looked and felt new. Jerry also mentioned that class 43-H was halfway to their graduation, and that the cadets of class of 43-I would be upperclassmen in just four to five weeks. It wasn't long before the men found themselves in front of a shiny BT-13 Vultee Valiant. As Jerry began to talk about the plane, the group circled in and around it. Felix noticed that the BT-13 had similar markings to the PT-22. Army was spelled out underneath the left wing, and the Army Air Force's circle and star insignia was prominently featured on the left and right side of the fuselage between the cockpit and the tail. The circle and star insignia was also featured atop the outer tip of the left wing and underneath the right wing. The plane's identification number of R-219 was located in bold fashion just below the cockpit. It was also found on the leading edge of the wings, and on the nose of the plane as well. Jerry then said, "This is a much heavier plane with more complex controls than what you've flown before. There are some gauges and gadgets located on the instrument panel that will be new to you. You men will be glad to know that you'll be able to fly this baby faster than the PT-22 with a top speed approaching 180 mph. The 450 horsepower engine will allow you to reach a ceiling of about 21,000 feet, and she'll get you about 700 miles when your fuel tanks are topped off."

Felix was getting increasingly more anxious while waiting to step up into the cockpit. Jerry placed his hands onto the propeller with two blades, and said, "This one is a bit different than the PT-22, and we'll teach you what to do with its dual positions. The variable pitch propeller will really help increase the efficiency and overall performance of the engine. The landing gear is fixed in place, just like you had before, with two wheels up front and one small tail wheel in the back." Finally, Felix stepped up onto the wing walk, and slid into the cockpit of the magnificent BT-13. He immediately noticed the additional gauges, and he took a few moments to fiddle with the controls within the confines of the cockpit. Unlike the PT-22, this plane had a canopy, and Felix was really hoping that it would provide more protection from the elements while flying at higher altitudes. Jerry proceeded to distribute a copy of the Pilot's Handbook of Flight Operating Instructions for the BT-13 to each of his men. He then finished his discussion about the plane with, "Don't let all of this information scare you. Sure, we've had plenty of washouts, accidents, and even a few deaths along the way, yet the Vultee is still a reliable and rather easy plane to fly. You're all going to learn how to fly more exigent maneuvers, but you'll be taught to do them safely. I aim to have the best safety record on base, and we're going to have the tightest formations out of any other flight here at Lemoore. We'll be taking her up for a spin tomorrow morning, so I need each of you to report to the Flight Room at 0700 hours."

As the cadets left the flight line, they were a bit troubled to hear about the deaths that had occurred in some of the classes that had preceded them. Felix felt the need to speak up, and he said, "Y'all just can't worry about everything. We'll be fine if we pay attention, stay alert, do what we're told, and practice as carefully as possible. Let's show 'em what we've got, and what we're made of." The afternoon was theirs to explore and partake in some good old recreation. As Felix walked around with his pals, he noticed that the Lemoore Army Air Field was located on a rather flat plot of land. It seemed as if they had built the base miles away from town with nothing but agricultural fields all around them. There were very few trees on the base, and the ones that were actually there were scattered around and weren't very tall. Felix missed the shade that the beautiful and well-established walnut trees provided back at SAAAB. The grounds weren't quite as green and appealing as Mesa Del Rey had been, but everything was clean and functional.

The men stumbled upon the baseball and softball diamonds, the basketball court, and the sandpit used for volleyball. They found the recreational areas to be outstanding, and Felix couldn't wait to participate in the intramural competitions. Next, they passed by the rope climb, and the area for group calisthenics. Colonel Phillips had said that camaraderie and teamwork would be key at Lemoore. The cadets figured that exercising, and playing sports together would be just what he had in mind. Felix figured that there would be plenty of time spent running and exercising in the sweltering heat of Kings County. Therefore, the men settled for a more easy-going afternoon indoors. They managed to find the bowling alley, and they also enjoyed shooting pool and playing ping-pong for hours. The weekend had been full of friendly antagonizing from the upperclassmen, but Felix found it all to be good clean fun.

It was Monday morning, 24 May 1943, and before heading to the Flight Room, the cadets stopped at the Parachute Building to receive their backpack parachute harnesses. Felix and his roommates then managed to make it to the Flight Room a few minutes before their meeting was to begin with Jerry. The layout was fairly similar to the one at Mesa Del Rey, but it was certainly larger in size. There were tall maps hanging on the walls, so Felix took a moment to see how close he was to Elsie. He estimated that Bloomington was about 250 miles from Lemoore, and he was glad that he was a little closer to Elsie than he was during his time at Mesa Del Rey. Felix then noticed the airways bulletin board, which listed flight assignments, and it also provided alerts, along with other important instructions for the pilots. The reports from the Air Weather Service were favorable that morning, thus the pilots were given the green light to fly. The pilot briefing only lasted about 15 minutes in order to accommodate the next group of cadets who were eagerly waiting outside. Felix was very excited as he walked out to the flight line with Jerry and his fellow pilots.

Felix was feeling eager to get up in the air with Jerry as he and the men in his flight drew straws to see who'd get to go first. He wasn't selected to fly first this time; therefore, he sat on a bench with the other men in an attempt to tamp down the anxiety that was flowing through his veins. Finally, the time came for Felix to get his turn inside of the BT-13. Before beginning the pre-flight check of the aircraft, Jerry reminded Felix to unlock the controls, and he also ensured that the engine switch was set to an off position. Everything appeared to be operable and in proper working order on the outside of the plane. Therefore, Felix quickly checked the fuel level on the wing before climbing into the front seat, while Jerry hopped into the rear seat. Felix checked Form 1A in the cockpit to verify that the plane had a current maintenance record, and he ensured that there weren't any warnings issued for the aircraft.

Jerry provided Felix with a brief overview on how to use the plug-in headset radio so that they could communicate with each other and the control tower. He then took a moment to ask Felix what was the callsign, a nickname, that he'd like to assign to himself. Thinking back to his childhood, he remembered that some of his friends used to call him "Scotty," and so that is what he told Jerry he'd prefer to be called while flying. Next, Felix proceeded to fill out his pertinent pilot information and some of the flight data on Form 1. Felix then fastened his seatbelt harness and shoulder straps before adjusting the position of his seat to ensure that he could easily reach the rudder pedals. Jerry was very thorough as he went step-by-step with Felix to review the takeoff procedures for the BT-13. In an effort to help ensure safety, he stressed the importance of manipulating the controls and testing the instruments before beginning to taxi. Jerry said, "We gotta keep 'em flying, so we need to keep both you and me safe."

The BT-13's engine was started from inside the cockpit, so Felix didn't need to worry about the crank or hand prop procedures. After priming the engine, and with his foot firmly on the brake, Felix adjusted the throttle before starting the engine. He felt marvelous knowing that he was just a few minutes away from being airborne. Felix was now ready to taxi to the takeoff lane by "S"ing his way through the crowded flight line. Jerry reminded him to taxi with his flaps up to prevent them from getting damaged by rocks or other debris that might get kicked up along the way. Felix checked his brakes to ensure that they worked, and Jerry was quite impressed to see him use only the rudder while taxiing. As they neared the takeoff lane, Jerry advised Felix on how to properly communicate with the tower in order to obtain the proper clearance for takeoff.

Felix paused for a few moments when he reached the takeoff lane in order to adjust a few remaining things. He quickly made sure the propeller was in HIGH RPM, and he checked that the mixture control was set to FULL RICH. After ensuring that the gas switch was set to the proper tank, he also adjusted the trim tabs to their proper position. Felix noted the direction of the wind and its approximate velocity. Jerry seemed pleased with Felix's diligence and his attention to detail; thus he gave him a thumbs up that he was clear to proceed to the runway. Felix used his entire field of vision to ensure that his path on the runway was clear and safe, and just like that, he found himself barreling down the runway. He continued to ease forward on the stick until the plane lifted itself off the ground. Felix felt proud that he'd successfully completed his first takeoff in the BT-13.

The base was located about nine miles west of downtown Lemoore, and Jerry knew that Felix hadn't yet gone into town. As such, Jerry directed him to reach an altitude of 3000 feet as they proceeded to fly over the town. Felix got a terrific bird's eye view of the surroundings, and he even spotted some railroad tracks that led to a train station. He was glad that the train would make it much easier for Elsie to come for a visit. Felix could see for many miles in every direction, and he was having the time of his life while flying with Jerry. Lemoore was clearly an agricultural community, and there were plenty of ranches and farms with their fields sectioned off into uniform plots. The image of the landscape beneath them was reminiscent of one of Viola's patchwork quilts. Farm equipment and machinery could be seen in nearly every direction below. For just a moment, Felix once again imagined himself operating his crop duster over the fields back home in San Saba County. He felt that it was a fitting time to share his dream of operating a crop dusting business after the war was over. Jerry replied through his radio headset that he liked the idea, and he proceeded to tell Felix that he believed that barley, wheat, corn, and an assortment of vegetables were being grown in the fields below them.

Jerry was satisfied as Felix ascended to an altitude of 5000 feet by performing a series of chandelles and lazy eights along the way. A chandelle is essentially a climbing maneuver where the pilot gains altitude as he makes a 180º turn. A pilot performs a lazy eight maneuver when he makes two 180º turns in opposite directions while climbing and gradually descending in a pattern, replicating the image of a figure-eight. Jerry reviewed the landing procedures with Felix as they slowly began to descend upon one of the six auxiliary fields located nearby by performing a series of gliding turns. After practicing a few additional landings and takeoffs, he had about ten minutes left in his one-hour time slot. Jerry instructed Felix that this was the best time to notify the tower that he'd like permission to land. Felix radioed the tower back at the Lemoore Army Air Field with his position, and he waited for clearance to land. He kept in contact with the control tower until just a few moments before landing. Felix gradually descended from the sky while maintaining his proper landing speed. He'd done it! Felix had piloted his Vultee Valiant to a near perfect landing as he passed by the six-story radio control tower. With the influx of planes spread across the multiple runways, Jerry reminded Felix to always clear the runway area as soon as possible after landing. He told him to remain alert, and to be on the lookout for air and ground traffic around him. Before leaving the cockpit, Felix filled out the duration of his flight on Form 1. After stepping down off the wing, Felix asked Jerry how he'd done. Jerry gave him a high five, and said, "You nailed it, Scotty!"

Felix experienced a whirlwind of emotions as he began his first full week at the Lemoore Army Air Field. In addition to being physically fit, he knew that it was equally important to be mentally and emotionally fit as well. On the one hand, Felix was very pleased that he was doing well with his training, and that he had no apparent problems with air sickness or vertigo. He was also quite euphoric after flying the new plane, but he was rather sad to be away from Elsie, and he was even feeling a little homesick. Felix had never been away from his folks or San Saba for this long before. He had missed Christmas, New Year's, Easter, and now he was about to spend his birthday away from his family. Felix had been so busy since his arrival at the Lemoore Army Air Field, he'd forgotten that he hadn't yet sent his new base information to his loved ones. Therefore, he stopped by the post exchange after his ground school classes had concluded for the day to pick up a candy bar, a few postcards, and some stationery. He also purchased a few one-cent stamps for the postcards, and he grabbed a dozen three-cent stamps for his letters. Felix found a few minutes to write a postcard to Elsie, and one to his folks before turning in for the night. Jerry had told his men that it was very important for them to get plenty of rest so that they'd be alert and focused. Felix did indeed get a good night's rest, and he dropped the postcards off at the base post office early the next morning before proceeding to the flight line. Felix was lucky to fly with Jerry every day that week, which earned him the right to begin his solo flight training.

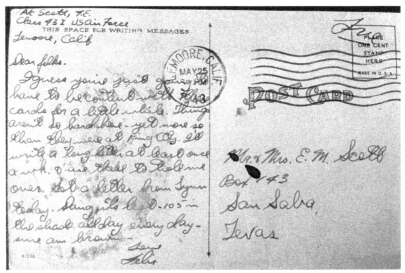

A postcard from Felix to his folks dated 25 May 1943. "Dear folks, I guess you're just going to have to be content with these cards for a little while. Things aren't so hard here-yet more so than they were at King City. I'll write a long letter at least once a week & use these to tide me over. Got a letter from Lynn today. Dang it's hot—105 in the shade all day every day-sure am brown. Love Felix.

The two-week quarantine period for the new cadets was still in effect on the fabulous day that Felix turned 23 years old. The day was Sunday, 30 May 1943, and Felix found himself confined to the base.

Although bummed that he couldn't go into town to celebrate, and dejected that Elsie couldn't come to see him in person, he figured that he'd find a way to make do. Felix's spirits quickly improved when he took a few moments to read through his mail. He was very pleased to read that Elsie's father had finally agreed to let the telephone company set up a phone line inside their home. After stuffing the letter with her phone number firmly into his pocket, Felix quickly ran to the nearest phone booth on base. He felt that he'd received the best birthday present after having a lovely conversation with Elsie, and after speaking with his folks as well. Hearing their voices and words of encouragement gave him the strength to power onward. Felix ended up catching a movie at the base theater, and he spent the rest of the evening shooting pool with his pals.

The base was buzzing when the men lined up to get paid the following day. Felix took $25 in cash, and he sent the rest home, figuring that June would be a busy month, and he wouldn't need too much money. He certainly felt the enthusiasm that had been building among the cadets regarding their upcoming trip into the town of Lemoore. The quarantine was finally over when Saturday, 5 Jun. 1943, rolled around. Felix was rather amazed that he'd found yet another town that was similar in size to San Saba. The streets were rather quiet that afternoon, and some of the buildings reminded him of the downtown area back home. Not really knowing where to go, the cadets spread out in several different directions. Felix and Roy headed up and down D Street looking for something fun to do. They found some nice gift shops, a pool hall, and the beautiful USO building over on C Street. They went inside to find a lovely staff that was very welcoming and accommodating. Felix and Roy enjoyed some delicious sandwiches along with some refreshing ice cold fountain drinks. They spent most of the afternoon playing ping-pong while listening to music on the jukebox inside the comfortable lounge. Felix figured that he'd probably spend a good portion of his upcoming weekends at the USO building with many of his fellow cadets. After having spent several hours at the USO, the men headed back into the downtown area, and they stumbled upon Mrs. Parker's Spanish Kitchen. Her tamales, enchiladas, and chili con queso were delectable, and rivaled those that his sister Johnnie Mae could make. After supper, they found the Lemoore Theater, and the men decided to watch *Raiders of San Joaquin* before heading back to the base. That Sunday, Felix spent some time talking on the phone with Elsie, he wrote a letter to his folks back home, and he studied in order to get ahead for the upcoming week of his ground school classes.

Jerry felt that his men were doing well overall, but he wasn't fully satisfied with their performance. He sensed that the growing number of pilot fatalities from the nation's training centers were holding them back from reaching their full potential. It was imperative that they begin to fly like they were in Basic training, and they needed to quickly take their skills to the next level. Bad news traveled fast, and the men weren't ignorant as to what was going on across America. None of the young cadets wanted to ever crash and die, but they surely didn't want to be killed while training on American soil. That wouldn't be the kind of legacy that any of them had in mind to leave their family members with. To courageously die in the midst of an epic battle would be an acceptable possibility to the cadets, and they knew that there was a real chance of that happening in the battlefields of the sky around the world.

In an attempt to ease the pilots' concerns, Jerry felt that he needed to discuss how to handle an emergency situation should the need ever arise. He began by reminding the cadets that the planes were expendable and could be replaced. Jerry was adamant, and he made it very clear that we weren't interested in replacing any of his pilots' lives. He then said, "Each emergency situation is unique, and many pilots have gotten confused and scared, which caused some of them to move the controls in a direction opposite to the intended protocols." He went on to mention that accidents due to equipment failure were unfortunate, and regrettably, they were even expected from time to time. However, Jerry was insistent that his cadets needed to do everything within their abilities to avoid an accident due to pilot error. Keeping calm, staying relaxed, and remaining level-headed, would give every pilot the best chance of recovering from a problem in the air so that both he and the plane could make it back to the ground safely.

There were many potential scenarios to discuss. Therefore, Jerry started with the most basic protection for his pilots, their parachutes. Jerry then said, "We pray that you'll never need to use it, but we've given each of you a parachute with the hope that it just might save your life one day. We fully expect you to use it if the need unexpectedly presents itself. If you find yourself in an emergency situation, do your best to avoid getting too excited so that you can use the skills that we'll teach you in order to deal with the problem. If time allows, dump your fuel, release your bombs where it is safe to do so, and toss out any unnecessary items from the cockpit that could be problematic during a forced landing. If you find yourself needing to eject, ditch the canopy, if possible, and quickly release your shoulder straps and safety belt, and, if doable, try to bail out from an inverted position. Remember that if your ship dips below 5,000 feet, it might be too late." The cadets were told that they needed to handle their parachutes with the utmost care, and Jerry emphasized that it was critical that they inspect them thoroughly before each flight. The men needed to ensure that the rip cord pins weren't bent, and they had to check that none of the canopy was visible from underneath its protective covering. Each pilot would also be responsible to make the necessary adjustments to their leg and chest straps should they become loose.

Jerry had some more words of wisdom to share with his men. He went on to say, "Time and altitude will be your best friends in the event of a problem. It's better to attempt a forced landing while you still retain some control of your airplane, rather than wait too long so that you now have to deal with an out of control situation. If your landing gear has become damaged, or if it won't deploy on one of your future planes, you must prepare yourself for a belly down landing. Before touching down, whether it's on a runway or on some makeshift field, try to keep your plane as level as possible. Be sure to use your flaps if they're still operable to reduce your airspeed, and remember to kill your engine just prior to touching down to help avoid the possibility of a fire." Jerry could tell that his men were paying close attention, but he didn't want to overwhelm them. Therefore, he ended the discussion with, "If you ever encounter a problem on takeoff, resist the urge to turn back to the base right away. For everyone's safety, fly straight ahead if possible, and be sure to promptly communicate with the control tower for the best course of action. Finally, it's imperative that you wear the proper clothing when flying. The warmer clothing will certainly serve you well, and it'll help to keep you alive when flying at higher altitudes. Keep in mind that in the event of a crash, you might need to walk a long way back to safety. You'll surely want to have your emergency kit, and proper shoes, to make your journey a little easier. If you ever happen to cause damage to one of Uncle Sam's planes, don't be afraid to report it to the crew chief immediately. If possible, be sure to move the plane to a secure place off the runway for an inspection and repairs."

Felix spent a majority of his flight time over the next few weeks flying solo, but he also enjoyed catching up, and learning something new from Jerry here and there. Flying in formation at Lemoore was undoubtedly more thrilling than it had been at Mesa Del Rey. With bigger and faster planes, it was also rather harrowing at times for Felix and the members of his flight as they practiced flying in many different formations. The men would take turns acting as the flight leader on the occasions when Jerry wasn't in the air with them. Flying above and within the clouds was heavenly to Felix, and being able to fly carefree brought him a great deal of happiness. He continued to focus on repetition of the basic maneuvers in order to develop added proficiency at them. Felix practiced countless takeoffs and landings, and he made sure that he flew in and out of each of the nearby auxiliary fields.

Much of the curriculum for Felix's ground school training had shifted towards the use of instruments in the cockpit. When he and his fellow flight members first walked into the Link Trainer Building on the morning of 21 Jun., the air was clearly abuzz. They found half a dozen of the Link trainer machines lined up in a row, and the men were certainly glad to escape the heat for some time inside the air-conditioned building. Seeing the Link trainers reminded Felix back to when he'd first stepped inside his pecan plane as a boy. However, he could immediately tell that the Link trainer was much more capable than his pecan plane. It was apparent that this was going to become a real man versus machine square off.

The Link trainer was a nifty little contraption that had no propeller. It clearly resembled a plane, but it was much smaller in scale. The machine was constructed with wood, and it had a hood that created a surreal experience for the pilot once it was closed. The Link trainer was operated by a rather sophisticated system of mechanical levers and organ bellows. The fuselage was painted blue, and it had small yellow wings. The tail was painted red, white, and blue, which made it look rather stylish and patriotic. The instruments that were found within the cockpit of the Link trainer could be customized to match those found on the plane that a pilot would be flying at the time. Each Link trainer was operated by a sergeant who served as the instructor for the machine. Each instructor sat outside of their machine, and they were tasked with controlling the Link trainer to simulate wind and other weather conditions.

The instructor was responsible for providing the cadet with an experience that would closely resemble an actual flight. The Link trainer could move from side to side, tilt up and down, and spin completely around if needed. When Felix climbed into the Link trainer for the first time, he had to put away all distractions in order to focus on being successful inside the machine. He quickly learned that it was much safer to practice new things inside the comfort of the Link trainer, rather than risk life and limb doing something in the plane itself. Felix was sure to spend a great deal of time inside the Link trainer as he continued along his training path. The Link trainer was a great training tool that required no gas, and there was practically no chance of injuries. In addition to what he'd learned at Mesa Del Rey, Felix now had to learn to fly with the directional gyro, and the artificial horizon as his primary flight instruments.

Jerry would fly with Felix periodically to check his performance with the plethora of maneuvers that he'd been assigned to master. Felix could tell that Jerry really enjoyed his role as a flight instructor, and he appreciated his by the book approach to everything being taught. After each morning briefing in the Flight Room, Felix knew what was expected of him that day. Jerry wanted each of his pilots to get the most of their time in the air, thus, he wanted them to follow a particular routine on most flights. Shortly after a regular takeoff, Felix would ascend while performing basic bank and turn maneuvers until he reached an altitude of 1000 feet. He'd then practice sharp turns, in addition to climbing and gliding turns, on his way to 3000 feet. Finally, Felix completed chandelles and lazy eights as he continued climbing to 5000 feet. Upon reaching 5000 feet, he had the freedom to perform his choice of acrobatic maneuvers. There would be plenty of gliding turns mixed with a series of high-speed dives as he descended back to the designated landing strip. Felix felt really official each time that he made contact with the radio tower. He'd quickly learned all the appropriate jargon to effectively communicate, and he got a real kick out of talking with his Texas twang.

It was really hot during Felix's time in Lemoore, and with very few trees on the base, shade was a hot commodity. He'd yet to experience any significant flight delays due to bad weather. On occasion, the cadets dealt with some foggy mornings, but there were clear blue skies once that burned off. This meant that Felix didn't have an opportunity to get real practice with his instruments during a bout of bad weather. Therefore, time in the Link trainer continued to be an excellent resource for dealing with that matter. Every now and then, when Felix would take off from one of the dirt airstrips at the Lemoore Army Air Field, he wondered if his Pa Millican would allow him to build a similar landing strip on his property. He could picture himself piloting a crop duster of his very own while his grandparents watched him take off and land behind their home. Felix figured that his grandfather would probably say yes, but he wanted to ask him in person the next time he made it back home. The ground school coursework had become more challenging for Felix, but he was doing well overall. He continued to hone his skills in Morse code, and he was becoming rather adept at navigating his BT-13 Vultee Valiant. Felix used the train tracks, busy roadways, and other natural landmarks to orient himself as he flew around the San Joaquin Valley.

Class 43-H graduated during the fourth week of June, and Felix was in complete disbelief to learn that five men who were part of their class there at the Lemoore Army Air Field had been killed during their nine-week session. They had lost three aviation cadets, just like himself, along with two officers as well. Felix remembered what Jerry had said about men who could be killed, but it didn't make it any easier to make sense of how such a tragedy could occur. Their graduation ceremony had many similarities to those that he'd seen previously. During the moment of silence for the fallen aviators, Felix couldn't stop thinking about the anguish that their family members would be dealing with. He reflected for a moment about what his own family would have to go through if it were him who they were honoring up on the stage. The marching band had nearly two dozen members, and there were men playing the drums, tuba, baritone, trombone, and clarinet. Felix couldn't play any of those instruments, so he didn't plan to join the band any time soon. However, he really enjoyed playing the piano in the Cadet Day Room. In just a few more weeks, Felix hoped that he too, would be parading around the review field.

After the graduation festivities had wrapped up, Felix was feeling rather ambivalent about how the afternoon had played out. He was just glad to be alive and well, and he was excited to be an upperclassman. It was somewhat inconvenient to move all of their personal belongings, but Felix and his classmates were pleased to be moved to the barracks that were reserved just for them. Calisthenics remained part of daily life for him and the other cadets. Felix decided to take up judo on the base in the event that he might have to defend himself one day if his plane were to go down. He realized that being an upperclassman meant that it was time to take his training to the next level. Jerry pushed his men to perform their routines with even greater speed, precision, and agility. Felix got a real thrill out of flying faster, but it meant that he had less time to orient himself when coming out of a loop, or when performing an Immelmann. Vertical dives were somewhat frightening to Felix, and he'd often find himself praying that his controls would work when it was time to pull off of a dive. Felix was thankful to be strapped into the cockpit with his seatbelt harness because the canopy on the BT-13 would often shake violently during some of his high-speed maneuvers.

Now that Felix and his flight mates had honed their skills in their BT-13s, it was time to advance their capabilities while flying in formation with Jerry as their flight leader. During the pre-flight meeting, Jerry planned to have the cadets start off in the echelon formation. Once airborne, the men began to fall into place along Jerry's right hand side. Each plane was staggered just a bit behind one another. When Jerry was satisfied with their performance, he dipped his wings to the left, and the men quickly swapped sides, moving into echelon formation along his left hand side. After the cadets finished flying in echelon formation, Jerry had them take turns moving into a three-ship V formation. Felix was good at giving a thumbs up to the man on his wing once they'd properly moved into position. The radio capabilities of the BT-13 helped Jerry provide occasional instructions, and praise for a job well done. The group generally finished their formation routine when the two remaining pilots joined the lead planes to form a five-ship V formation. The cadets looked like and felt like they were ready to go to war. Felix thought that it was the perfect moment to be a bit humorous when he spoke into his radio microphone, and said, "Any of you boys feel like fueling up so that we can pay a little visit to those Japs this afternoon?" He got a few chuckles from his pals, but it didn't take long before Jerry replied with, "Negative, Scotty. It's too far, and, besides, you men haven't had your armaments training yet. Return to base immediately, over." Felix acknowledged Jerry's command with an emphatic "Roger that," and he then returned to the base as ordered. After landing, he was feeling more confident than ever, and he once again wondered if the war would be over before he got a chance to fight.

Like Randolph, Jerry had also instructed his cadets to stay away from flying along the coast, especially while in formation. He didn't want his men to cause unnecessary alarm to the citizens on the ground since they might be perceived as a potential enemy invasion. Thankfully, the folks manning the aircraft warning station in downtown Lemoore knew how to properly identify the BT-13s and other American aircraft. Felix found that flying in formation was both emotionally and physically draining. He could hold his position in the formation well enough, but he seemed to be a little nervous with the other pilots being in such close proximity to him. Felix certainly didn't want to touch wings, or get his propeller tangled into any part of the plane next to him. He knew that one wrong move could be disastrous.

Felix was glad that he was able to speak with Elsie by phone every weekend. Hearing her cheerful voice was great, but he longed for her to be in his arms once again. Felix was thrilled that Elsie had accepted his offer to come and visit him there in Lemoore. Plans had been finalized, and she was due to arrive by train on the afternoon of Friday, 25 Jun. 1943. Felix figured that he'd be very busy before her arrival, and he made sure that he was on schedule with his flight hours, and that he was caught up with all of his course work. He hadn't received any disciplinary action, so he was excited to have a pass for the whole weekend. However, Felix was certainly upset that he couldn't get out of class early enough to meet Elsie at the train station when she arrived.

Nevertheless, Felix bummed a ride into Lemoore as soon as he was done with his classes that Friday afternoon. He'd arranged for them to stay at the Lucerne Hotel there in town. When Felix exited the car, he looked up to see Elsie standing on the second story balcony, looking ever so cute. He stopped at the front desk just long enough to identify himself before running up the stairs to give her a big hug and a kiss. It was quite evident that they'd missed each other, and they were truly excited to be together again. Felix had really liked the quality and selection of food at Mrs. Parker's Spanish Kitchen, so that is where they headed for supper. After seeing a show at the Lemoore Theater, Elsie had mentioned that the train had been overcrowded, and people were standing about in the aisleway. Being that she was hot, tired, and plum worn out, they decided to save the tour of the town for another time. The young couple returned to the hotel, and after changing into something more comfortable, they enjoyed a splendid evening out on the balcony as they laughed and watched the stars twinkling against the backdrop of a full moon. Felix was eager to share all that he'd accomplished during the week, and, before long, they turned in for the night.

Early the next morning, Felix and Elsie made their way to a bus that would take them to San Francisco. He and many other cadets, along with their significant others, made the four hour trip into the heart of San Francisco. Felix had purchased tickets for the all-inclusive sightseeing adventure, complete with a stop at many of the most popular and scenic spots in town. After dropping off their belongings at the Sir Francis Drake Hotel, Felix and Elsie walked towards Union Square. They crossed Post Street, and then they stopped for a moment at the corner of Powell and Geary Street to marvel at just how tall their hotel was since neither of them had ever seen anything quite like it before.

Tall buildings were abound, cable cars were whizzing by, and people were going about their day as if they didn't have a care in the world. After enjoying some clam chowder and sandwiches at a nearby restaurant, the group hopped back on the bus for an afternoon trip to the San Francisco Zoo. They spent four hours traversing the beautiful grounds and viewing the wonderful exhibits. Everyone then boarded the bus for a drive through Chinatown, followed by a stop for supper at Fisherman's Wharf. Felix wasn't sure when he'd ever get back to San Francisco, so he wanted to experience some local seafood. Therefore, he ordered a large sampler plate of crab legs, oysters, and lobster tails for him and Elsie to share. Felix figured that a fine bottle of Sauvignon Blanc ought to go nicely with their meal, and would help set the mood for another romantic evening. The last journey of the evening was a trip across the Golden Gate Bridge and back. The views were stunning as they took in the beauty of San Francisco. As Felix reached the middle of the bridge, he had a sudden feeling of uneasiness come over him. He certainly didn't think that he was carsick, and he felt that it was probably too soon to have food poisoning. Felix chopped it up to being a fluke, but he experienced the same feeling on the return trip over the bridge.

When the bus returned to the hotel, there were servicemen everywhere. Apparently, this was a popular place for soldiers who were on leave, and for others who were heading off to, or returning from, the war. Felix and Elsie gazed out the window of their 14th floor hotel room. Elsie was amazed at just how stunning the city lights were. Felix could only imagine the hell and destruction that he was potentially going to see within some of the finest cities in the war-torn countries around the world. He was certainly glad that the Japanese and Germans hadn't yet brought the fight to the United States. The young couple stayed up late finishing the bottle of wine, and they enjoyed sharing countless stories with one another. Elsie felt very comfortable being around Felix, and he was entirely smitten with her. Since they were having such a grand time in the hotel room, they really had to hurry so they didn't miss the noon bus. There was just enough time for them to grab a bite to eat from a nearby deli before hopping aboard the bus for the ride back to Lemoore.

As they headed south on US Route 101, Felix wished that he could just continue on down the road to Southern California with Elsie. The dream quickly faded as he knew that he had some unfinished business with the Axis powers that were waiting overseas. There was plenty of time for Felix and Elsie to discuss plans for her return trip to Lemoore for his upcoming graduation from Basic training. He provided her with some money for a train ticket, and they reserved a room at the Lucerne Hotel for her upcoming trip in July. Felix needed to be back on the base by Sunday evening, which meant that Elsie would have to spend her final night in Lemoore by herself. Before having to catch a ride back to the base, they shared a fabulous supper. While walking back to the hotel, Felix pointed to an area in the sky just outside of town. Since Elsie's train didn't leave until around 1000 hours the next morning, Felix told her that he'd be sure to get his flight time at 0800 hours. He wanted her to watch him show off, and perform some of his maneuvers in the sky before she headed home. Elsie thoroughly enjoyed watching Felix fly his plane, but she repeatedly said a few prayers as he performed his loops, rolls, spins, and dives. She was glad that he hadn't crashed, but she was sad as Felix rocked his wings from side to side as to say goodbye before proceeding out of sight. Elsie was elated to be part of Felix's life, and she was very happy that he was doing what he loved.

There were no leave passes granted for the first weekend in July, for it would be Independence Day on Sunday, 4 Jul. 1943. Felix wanted to make sure that he wished his sister Pauline a happy birthday on 3 Jul. He thanked her for sending newspaper articles and comic strips to him regularly. Felix was also delighted to speak with his folks since they happened to be over at Pauline's place to celebrate her special day. The cadets were required to spend most of Saturday practicing their routines for the air show, which was to be held the following day. Colonel Phillips had sent an open invitation to the citizens of Lemoore, inviting them to an open house that was going to be held at the base on the Fourth of July. An afternoon of fun was planned, which included base tours, a peak into the Link Trainer Room, a trip around the parking ramp, and one-on-one time with a cadet for any young men wanting to become a future pilot. There was plenty of great food, live music from the band, and even a parade, held before Retreat, to end the festivities in front of the base headquarters. At the end of the long day, the cadets were given special permission to go into town for a few hours. When Felix heard that they were showing *The Pride of the Yankees* down at the Lemoore Theater, he knew that he just had to go see it. Even though the film didn't feature Joe DiMaggio, Felix really enjoyed the movie. On his way back to the base, the exploding fireworks in the sky above him capped off a terrific weekend.

Any remaining excitement from the Fourth of July celebration was wiped out on 9 Jul. 1943. Word that a cadet and his instructor had been killed in a plane accident near one of the auxiliary fields sent shockwaves and sorrow throughout the base. Jerry once again reminded his men that flying was inherently dangerous, and that they were tempting fate nearly every day. He insisted that safety remain as their number one priority, and that they needed to carry on with their training. There were only two weeks of training left, and Felix was as ready as he could be heading into the final phase of Basic training. Felix had pretty much mastered the regular tricks and maneuvers during his normal flight routine. Jerry began to integrate some long distance flights into the training program, and Felix was excited to learn that he could be flying as many as 400–500 miles or so on one flight.

Felix had already accomplished many things as a young pilot, and the next milestone would be his first night flight. The thought of flying in the dark was both exhilarating and scary at the same time. Felix felt a great deal of anxiety wondering if he'd fly with a full moon, or on a pitch black night. The cadets went through a lengthy training regimen in preparation for their big night, and they were given a slew of tips to better their night vision. Of course, there was plenty of time under the hood in the Link trainer, and even the mess hall did their part by offering a nice selection of food loaded with vitamin A. The men were told to relax in a dark room for at least 30 minutes prior to takeoff, and they were instructed to use their flashlight with a red bulb within the cockpit to glance at their charts, maps, and notes. As fate would have it, Felix was assigned to make his first night flight in near total darkness. After walking out of the Flight Room, he looked up into the sky to see a scant sliver of the moon, and he could only find a few scattered stars nestled in between the clouds. The lightless evening was eerily mesmerizing, yet he had psyched himself up, and he felt ready for the challenge. Felix and Jerry, along with several other instructors and cadets were driven by truck out to a local auxiliary field. With everyone's safety in mind, the cadets would perform their first evening of night flying from there, rather than from the main base. The flight would also be a bit more challenging, since there wouldn't be any city or base lights nearby.

Felix went through his typical pre-flight check, and he made sure that the landing lights on the wings were operable. He then climbed into the cockpit while Jerry hopped into the seat right behind him. He double checked his gauges and controls because he knew that failing to do so could be disastrous. Jerry tapped Felix on the shoulder, and said, "Trust your instruments. You've gotten really good at checking them carefully before each flight. If you're all buckled up, let's see what you've got." The dozens and dozens of hours spent flying with instruments was about to pay off. There was a little trembling in his knees, and some shaking in his hands. Felix paused for a brief moment to take a deep breath, and he proceeded to wipe the sweat from his forehead. He then made his way down the airstrip with no trouble, and he began to fly a circular course around the field. The plan for the evening was to practice multiple takeoffs and landings until Jerry was satisfied. To make things just a little more difficult, Jerry only allowed Felix to use the landing lights when he was just about to touch down upon the dirt runway. Felix only needed two more night fights with Jerry before he'd be cleared to solo at night.

Felix had hoped that his third night flight would go even better than the first two. In order to receive a "qualified" rating on his instrument flight check, he knew that Jerry planned to mix things up a bit for him. Shortly after takeoff, Felix was told to fly north for ten minutes while steadily climbing to 5,000 feet. Next, Jerry kept a watchful eye on Felix's ability to keep the plane level as he had him complete a series of 90° and 180° turns in different directions. Although quite nerve-racking, Felix had performed all of his additional maneuvers well. He even impressed Jerry by successfully recovering from a stall, all within the dark of the night. Felix became increasingly anxious as he awaited the final element of his flight check. He had no idea what was about to happen when Jerry took control of the aircraft. Jerry proceeded to roll the plane into an inverted flat spin. Felix quickly realized what was going on, and it didn't take long for him to regain control of the Vultee Valiant. After successfully touching down, Jerry signed Felix's instrument card, and he praised him for a job well done. Felix had learned firsthand just how important his instruments could be, and he was so excited to finally be able to explore the night skies by himself.

Each consecutive night flight was a bit longer than the previous one, and Felix's confidence also increased with each successful flight. During the last week of training, he had four night flights in a row. Jerry had another final exam of sorts planned for Felix and the other cadets under his command. Jerry flew with Felix during the last two flights of his Basic training experience. They began with a morning flight where each maneuver was performed to Jerry's satisfaction. As luck would have it, a fairly significant crosswind had suddenly developed. Therefore, Jerry seized the opportunity to have Felix practice his landings to see how he'd deal with it. After noticing that the windsock was blowing mightily from left to right, Felix let Jerry know that he hadn't landed into a crosswind quite like this one before. Jerry had an idea, and he figured that he could take care of teaching two things at the same time. He realized that it would be best for Felix to perform a few go-around procedures so that he could practice his approach into the crosswind. Rather than approaching the center line of the runway head on, Felix approached the runway at a slight angle with the nose of his aircraft pointed left into the wind. With each pass at the airstrip, and with a little trial and error, Jerry was satisfied that Felix had seemingly mastered the go-around procedure. Felix also realized its importance since it might become necessary for him to abort a future landing at the last minute for a number of reasons.

Jerry felt that Felix was now ready to attempt an actual landing into the crosswind. With all of Jerry's tips and advice, Felix was feeling quite confident as he approached the auxiliary airstrip. Jerry advised him to aim just to the left of the centerline on the runway so that the wind drift would hopefully push him right where he needed to be as he attempted to touch down directly onto the centerline. If he had aimed straight for the centerline instead, the wind might've very well pushed him off to the right of the runway, and into the scrub brush.

Just before touching down, and with the nose of his Vultee Valiant still pointed left into the wind, Felix applied the right rudder to move the nose to the right. He then used the left aileron to push the tip of the left wing downward into the wind, in order to complete a successful landing, much to Jerry's delight. Felix's final time in the air at the Lemoore Army Air Field was a night flight, and he had once again handled all the tricks that Jerry had thrown at him. After landing for the last time in the BT-13, Felix took a moment to thank Jerry for all of his time and hard work over the past nine weeks. Felix gave him a high five, and he shook his hand before heading back to the barracks for some well-deserved sleep.

Felix had passed his final flight check with flying colors, and his skills as an aviator were evident in the BT-13. He was very glad to have survived his Basic training course with no accidents, mishaps, near misses, or even a close call. Felix wasn't exactly sure how many cadets had washed out, but he figured that there had to have been at least a few dozen or so. He still felt really bad for the families of the cadet and the instructor who had died two weeks earlier. Felix ended up with 27.25 hours of dual training time, and 49 hours of solo flying time, which was enough to graduate. He felt invigorated, and he was now more than ready to move on to his Advanced training. Felix's flight log book was beginning to fill up, but there was still plenty of room to log more flights as he continued down the path to war.

Elsie arrived at the Lemoore train station on Saturday morning, 24 Jul. 1943. Felix was definitely there to meet her at the station this time, and it didn't take long for him to spot his gorgeous girlfriend. Elsie was very happy to see him as well, and she quickly ran towards him. Felix gave her a big hug with a kiss, and he then grabbed ahold of her suitcase. After dropping off their things at the Lucerne Hotel, Felix grabbed Elsie's hand in order to take her on the tour of downtown Lemoore that she'd missed on her previous trip. They decided to catch a matinee of the musical comedy *Tahiti Honey* at the Lemoore Theater before stopping at a cute little café for supper.

Felix had flown over the Kings Canyon, Sequoia, and Yosemite National Parks many times, and he was truly amazed at the raw beauty that was visible from his cockpit. He knew that he just had to get a closer look to see some of the wonderful things that might lie underneath the endless canopy of trees. Therefore, while Felix and Elsie were in town, he purchased tickets from the same tour company that had taken them to San Francisco. They were very excited before dawn on Sunday morning as they boarded a bus that was bound for the Sequoia National Park. They spent the entire day traversing the rugged canyons, and hiking the scenic trails. There were a few moments when they just stood in awe of the majestic and magnificent sequoia trees. It had been a long, but marvelous day, and neither Felix nor Elsie wanted to leave. They ended up boarding the bus on time for their return trip, and they were certainly glad to get back to the hotel to relax and unwind.

Early that Monday morning, Felix needed to be back on the base for a very important meeting with Jerry and his squadron commander. The hotel staff had been kind enough to iron his jacket, shirt, and slacks. Elsie thought that Felix looked sharp, and she gave her approval after he got dressed. After a light breakfast, Elsie gave him a good luck kiss, and he was beaming with confidence when he caught a ride back to the base. Felix had filled out a questionnaire a few weeks earlier that had asked him to designate his preference for wanting to fly bombers or fighters during his upcoming Advanced training course. Felix was about to find out the decision that had been made by the command staff there at the Lemoore Army Air Field. The decision would be significant because it would affect the rest of his training, and his career as a pilot in the United States Army Air Forces.

Felix waited anxiously in a room with many other cadets including Eugene and Arthur. Roy had just exited from a door that Felix was about to enter. Felix inquisitively asked, "So, what did you get?" Roy joyfully replied, "I got selected for multi-engine training. They're gonna teach me how to fly the B-17 and the B-24 bombers." Felix congratulated him with a high five, and a pat on the back. He then stood upright as tall as he could, and he proceeded to walk quickly to the desk where Jerry and his squadron commander were seated. After saluting, Felix stood at attention with his heels together, chest out, head up, and his arms by his side. The men got right to the point, and Jerry began with, "Felix, you've proven yourself in the classroom and in the skies. We have taken into account your overall performance in both Primary, and here at Basic. You have the right physique, skills, and mindset to be a fighter pilot. Congratulations, Felix. You are heading to single-engine Advanced fighter training." Felix wanted to jump up and down and scream, but he managed to contain himself. He quickly saluted his superiors, and then thanked them for the terrific news.

The graduation ceremony and class dance was all that was left for Felix at the Lemoore Army Air Field. He'd arranged for Elsie to stop by the Lemoore Flower Shop to pick up her corsage before making her way to the base. Felix was there waiting for her at the guard post when she arrived by cab. When Elsie stepped out of the car, he thought that she looked absolutely sensational in her long red dress, white heels, pearl necklace, and her corsage adorned with white roses and blue delphiniums. Her outfit was quite patriotic, lovely, and entirely appropriate for the occasion.

Felix was able to get Elsie past the guard post as his guest for the ceremony. After reaching for her hand, he then escorted her to the field adjacent to the flight line, where they found plenty of chairs that were lined up for the guests and family members. It was still rather warm outside when the ceremony began promptly at 1600 hours. All of those in attendance appreciated that the staff wasn't too long-winded, and that the ceremony didn't last overly long. The fly-over and airshow was top-notch, but Felix felt that it wasn't quite as thrilling as the one held at Mesa Del Rey. While the band played on, the graduates of class 43-I proudly paraded by the review stand as the underclassmen of class 43-J cheered loudly.

Everyone was glad to get out of the sun and into the building where the class dance and dinner was being held. There were plenty of girls in attendance, but Felix truly believed that the one in his arms was the cutest one there. He proudly introduced Elsie to Jerry, his roommates, and to several other friends with whom he'd been training with. The buffet style dinner was fabulous, and the band played for many hours while Felix and Elsie danced long into the night. Felix was surely going to miss all of the friends that he'd made during his stay at the Lemoore Army Air Field. Although he knew that it would be unlikely, he certainly hoped that they'd all make it home from the godforsaken war that was raging around the world.

Felix and Elsie returned to their room at the Lucerne Hotel, unsure of how long it might be before they'd be together again. They certainly wasted no time making the most of their last few hours together. Once again, Felix found himself trying to delay the inevitable for as long as he could. Regrettably, the time had come for them to get dressed, and they quickly collected their things, because they both had trains to catch. Elsie's train was the first to leave town that morning. Before boarding, she gave Felix a long goodbye kiss, and she wished him the best of luck at his Advanced training base. Elsie looked him directly in the eyes, and said, "I'm so proud of you, Felix. You're a damn fine pilot, and I want you to do your best. Study hard, be safe, and I hope to see you again real soon. You can certainly bet that I'll be there to pin those wings onto your chest at your graduation." Felix tearfully waved goodbye as Elsie climbed aboard her train. He knew that he'd be more than likely heading to Arizona for the next round of training, and he had a feeling that it might be quite some time before he held Elsie in his arms once again. After boarding his train, Felix took some time to write a long letter to his folks back home to let them know what had happened over the last week, and that he was on the move once again. He was incredibly excited that he was about to be flying a faster and more powerful fighter plane. He figured that he'd mail the letter once he officially received the address information for his new post. Felix lay back in his seat and proceeded to take a nap, knowing that there was going to be plenty of hard work ahead of him.

CHAPTER 12

Wings

The train ride from Lemoore to Phoenix, Arizona, took more than nine hours. There were plenty of graduates from the Lemoore Army Air Field on the train with Felix when it came to a stop on the afternoon of 27 Jul. 1943. The men who were on the train with Felix were taken to an area next to the train station to await transportation. From the looks of things, it appeared that cadets from other Basic training bases had already arrived. As the deuce and half trucks began to line up, Felix noticed a clear sky, dry weather, plenty of visibility, and a light breeze. There was an orderly process to get all of the cadets onto the trucks for the 15 mile ride out to Luke Field.

The convoy of trucks headed west out of Phoenix. After turning left off of Litchfield Road, they stopped at the large guard post. Felix looked out the window, and he saw several military policeman buzzing around the entrance to the base. He noticed "LUKE FIELD" was spelled out in capital letters on an embankment to his left. It was beginning to get dark by the time the men got off the trucks, and had collected their belongings. The cadets were all called to attention for a brief speech by the Commanding Officer of the base, Colonel John K. Nissley. He began with, "Good evening. I'd like to welcome you to Luke Field. We're the largest single-engine fighter training base in the United States Army Air Forces. Here, you'll receive your Advanced training, where we'll test you both mentally and physically. For those who have the endurance, grit, and skills to complete our nine week course, you'll graduate, and you'll also receive a pair of our coveted silver wings along with your commission as a second lieutenant. You men are valued additions to this post, and I'm confident that you'll serve as pivotal aviators with the most powerful Air Force in the world. We're now going to get you assigned to your squadrons, your quarters, and then, we'll get you some chow."

Just like that, the men were quickly placed into either group one or two, and they were further placed into one of eight squadrons. Each of the squadron commanders held up a small sign so that the men could easily congregate before heading to their assigned barracks. Felix grabbed his bags, and he began talking with another fellow as the other cadets began to join his group. All of a sudden, a man approached Felix from behind, and he began to shake both of his shoulders. As Felix turned around to see what the hell was going on, the man enthusiastically said, "Hey Felix, Buddy Ol' Pal. Are they gonna let you fly fighters in Uncle Sam's Army?" Felix was thrilled to see that the man was none other than his good friend, Ray Simon, from his time back at SAAAB. Felix excitedly replied with, "I reckon they are. It's so good to see you. How's life been treating you?

As the men made their way to their quarters, Felix and Ray quickly caught up as if they hadn't been apart for the last 18 weeks. Felix could see that there were two-story barracks everywhere, and it appeared that there were many more barracks than those found at King City and Lemoore combined. Once inside, the men found two rows of bunk beds lined up with footlockers on the floor. Felix pulled out his lucky 1938 Buffalo nickel, and he asked Ray to choose heads or tails to see who could have the bottom bunk. Felix figured that he'd be tuckered after a long day of training, and he didn't think that he needed to exert any additional energy by climbing up to the top bunk. Luckily for Felix, he won the coin toss, and Ray made his way up to the top bunk. The simple metal bed frame with a thin mattress wasn't luxurious, but it would serve as home for the next couple of months. After unpacking their belongings, Felix and the rest of the men in his squadron made their way to the mess hall. The food was great, and the meal clearly helped satisfy Felix's hunger pains after a very long day. However, Felix found the lively conversation, and joking around with Ray, to be entirely more satisfying.

Early the next morning on 28 Jul. 1943, the cadets were assembled together once again for some further introductions. Major Hugh A. Griffith, Director of Flying, began with, "Good morning to you men of class of 43-I. We're very glad to have you here, and we know that you're eager to get on with your training. You men will soon be flying an even more powerful plane than you flew during Basic, and it will closely resemble the features and capabilities of an actual combat plane. We're going to teach you how to fly the AT-6C, and if you prove yourselves, we'll provide you with the opportunity to fly the P-40 as well. Additionally, you'll become familiar with the oxygen system found on these planes. We'll continue formation flying, but at higher altitudes, and with even more planes than ever before. As you well know from your previous posts, safety will remain as our top priority for all of you cadets. You'll also be tested on your navigation skills along with your ability to use the instruments in the new planes. Of course, there will be acrobatics, but at greater speeds, and with an elevated degree of difficulty. After you've become comfortable in my planes, we'll train you on air to air, and air to ground combat techniques with live machine guns." Both Felix and Ray loved the sound of that! Felix was very excited to hear that he'd have an opportunity to learn how to fly the two new planes, and he hungered for an opportunity to get a crack at flying at even faster speeds.

The AT in AT-6C stood for Advanced Trainer, and the P in P-40 stood for Pursuit. A copy of the Pilot's Handbook of Flight Operating Instructions for the AT-6C was passed out to each of the cadets. Next up, was Major John P. Jones, Director of Ground Training. "Good morning, men. Surely, you'll be glad to know that your ground school training will continue here at Luke Field. Be prepared to learn about all of the new instruments, and we'll help you become very familiar with the latest radio equipment. You'll continue to hone your flight planning skills in preparation for much longer flights, and each of you will realize the importance of knowing how to more accurately compute your fuel usage and range. There will be plenty of weather related courses, where we'll dive deeper into topics pertaining to the sky, visibility, barometric pressure, ceiling, wind, and the many different types of clouds. Besides your classroom instruction, you boys will spend some time in our engine and maintenance shop to learn how your plane is powered, and how we keep 'em flying. Finally, you'll spend more time inside our Link trainers to further develop your piloting skills with instruments. Essentially, we're building on the foundation that has already been established at your previous posts." Felix and the other cadets were then issued an Advanced Instrument Flying manual. He was ready for what the instructors were about to throw at him, and he was prepared to soak it all up like a sponge. By looking at the size of the manuals that they had just been given, Felix was hoping that Ray would once again prove to be an invaluable study buddy as they worked through the more difficult material.

Felix's final introduction of the morning involved meeting the chief flight instructor, and the instructors for his squadron. After that, the men in his squadron were given a tour of the base. They traversed the maze of endless buildings before ending up on the parking ramp. Felix found the flight line to be bustling with activity, and he was eager to get back up in the air. He thought that the surroundings at Luke Field resembled those found on the grounds back at SAAAB. However, this base had planes, and, boy, there sure were planes everywhere. Felix estimated that there must've been double the amount of planes that were found at the Lemoore Army Air Field. Although Luke Field was a new base for Felix, it had many of the same old things. It was a sprawling base, and it was apparent that there would be plenty of activities, and places to unwind during any free time that he might get. He noticed the two theaters, the service club, the exchange, a fabulous pool with diving boards, and even a bowling alley. As Felix walked around with the men in his squadron, they passed several other squadrons whose cadets had gathered to meet with their flight instructors. He estimated that there were close to 500 cadets in his class if he counted the two dozen or so Chinese nationals who had come to Luke Field for training.

Class 43-I yearbook photo at Luke Field.

There were no chairs for the meetings held by the squadron command staff. Instead, several of the flight instructors stood up on the wing walk while the cadets were told to gather around on both sides of the left wing of the remarkable plane sitting idly before them. A roll call commenced, and Felix was the first cadet assigned to First Lieutenant Fred Duggins. Ray gave Felix a high five after his name was selected as the last man assigned to Lieutenant Duggins. The men listened attentively to what Fred's expectations were, and what the training curriculum would entail. The cadets hollered loudly when they heard that there would be approximately 70 to 80 hours of flight time at Luke Field, and at least 20 more flying hours at the Gila Bend Gunnery Range. Felix was just chomping at the bit to get inside the cockpit of the magnificent AT-6C Texan. He surely thought that it was rather funny that a Texan would be flying a Texan. Ray chuckled, and he said, "The AT-6C Texan certainly has a much better ring to it than if it were an AT-6C North Dakotan." Felix looked around the plane, and he noticed that it had essentially the same US ARMY markings as the BT-13. The circle and star insignia was found on both sides of the fuselage, and on the tips of the wings as well. The plane was marked with a large X-320 on the fuselage, and there was a different number found on the tail.

The instructors took turns describing the features and functionality of the plane, and they explained the various instruments that would be found within the cockpit with a tandem seat configuration. The AT-6C featured a two blade propeller along with a wooden radio antenna, which was positioned just off to the right of the foremost cockpit. The radio antenna cable ran all the way to the rear of the plane, and it was fastened securely to the tip of the tail. Felix was impressed that the Texan had retractable front landing gear, and the much smaller landing wheel located under the tail was fixed in place just like on the previous planes that he'd flown. He noticed the location of the navigation lights that were found on the top and bottom of both wing tips, and one at the top of the tail. Felix figured that the red lights out on the left wing, the green lights out on the right wing, and the white lights back on the tail would help to keep him safe while flying in formation at night. Felix then ran the palm of his hand along the leading edge of each wing. He glanced at the landing lights that were located on each wing, and he saw that the passing light was found next to the landing light in the outer panel of the left wing. Felix then spotted the red, green, and amber recognition lights that were found underneath the fuselage just behind the rear cockpit. There was also a white recognition light found on top of the fuselage just in front of the tail. These lights could be used for signaling purposes, but they were to be mainly used as a way for folks on the ground, and for other pilots to recognize that the Texan wasn't an enemy aircraft.

Next, the instructors reviewed the oxygen delivery system, and then it was finally time for Felix to get his turn inside the cockpit. His eyes were immediately drawn towards the switches for the machine guns, and for the couple of bombs that the plane could carry. Felix was impressed, but he was perhaps a little overwhelmed with the 100+ levers, switches, gauges, and controls found on the main instrument panel board, and within the cockpit. There sure were a lot of internal and external lights, but Felix felt confident that he'd figure it all out in no time flat. He fiddled with the rudder and brake pedals, the control stick that was made from a fine piece of hickory, the trim tab and flap controls, and the escape latch and hood release levers. To fully complete his initial experience within the cockpit of the AT-6C, he used his index finger to touch or tap every gauge and switch. Felix exited the cockpit just as the instructors were finishing their introduction to the Texan. He was excited to hear that the nine-cylinder air-cooled engine could produce nearly 600 horsepower, and he was thrilled to no end to learn that he may soon be able to hit a top speed approaching 200 mph. Finally, the men were told that they'd be able to fly the AT-6C for approximately 750 miles on a full tank of fuel, and it could reach an altitude of about 21,000 feet.

During the afternoon meal, Felix met an Australian, two British flyers, and even a fellow Aggie named Louis Hensley. He was quick to make some new friends, and he enjoyed the many laughs shared during their conversations. The mess hall seemed to encourage healthy eating by placing a fruit bowl near the exit, and Felix was glad to grab an orange on the way out. The men then headed directly to the flight surgeon's office where they spent the afternoon getting another physical, and luckily for them, they didn't need to get any shots that day. After that, Felix and Ray spent the rest of the day participating in a variety of team sports with their squadron mates. They played basketball, volleyball, and then Felix even showed off his marksmanship with the shotgun over at the clay pigeon shooting range. After supper that evening, Felix made sure that he knew where all of the ground school classrooms were located.

It was 29 Jul. 1943, when Felix made his first trip to the post exchange. He picked up some stationery and pipe tobacco before heading back to the barracks. Felix then took some time to write a long letter to Elsie and to his folks. He let them know that he'd arrived safely at Luke Field, and that he'd be starting the final leg of his flight training the following day. Felix figured that it would be a good idea for him to take some time to review the Pilot's Handbook of Flight Operating Instructions for the AT-6C before heading to the classroom for an afternoon discussion about the Texan. This time, the instructors primarily focused on the engine, and the process necessary to start it. There were plenty of schematics hanging on the walls, and a cut out of the instrument control panel from the Texan was also located inside the classroom. Before the day's session was over, they went on to have an informative discussion pertaining to the fluid control gauges, magnetic compass, directional gyro, bank and turn indicator, rate of climb indicator, and the hydraulic system. The classroom instruction concluded for the day with an explanation of how the cockpit interphone radio worked. The instructors wanted to be sure that the cadets were fully comfortable with all of the instruments and controls that were available to them within the cockpit.

Felix thought that Lemoore was hot, but it seemed as if the temperature at Luke Field was even hotter. The heat didn't prevent the men from assembling on the dirt exercise field that was laden with weeds for a late afternoon of group calisthenics. Before heading back to the barracks to prepare for supper, Felix and Ray headed to the obstacle course to see who could establish early bragging rights for having the fastest times. The stages throughout the course were quite challenging, and it made for an exciting way to wind down the day.

Once again, Felix was assigned the morning time slot to complete his required flying hours, and his classroom training was scheduled for the afternoon. He could hardly eat breakfast on the morning of 30 Jul. 1943 with all of the enthusiasm that had been building inside him. Flying a new plane never got old for Felix, so he practically ran to the Flight Room for the pre-flight briefing. Major Griffith led the discussion by informing the cadets that they needed to be constantly aware of their surroundings since they wouldn't be piloting the only planes in the airspace above Maricopa County. They needed to conform to local air traffic patterns and regulations due to the location of the civilian Sky Harbor Municipal Airport that was located just to the east of Phoenix. The men were told that it was fairly common for military planes of all sorts to fly in and out of Sky Harbor for refueling purposes. They'd also need to contend with the "dodos" and rookie pilots over at the nearby Primary training bases. Thunderbird

Field I was located in Glendale, which was northwest of Phoenix, and Thunderbird Field II was located in Scottsdale, which was located northeast of Phoenix. Felix was used to having mostly unfettered access to the sky, so having to contend with other types of military and civilian planes was just another thing that he'd need to deal with while flying. Major Griffith continued the conversation by providing the radio frequencies that the men were to use to be in contact with the control tower. He then discussed the flight plan, and the terrain that they'd be flying over. Major Griffith pointed out the warnings on the blackboard before revealing the locations of the eight auxiliary fields found on the Regional Aeronautical Chart. Finally, he assigned the group to several different auxiliary fields located to the north and south of Luke Field. For everyone's safety, Major Griffith felt that it was best for them to practice their takeoffs and landings from the less congested airstrips.

The briefing had concluded, and the time had come for Felix and Fred to make their way to the flight line. They managed to find the plane that had been assigned to them, and Felix thought that it looked amazing as the sun reflected off of its shiny metal frame. Fred looked on with a watchful eye as Felix made his way around the Texan to perform his pre-flight check of the aircraft. He began by inspecting the leading edge of the left wing, and he meticulously looked for possible fluid leaks. He also looked for any sort of damage to the wings and fuselage. Felix then inspected the propeller from a safe distance, and he also checked the landing gear along with the tail wheel. After taking a good look at the rest of the tantalizing Texan, Felix ended up at the right wing. He inspected his parachute straps before proceeding to verify that the oil and fuel levels were full.

Felix stepped up onto the wing walk, and happily slid into the front cockpit. He immediately fastened his safety belt, and then secured his shoulder straps by locking them in place. Felix adjusted the seat position in order to be able to reach the pedals comfortably, and he made sure to check all of the controls to ensure that they were operable. Fred hopped into the rear cockpit as Felix glanced at Form 1A to verify that there were no maintenance issues with the plane. He then logged the date, destination, his name, and so forth on Form 1 before beginning to taxi. After successfully firing up the engine, Felix didn't hear or see anything that caused any concern as he was carefully listening to Fred's instructions. All of the instruments appeared to be operational after the engine had been given a chance to warm up. It was a mighty hot day, and in order to keep the engine from overheating while they reviewed the takeoff procedures, Fred asked Felix to position the nose of the plane into the wind. Fred reminded Felix to be aware of the location for the emergency brake, and he then gave him a thumbs up.

It was certainly exciting to be only moments away from takeoff. Fred instructed Felix to hold his spot on the parking ramp, and to wait for clearance from the flagman who was directing traffic on the ground in front of them.

After connecting his headset to the cockpit radio, he felt that it was entirely more appropriate this time to talk with the control tower with a touch of his Texas twang from within the Texan. Felix ensured that everything was working properly by contacting the control tower with, "Luke Field tower, this is 0263. Over." There was some back-and-forth conversation with the tower before Felix heard the words that he'd been waiting patiently for. Crackling through his radio headset came, "0263, you're cleared to taxi to the takeoff lane. Over." Felix acknowledged the tower, and then the flagman quickly gave him the clearance to proceed off of the parking ramp. He made sure that he used only a reasonable speed while taxiing, which wasn't much faster than a man walking briskly as if he was late for church. Fred liked what he'd seen up to that point as Felix made his way to the takeoff lane by "S"ing his way ever so smoothly and safely. After reaching the takeoff lane, Felix paused for just a moment until he heard the crackle once again from his radio headset. "0263, you've been cleared for takeoff. Have a nice flight, Scotty. Over."

Fred cautioned Felix that the runway was almost always bustling with activity. Therefore, he did his best to have a 360° field of vision by looking around from side to side, in front of and behind him, and, of course, above him. Felix revved the engine just a bit, and he slowly began to move off of the takeoff lane, and onto the runway. He was entirely jubilant as he felt the wheels become freed from the grasp of the scorching hot runway. It was evident that his hard work and preparation had paid off for a successful takeoff. After retracting the landing gear, Fred reminded Felix that an unexpected emergency or equipment failure could always be a real possibility. They then reviewed the basic emergency exit process from within the cockpit. Fred instructed Felix that it was ok to bail out if he couldn't control the plane due to an engine failure, or in the event of an uncontrollable fire. Fred then said, "It's always important to look around for a place to land if the need arises. You never know what might happen when flying over, and through the Valley of the Sun."

Fred pointed out the location of the Goodyear auxiliary field before they made their way to land at the Beardsley auxiliary field. There were multiple runways at Beardsley Field, so Felix had no trouble getting clearance from their tower to land. He was always a little nervous when landing a new plane for the first time. Felix used the entirety of his piloting ability and skill to properly enter the traffic pattern in order to set up his approach for a well-executed landing. Fred was impressed that Felix had maintained the proper landing speed, and he'd even managed to touch down on the first third of the runway. He was also thankful that he didn't need to remind Felix to lower the landing gear before landing in the Texan.

A pilot always hopes for a smooth wheels down landing, and he or she would surely want to avoid a wheels up landing at all costs. It might've been repetitious to some, but the numerous takeoffs and landings were thrilling to Felix on that marvelous day. He was very diligent about recording each of his flights into his pilot's flight log book. The book recorded the date, type of plane flown, whether it was a dual or solo flight, and the duration of the flight. Felix figured that it might take a week or two in order for him to amass the required minimum number of landings in the AT-6C to be officially cleared to fly solo. As the week went on, Felix enjoyed demonstrating his skills as he performed his routine maneuvers with Fred, and he was eager to learn more tricks in the coming weeks. Felix knew that there was plenty of hard work and dual flights remaining, but he was glad to be doing well, and he hoped that he was making a positive impression on Fred.

Ground school training was going well for Felix, but there was still plenty to learn. He had to memorize the Aeronautical Chart symbols as well as the nearly three dozen or so symbols that were found on the weather maps. Felix continued to become more skilled at using the D-4 computer, which was a small non-electrical device that allowed him to manually compute travel time, distance, and airspeed. He'd first used this device during his stay at Mesa Del Rey, and he hoped that one day, he'd be better than Ray at using the little gadget. The cadets continued to practice their International Morse code skills so that they could recognize the sights and sounds of the numbers and letters quicker as time went by.

D-4 time & distance computer. An integral contraption that a pilot would use for planning a flight. The reverse side helped calculate the time needed to travel a certain distance. Photo courtesy of the Jernigan Collection-King City, CA.

Felix had no idea that there was so much to learn when it came to the weather, but he was committed to reading every page of his Flying the Weather manual. Felix wondered how there could really be so many different types of clouds. Cumulus and stratus clouds would typically be found at altitudes below 6,500 feet. Then, there were the altocumulus, nimbostratus, and altostratus clouds that would be found at altitudes between 6,500-20,000 feet. Finally, cirrus, cirrocumulus, and cirrostratus clouds would be typically found at altitudes above 20,000 feet. The young pilots then learned about all of the things that they would find within the troposphere, which is the lowest layer of the earth's atmosphere. The troposphere extends from the ground up to an average altitude of about 36,000 feet globally. The cadets were told that there'd be significant variances to the height of the troposphere, depending on what region of the world they were in. The key takeaway was that this is where a pilot would deal with weather elements like fog, snow, rain, sleet, hail, drizzle, dust, clouds, thunderstorms, smoke, and other things that might inhibit their ability to fly safely. Many of these weather elements could reduce visibility to nearly zero, which could be disastrous for the pilot. Ray turned his head, and he looked out of the classroom window to see clear blue skies outside. He then said to Felix, "I suppose that we won't be dealing with many of these problems anytime soon when we're blessed with such a gorgeous day like this." Felix smiled, and said, "Yeh, I reckon you're probably right, but you never know what we might find when we get overseas." At supper that evening, Felix shared the harrowing events of the 1938 storm that had seemingly come out of the blue to strike San Saba County. He told his pals that he'd never seen anything quite like it with the devastating wind, rain, thunder, and so forth. Felix let them know that they needed to prepare for the worst weather conditions possible, and that they shouldn't be lulled into a false sense of security while flying.

Fred stressed the importance of always knowing their location while flying, and to be alert to any changes in the weather conditions. The instructors had taught the cadets that it would be a best practice to go around or turn around if they encountered bad weather unless they were on a critical war mission. It was important for them to find the best altitude where the wind and weather elements would be optimal. They also had to pay close attention to the weather officer's reports to know when it was too windy or too dangerous to fly safely. Felix hoped that with all of his training, and by trusting his instruments, he'd be able to complete and return from his missions.

There was always plenty of time spent on flight preparation in order to help ensure everyone's safety. Since the cadets would be flying longer distances, they also needed to be aware of the weather reports for their intended destinations, and any possible stops along the way. They were reminded that it would be a good idea to double check the weather reports prior to taking off. The area surrounding Luke Field was mostly flat like Lemoore, but there were visible mountains all around the area. Therefore, Felix needed to account for the maximum elevation of the neighboring mountains in his flight plan, and he also had to consider the features of the terrain that he'd be flying over. Felix was instructed to set specific checkpoints along the way to ensure that he maintained his proper course. The Link trainer continued to be an invaluable tool for him to practice flying with the use of his instruments, and to experience simulated bad weather conditions.

Having flown over Phoenix a few times, Felix could tell that it was a fairly large city, and he wondered what he might find in town. However, he had his eyes on the prize, and to Felix, that would be for him to receive his pilot's wings. Therefore, Felix wasn't about to mess this thing up at this point. Rather than spending the weekend partying with his pals, he spent additional time studying. The ground school quizzes were quite challenging, and they required a good deal of math and thought in order to come up with the correct answers. A phone call to his folks back home, and one to Elsie, provided him with emotional support, encouragement, and a brief respite from his coursework. A few matches of tennis, and a couple of trips to the movie theater with Ray also helped Felix to find the right balance that he needed to deal with his demanding schedule. He was already making plans for Elsie to come out for a visit over an upcoming weekend. Felix was really looking forward to seeing her again, and he figured that they could explore the Phoenix area together at that time. It had been nearly eight months since Felix had seen any of his family from San Saba, and he'd been told that he'd get some leave after graduating. With a little less than eight weeks left of his Advanced training, Felix was prepared to put in the time to accomplish his goal of graduating, so that he could take the war to the Japanese, or to the Nazis.

Felix had become friendly with the different plane captains that he interacted with. These captains didn't fly the planes, but rather they were responsible to ensure the overall readiness of the aircraft, and to make certain that each plane had been serviced prior to take-off. He was also very appreciative of the line chief, and the rest of the maintenance crew. Felix knew that they had a demanding job, having to work out in the scorching Arizona heat on a regular basis. Whenever possible, he thanked them for keeping the planes in tip-top condition, and for allowing him the opportunity to fly nearly every day.

Felix had established a good daily routine that began at the Flight Room early each morning. He made it a point to obtain the most recent weather maps and forecast information. In addition, he always checked the bulletin board for any red or orange flag warnings. Felix knew that he could generally count on it being hot and sunny more often than not there in the Phoenix area. He received the wind pattern data every day to help determine the best cruising altitude because he knew that wind aloft could be much different than what he felt on the ground. Felix double-checked that he'd looked at the correct navigational charts for his flight plan before heading to his plane for each flight. He realized the importance of adhering to his flight plan, and he figured that by avoiding deviations, and if he was mindful of other air traffic, he'd hopefully remain safe, and out of harm's way. Using good judgment, and trying not to be careless was equally important in order to be able to fly another day. Felix figured that his mother and father back home would also appreciate that.

It was 9 Aug. 1943, and Felix was about to make his first solo flight in the AT-6C Texan. He was certainly looking forward to having the freedom to fly by himself once again. When flying solo, Felix knew that he had to check the rear cockpit for any loose controls, seatbelts, or anything else that might pose a risk to him while up in the air. Felix quickly completed his pre-flight check of the Texan, and he reviewed every line on his takeoff instructions checklist. He had seemingly become an old pro when it came to communicating with the control tower. Upon receiving clearance for takeoff, it didn't take long for Felix to become airborne once again, but this time, he was flying solo over the Sonoran Desert below him. He planned to use the time during his first solo flight in the Texan to really take in the scenery, and true beauty of the greater Phoenix area. Felix began by making the short trip over the Phoenix Mountains Preserve, and he then buzzed Piestewa Peak. He noticed that there were plenty of ranch and agricultural fields spread throughout the area. Felix was pretty diligent about checking in with the control tower as he reached the various checkpoints on his flight plan. He proceeded to fly over the top of Camelback Mountain, and he then made his way along the Salt River. Felix remained at a safe altitude as he flew over the river because he'd been told many times never to buzz any body of water. Although he didn't get too close to the surface of the river, he was pretty sure that he had surprised some of the local fishermen as he streaked past them.

Although the desert landscape was different, it was similar enough for Felix to dream of being back home, flying all over San Saba County. However, he certainly didn't feel as if he was in a crop duster, and piloting the Texan made him believe that he'd become an actual fighter pilot. Felix saw plenty of mesquite trees along with saguaro and prickly pear cacti. He also saw the bright red flowers of the ocotillo beneath him. The yellow desert marigolds, the purple New Mexico thistle, and the orangish/red barrel cactus made for a breathtaking view from above. The vibrant colors of the Sonoran Desert flora were simply marvelous. Felix spotted some desert bighorn sheep, and a small herd of mule deer seeking shelter from the sun under the cat claw acacia and foothill palo verde trees. He had to remind himself that he wasn't there to hunt any animals. Instead, he was there to train so that he could go and fight the Axis powers around the world. Finally, he saw several red-tailed hawks circling around looking for some of the monstrous tarantulas, centipedes, rattlesnakes, and scorpions that he knew would be crawling on the desert floor below. Felix had a blast while piloting the AT-6C that day, and he safely returned to base with a memorable experience that was sure to last a lifetime.

Since Felix had the late morning flight that day, he decided to visit the quick lunch counter before heading to his ground school classes. The service there was fast, and they offered a variety of delectable choices. It was also a terrific place to hang out, and socialize for a spell with his fellow aviators. Felix ordered a chili cheese dog along with a soda when he happened to spot Louis standing near the end of the long counter. He decided to join Louis, and it didn't take long before they got to talking about planes, and their girls. Felix then mentioned that he was planning to see Elsie in the coming weeks. Louis chuckled a bit, and said, "Where is she going to stay? Are you going to try and hide her in your footlocker?" Felix smiled, and replied, "I was planning to get us a hotel room somewhere in downtown Phoenix. They have hotels there in Phoenix, right?" Louis replied, "Yes, there are hotels, but those bombardier fellas over at Williams Field, the dodos at the Thunderbird Fields, and those boys over at that Naval Air facility all have the same idea. I've heard that it can be challenging to get an affordable room anywhere in the downtown area. You might have to settle for one of those flea bag motels closer to base, or step up, and stay at one of the fancier and more expensive hotels." Felix was somewhat dismayed after hearing this information, but he wasn't willing to give up without trying.

It was Saturday, 14 Aug. 1943, when Felix hopped on a bus for a ride into downtown Phoenix. There seemed to be plenty of places open for business, and there were people moving about in every direction. Felix began walking along East Van Buren Street, and he then headed north on 3rd Street. After heading west on East Fillmore Street, he ventured into the Westward Ho, which was near the corner of Central Avenue and Fillmore Street. Felix thought that it was a very nice hotel, and surprisingly, they did have some rooms available. They were a bit pricey, so he continued south on Central Avenue until he arrived at the Hotel San Carlos. Felix really liked the look, and overall atmosphere at the Hotel San Carlos. They too had some availability, but he decided to keep looking. He then headed a few blocks south until he reached the Hotel Adams. Felix felt that he'd developed an instant rapport while speaking with the gentleman at the front desk. Although the rooms were indeed a little expensive, Felix was willing to splurge, since he really didn't know how many more weekends he'd have with Elsie before heading off to war. He explained that he needed a room for the Saturday night at the end of the month for him and his girlfriend. The man at the front desk winked, and said, "I'll always do my best to find a room for a serviceman and his wife." Felix seemed to understand the subtle hint, and replied, "Thank you sir, the reservation would be for me and my wife, Mr. and Mrs. Felix E. Scott." After the words had come right out of his mouth, Felix clearly liked the sound and thought of that. The clerk reserved the room, and he provided Felix with a receipt stating that his reservation was paid in full. While there at the hotel, Felix also made a reservation for two rooms for his upcoming graduation ceremony. He mentioned to the clerk that his "wife" and his parents would be coming to Phoenix for the special day. The clerk thanked Felix for his service, and wished him luck with the rest of his training.

With just two weeks to go before Elsie arrived for her visit, Felix had a great deal of flying to get in. He'd noticed that the new Army Air Forces insignia had been painted onto nearly all of the planes out on the flight line. Essentially, the white star remained inside the blue circle, but there was now a white rectangular bar with a blue border running through the center of the roundel. Between time spent in the Link trainer and actual flying time, he planned on logging two to three hours per day. Fred was impressed with Felix's ability to perform the high-speed vertical dives, spins, and turns in the AT-6C. The plane was very responsive as Felix effortlessly handled recovering from stalls, but he needed to remember to keep the canopy closed while doing so. Felix became quite skilled at his short field takeoffs, and he handled his simulated forced landings like a champ.

Felix and the other cadets had regular instruction on the use of their oxygen equipment in order to keep them safe at the higher altitudes. Since a supplemental source of oxygen was typically needed at altitudes above 12,000 feet, Fred reminded his pilots to affix their fancy oxygen masks to their faces before taking off in the event that they planned on reaching the higher altitudes during a flight. If they were participating in a high altitude night flight, he suggested that they begin receiving the oxygen before taking off. By being prepared ahead of time, the pilots wouldn't need to fiddle with their masks while trying to safely fly their planes at a high-speed and altitude.

Formation flying was even more exciting at Luke Field than it was at Lemoore, and for Felix, it was at a whole new level. It was quite a thrill to fly in a formation of up to twelve ships at altitudes between

18,000 to 20,000 feet. On occasion, more than twelve ships would be in the flight, which made for an even more amazing experience. The sound was near deafening with that many ships grouped together. The sight was certainly impressive, and Felix knew that any enemy wouldn't want to be on the receiving end of a fighter squadron like that. Flying faster than ever before, and with just a few feet separating him from another plane, Felix had to always be alert. He needed to keep a light touch on the stick, so that he wouldn't over react, and cause a catastrophic accident. Although there were plenty of large formation flights, Felix regularly participated in more three-ship, and even some two-ship combat formations.

At times, Felix wished that he could trade his leather flight helmet for his cowboy hat. He relished the thrill of being an air cowboy every time he flew in his Texan. There was rarely a dull moment for Felix and his pals around the base. Felix would normally be flying, reading, studying, writing letters, or hanging out with the other pilots from 0700 hours until noon. Afterwards, calisthenics, drill, and ground school classes would run until 1700 hours with supper, taps, and bed to wind down the evening. Felix ordered his new officer's uniform from the PX, and he rang up quite a bill with a new blouse, trousers, a few shirts, a new service cap, and a pair of shiny new shoes. He and his pals were surely glad to hear that Uncle Sam would cover some of the cost. The men weren't thrilled about having to take some additional evening classes and lectures, but it was just one more step in the path to receive their wings. The days were long and arduous for Felix, but he didn't complain.

Felix figured that skeet shooting with the 12 gauge shotgun was just for fun and recreation. However, the staff at Luke Field was essentially preparing the men for their upcoming aerial gunnery and combat maneuvering class. The flight of the clay pigeons mimicked the view that a pilot would have of an enemy aircraft flying by. The process was designed to help train the pilot's eyes to lead the target when firing from the cockpit. Felix had been hunting ducks and pheasants nearly his whole life, so this was just another area that he planned to excel at. He was really looking forward to the aerial gunnery class, but the upcoming instrument flying course didn't have him jumping for joy. August had been a rough month for Felix and the other cadets at Luke Field. Five training officers and one cadet had been killed during the month in four different accidents. Felix understood that his training was dangerous, and that his life was in jeopardy with each flight. He certainly didn't plan on anything happening to himself, but he decided to write a letter to his mother, which provided her with a list of friends with whom he had trained with, and for some whom he had gone to school with at Texas AMC, all of whom should be notified in the event of his death. Felix was sure that his mother would worry even more when she received the letter, but it provided him with peace of mind. He also knew that it would be prudent for him to begin paying for the pilot's life insurance after he graduated with his wings.

Frustration was running through Felix's veins when he learned that he couldn't get more than one night away from the post. Therefore, he asked Elsie to arrive at Union Station in Phoenix on Saturday 28 Aug. 1943. Needless to say, he was very glad to see Elsie step off the train and into his arms. Felix grabbed her luggage, and they began to walk hand-in-hand towards the Hotel Adams, which was about 15 minutes away. There were cars everywhere, and many folks were out and about for a stroll on the sidewalks. They walked up 3rd Avenue, and they then proceeded east on Adams, where they stumbled upon the Orpheum Theater. It looked magnificent from the outside, and they could only imagine what it looked like on the inside. Felix asked Elsie if she'd like to see a show, and she happily agreed with the offer. He promptly purchased two tickets to see the 3 p.m. showing of *Dixie*. Felix had already checked into the hotel prior to picking up Elsie, so they proceeded directly to the room to drop off her luggage. They were both hungry, so they decided to walk over to the nearby Busy Bee Café. Afterwards, they explored more of the downtown area before heading back to the theater to see the show.

They really enjoyed the musical, and all of the dancing and singing in the film got them in the mood to dance. Felix remembered that he'd seen a sign at the Hotel Adams advertising live music and dancing later that evening. The young couple returned to the five-story hotel to change into some fresh clothes before heading to the restaurant downstairs. The hotel had wide hallways, and it featured an expansive lobby. The decor was quite exquisite, and the food was rather delicious. Felix was eager to spend some quality time with Elsie out on the dance floor, so they proceeded towards the sound emanating from the Corinthian Room. They danced for hours to the music of Tommy Blake and his Orchestra before heading upstairs to bed. The room was air-conditioned, which was certainly a refreshing way to unwind from a long day.

The morning came all too soon for Felix, since he was so accustomed to getting up early. Elsie was still sleeping, so he decided to go down to the lobby for some coffee. While sitting in a comfortable leather chair, he enjoyed the quiet time to read through the morning edition of the *Arizona Republic*. Felix was able to catch up on the latest events and news about the war, and he was very glad to read that Germany and Japan were having ongoing problems with the Allied forces. Once again, Felix wondered if the war would be over before he got a chance to experience some actual combat. After finishing with the paper, he headed back upstairs to find Elsie getting dressed. They then proceeded to take a short stroll over to the Saratoga Café for brunch. The staff at the front desk agreed to hold onto their luggage while Felix and Elsie went about shopping and exploring.

It didn't take long for it to get hot outside, so they walked to a nearby canal to cool off, and splash around for a bit. Felix mentioned to Elsie how he'd grown up having such a great time splashing in the local ponds and rivers around San Saba. He told Elsie that he planned to take her there to see his little town of San Saba once he got his wings. Elsie seemed to be agreeable to the idea as she proceeded to get Felix all wet. The day began to wind down, and Felix needed to get Elsie back to the train station. They grabbed a bite to eat at the Hotel Adams before retrieving their luggage. Elsie gave Felix a nice kiss, and then said, "You've made it so far. I'm very proud of you, and I know that you're going to finish strong. You need to stay focused, and apply yourself so that I can come back here to pin those wings upon your chest." With that, Felix gave her a hug and kissed her goodbye. Felix was sad to see Elsie go, but he knew that if all went well, she'd be back in just four weeks. He was able to return to base on time, and he got right to work studying before bed. It was going to be a busy month ahead, and Felix was eager to get it going.

Felix was thrilled to learn that he'd passed his flight check in the AT-6C on 30 Aug.1943. Fred was satisfied that Felix had proven himself proficient at performing all of his high-speed maneuvers, and he felt that he handled the Texan quite skillfully. It was now time for Felix, and the cadets of class 43-I to begin a 10-day stretch where they'd focus on flying entirely with instruments. Felix had spent many hours inside the Link trainer, and a great deal of time in ground school in preparation for his first actual "blind flight" on 2 Sep. 1943. After Felix climbed into the cockpit, a hood was attached to the canopy directly above him. It quickly became dark inside, and he was no longer able to see anything outside of the cockpit. Therefore, he had to use his flashlight to see his flight plan, map, and notes. Felix was now going to have to rely on his training in order to take off, fly an assigned course, and eventually land the plane, all from underneath the hooded canopy. This experience had all of the makings to become a harrowing ordeal, since he was no longer within the safety of the Link trainer. Felix was anxious, and even nervous about the flight. He realized the inherent risk of this activity, but he felt that he was fully capable to complete the mission. Luckily for Felix, and in the spirit of teamwork, Fred let each of his pilots take his place by choosing a fellow cadet to ride along in the rear seat. Without a doubt, Ray was chosen to fly with Felix in the rear seat without a hooded canopy so that he could assist in the event that something went wrong during the flight. Before beginning to taxi off the parking ramp, Ray was quite encouraging, and he provided Felix with assurance that all would go well.

The blind flight went better than expected for Felix, and he was surely glad to have walked away unscathed. The experience actually boosted his confidence, and he was ready for the next challenge. After supper that evening, Felix called his father to wish him a happy birthday. Ernest was very glad to hear about the successful flight, and Felix was eager to find out how he'd celebrated his special day. They both agreed that it was probably best that Viola didn't need to hear about flying blind. There were several more blind flights over the next couple of days, and Felix proudly reciprocated by riding along with Ray for his blind flights. Having passed this stage of the course, Felix and Ray now had to prepare for their upcoming night flights, and their high altitude long distance night flights.

With the hood removed, Felix felt pretty comfortable piloting his Texan at night. He certainly had to rely on his instruments, since there weren't too many visual landmarks or city lights once they got out of the greater Phoenix area. The men flew all over Arizona during their "cross country" flight training. Felix certainly lucked out on one evening by having a full moon illuminate the sky as they flew over the Grand Canyon at about 18,000 feet. The view of the Grand Canyon below was extraordinary, even in the dark. They then headed south over the mountain communities of Flagstaff and Sedona before heading back to Luke Field. Felix used his radio navigational aids throughout his night flights. Whenever possible, he used light lines such as highways, busy roads, and nearby auxiliary fields as a check to ensure that he was headed in the right direction. Felix was very thankful that he hadn't needed to use his parachute for a bail out situation at any point during his training. Overall, Felix felt safe while flying at night, but he was glad to have received instructions on the proper method of pulling the rip cord to deploy the parachute. Additionally, he paid close attention to the discussion on how to deal with different emergency situations that might arise while flying at night. Felix ended up with a total of five night flights, and he was very pleased to have passed the instrument flying course and written exam with flying colors.

After nearly nine months of training, Felix was finally going to partake in live fire exercises from an airplane. On the morning of 9 Sep. 1943, Felix called his sister, Johnnie Mae, to wish her a happy birthday. He told her that he was just chomping at the bit to be able to shoot targets from the two .30 caliber machine guns mounted on the AT-6C. However, with all of the recent accidents and deaths at the base, Felix mentioned that he was fearful that something terrible could happen with all the bullets flying through the air. Johnnie Mae let Felix know that she wouldn't tell their mother about this stage of his training. It was time for Felix and the other cadets to board the bus that would take them to the Gila Bend gunnery range. During the one hour bus ride toward Arizona's southern tip, Felix imagined all of the cool things that he was about to experience during the 10 day gunnery training course.

There were plenty of things to keep Felix and the other men occupied on the first day of gunnery training. They'd previously been introduced to the Browning .30 caliber machine gun during their ground school time at Luke Field. It was more of a formality to some degree, but the cadets had to demonstrate their ability to dismantle, and reassemble the gun. Additionally, Felix needed to qualify on his marksmanship skill with the .30 caliber machine gun while shooting from the ground. Ground school courses continued at Gila Bend with an emphasis on using the blinker lights for Morse code, aircraft recognition, combat tactics, and the mathematical skills needed to effectively shoot down enemy aircraft.

The following morning, Felix was beyond thrilled when he climbed into the cockpit of his mighty Texan on the Gila Bend flight line. He immediately noticed the Browning M-2 .30 caliber machine gun mounted on the engine cowling just to the right of his windshield. Felix also noticed an additional .30 caliber machine gun positioned on the outer right wing panel of the aircraft. He felt the trigger for the machine guns on the grip of the control stick, and the bomb release switch was found atop the grip. While clutching the grip, he quickly pictured himself in a dogfight with multiple enemy aircraft. Felix then took off with an instructor in the rear cockpit so that he could become acclimated with the gunnery range, and the area surrounding Gila Bend. Having the opportunity to briefly fire the machine guns for the first time was electrifying to Felix. The plane shook as the guns fired, and he could feel the vibrations of the shots pulsating throughout his body. Felix figured that this experience would never get old, and he was most definitely having a blast.

Felix and the other cadets were assigned a time to clean the guns, and protect them with an oil preservative. They also spent time with the line crew to learn how other maintenance was performed on the guns, and they were shown how the bullets were loaded into the ammunition boxes prior to a flight. Felix was amazed at how efficiently the crew loaded the 200 rounds per gun to prepare for a training flight. He could only imagine what type of damage would be inflicted with 400 rounds firing down upon a target. When it would become necessary to score hits on targets, the tips of the bullets would be painted with different colors to track the results for each pilot.

There was plenty to learn in the classroom about the science, and art of aerial gunnery techniques. Felix was issued several training aids including the Fighter Pilot Gunnery manual, and the Browning .30 caliber Machine Gun manual. Velocity, angles, aerodynamic drag, and projectile gravity drop were all important factors to be successful with a machine gun from the cockpit. Felix needed to become skilled at sighting a moving target through his gunsight. He also needed to learn how to estimate the crossing speed, and the range of an enemy target. In order to have the bullet successfully hit its target, he needed to understand the path of a bullet, and he had to be able to track and lead the intended target.

Felix spent many hours at the ground range firing on moving targets before officially beginning his training on the aerial target range. He and the other men trained during the day, and also at night. Tracer bullets were utilized to help the cadets get a greater concentration of hits on their targets. Felix was ecstatic to begin his actual air-to-air, and combat maneuvering training. Simulated dogfights were pretty risky, since they used other ships within their flight as practice. Constant radio communication with one another was necessary to avoid disaster. Felix learned many different dogfighting strategies, but he realized that the enemy could be totally unpredictable in reality. He was always on the lookout for a potential bogey on his six (tail), and he needed to be aware of what was above, and below him as well. Felix trusted that his training and instincts would keep him alive in the event that real enemy bullets were being fired his way. The instructors were looking for how well the cadets handled the quicker planes under stress, their ease at performing maneuvers with other planes nearby, and how they handled sudden changes within the "hostile" environment.

As part of his pre-flight check of the aircraft, Felix needed to inspect the guns to be sure that they'd been cleaned, that they were loaded, and that they'd be ready to fire when needed. He also inspected the N-3B optical gun sight to ensure that it would be operable for his training exercise. The cadets were taught the importance to seize the opportunity for a clear shot, and to pull the trigger when the reticle appeared to be covering the target. Before firing the guns, Felix turned the gun safety and selector switches to the ON position, and it was certainly important to place them into the OFF position before landing. There was plenty of time and practice spent focusing on grouping shots together in short bursts. The main objective was to conserve ammunition in order to be as effective as possible during training, and ultimately when at war. The cadets were asked to limit bursts to 25 rounds or less, and they were advised not to exceed bursts of 75 rounds or more in an attempt to keep the guns from overheating. When possible, the men were told to wait a few moments in between bursts, and they were reminded to never empty their entire ammo box at once, unless their life was in danger.

The two guns aboard the AT-6C could be fired individually, or simultaneously, if there was a need to inflict a greater amount of damage on the target. Felix thoroughly enjoyed diving down to strafe the wooden ground targets while flying at a low level. He'd quickly fire his guns, and then climb at a high rate of speed before the plane behind him took his turn. With plenty of repetition, Felix had become outstanding at firing his machine guns upon the ground targets with a fairly high degree of accuracy. There was very little room for error being so low to the ground, but he didn't let his nerves get to him. Shooting at moving targets in the air, while he himself was moving, was certainly more challenging to Felix. There were several different types of cloth targets that could be towed behind another plane. The pilots clearly needed to focus, and pay close attention in order to keep the bullets on target versus hitting the plane that was pulling them. They trained over and over again at different speeds, ranges, and they learned the proper lead time, depending on if they were approaching the target from a 30º, 45º, 60º, or 90º angle. Felix realized that flying at higher altitudes provided a prime vantage point to be able to spot potential enemy planes below. He'd regularly fire between 200–400 rounds per day while on a training flight.

The time seemed to have flown by during Felix's stay in Gila Bend. The last day of his gunnery training was on 19 Sep. 1943. Before saying his final goodbyes to the men, the flight instructor within Felix's group said, "With the combination of ongoing learning, and with even more practice, each of you are well on the way to becoming the best pilots in the world. All I ask is that you remember these three basic things every day. Be sure to fly your plane instinctively without overreacting, precisely locate your intended destination or target, and then destroy the enemy's position or aircraft before returning to base safely." Felix had scored high enough on hits to his ground and air targets, and he was exhausted after logging the 20 flying hours required of him at Gila Bend. Felix also passed the final examination for the Aerial Gunnery training, and he was ready to head back to Luke Field for the final 11 days of training.

Upon returning from Gila Bend, Felix and Ray were told that they'd been selected to receive training in the P-40 Curtis Warhawk. Felix was thrilled that Major Griffith was a man of his word by providing them with training in the P-40. The training on the new plane was going to be abbreviated, and Felix knew that he'd really need to step up his game. Each man was given a copy of the Pilot's Handbook of Flight Operating Instructions for the P-40C, and they were told to familiarize themselves with it that evening. The Warhawk wasn't just another plane, but rather it was a full-fledged fighter plane. Felix wasn't so thrilled about the daily round-trip bus ride that would take them to the auxiliary field No.1, which was known as Wittman Field. However, he figured that having the free time to joke around with Ray and his pals would make the bus ride enjoyable after all. The auxiliary field was northwest of Luke Field, and it had several runways that were arranged in a triangular fashion. Felix and the cadets arrived at Wittman Field on the morning of 20 Sep. 1943, to find a control tower, and plenty of impressive P-40C airplanes arranged neatly on the flight line. He'd flown near the field many times, but he'd never landed there before.

Felix and the men were given an introduction to the P-40C, and they were quizzed on what they were to have learned from their instruction manual. Since the cadets would soon be receiving their wings, the instructors didn't spend too much time on the basic components of the plane. Rather, they got right to the point by having a thorough discussion of the things that would be necessary for them to take off, to fly, and to land safely in the Warhawk. Felix walked around the majestic plane as if he'd fallen in love with a new girlfriend. He marveled at its overall beauty, and more lethal armament capabilities. Felix was quite impressed when he saw two Browning M-2 .30 caliber machine guns on each wing, and two .50 caliber machine guns affixed to the engine cowling at the front of the plane. It didn't take long for him to notice that there was no room for an onboard instructor in the P-40C, since it had just a single-seat cockpit. Felix was excited when he slid into the Warhawk's cockpit for an opportunity to poke around, and fiddle with all of the controls. He noticed that the instrument panel was arranged nicely, and he got a firsthand look at the gauges, switches, knobs, and levers. While sitting behind the armored windscreen, Felix imagined how much fun it would be to get her up in the air.

Felix being pulled by a tug while standing in a P-40.

The afternoon was spent with the line crew as they gave a demonstration on how the machine guns were loaded and serviced. The cadets were then shown where all of the vital fluids were located, and the mechanics took their turn by describing how the engine was put together. The men were thoroughly impressed that the engine could deliver 1200 horsepower, yet they were cautioned that the Warhawk could overheat on occasion. The 12-cylinder liquid cooled engine could help the pilots reach speeds in excess of 300 mph, which was significantly faster than the AT-6C. This was the first plane that Felix would fly with a 3-blade propeller. The overall ceiling on the P-40C was greater than the Texan, but it performed most optimally at altitudes between 10,000 and 15,000 feet. Felix noticed the sizable drop tank that was located under the belly, which helped increase the range of the P-40C. While standing on the wing walk, the line chief said, "The Warhawk is faster than anything that you boys have flown thus far. She's very versatile, yet sturdy as well. You'll find that the Warhawk responds quickly, handles well overall, and she has a dive speed that just might knock your socks off! I've been told that if you can learn to fly this baby well, you'll be able to handle the P-47 and P-51 with no problem." The cadets were then told to get plenty of rest since they'd get their first opportunity to fly the P-40C early the next morning.

Being that there was limited visibility over the nose of the Warhawk, Felix was a little nervous as he was about to take off for the first time. Additionally, it was rather difficult to see what was behind him, so communication with the tower would be crucial for a safe takeoff and landing. Once in the air, Felix found the plane to be a relatively slow climber, but he thought that the plane handled gracefully, and he agreed that it performed well at high-speeds. Felix got such a kick out of pushing the throttle forward to test the speed limits of his newest war machine. Although there was no one on board with him, there was an instructor in the air with Felix. Captain Drew Gustafson was the flight instructor assigned to Felix, and it was sort of like playing follow the leader, P-40 style. Drew trailed behind Felix, and he closely watched him perform every maneuver that was asked of him through his radio headset. The nearly one hour flight went by quickly, and without a great deal of difficulty. Much to Felix's surprise, he executed a near perfect landing, and Captain Gustafson seemed pleased with his abilities. Felix and Ray were certainly perturbed to learn that they wouldn't be participating in any live fire exercises while using the guns aboard the Warhawk during their time at Wittman Field. However, the cadets were told that they could expect plenty of gunnery training at their next base when they reported for their Operational Training Unit (OTU) assignment.

Over the next several days, Felix continued to perform, and practice his maneuvers at greater speeds. His last day spent in the P-40C while in Arizona was on Sunday, 26 Sep. 1943. Being that Felix had no specific tasks left to accomplish that day, he decided to set his flight plan to include a stop at the Three Sisters rock formation located in the southern area of the Superstition Mountains. Since Felix's three sisters couldn't travel to Phoenix for his upcoming graduation, he felt that it was entirely fitting to perform his maneuvers and acrobatics above the rock formation as if they were somehow watching. Felix had a blast as he performed his one-man aerial show. Although Aletha, Johnnie Mae, and Pauline couldn't physically see his prowess, he knew that they were rooting for him back home.

Nearly two years after the dastardly attack on Pearl Harbor, Felix was getting closer to exacting the revenge against the Japanese that he so fervently sought. Graduation was just days away, and Felix knew that he needed to perform well in his final flight checks. He was fairly certain that he'd ace the flights with Fred, and he was happy with his individual success. However, Felix and many of the other cadets were sad, and still reeling from the recent deaths of a Lieutenant and a cadet. The untimely deaths resulted from two different plane crashes that occurred on 17 Sep. and 23 Sep. Felix felt terrible for the fallen pilots and their families, but he knew that he must carry on.

Felix had managed to successfully complete all that Fred had thrown at him on their final flight together. In the end, they had tallied 28 flying hours together in the Texan. In addition, Felix obtained

60.25 solo flying hours during the day, and he logged another 8.25 hours at night in the AT-6C. Felix managed to get 10.25 hours in the P-40C for a grand total of 106.75 flying hours combined between the two planes. He'd exceeded the minimum amount of flying hours required of him, and Felix was very pleased with his hard work. He seemed to have the flying piece down pat, but he was a little concerned with the looming comprehensive written final exam. Felix reviewed his manuals, his workbooks, and he'd even spent many hours with Ray quizzing each other. His effort and hard work paid off as Felix passed the final exam with flying colors. He was very proud that he was able to retain all the facts, figures, and mathematical calculations needed to complete the requirements for graduation. Felix's new officer's uniform had arrived at the post exchange, and he was eager to begin wearing it on graduation day.

The last day of September was special to Felix in many ways. He was given permission to leave the base after the graduation rehearsal had taken place. Felix made sure to stop by Lieutenant Staley's desk to collect his monthly salary. He signed his name for the last time as an aviation cadet, and he collected his $105 in cash. Felix was looking forward to the bump in pay moving forward since he'd now be a second lieutenant. After grabbing a bite to eat at the quick lunch counter, Felix bummed a ride bound for downtown Phoenix. Elsie and his folks were due to arrive on different trains later that afternoon at Union Station.

Felix was overjoyed to embrace Elsie after she made her way off the train. Walking hand-in-hand, they made their way towards the platform where Ernest and Viola were due to arrive at. Their journey was much longer than Elsie's, but the Scotts were due in within an hour or so of Elsie's arrival. Felix was smiling from cheek to cheek as his folks appeared from the crush of people exiting the train. He hugged his mother and father for what seemed like a few minutes before introducing them to his beautiful Czechoslovakian girlfriend. Elsie seemed to have an instant connection with Mr. and Mrs. Scott, and she immediately began chatting it up with Viola. Felix was busy filling his father in with all of the recent happenings that had taken place over the previous few weeks on the base.

The group began walking towards the Hotel Adams, and Felix pointed out the Orpheum Theater to his folks as they passed by. Felix checked in at the front desk, and he obtained the keys for the two rooms that he'd reserved. Everyone was hungry, so after leaving their luggage in the rooms, Felix led them to the Saratoga Café for a scrumptious supper. Afterwards, the group proceeded to trek around downtown Phoenix, and Felix made sure that he kept his arm interlocked with Elsie's the whole time. As they strolled along the sidewalk, Ernest noticed a store that sold Navajo, and other Native American items and artifacts. Felix just had to go inside to see what they had for sale. Naturally, he and Ernest looked at the arrowheads and other edged weapons. Felix then asked his father, "Is my collection still stored safely in my dresser drawer? Are my most prized pieces still hanging on the wall?" Ernest placed his hand onto Felix's shoulder as a means of reassurance, and replied, "Yes, you betcha son!" Meanwhile, Elsie and Viola looked at the wonderful jewelry that was displayed inside of the glass showcases. Felix could never resist spoiling Elsie, and with the wad of money burning a hole in his pocket, he just had to buy her a silver bracelet with beautiful turquoise inlays. Upon returning to the hotel, everyone proceeded to the sitting area near the lobby for an evening of pleasant conversation. Felix opted not to attend the class dance that was held on the base because he wanted to spend the time catching up with his folks and Elsie.

Felix gave copies of this photo to all of his family members back home in Texas, and he also sent a copy to some of his buddies across the country as well. He was very proud to give Elsie a copy too.

It had been more than nine long months since Felix had first set foot on the post in Santa Ana, CA. The journey along the way had been both tough and exciting at the same time. Felix hardly slept that night because he knew that in just a few hours' time, his silver wings would finally be pinned upon his chest. He was a forward thinker, and as such, Felix arranged for a ride to Luke Field on the morning of 1 Oct. 1943. A training officer who lived near the downtown area swung by the hotel to pick up Felix and his guests. It was a little tight in the car, but everyone made it safely to the base. Since they'd arrived a little early, Felix gave them a brief tour as they made their way towards the concert green for the ceremony that was to begin at 0900 hours.

Colonel Nissley gave the graduation address to the cadets and their families. There were a few more than 400 proud graduates in class 43-I at Luke Field that morning.

After the speakers were finished, the graduates gathered with the members of the Women's Auxiliary Corps on base for a review, and parade in front of the guests in attendance. The band played on as the group marched in unison past the Headquarters Building, and along the flight line. As Viola watched the review, it brought back some fond memories of the few that she'd seen at Texas AMC. She'd wished that Felix would've graduated from college so that she could've seen the impressive graduation review held there on campus. Viola certainly tried to hide the mixed emotions that were running feverishly throughout her body. On the one hand, she was very proud of Felix's accomplishment, and she realized just how hard he'd worked to earn his wings. In reality though, Viola was a mess wondering what country Felix was going to end up in, and what the future held for her only son.

Front of the graduation card given to Felix by his favorite cousin Chauncey.

The Scotts thought that the review was nice, but they weren't really blown away. However, the aerial review, and fly over that followed was unlike anything that they'd ever seen before. There were countless P-38s, P-39s, P-40s, and even a few P-51s executing daring high-speed maneuvers in the sky right above them. Felix wasn't sure where the trio of B-17 bombers had come from, but he certainly enjoyed their thunderous flyover in a tight formation overhead. There were plenty of planes in the sky performing dazzling acrobatics in nearly every direction around the crowd. The final flyover formation with dozens of planes grouped together was astonishing to all those who witnessed it. At the conclusion of the ceremony, Felix managed to find Elsie and his folks among the throng of people scattered about the area. Elsie gave him a big hug and a kiss, and his folks followed with their congratulatory embraces as well.

Felix proudly wearing his new wings on graduation day at Luke Field.

Felix was beyond thrilled to show off the silver wings that were nestled securely in the palm of his hand. He then handed them to Elsie so that she could pin them upon his chest. Finally, Felix officially looked the part of a newly commissioned second lieutenant with his wings and new brass pins affixed to his coat. There were plenty of handshakes and high fives to go around as Felix saw men from his class pass by. Ernest proudly took plenty of pictures of Felix, and, of course, there were some with Elsie, his mother, and his pals as well.

Everyone was thankful that they were able to get a ride from the training officer back to the hotel. They could've taken a bus back to Phoenix, but the line was so long, and they were starving. Felix remembered that the food and service had been great at the Busy Bee Café, so that's where they went. During the course of their meal, Felix mentioned to his folks that he'd be on leave until about 16 Oct. 1943. Viola had a hard time containing her enthusiasm as she was obviously bursting with joy. Ernest was pleased to hear the good news as well, and he figured that all of the family back home would also love to see Felix. He then asked his folks if it would be ok if Elsie accompanied them back to San Saba for a visit. Felix was very glad that they said yes, because he had already asked Elsie to bring an extra suitcase figuring that they'd be agreeable to having company.

Felix needed to return to Luke Field early on 2 Oct. 1943 for processing, and he could only imagine the stories that his folks were going to share with Elsie while he was gone. He quickly learned the new seven digit serial number that was issued to him as an officer, and he promptly filled out the required paperwork that had been given to him. Felix's proficiency card looked much better than did his transcript from Texas AMC. There were no letter grades, but rather a few Above Average, many Average, and luckily, no Below Average marks on the form. The form contained his marks for the Primary, the Basic, and the Advanced levels of training. The scores marked his proficiency in military rules and regulations, academics, and all of the specific areas that were relevant to being a pilot. Next, he received a Certificate of Proficiency, which provided a numeric grade for the ground school courses that he'd taken there at Luke Field. It also listed the cumulative hours that he'd flown during his time at Mesa Del Rey, the Lemoore Army Air Field, and at Luke Field. Felix was pleased that the form showed that he'd officially received a Satisfactory rating during his journey to obtain his wings. He was certainly anxious as he stood in line to receive his orders for his next post, which would be with an Operational Training Unit (OTU). It was hard for him to believe, but the rumor was that the graduates would find the training that was waiting for them to be even more difficult than what they'd already experienced.

The excitement quickly waned when Felix learned that his orders would take him to Tallahassee, Florida. He suddenly felt thoroughly dejected knowing that there wouldn't be any weekend getaways with Elsie when he was going to be training on the other side of the country. Felix figured that he'd hold off on telling Elsie about his orders until they arrived in San Saba. He quickly cleared out his footlocker, and he removed all of his belongings from the closet. His rack was left just as he'd found it with the sheets and blanket folded neatly on top of the mattress. As Felix walked out of the barracks for the final time, he happened to see Ray heading his way. The two men stopped for a couple of minutes to share a few laughs, and to say their goodbyes. Felix mentioned that he was headed to Dale Mabry Field in Florida, and he was thrilled to no end when Ray showed him his orders that confirmed that he was headed there as well. They wished each other a great couple of weeks while on leave, and they planned to meet up again upon their arrival at their new post. Felix bid a final farewell to the other men and staff that he saw before heading back to Phoenix. He knew that the war would take him and his pals all over the world. Sadly, there was a clear sense that many within his class would never return home from the unrelenting war.

Once Felix arrived back at the hotel, he found Elsie and his folks having a grand old time chatting it up over dinner. After joining them for a fine dessert, they retrieved their luggage, and headed for Union Station. Prior to boarding the train, Felix and Elsie stopped by the newsstand for some snacks and magazines. He picked up the newest edition of *Air Trails* and a *Sky Raiders* comic book. Elsie purchased the two most recent copies of *Life* and a *Saturday Evening Post*. They then headed to the platform where Ernest and Viola were waiting. Everyone gathered their belongings, and they prepared to board the afternoon train bound for San Saba.

It was pretty late on 3 Oct. when Elsie and the Scotts arrived in San Saba. Thankfully, Pauline was waiting there at the train station so that she could get everyone home quickly. Felix was proud to introduce Elsie to Pauline, and he assured her that they'd hang out during their stay in San Saba. While making the short drive over to the Scott home on South Live Oak Street, Felix asked Pauline, "How well have the Aggies been playing?" Pauline cheerfully replied, "They've scored a lot of points to win their first two games of the year. It could be a strong year for the Aggies, but it's still too early to tell."

Felix was thankful to wake up in his own bed, and to wear his regular clothes once again. He donned his plain khaki pants with a button up striped shirt, and he just had to place his favorite cowboy hat back upon his head. Early that Monday morning, Felix and Elsie walked down the street to Johnnie Mae's café. Elsie thought that it was terrific that Johnnie Mae was able to handle the demands of the restaurant while making time to visit with them. Johnnie Mae and

Elsie seemed to really enjoy conversing with one another. Over breakfast, Felix caught up on the world events, and the war happenings by reading the most current edition of *The San Saba News*.

It was cooler outside than Elsie thought it would be, so Felix decided that they'd walk across the street, and into Harry's Boots. After showing Elsie around the store, Felix ended up purchasing a fine wool coat that featured many images of wild horses for her. He was excited to show off, and drive his beloved car and truck, so they proceeded directly home. Felix quickly tore the tarp off the '37 Ford to find that it was in remarkable condition. It was clean, and the tires were full of air just like Ernest had promised. So, off they went for a cruise around town, and, of course, they stopped in at Mrs. Howard's bakery, and at the AAA office to say hello. Felix's former bosses were thrilled to see him, and they enjoyed meeting a fine young woman in Elsie. They were glad that he'd made it this far with his training, and they both wished him continued luck and success moving forward. Next, they drove by the High School, the football field, and many of his other favorite hangouts that he'd had while growing up. Elsie then hung on for dear life as Felix put the pedal to the metal while they were en route to Bend for dinner with his grandparents. Felix had to remember that he was now driving a car, and not flying a plane, thus he ended up slowing down for Elsie's benefit. Elsie began to wonder where the long dusty road was taking them since they'd been traveling for nearly an hour in what seemed like the middle of nowhere. Felix assured her that he'd been there a million times, and they arrived safely shortly thereafter at the River Bend farm.

Ma and Pa were just tickled to meet Elsie. Of course, Felix had brought other girls by their home before, but they found Elsie to be a remarkable young woman the moment they first met her. After a fine fried chicken dinner, Felix and Elsie took a horseback ride through the pecan orchards. They continued along the river banks, and they stopped at several points to walk around the vast property. Unfortunately, it was too cold for wading or for a plunge into the river via the tire swing that was tied to a tree branch nearby. Felix told Elsie about all of the fun that he'd had with his cousin Chauncey there on the farm, and in the river. He was sad that he wasn't able to visit with Chauncey due to his recent enlistment in the United States Marine Corps. They had a fabulous time visiting with Ma and Pa, and they were certainly looking forward to the fish fry that was to be held with all of the family on Saturday, 9 Oct. Felix then took Elsie to a few of his favorite spots around Bend before heading back home. Over supper, Felix let his parents know that Elsie could stay until 16 Oct., when he too would have to leave. He also mentioned that he planned to take her to San Antonio for several days.

As dawn began to break on the morning of 5 Oct., Felix pulled the cover off of his '41 Chevy truck to find that it was also clean and well-kept. After a bountiful breakfast, they placed their bags into the bed of the truck. After helping Elsie into the cab of the truck, Felix hopped in, and they waved goodbye to Ernest and Viola, who were standing on the porch. Before leaving San Saba, Felix stopped at the San Saba National Bank to withdraw some extra cash for the trip. Having Elsie sit right beside him on the bench seat made the ride quite enjoyable. After cruising around the downtown area of San Antonio for a bit, Felix found a place to park on East Crockett Street. He moved their bags into the cab before they proceeded to walk about the area looking for a hotel. Felix had picked all of their prior hotels, and this time, he told Elsie that she could choose where they'd stay. Being that they were practically standing in front of the Alamo, Felix and Elsie took the opportunity to explore the area around the historic site. Elsie thought that it was sad that so many men had died during the battle for the Alamo back in 1836. Felix then said, "Yes, there were a lot of brave men who died that day. Like many Americans, I also feel that it's important to stand up, and fight for what is right. I'm ready to do my part to bring the full might of the Army Air Forces to the doorsteps of our enemies abroad." Elsie then grabbed Felix's hand, and said, "Well, I'm not ready to let you go just yet."

There was a line that stretched out to the sidewalk at a nearby Mexican food restaurant. Felix and Elsie were hoping that the food tasted as good as the smell that was wafting out the windows towards them. The enchiladas and fresh guacamole were well worth the wait. After dinner, they continued their search for a place to stay. There were several hotels in the area, but Elsie had decided upon the Menger Hotel. Felix thought that Elsie had made a fine choice, although it was going to hit him rather hard in the pocket book. He was glad that he'd decided to have the extra cash on hand. Felix paid for Tuesday, Wednesday, and Thursday night, and he was happy that the room was a little cheaper being that they were there during the middle of the week. There were luxurious, and well-appointed furnishings, throughout the lobby, sitting areas, and hallways. Felix and Elsie had selected a standard room, but even that was rather opulent and entirely comfortable. They both agreed that this had to have been one of the finest hotels that they'd stayed in yet.

During their stay in San Antonio, Felix and Elsie attended a theatrical production, and they even saw a movie at the Aztec Theater. There was plenty of live music up and down the streets, and they found a marvelous mariachi band performing at a park that was close by. They seized the opportunity to dance wherever they had a chance. Finding a place under a shade tree proved to be quite relaxing while other musicians played a variety of music. As they continued their walk through town, Felix and Elsie stumbled upon a nearby canal that appeared to be an up-and-coming focal point for the city. There were new shops and restaurants being constructed along the walkways near the water. Felix imagined that this place would turn out to be spectacular, and he hoped to return one day to see how it had all turned out. Mexican food seemed to be the daily choice for the young couple, but they made every effort to try a different dish each meal.

Felix still found it to be rather odd to be walking around in his regular clothing when he'd worked so hard to earn his wings to go upon his officer's uniform. However, he figured that there would be plenty of other opportunities for him to proudly show off his new attire down the road. For now, he just wanted to be a regular guy out having fun with his adorable girlfriend. On the final morning of their stay, they decided to visit the San Antonio Zoo. Felix and Elsie enjoyed the wide variety of animals, and their leisurely walk throughout the beautiful grounds.

With the holidays approaching once again, Felix knew very well that he wouldn't be home to celebrate with his family or with Elsie. Therefore, he thought that it would be a great idea to do some early Christmas shopping. Felix and Elsie traversed many city blocks looking for just the right present for each other, and for their family members. When Felix passed by the Lucchese boot store, he just knew that he had to go inside. He told Elsie all about his senior boots that he'd proudly worn for just one semester. Unfortunately, the boots were pretty specific to his Texas AMC uniform, and they'd look a bit odd if worn with something else. Nevertheless, he loved the quality and comfort that the Lucchese boots offered, so he figured that Elsie ought to have a pair to go with her new coat. Felix then placed his arm over her shoulder, and said, "Babe, when I get back from this war, maybe you'll settle down with me here in Texas. You gotta look like a Texan to best fit in round these parts, and I'm certain that they'll look amazing on you." Elsie loved being spoiled, and she graciously played along by picking out a fine pair of boots. Having purchased several bags worth of presents in downtown San Antonio, Felix felt that it was time to head back to San Saba.

When Felix pulled into his driveway on that Friday night, he was excited to see Aletha's car parked next to his father's shop. Elsie was just about six months older than Aletha, and he figured that they'd have the most in common out of his three sisters. Felix's assumption was right. Aletha and Elsie spent many hours talking, laughing, and cooking late into the night in preparation for the family get together, and fish fry that was to be held that Saturday afternoon. Aletha took a genuine interest in learning how Elsie effortlessly made dozens of Czechoslovakian spice cookies, and a sponge cake filled with fresh cherries all from memory. Not to be outdone, Aletha showed Elsie how to make a platter full of snappy turtles. She used her creativity to craft the sugar cookies into miniature turtles. Sliced pecans were used for the arms, legs, and head, and the delicious chocolate frosting that was used for the shell was just divine.

The fish fry turned out to be fabulous, and Felix felt that it rivaled the one that was held just prior to him leaving for Santa Ana. Nearly all of the family members attended the supper, and boy, each of them sure brought some delicious food and desserts. Viola had invited a few of her neighbors, and the gathering became much livelier after supper. Pa was on the mandolin, Felix was on his violin, Ernest played the piano, AJ played the trombone, and Ted joined in with his harmonica. Viola asked Elsie if she could sing, and before you knew it, she was singing songs, and even some church hymns right along with most of the other kinfolk.

Felix wanted Elsie to experience a Sunday service in a small town church. They were glad that Aletha tagged along with Ernest and Viola for their trip out to the Bend Methodist Church. Ma and Pa met everyone there for a wonderful service that morning. Felix let Elsie know how much the little church meant to him, and that he'd been attending services there nearly his whole life. After a fine dinner over at the River Bend farm, it was time for Aletha to head back to nursing school. Felix and Elsie had made plans to spend their last week in San Saba doing many fun and relaxing things. Viola offered to prepare some delicious sandwiches, and she baked fresh chocolate chip cookies for their adventure on Monday afternoon. Felix grabbed the picnic basket, a few fishing poles along with the tackle box, and he threw everything into the back of his truck. He and Elsie then made the drive over to Richland Springs to see the Regency Bridge. After picnicking on the large rocks that were just off to the side of the suspension bridge, Felix and Elsie walked upon the thick wooden planks until they reached the center. He promptly affixed the bobbers, weights, and worms before showing her how to drop their lines into the chilly Colorado River below. Between the two of them, they caught plenty of fish for supper, and they had a splendid time while doing so.

Felix walked with Elsie over to Johnnie Mae's cafe for dinner on 12 Oct. 1943. Elsie thought that the tamales were better than anything they'd had in San Antonio. Johnnie Mae was always looking out for Felix, and she had the latest newspapers saved for him. He was glad to read that the New York Yankees had just won the World Series, even without Joe DiMaggio. After reading all about the highlights of the series, Felix couldn't resist bragging to the men in the cafe that he'd met Joe DiMaggio in person while stationed at SAAAB, and that he even had an autographed picture to boot. Felix had a blast taking Elsie to see a movie at the Palace Theater there in downtown San Saba. Afterwards, they walked around the Courthouse Square, and visited several of the nearby shops. While walking down East Wallace Street, they stopped in front of Kimbrough's Jewelry store to look at the dazzling diamond jewelry that was on display behind the large glass window. Felix noticed a beautiful diamond engagement ring featured prominently on top of a small velvet pedestal. Part of him really wanted to march inside and purchase it. He thought that a marriage proposal under the giant Wedding Oak tree would be a fitting end to Elsie's trip to San Saba. However, the fantasy quickly vanished from his mindset, and he and Elsie continued on towards the Scott home. Felix had to mentally remind himself that he was heading off to war, and his fate was yet to be determined. He certainly dreaded the thought of having to leave Elsie behind, and he most definitely didn't want to burden her with the possibility of becoming a widow. Besides, Felix himself would be leaving town, and the country soon, and he had no idea when he'd be able to get back to Texas or California, for that matter.

 On the walk back to the Scott home, Felix figured that it was time to let Elsie know about his orders that would take him to Florida. Elsie was undoubtedly saddened to hear the news, but she took the optimistic approach, and she chose to be supportive of Felix's upcoming journey. She took him by the hand, and said, "My darling Felix, I just knew that something was troubling you. Remember that you've come so far as a pilot. You've worked extremely hard, and I truly believe in your abilities. The good Lord will keep you safe, and, who knows, hopefully this war will be over right quick. Don't you worry one bit about me, as I'll be rooting for you while you're gone, and I'll pray every night that we'll be back together again soon." Elsie was probably naïve to some extent, because in reality, there was no end in sight to the battles raging across Europe, and in the Pacific. Felix and Elsie spent the rest of the evening playing dominoes, and Ernest even gave her a few pointers on playing the piano. Viola served a fabulous fried chicken dinner along with macaroni and cheese, biscuits, and gravy. The apple pie and homemade vanilla ice cream capped off a very pleasant evening at the Scott home.

With his time winding down in San Saba, Felix felt that he needed to spend a little more time at the River Bend farm before heading to Florida. Therefore, he and Elsie made the trip to Bend on Thursday, 14 Oct. to spend the evening with his grandparents. Spending time at the River Bend farm, and seeing many of his cousins and aunties was never a dull moment. Felix just couldn't get used to Chauncey not being there, but he wished the best for him with his ongoing training in the Marine Corps. He planned to continue writing letters of encouragement to Chauncey, knowing full well that military training would be rough and demanding. Dimmitt was serving in Australia, and Dardon was fighting over in Europe somewhere. Felix's uncles were very encouraging, and they took bets on how many enemy planes Felix would shoot down. He spent a few hours on the front porch with the menfolk sharing stories about his training, and the thrills that he'd had while flying each of the different planes. Felix even mustered up enough courage to ask Pa about helping him start his crop dusting business after the war. He was pleasantly surprised to hear his grandfather say that he thought that it was a splendid idea. Felix was overjoyed when he saw his parents pull up with Aletha in their car. It was a real treat for him to be able to spend some more quality time with them. Felix adored all of his family, and each of them were very proud of him. They all told Felix that he'd be in their prayers every day until he returned home safely.

There was just one day remaining before Felix had to board the train for Florida, and he couldn't seem to shake the nagging feeling that he had deep within him. Felix knew that he'd be heading into a hornet's nest, and at some point, his folks would be plenty worried about him. He was certain that there would be a plethora of rough patches, and turbulence ahead as he prepared to begin his first tour of duty. When Felix had left home for school over at College Station, he knew that he'd be coming home for the holidays, summers, and so forth. He understood the reality that he might never return to San Saba, and that weighed upon him heavily.

Felix spent his last full day in San Saba visiting with his friends, and a few of his neighbors. When he and Elsie returned home that afternoon, Viola asked him to put his military uniform on for a special evening. Felix was very proud to slip on his service coat with his shiny silver wings featured prominently above his left jacket pocket. When he and Elsie climbed into the car, Felix had no idea where his folks were taking him. It didn't take long before the car stopped in a space reserved for the special guest of honor directly in front of Ketchum's Kitchen. Johnnie Mae had closed the restaurant to the public that evening for a very special gathering of friends and family only. Several of her friends offered to assist with the cooking and serving so that Johnnie Mae could enjoy the evening as well. Felix probably did more socializing than dining that evening. The jukebox played on late into the night as Felix danced with Elsie and his sisters. He made sure to mingle with everyone in attendance, and there were a few tears shed as he said his goodbyes to all of those who had come to the party.

The celebration helped to reinvigorate Felix, and he was now eager to continue on with the next leg of his training. However, knowing that Elsie was headed back to her home in California, he tossed and turned throughout the night. Felix woke up rather early on 16 Oct. 1943 to make sure that all his military clothing was packed inside his duffel bags. He was stocked up with razors, lighters, and even some film for his camera. After breakfast, he and Elsie went outside to spend a few moments inside of his '37 Ford. Felix remembered all of the good times, and even a few of the sad times that he'd spent in the car that he called "Elizabeth." He gently shut the door feeling as if he didn't want to let go of the door handle. With Elsie's help, he begrudgingly placed a tarp completely over the vehicle.

Elsie's train was due to leave at 1000 hours, and Felix wanted to spend the last few precious moments with her privately. Therefore, they decided to take a leisurely walk over to the train station. Ernest and Viola planned to meet them there, and Ernest offered to drive her luggage over to the station. There were plenty of tears rolling down their faces as they made the short journey from South Live Oak Street. Felix was glad that they'd chosen to walk because he was able to get plenty of hugs and kisses along the way. By the time they arrived at the train station, Felix and Elsie were in good spirits, and there were no more tears. Ernest grabbed Elsie's luggage and placed it near the tracks. Viola gave her a bag full of fresh baked goodies for her trip home. Felix knew that he'd be able to write to Elsie often, but he was pretty sure that he wouldn't be able to speak with her over the phone once he was deployed overseas. He had a lingering doubt in the back of his mind if he'd ever be able to hold Elsie in his arms again.

To Felix, being separated from Elsie and his family was just another reason for him to hate the Japanese and Germans even more. As the train came to a screeching stop on the tracks in front of them, Felix did his best to say goodbye without beginning to cry. He gave Elsie one last kiss, and he most definitely wished that the hug could've lasted much longer. Elsie thanked Ernest and Viola for their hospitality, and she hugged them before boarding the train. She took a window seat in order to wave as long as possible as the train left San Saba.

Ernest and Viola offered Felix a ride home from the train station, but he politely declined. He figured that a walk back through town would help to clear his mind, since he was already missing Elsie. When he made it home, he was glad to find that Pauline and Johnnie Mae had arrived to spend some time with him during his last few hours in San Saba. Felix really enjoyed hanging out with all of his sisters. He loved talking about Aggie football with Pauline, and having a few shots of whiskey with her was a real treat as well. The Aggies had won their first three games of the year, and Pauline promised to send him articles regarding their progress throughout the rest of the season. Figuring that Felix might be hungry while on his train ride, Johnnie Mae had baked him some fresh biscuits, and Aletha had made him a bag full of sugar cookies.

After having had the final opportunity to get his fill of his mother's home cooking, Felix figured that it was time to leave. In true military fashion, he made sure that his room was tidy, and that the bed was properly made. Felix then took a good look at his things that were arranged neatly around the room. He slowly closed his bedroom door, wondering what God had planned for him before he'd be home to open it once again. Ernest and Viola were joylessly waiting outside, yet they were prepared to head back to the train station. After snapping a few last pictures of everyone, Felix tossed his bags into the back of his '41 Chevy truck, and off they went. Aletha, Pauline, and Johnnie Mae trailed behind them in her '41 Chevy truck as well. When they arrived at the train station, Felix told his mother and father that he was going to miss them, and his truck very much. Ernest then chimed in with, "Well son, I bet one of those shiny new P-51s will sure tickle your fancy." Felix laughed, and said, "Yeah, you're probably right, Pop, but I want you to take good care of her while I'm gone." He then took off his cowboy hat, and placed it on top of the dashboard. He looked into the rear view mirror to ensure that his service cap was arranged properly upon his head. Felix was glad that Ma and

Pa had brought his Aunt Betsy, and his Aunt Jesse out to the train station to say goodbye. He bid farewell to everyone, and he just had to pick up little Felix Wayne one more time. Each of his sisters made sure to give Felix one last hug. Viola tried to keep her composure, but how does a mother appropriately say goodbye to her son who is about to go off to war?

Pauline (on the left) and Felix standing with Johnnie Mae and her beloved 1941 red Chevrolet truck named "Lucille." She loved her truck, and unlike her brother, she wasn't concerned with a little San Saba dirt on it. One of the last pictures taken of Felix before leaving for Florida.

Viola gently grabbed Felix by the arm, and she turned him around so that she could look directly into his eyes. She then slid the simple gold wedding band off of her left ring finger. Viola placed the ring into Felix's right palm, and said, "Son, I want you to keep this safe. Knowing that you'll keep it safe will allow me to know that you're safe. This ring will be a small reminder of our love for you, and

I want you to keep it close to your heart while you're away. Felix, I need you to come back home to me." Felix pulled the chain with his dog tags off his neck, and he secured the ring onto the chain. He then said, "Mother, you know that I love you, and I'll do my darnedest to fly safely, and I'll always try to stay one step ahead of the enemy. I'll guard this ring with my life, and I'll be sure to keep it close to my heart every day." After slipping the chain back inside his shirt, Felix gave his mother a big hug, and a kiss goodbye. Ernest also gave him a hug, and a pat on the back as Felix climbed aboard the train. Just like Elsie had done, Felix grabbed a window seat so that he could see his family. He tried to refrain from crying as the train began to move, and it didn't take long for him to lose sight of his loving family that was still waving from the train station. Felix smiled as he peered into the bag of goodies that Viola had given to him, and he did his best to get comfortable as he began the journey towards Dale Mabry Field.

CHAPTER 13

Florida Flyboys

It was pretty late in the evening on 17 Oct. 1943, when Felix arrived at the train station in Tallahassee, Florida. He was pretty worn out from having been confined to the passenger train for the better part of a day and a half, but he was glad to have met three fellow servicemen who were also heading to Dale Mabry Field. After stuffing their bags into the trunk, the group hopped into a Yellow Cab, and they explained to the driver that they'd just arrived in town for pilot training. The driver knew of a perfect location that was just a few miles away from Dale Mabry Field. The motel wasn't fancy, but the men were needing to get only a few hours of sleep before beginning their next stage of training early the next morning.

It was Monday, 18 Oct. 1943, and it didn't take long for Felix to be officially assigned to the Third Air Force, III Fighter Command, and to the 439th Fighter Squadron. He and the other pilots began to congregate onto the drill field as they waited for the rest of the men to arrive. Felix continued to scan the crowd looking for any familiar faces, and for his good buddy, Ray Simon. He was quite relieved to see Ray finally step off a truck that had just arrived from the train station. Although Ray was equally tuckered out, his smile was ever-present. The two men quickly exchanged details of their time while on leave as they waited anxiously for someone from the command staff to address the crowd that had grown sizably. The Operations Officer, Captain Harold Paulin, stood up at the podium in front of the men who had assembled in formation. "Good morning everyone. I'd like to welcome all of you newly commissioned officers to Dale Mabry Field. I hope that you had a relaxing two weeks off because you're about to experience a rigorous schedule of ground school courses. Many of you will only be here for about 4–6 weeks, and it's likely that you might not get back into the cockpit until you reach your next post. We'll spend a great deal of time and effort figuring out where each of you will be sent to complete the next phase of your training before heading overseas. Be attentive, be prepared to work hard, and remember to always do your best." Felix and Ray were rather dumbfounded as they looked at each other after hearing that they might not be given the opportunity to fly for a spell. Nevertheless, the young pilots figured that the staff knew best, and they were committed to doing what they were told, and they planned to give it their all.

After finishing up their paperwork, the men were officially processed onto the base. Next, the squadron commanders led an orientation where they also took a moment to welcome all of the new pilots. Dale Mabry Field was nearly three and a half miles west of Tallahassee, and it was located towards the northern tip of Florida, just a little south of the border with Georgia. The men were told that there were more than 3,000 people on the base, consisting of staff, students, and a plethora of support personnel. A fairly large detachment of airplane mechanics would be training there on the base as well. Felix could tell that there were more than one hundred buildings of all sorts scattered throughout the post, and he loathed that he would once again have to remember where all the important ones were located. As they made their way along the flight line, Felix and Ray had a hard time counting all of the planes since they were spread out on parking ramps across the sprawling base. After noticing several multi-directional runways, they were very excited to see plenty of P-39s, P-40s, and even some P-47s. Once inside the barracks, the men found two rows of single beds on the first and second floors. Shoes were then stowed neatly under the bed, and their clothes were hung on a rod, which dangled from the ceiling above their pillow. Everyone tied their barracks bags to a hook that was found on the wall beside each of the beds, and their personal things were placed into individual footlockers.

Felix and Ray weren't all that surprised that they needed to pay a visit to the flight surgeon's office early the next morning. Luckily, they weren't there all day, but they had to get vaccinated against yellow fever, typhus, and cholera. Felix knew that the training would be rigorous, and there'd be no hand holding as they prepared him for war. The pilots among Felix's and Ray's squadron eased into their ground school curriculum with a series of films pertaining to performing acrobatics, and flying in the P-40. The instructors made sure that each of the men had the most current version of the Pilots' Information File manual. Many of the training courses were to be more like seminars that would last for a few days, instead of the couple of weeks format that they'd been used to. There were a few refresher topics such as aircraft recognition, parachutes, navigation, and meteorology. In addition to time on the firing range, the pilots were going to dive into subjects like signal communication, chemical warfare, combat intelligence, and medical training. They were also going to take an in-depth look at some safety related topics such as woodsmanship, seamanship, ditching, and the best practices to avoid aircraft accidents.

It was 30 Oct., and Felix was feeling a little apprehensive about having to make another trip into the altitude chamber. He and Ray hadn't been inside the machine since they were at SAAAB back in December of 1942. The morning began with a lecture on what they were to expect from the physiology of high-altitude exposure. The men were concerned about what tricks the instructors had planned that would play all sorts of havoc on their bodies. After taking their seats, Ray gave Felix a fist bump and a high five before the door was closed. They steadily climbed to a simulated altitude of 5,000 feet before returning to where they had begun. Then, as they began to climb again, and as they approached 10,000 feet, they began to intermittently use their A-10 oxygen masks. The men were told that they could expect to use the latest version, the A-14 oxygen masks, for actual flights when they arrived at their next post. They continued onward to an altitude of 18,000 feet, and after holding there for a bit, they climbed upward to 30,000 feet. After topping out at about 38,000 feet, the men slowly experienced the descent back towards the ground level. Their experience inside the altitude chamber had lasted nearly two hours before the door had swung open. After a short debriefing of their journey, Felix and Ray headed to the mess hall to celebrate the fact that they'd walked away without any problems.

The weeks had flown by, and just as Felix had become fully acclimated to his new surroundings, it was time for him to be processed out of the Dale Mabry Replacement Depot. Just after dawn on the morning of Saturday, 20 Nov., the squadron commanders had gathered the men into one large group. They then took turns yelling out the names of each of their men, and the location of the new base that they were being assigned to. Felix listened attentively when he heard his name being called, and he was quickly informed that he was being sent 300 miles south to Sarasota, Florida. It didn't take long before Ray's name was called, and as luck would have it, he too, would be headed to Sarasota. The pilots were told to return to the barracks to immediately gather their things since they'd be leaving right away. Within the hour, Felix and Ray had boarded a train along with dozens of other men who were en route to their tactical training group at the Sarasota Army Air Field. Having carefully studied the entire map of Florida, the young men were thrilled to be heading to their new post due to its proximity to the beautiful sandy beaches, and to the Sarasota Bay.

Felix and Ray didn't have to report to the Sarasota Army Air Field until 0800 hours on the morning of Tuesday, 23 Nov. Therefore, they planned to make the most out of their two full days off. After stepping off the train, Felix asked the conductor for directions to the best hotel in the area. Since Felix and Ray planned to share the room with a few other fellas, they figured that they could afford to splurge a little. They were instructed to head west on Main Street towards the waterfront. Felix and Ray, along with Walter Schuck and Jamison Shotwell, walked for about 15 minutes until the Mira Mar Hotel came into view. Although it was beginning to get dark, everyone could tell that it was a large and luxurious hotel. When the men arrived at the front desk, the room turned out to be a bit more expensive than they'd expected. Felix then said, "Look fellas, I've stayed in several fine hotels during the past year or so, and I must say that this one is in a magnificent spot right next to the ocean. Just think of how amazing it'll be to relax on the sandy beach with a few cold drinks in our hands. I'll even bet that you boys will find some of the most beautiful girls in all of Florida out on that beach." The men were convinced that Felix was spot on, and they just couldn't say no at that point. Thus, Felix grabbed the key, and after entering their room, everyone marveled at their view just as the sun crept out of sight over the glistening water in front of them.

Felix woke up early the next morning to go for a run along the sandy coastline. The views and scenery were breathtaking as the sun began to rise, which allowed him to take in all of the beauty that Sarasota had to offer. There was an abundant supply of palm trees and lush green foliage throughout the area. As Felix continued his run, he passed by the pier, and he reminisced about the wonderful time that he'd had with Elsie back in Balboa, California. He was glad to be training near an ocean once again, but he just wished that it was near the Pacific Ocean instead. Upon returning to the hotel, Felix and his pals ventured down to the beach to find some comfortable lounge chairs underneath a large shady palapa. It turned out that Felix was a man of his word, as the men did indeed have a fabulous day working on their tans, flirting with girls, and enjoying a much needed break from their training. Later that evening, they all had a delightful discussion about their previous training locations, close calls as rookie pilots, and the overall thrills that they'd experienced while flying thus far. Felix really enjoyed their company, and the men agreed to take a trip over to Lido Key the following morning.

Ray took a picture of Felix and their pal Walter while enjoying a day on Lido Beach, FL.

On the morning of 22 Nov., the group walked down to the marina to rent a small motor boat. It didn't take that long for Felix and his pals to arrive at the Lido Beach and Casino. They enjoyed a wonderful afternoon lounging around on the pristine shore of the sandy beach. Felix figured that it was probably best that he not tell Elsie about all of the good looking young ladies that were getting some sun on the beach. He certainly enjoyed a few cold beers while watching a plethora of sail boats pass by in front of the group. Later on that day, Felix showed off a bit by doing backflips off the high dive at the pool located there at the casino. He was glad that he was finally able to find something that he was just a little better at than Ray. Upon returning to the Mira Mar Hotel on that Monday evening, Felix knew that the fun and games were probably over for some time to come. Early the next morning, the men waited outside of the hotel lobby for a cab that would take them north to the Sarasota Army Air Field. It wasn't long before Felix saw the small, and rather nondescript, sign for the base, and just like that, he was about to begin the last stage of his training before heading off to war.

By now, the men were well accustomed to the process of being welcomed at a new base. Once all of the pilots had assembled into formation, the Commanding Officer of the base, Lieutenant Colonel Jack Jenkins, began to speak. Felix's mind steadily wandered towards the planes that were sitting idly upon the flight line nearby. He was just itching to get back into the air, and he seemed rather bored, having heard a similar welcome message at all of his previous bases. However, Lieutenant Colonel Jenkins quickly caught Felix's attention when he said, "Over the next couple of months, you men will receive the most comprehensive training yet. The primary focus of your training will revolve around flying as a seasoned combat group, and by learning how to work together as a cohesive team. Everything that you've learned until now will be crucial as you tackle the months ahead. This is where we'll do our very best to prepare each of you for your assignment to an overseas theater of war." The young pilots were then told that they'd officially been assigned to the 3rd Air Force, III

Fighter Command, 337th Fighter Group, and to the 98th Fighter Squadron. The fact that the end of his training was near really resonated with Felix, and he was eager to get going.

The welcoming session continued when the Director of Training, Captain T. J. Clark, began to address the newest arrivals to the Sarasota Army Air Field. "Over the next 11 weeks, my very worthy team of instructors will provide you men with nearly 220 hours of classroom and hands-on training. We'll begin by familiarizing yourselves with detailed maps of the terrain in our local area. I'm certain that you boys are eager to get back up in the air, and we'll be sure to cover our communication protocols, our emergency airfields and facilities, and our taxiing and landing procedures. Before long, you'll be flying the P-40K, and the P-40N. You can bet that you'll be receiving the latest version of the Pilot's Handbook of Flight Operating Instructions for these planes. If you can prove yourselves capable, you'll most definitely enjoy time on our ground strafing and bombing ranges. You'll learn the importance of air discipline, and the latest methods of advanced fighter tactics. There will be plenty of time spent in the Link trainer, and you'll be taught just about everything there is to know about the theory of sighting and bombing procedures. Our line crew will provide plenty of instruction pertaining to the armament capabilities of the P-40s that you'll be flying. I'm sure that each of you will also enjoy the many hours spent practicing your skills with Morse code. Finally, you'll probably find the gun camera film assessment sessions to be fascinating, and there will surely be some lively discussions pertaining to the debriefing and critiquing of your various missions. Of course, you can count on plenty of physical training, skeet shooting, and drill practice. This phase of your training will be both mentally and physically exhausting. We'll be watching closely at every step, and you surely don't want to know what will happen if you cannot cut the mustard around here. So tell me, are y'all ready to get this show on the road?" The men cheered loudly, and they showed a great deal of excitement by waving their caps high into the air. Everyone seemed eager to begin the training program that had just been presented to them.

After being assigned to Flight B, Felix and Ray found their barracks, and they got settled in quickly. After supper, they walked all over the base to acclimate themselves with the locations of the important buildings, and, of course, the recreational facilities. It was 24 Nov., and the day began with yet another trip to the flight surgeon's office. Luckily, Felix and Ray didn't need any further shots this time around, and they were very glad when First Lieutenant Sydney Tauber proclaimed that they were both physically and mentally qualified to engage in flying activities. Afterwards, they got right to work with time spent inside of the Link trainer, in the classroom, and they concluded their day with a brief trip to the maintenance shop.

Waking up in Florida on Thanksgiving Day surely wasn't the ideal situation for Felix. Having celebrated all of the previous holidays away from home over the past 11 months, Felix had become rather ambivalent to the situation. He was sad that he was once again away from his loved ones, but he was happy that he was one step closer to fighting for his country. To Felix and Ray, Thanksgiving turned out to be just another day. However, the fabulous turkey supper with all of the fixings certainly boosted morale, and it created many smiles among the men that evening. It was evident that as a member of the military, Felix wasn't going to be spending any of the other upcoming holidays with Elsie or his family. Felix took a few moments before bed to write a letter to his folks, and one to Elsie in order to provide them with his new mailing address. He planned to give each of them a quick call over the weekend to make sure that they knew that they were always in his thoughts, and in his heart.

On the morning of 27 Nov., Felix's superiors wanted to see him demonstrate his skills as an aviator first hand. Even though, he hadn't flown a plane since leaving Luke Field, Felix really didn't feel as if he had lost his touch, or his ability as a pilot. He was incredibly eager to show the squadron commanders that he'd be a valuable addition to the group. Needless to say, he wasn't overly thrilled with having an instructor in the rear seat of the AT-6 Texan, but he was thoroughly excited to be back up in the air. Flying near the beautiful Florida Coastline was incredibly entertaining for Felix, and as he'd figured, there were no problems with his acrobatics, basic maneuvers, or with his landing. Felix was glad to have received clearance to move forward with solo flights, and he felt that he'd proven that he was a good man to have around. Over supper that evening, Felix and Ray discussed their first flight over Florida, and they were told to be prepared to fly the P-40K within a matter of days.

Ray Simon relaxing on base in Sarasota, Florida. Photo provided by the Ray Simon family.

Ray Simon (pictured on left) with Felix Scott in front of a P-40.

The next morning, the men were given an opportunity to re-acclimate themselves with the configuration and layout of the cockpit found on the P-40 Warhawk. Afterwards, Felix immediately realized that the instructors weren't messing around when they blindfolded each man before testing everyone on the location of the critical components and controls within the cockpit. Felix had to certify that he fully understood the entire Pilot's Handbook of Flight Operating Instructions manual for the P-40K. He also had to attest that he had a thorough working knowledge of the instruments, controls, fuel and fluid systems, oxygen system, engine, and the radio equipment found on the P-40K. Felix and Ray then spent the afternoon with the fellas from the maintenance shop, where they received some hands on practice servicing an engine for a P-40K. Learning how to change the tires, and being shown how to add fuel along with the other fluids, made for an interesting afternoon. After confirming that each man understood all of the flying regulations there on the base, their flight commander signed off on the appropriate paperwork, which paved the way for Felix and Ray to begin flying the P-40K on 29 Nov. 1943.

When 1 Dec. arrived, Felix made his way around the base to collect his mail, and his full monthly salary as a second lieutenant. After reading a wonderful letter from Elsie, he just had to open the package from Pauline. Indeed, she was true to her word, and she'd sent several articles regarding the recent football games for Felix's beloved Aggies. It didn't take long for Felix to catch up on their winning streak, and he was glad to see that they'd been piling up plenty of shutouts. Going into the annual rivalry game with the University of Texas, the Aggies were undefeated once again. With the big Thanksgiving Day game being held at Kyle Field, everyone assumed that the Aggies would find a way to win. Felix, on the other hand, knew plenty well how some of the previous matchups had ended up, and how the Aggies had been repeatedly heartbroken at the hands of the Longhorns. As fate would have it, on 25 Nov. 1943, the Aggies had once again lost to the Longhorns by two touchdowns. Felix just couldn't believe what he'd just read, and he felt terrible about the loss for the team, the fans, and for the cadets who were back on campus. Felix could only imagine what four letter words that Pauline was screaming into the radio as the game got out of hand. He clearly understood that there were no guarantees in life with anything, and he expected that the Aggies would be ready to give it another go the following season. Felix believed that his Aggies would still have a shot at playing in one of the upcoming bowl games, and he remained optimistic that they could salvage the season with one last win.

 Felix was going to be asked to push the Warhawk to its limits, and he knew that he'd have to do so safely. The training routine there at the Sarasota Army Air Field was pretty familiar to what he'd experienced at his previous bases. Taking what he'd learned from the classroom, and then having the opportunity to practice it up in the air was quite a thrill for Felix. He continuously studied the topography of the central Florida coast line, and he committed all of the local landmarks to memory. Flying over the numerous Florida Keys, and seeing the stunning blue ocean below was an amazing experience for sure. Felix quickly came to learn that there were a large number of military installations all over the state of Florida. Just like at his previous bases, Felix had to become entirely familiar with the locations of the auxiliary fields and bases near the Sarasota Army Air Field. The Punta Gorda and Fort Myers Army Airfields were located south of Sarasota. The Pinellas Army Airfield was to the north, and the Lake Wales Army Airfield was to the east. There were four runways at the Sarasota Army Air Field which allowed for takeoffs and landings in several different directions, depending on the wind conditions.

The weeks were flying by, and Felix was happy when he climbed into his warbird nearly every day. With all of the activity going on around him, additional focus and attention was necessary each time Felix took off and landed with the P-40K. Felix was becoming very proficient at performing his high-speed maneuvers in the Warhawk. His individual talent and capabilities were about to be fully integrated into the overall squadron's potential. Collectively, Felix and the other members of his squadron practiced flying "top cover" above a formation of bombers, which were also practicing in the area. This was a very important role for fighter pilots, as they would provide protection, and act as an escort for the bombers that were about to carry out their missions. Felix couldn't wait to fly a more robust war machine, since the P-40 variants didn't operate all that well at the higher altitudes.

Flying in formation at a leisurely speed back in Lemoore was relatively easy. Flying in formation at more than 300 mph was completely nerve-racking, to say the least. Felix's squadron continually practiced line abreast, finger four, box, and V-shaped formations. He and Ray enjoyed every opportunity that they had to fly side by side with one another. Some of the combat formations would involve as little as three planes, while others numbered a dozen or more. On a few occasions, Felix felt like the entire wing of pilots were flying in formation. Regardless of the formation type or size, each pilot was required to work as a team with the flight leader, element leader, and wingmen. Along with maintaining a safe distance to a wingman, each pilot was responsible for looking out for possible enemy aircraft. Being able to spot potential enemy planes at a long distance was imperative for the security of all the Allied planes within the formation. Felix possessed a strong sense of situational awareness, and he had exceptional eyesight which helped him to perform well during each formation flight. Felix and Ray were having the time of their lives when their squadron practiced combat exercises at altitudes as high as 22,000 feet, or as low as just 200 feet. At the end of each day, Felix and Ray felt that if they had survived their mission, then that equaled success.

Keeping up with the actions and events involving the war was very important to Felix. There were regular base briefings regarding the advances and failures of the Axis powers. He really enjoyed getting letters along with articles from Johnnie Mae pertaining to important worldwide happenings. Reading about bombs being dropped on Berlin, and Marines assaulting the Japanese forces on Tarawa, made Felix feel like the United States and its Allies were beginning to gain the upper hand in the war. In the classroom, Felix and the men watched two more installments of the *Why We Fight* film series that he began watching while at SAAAB. They watched episode four, *The Battle of Britain,* and then episode five, *The Battle of Russia.* After viewing episode four, Felix was amazed at just how epic of a battle it must've been for the skies over Great Britain. France had recently fallen to the Nazis, and then the Luftwaffe began their unrelenting strikes upon Great Britain in July of 1940. The chaotic battle in the sky raged on for several months. Countless planes from the Royal Air Force (RAF) had been lost, but it would be safe to say that the Germans undoubtedly lost many more fighters and bombers during the battle. Regrettably, an untold number of British citizens lost their lives during the senseless bombing attacks brought by the German Luftwaffe.

Felix felt that he'd learned just about all that he needed to know from the ground school portion of his training. He was certainly chomping at the bit to move on to one of the many theaters of war overseas. Since Felix wasn't yet in actual combat, he had to be satisfied with just reading about the heroics and accomplishments of the distinguished pilots who had achieved the status of a flying ace. To be officially recognized as an ace, a pilot needed to have shot down at least five enemy aircraft during air to air combat. Since the early days of his childhood, Felix had dreamed of becoming an ace one day, and he hoped that it would be much sooner than later. He was looking forward to getting out to the aerial gunnery range in order to unleash the devastating firepower that the P-40K could inflict. There were three .50 caliber machine guns on each wing, and improvements had been made to the onboard ammunition boxes to keep the guns firing effectively and efficiently. Felix planned to do everything necessary to help ensure that he was going to be the victor, and not the victim, when it became time for him to fight.

As the weeks continued to drag on, Felix was getting increasingly restless and anxious. He and the other pilots at the Sarasota Army Air Field were challenged both physically and mentally every day. The rigorous PT regimens helped to keep Felix fit, healthy, and sharp, yet trying to beat Ray to the finish line at the obstacle course generally seemed pointless. Many of the pilots found that the training flights, and high stress maneuvers were exhausting. Even though the men weren't at war in a combat zone, they were practicing as if they were on real life missions in order to get the most out of each experience.

Felix looked forward to whatever downtime he could attain. Whether it was horseshoes, basketball, a brief nap, or even some tennis with Ray, Felix relished every opportunity to relax and have fun. He especially looked forward to each Saturday when he'd call his folks back home in San Saba. Felix tried to call around the same time each week in the event that one or more of his sisters might be there at the Scott home. Sundays were certainly reserved for a little extra sleep, and for a call to Elsie. Felix would do his best to talk with Elsie until his quarters ran out because her voice, and words of encouragement, were very refreshing to him.

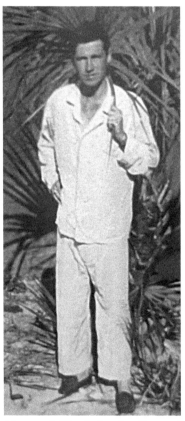

Felix Scott relaxing in his casual attire during free time on base while in Sarasota.

It was rather hard for Felix to fathom that he'd already spent a year in training, and that yet another Christmas had arrived with him being away from his family. Luckily, Christmas fell on a Saturday in 1943, and it was quite evident that the men were thrilled to have been given a weekend pass. Felix and Ray spent the day relaxing, and strolling around in downtown Sarasota. Seeing parents out walking with their children, and others holding hands with a loved one, made the men feel a little out of sorts. However, they wholeheartedly realized the importance of what they were training for, and why they were prepared to go to war. Felix and Ray shared the belief that America was worth protecting, and they could only hope that someday soon, they too, would be celebrating with their loved ones. They were both ecstatic to find a few telephone booths off the beaten path. Felix spent his pocket full of coins calling Elsie and his folks, while Ray reached out to his loved ones in North Dakota. As Felix sat at the long table for supper that evening, all of the food, laughter, and the large group of people made him feel like he was really celebrating back home with his family.

All of a sudden, it was 1 Jan. 1944, and Felix was fired up to find a bar that was broadcasting the Orange Bowl game over the radio. Logistically, it was too far and complicated to get all the way down to Miami to watch the game in person. Felix's Aggies were squaring off against the LSU Tigers. He was thrilled to meet a few other former Aggies there at the bar, and they enjoyed yelling the Texas AMC school songs as the game wore on. Those few hours brought back tons of fond memories from his time at Texas AMC. Although the Aggies lost the tightly contested game, Felix was invigorated as he was set to begin the most anticipated phase of his training.

On 2 Jan., the time had come for Felix and Ray to begin live fire exercises in the P-40N, and the pilots were told that they could expect to fly that particular variant whenever they were participating in exercises over the bombing and strafing ranges. Of course, the men were glad that it could fly a little faster, climb a little higher, and go a little further. However, they were somewhat disappointed that the P-40N had reduced its armament capability to just two .50 caliber machine guns per wing. The P-40N could still carry a combination of 100, 300, and 500 pound bombs, but the total bomb weight couldn't exceed 1,500 pounds. Becoming a top-notch fighter pilot required a great deal of practice, and the men were about to get plenty of additional time on the bombing and strafing ranges. There were plenty of unpopulated areas in Florida, and the Army had established several places in Sarasota County for the pilots to train at. Felix and Ray had gone through an abbreviated bombardier class while in ground school there at the Sarasota Army Air Field. They were taught how to properly use the optical reflection gun sight, and there was plenty of time spent studying the theories, and mathematical calculations needed to be successful on the bombing range. Felix and the other pilots paid close attention as they learned about fragmentation, cluster, incendiary, and chemical bombs. They learned that the large bombers such as the B-17 dropped their bombs while flying horizontally, while they, as pilots, were mostly going to drop their bombs in a much more vertical manner. It was very important that they understood the optimal altitude to release their bombs when dive bombing so that they could avoid the danger area that might take them too close to the intended target. There was a comprehensive discussion pertaining to the procedures for low level diving, skip bombing, and dive bombing from higher altitudes. By the end of the class, the men knew nearly everything there was to know about the process to load, arm, and disarm the bombs that could be underneath their planes. Felix had evolved into an excellent pilot, and he'd developed a keen sense of handling stress under pressure. He felt that he was ready for the challenges that lay ahead.

Felix piloting a P-40 off the coast of Florida.

The thought of dropping bombs, and blowing stuff up was such a thrill for Felix. Needless to say, his spirits were quickly dampened when he found out that they'd be primarily using practice bombs that contained a smoke filled cartridge rather than actual explosives. Ultimately, he understood that it was probably best to save the real bombs for the Nazis and Japanese. However, the men were told that if they did well in their training, they might have the opportunity to drop a live bomb or two near the end of their time in Sarasota. It was the responsibility of each pilot to know what was on his plane, and the men were told that the practice bombs featured a light blue color scheme. Felix was very methodical before each flight to the bombing range, and after completing his typical pre-flight inspection, he then needed to be sure to check that the bombs were properly attached to the racks underneath the wings.

Once inside the cockpit, Felix felt confident that he could handle all of the armaments skillfully. After reaching an altitude between 5,000 to 10,000 feet, he'd initiate a high-speed dive towards his target. It was completely satisfying to him when he'd hit his target with a speed in excess of 200 mph. Felix was having a blast dropping bombs on the targets made of three concentric rings. There was nothing better than actually applying the principles and theories up in the air that had been learned in the classroom. Felix was certainly not perfect, and it took multiple drops before he began to consistently hit his targets within the rings. Seeing the white smoke rise up from the point of detonation was exhilarating, and he could only imagine the feeling that he'd have when given the opportunity to drop a real 500 pound bomb on a live enemy target. However, Felix dreaded the idea of having to drop bombs over large cities knowing that there could be plenty of collateral damage. This weighed upon him a great deal, and he vowed to put his best effort into his training so that he could be as precise as possible when dropping a bomb.

During January, Felix spent many weeks at the bombing and strafing ranges in Venice, Florida, which was about 20 miles south of Sarasota. Upon takeoff, Felix had hundreds of rounds on board to feed the hungry .50 caliber Browning machine guns found out on the wings. He really couldn't decide which was more fun, strafing targets or blowing them up. Since the machine guns were spitting out live rounds, Felix ultimately had the most fun at the strafing ranges. The rectangular wooden targets on the ground were painted with a white background that included a large red circle in the middle. Felix wasn't sure if this was just a coincidence, but the targets seemed to resemble the image of a Japanese flag. Either way, he enjoyed filling the targets full of bullets, imagining as if they were Japanese strongholds. Felix would repeat the process of diving, firing, and climbing until he was out of bullets, or almost out of gas.

Felix really liked flying with his squadron so that he could learn new skills that would help him to obtain a tactical advantage if he were to ever encounter enemy planes. It was important for the pilots to take risks, but there was no need to be reckless during a flight. Felix felt rather savvy as he learned, and practiced the new air to air combat techniques. He really felt glad that he'd been given an opportunity to take the fight to the enemy through the air. Being able to perform vertical hit and runs from high altitudes could prove deadly to any unsuspecting enemy aircraft flying below him. At supper one evening, Felix was talking to Ray about how incredible he thought that it would be to have an opportunity to take off from an aircraft carrier. He undoubtedly figured that it would be rather harrowing to attempt to land upon one. Realizing that this opportunity would be reserved mostly for his naval counterparts, Felix could only dream that one day, he just might get the chance.

Felix preparing for a flight in a P-40 Warhawk at the Sarasota Army Air Field.

With only a few weeks of training left there in Florida, Felix realized that he probably wouldn't get an opportunity to fly the twin engine P-38 Lightning. He thought that the design was really neat, and he felt that it would be a hoot if he was given a chance to take it for a spin. Felix was still unsure which plane he'd fly in actual combat, and he had no idea which theater of operation he'd end up in. However, he was crossing his fingers that he'd be able to fly the powerful P-47 Thunderbolt, or the sleek P-51 Mustang once he finally got into the war. Felix knew that there were plenty of inherent dangers when it came to flying the more advanced planes. Therefore, he opted to continue paying the life insurance premiums out of his own pocket in the event of some unexpected disaster.

With his time in Sarasota winding down, Felix felt that the daily flights were becoming routine, and even the time spent at the bombing range was becoming rather mundane. He and Ray were anxious about getting into the war, and they were told to expect their orders to a station on foreign soil at any time. The morning of 28 Jan. 1944 started out just like any other day in Florida. Felix left the Flight Room with a flight plan that would take him south, down the coast of Florida and back, for a routine training mission. There were scattered clouds, and the visibility was three to five miles due to a morning haze that had blanketed the area. When Felix took off from the Sarasota Army Air Field at around 1000 hours, the wind speed was rather negligible at less than 10 mph. At about 1100 hours, he was heading north, and he was well on his way back towards the Sarasota Army Air Field. The flight had been uneventful up until that point, but things were about to become frightening really quick.

Felix was about 20 miles southeast of Punta Gorda when he was forced to use the manual propeller control after the engine in his

P-40K began to run rough. At that point, he was cruising along at an altitude of about 3000 feet when smoke and flames began to emerge from the engine compartment. Suddenly, Felix's experience within the cockpit of the P-40K became quite harrowing. He'd managed to change his heading directly towards the Punta Gorda Army Air Field, and he was preparing to make a forced landing. Felix made contact with the control tower, and he received clearance for an emergency landing. On the final approach to runway 27 at the Punta Gorda Army Air Field, the engine abruptly stopped, and he proceeded to glide the rest of the way in. Even with a nearly dead stick, Felix managed to make a wheels down landing with the engine still smoking. He was able to get the plane safely off the runway before climbing out in a hurry. The base fire department arrived quickly, and they promptly extinguished the engine fire.

Although there was major damage to the engine, Felix wasn't hurt, but he was certainly shaken. He attributed his survival to the excellent training that he'd been given, which kept him calm so that he could follow the proper emergency protocols. After filling out a slew of paperwork pertaining to the incident, and answering lots of questions about what had happened, Felix was able to catch a ride in an AT-6 with a pilot who was heading to the Sarasota Army Air Field. When Felix got back to the base, he had quite a story to share with Ray, and the rest of the guys in his squadron. There was an investigation, and the Office of Flying Safety determined that Felix wasn't at fault. They concluded that there had been a bearing failure, which caused a rod to be thrown through the crank case, resulting in two large holes. Felix wasn't sure how Elsie or his parents would react to the near catastrophic incident. Therefore, he spent most of that Friday night thinking about what he could say that wouldn't cause them to worry any more than they already were.

Felix was thrilled to be posing for a picture in a P-47 Thunderbolt. Sarasota, Florida 1944.

The conversations that Felix had with Elsie and his folks that weekend went much better than he'd expected. Felix did a pretty good job spinning the incident in a way that didn't sound too frightening. He let them know that his training and skills as a pilot got him through to see another day. It was safe to say that he was a little nervous to get back into the cockpit on that next Monday morning. Luckily for Felix, his remaining flights at the Sarasota Army Air Field were uneventful, and he continued to excel at the strafing and bombing ranges. On 1 Feb. 1944, Felix received his orders that would take him to the China/Burma/India (CBI) theater for his Replacement Training Unit (RTU) assignment. When Felix learned that Ray had also been given orders to the CBI, he just couldn't believe it. Including their time in Florida, Felix had trained with Ray at more than half of his training bases. They'd developed an amazing friendship, and their time together had grown into a bond that felt as if they were real life brothers. Although they were feeling uneasy about going off to war, they both knew that they had each other's back, and they each felt safe whenever they'd fly together. After more than a year of training, Felix and Ray were one step closer to actual combat against the Japanese.

Felix spent his last week in Sarasota preparing to go to war. There were so many things that he needed to deal with on base prior to his deployment. Felix and Ray, along with the other men who were headed for overseas duty, attended classes that included advanced sanitation, first aid, and precautionary measures involving general/sex hygiene. The men had to pay another visit to the flight surgeon's office on 9 Feb. to get yet another physical. Felix and Ray found it to be rather unnerving when they had to make sure that their dental records were complete in the event that they might be needed to identify their remains down the road. They gave each other a high five after the Flight Surgeon, Samuel Marker, declared them fit for overseas duty. There was plenty of paperwork that still needed to be completed, and collected for their files. Felix and Ray made sure that they had their special orders, which assigned them to active duty, and their personnel orders, which rated them as pilots. They also ensured that their immunization record, and pilot physical record cards were safely stowed in their files. After verifying that they had their officer's identification card and identification tags, they double checked that they had their transfer paperwork, last will and testament, power of attorney, and the receipt confirming that their life insurance premium was paid.

Although it was getting late on Wednesday, 9 Feb., Felix had made prior arrangements to make calls to his family, and to Elsie, to say goodbye. The phone calls to Texas, and to California were longer than usual, and there were plenty of tears shed on both ends of the phone lines that evening. Felix really didn't want to hang up because he knew that going off to war meant that it could be the last time he'd ever get to hear the voices of his loved ones. He told everyone that he loved them very much, and that he'd write long letters while aboard the ship. Felix tried to explain the general area that he was headed off to, but Elsie and his folks knew only that it was very far away. Ernest told Felix that he was proud of him. Viola asked him to be careful, and she reminded him to say his prayers every day. Pauline said that she'd mail him plenty of comic strips, and Johnnie Mae offered to mail AJ's model airplane magazines when he was through with them. Felix felt glad that he was able to have a nice conversation with Aletha as well. She ended the conversation with, "You're the only brother that I have, so you better come home in one piece, you hear?" Elsie concluded her call with, "My darling Felix, you're a remarkable man, and I'm going to patiently wait until you return home safely to me. I love you very much, and you'll be in my thoughts and prayers every day." Felix closed each call with a reassurance that he'd be as safe as possible, and that he'd do his part to bring the war to an end real soon. Felix was bummed that he didn't get to say goodbye to his aunts, uncles, grandparents, and, of course, to Chauncey.

Felix couldn't sleep a wink that evening due to all the things that were racing through his head. It had been more than two years since the bombing of Pearl Harbor, and he had no idea that it would take him that long to be in a position where he could finally go fight for his country. Felix was delighted that his wish to get into the war had finally come to fruition, but he had no idea that the emotional toll was going to be so impactful on his heart and soul. He was going to miss his grandfather's wisdom, and his father's guidance. Felix was going to miss his grandmother's cooking, and his mother's joyful laughter. He was surely going to miss all of his sisters, his dear friends, and his nephew too. Felix was certainly going to yearn for the sweet smell of Elsie's perfume, her gentle kisses, and her genuine personality. When the morning bugle rang out for Reveille on 10 Feb. 1944, Felix knew that it was time for his next adventure to begin. He could only hope for the best, and he vowed to make his family and loved ones proud.

Felix and Ray gathered all of their belongings before climbing aboard the truck that would take them to the ship that would deliver them at the doorstep of the war with Japan and the rest of the Axis powers.

CHAPTER 14

Completing the Mission

It was approaching supper time when Mack finished with his presentation regarding Felix's path to obtaining his wings. Everyone was heartbroken when Mack passed around the newspaper clippings that provided some of the details regarding Felix's death and funeral. After reading through the articles, Sam asked aloud, "I wonder what really happened to Felix that day? Was it an unfortunate accident, or was he killed in action?" Mack's Uncle Bruce stood up, and said, "I can only imagine how excited Felix was to graduate as a fighter pilot." Sue Ann nodded her head in agreement, and said, "Once again, a wonderful relationship cut short. I feel terrible that he lost his life, and I feel so bad for his folks, for Elsie, and, of course, for Felix." Frank chimed in by saying, "Felix was living his dream. It sounds like he led an exciting life up until the very end." Sam then stood up, and said to Mack, "I was so enthralled as you meticulously led us through all of the stages in Felix's life. I feel like I'm left with wanting more, but sadly, there's no more to tell. You did a magnificent job, and I bet that Felix would appreciate you for all of your efforts." Mack replied, "I believe that Felix was certainly an amazing pilot, and an even better man. Going through his things has inspired me to try and become a pilot as well. I'm going to make it a point to do something special with my life, and with some of his belongings."

During the remaining days at his Uncle Bruce's place, Mack spent some time really digging into the yearbooks from Felix's Primary and Advanced training classes. He looked at each face on the pages, and wondered how many of those men had died during the war. Each smiling pilot was full of promise and ambition, and sadly, there were surely many families like Felix's who were left grieving over the loss of their loved one. Mack felt a deep sense of appreciation for their sacrifice and service. He could only imagine the lives that Felix, and the other men could've lived if it hadn't been for the war. Mack then looked through Felix's yearbook from Texas AMC with a focus not only on the cadets, but at the school itself. He knew that the school had now become known as Texas A&M, and to this day, he was certain that it was still very proud of its storied traditions, and of the many war heroes who had spent time there.

Mack was about to start his senior year at Mustang High School, and he knew that he'd be submitting his college applications very soon. He figured that it was a sure thing that he'd get accepted to the University of Oklahoma (OU), being that it was only 30 minutes from his home. His father and grandfather had both been Sooners over in Norman, Oklahoma. After having gone through a great deal of Felix's things, Mack began to see some similarities in his life to things that Felix had experienced in his own life. Maybe it was just coincidental, but Mack began to wonder if it was really meant to be that he'd stumbled upon all of Felix's belongings. After sitting down next to his father at supper that evening, he intended to have a conversation with him about his newfound interest in possibly attending Texas A&M. Mack began with, "I found out that Texas A&M is actually older than OU, and they both have legendary football teams along with solid academic programs." Sam was a little surprised at

Mack's sudden interest in Texas A&M, but he encouraged him to research it further before making a decision.

Mack woke up early the next morning with what he thought was a terrific idea. He proceeded to ask his father if they could take a day trip over to College Station to visit the Texas A&M campus. How could Sam say no, being that he'd just asked Mack to research the school the previous evening? Therefore, after breakfast, they began the three hour drive over to Brazos County. Mack felt a little overwhelmed when he stepped out of his father's truck, and onto the illustrious grounds of Texas A&M. Being that it was summertime, the student population on campus was much less than on a typical day during the regular school year. Mack planned to check out all of the places and buildings that he was interested in. He pulled up a campus map on his phone, and they began their journey. Before the day was over, Mack also wanted to look out for some of the structures that dated back to Felix's time as an Aggie.

After orienting themselves to their location on campus, Mack and Sam's first stop was at the Sanders Corps of Cadets Center. They were very excited as they proceeded to view all of the exhibits that were on display inside the building. The staff members were quite accommodating, friendly, and knowledgeable. Mack and Sam were amazed to learn that just over 20,000 Aggies had served during WWII, and they were told that this number was greater than any other American military school at that time. They were saddened to find out that Felix was one of the 953 Aggies who died while serving during WWII. Mack and Sam were thoroughly impressed with the quality, and selection of the items that were featured within the beautiful glass showcases. On the way out, Mack said to his father, "If I end up coming to school here, I just might donate some of Felix's college related items to this wonderful place." Sam liked Mack's idea, and they continued on. Next, they saw the old YMCA building, the Sbisa Dining Hall, and, of course, Kyle Field. It was clearly the largest and most magnificent stadium that Mack had ever seen, and he was certain that Felix would've been impressed with the enormous structure.

Mack making a wish before placing old pennies upon the foot of the Sully Ross statue at Texas A&M for good luck.

As Mack stood next to the Sully Ross statue, he imagined Felix standing in the very same spot so many decades ago. On the way to the residence halls, Mack checked his notes to verify which dorm Felix had lived in. He was thrilled to see that the Gainer Residence Hall was still standing. Although they couldn't venture inside, and up to the third or fourth floor, Mack was content to see one of the buildings that Felix had called home. He could almost picture Felix carrying his bags as he walked out the door for the last time with Buzz back in

January of 1942. A walk over to the Memorial Student Center (MSC) was the last stop of the day for their tour of the campus. The building seemed like a perfect place for students to hang out, socialize, and relax. The Memorial Student Center didn't date back to Felix's time; however it was quite impressive, and it held many tributes and memorials to those Aggies who had given their lives in the service of their country during wars past. Mack and Sam methodically searched for Felix's name by looking at each and every plaque located within the building. Finally, Sam spotted a very long memorial that represented each class year in which Aggies were killed during WWII.

Felix's name is featured on a memorial found inside the Memorial Student Center at Texas A&M.

The large plaque was affixed to a wall, and the class of 1942 section featured Felix's name along with the names of his 95 classmates who had also perished during the course of the war. After staring at Felix's name for several minutes, Mack realized that Felix would always be with him in spirit if he was lucky enough to be accepted as a student there at Texas A&M. Mack and Sam were thankful that the lives of the fallen soldiers were recognized appropriately, and they were glad that their legacy would live on forever. After snapping a few last pictures, they slowly made their way back to the parking structure while taking in all of the beauty and grandeur that the Aggie campus had to offer.

The trip to Richland Springs was just supposed to be an opportunity for Mack to relax, and to visit with his family. However, he left with a pile of goodies, and a clear sense of what he wanted to do with his life. Mack was still blown away that he'd ended up with Felix's '41 Chevy along with the cedar chest, the footlocker, and the suitcase, all of which were loaded into the bed of his truck. It was time for Mack and Sam to say goodbye to Bruce and Sue Ann. Mack thanked them for their hospitality, and for their assistance with all of Felix's things. Sam pulled out onto the street, and Mack pulled up right behind him. They then honked their horns, and waved out the windows as they began their journey back to Mustang, Oklahoma. For the trip home, Mack had placed Felix's service cap and jacket on the seat beside him. In a rather eerie sort of way, Mack could seemingly feel Felix's energy and spirit within the cab of the truck. While Mack was cruising along behind his father, he imagined Felix's hands on the steering wheel, piloting his blue beauty all over the roads of Central Texas.

The ride home provided Mack with an opportunity to really ponder his choices pertaining to the upcoming college application process. As he headed north on State Highway 183, he called his girlfriend, Barbara, to discuss his visit to Texas A&M. After telling her about all of the terrific things found on the campus, Mack mentioned that he was considering applying to Texas A&M. Barbara then asked, "I thought that we were going to go to OU together?" Mack replied, "Well babe, Texas A&M has an awesome campus, and I bet you'd really like it too. I haven't fully made up my mind yet. I just wanted to tell you about it, and maybe we can apply there as an option." Barbara wasn't yet convinced, but she listened to what Mack had to say, and she told him that she'd also consider it.

Mack was glad to be back home, and he had a fabulous time unpacking the truck. After placing the items safely inside the garage, Mack showed his mom, Lucy, all of the marvelous things that he'd purchased at the auction. Their vacation to Richland Springs had been a blast, but it had also taxed Mack both mentally and physically. However, he looked forward to showing off Felix's worldly possessions to all of his friends, neighbors, and classmates as well. Mack spent the next few days contemplating what to do with all of Felix's belongings. How could he best honor the legacy and memory of Felix Scott? For the time being, Mack decided to leave Felix's things in the garage as he prepared to begin his senior year of high school.

Barbara had become convinced to apply to Texas A&M, and much to Mack's surprise, they both received acceptance letters to the University of Oklahoma, and also to Texas A&M. Mack had also looked into the possibility of obtaining an appointment to the Air Force Academy, but he found out that it was going to be a lengthy process. There were multiple options on the table, and it was time for Mack to make a decision. Should he go to OU, Texas A&M, or should he follow in Felix's footsteps, and join the Air Force to pursue a career as a fighter pilot? Once again, Mack thumbed through Felix's photos, magazines, and yearbooks, looking at the pictures from his time in pre-flight training through the time when he left Sarasota. He was looking for inspiration and guidance from Felix before making such a life-changing decision. All things considered, Mack figured that the University of Oklahoma would probably be the best choice for him since it was close to home and to his family.

Some of Felix's USAAF yearbooks, Pilots' Information File, and a few of his magazines.

Mack had dreamed about the possibility of flying some of the most sophisticated fighter jets in the world. The thought of flying an F-16 Fighting Falcon as part of the famed U.S. Air Force Thunderbirds, or an F-35 Lightning II stealth fighter really intrigued him. However, Mack realized that flying passenger jets would be far safer than piloting a fighter jet in any of the world conflicts that the United States might find themselves involved in. He ultimately decided to forgo the Air Force career path, giving up the chance to become a fighter pilot. After several days of contemplation and a few laborious discussions with Barbara, they decided to accept the offers from OU. Mack was very excited to be accepted into the OU School of Aviation, and he figured that he'd be flying, and that's what really mattered most in the end. Barbara was accepted into the Aerospace Engineering program at OU. Mack planned to work towards obtaining his Bachelor of Science degree with a major in Aviation. He was going to earn his pilot's license, and use that to pursue a career as a commercial airline pilot. Mack figured that Felix would be proud with his choice, and he felt honored that Felix would be his spiritual copilot as he was about to embark on his schooling at the University of Oklahoma.

Mack's senior year of high school had flown by, and it was time for him to graduate in May of 2019. He had excelled both academically and socially, which led him to be near the top of his class. Everyone on campus knew that Mack and Barbara were one of the most popular couples in the senior class. Those who knew Mack best, realized that he liked the limelight, and that he wasn't bashful. However, nobody expected what was going to happen on graduation day. At the conclusion of the high school commencement ceremony, Mack quickly ran up onto the stage and grabbed the microphone from the podium. He then faced the audience, and said, "Hello everyone, may I kindly ask for just a few more minutes of your time?" Mack looked directly into the front row, and he asked Barbara to join him up on the stage. Although she had a puzzled look on her face, Barbara excitedly ran up the small steps, and stood with Mack at the podium. Mack then said, "Barbara my dear, you and I have come a long way together here at Mustang High School. We're heading to OU together so that you can learn how to design new planes, while I'm going to learn how to fly them." Suddenly, Mack proceeded to get down on one knee, and said, "I think we make a great team, you and me.

I love you very much, and I'd like to ask you if you'll marry me?" The crowd was silent as they anxiously waited on the edge of their seats for her reply. As Mack looked directly into Barbara's eyes, he pulled out a fancy ring box from his pocket. He then lifted the ring from the black velvet cushion, and the crowd began to cheer loudly when Barbara fervently said "Yes." Everyone applauded for the young couple as they made their way back towards their classmates while smiling from cheek to cheek.

The summer of 2019 had begun, and Mack decided that he wanted to take a road trip with his fiancé. Barbara also liked history very much, and she was excited to embark on the trip where they planned to visit many of the places where Felix had trained at. They had a terrific time planning the route, and they came up with a budget after pooling the money that they'd received for graduation. Mack made sure to get the '41 Chevy checked out to ensure that it was safe for the long journey. Reminiscent of Felix's trip with Elsie to San Antonio, they tossed their luggage into the bed of the truck and off they went. It was rather early on 15 Jun. 2019, as Mack and Barbara made their way towards Amarillo on I-40 West. While filling up his tank with gas, Mack let Barbara know about the time Felix had made his way to Amarillo looking for Francine. Barbara didn't like how the story ended for Felix on that day, but she thought that it would be fun to cruise by Francine's former house on Jackson street. They ended up in Albuquerque for the evening, and they planned to get to Phoenix around noon the following day.

The Hotel Adams wasn't an option for Mack and Barbara since it had been leveled long ago, and it had been rebuilt under a different name. After a short drive around downtown Phoenix, the young couple managed to find their hotel, and it happened to be rather close to the Orpheum Theater. Afterwards, Mack and Barbara enjoyed walking around the CityScape where they ate some terrific Mexican food at Chico Malo. They then strolled along the fence line to get a peek at the shuttered Union Station while trying to picture Felix waiting for Elsie and his folks as he prepared to graduate from Luke Field. Later that evening, they drove by Luke Air Force Base, which was known as Luke Field during Felix's time. Mack parked his truck in an area outside the base so that they could sit and watch for planes in the sky. He imagined that Felix would've had a blast flying all over the Valley of the Sun, and in the air space right above them.

Mack was thrilled to wake up on the morning of 17 Jun. 2019. He and Barbara were going to make the six hour drive out to Orange County, which was located in beautiful Southern California. They intended to visit the place where it had all started for Felix back in December of 1942. Although the Balboa Inn had changed over the years; Mack could imagine Felix and Elsie standing at the front desk as he checked into the hotel. Mack realized that Felix had stayed there on several occasions, and after seeing the beautiful surroundings, he could understand why. The view of the ocean from their second story room was picturesque, and the proximity to the beach was amazing. Mack and Barbara spent the entire afternoon biking and roller skating along the Balboa Coastline and peninsula. They had a terrific evening at the Balboa Fun Zone, and they took guesses as to where Felix and Elsie had first met. Afterwards, they hopped into his truck for a short ride up the peninsula, where they enjoyed a fabulous seafood supper at the Bluewater Grill. They had a terrific view from their table as they watched the sunset fade into the sea. Barbara wanted to visit Disneyland, so that is where they went on 18 Jun. 2019. The park was certainly crowded, but all of the rides, parades, attractions, and the shows made for a very entertaining day. After checking out of the hotel the following morning, Mack felt sad that Felix wasn't able to return to California in order to enjoy more time in this fantastic city with Elsie.

It was 19 Jun. 2019, when Mack and Barbara headed to the Heroes Hall Museum in Costa Mesa, California. They found the museum to be located inside of a renovated Santa Ana Army Air Base barracks building. It was one of the few remaining structures to be found on the site of what is left of the former military base. The building held magnificent displays on both the first and second floors. Mack just couldn't believe that he was walking around the same grounds that Felix had trained at back in late 1942, and into the early 1943. Could it be possible that he was standing in the actual barracks building that Felix and Ray had called home? Mack got to talking with one of the staff members about Felix, and the items that he'd discovered. Before leaving the museum, Mack obtained the docent's business card, and he let the man know that he might be sending some of Felix's belongings their way.

After grabbing some sandwiches, Mack and Barbara headed northeast over to Chino, California. Fighting the freeway traffic nightmare for nearly two hours would prove worthwhile when they pulled into the parking lot of the Planes of Fame Air Museum. Mack had heard that they had the only authentic P-51A that could still fly there on display. Being that the Mustang had survived the many decades since WWII, he knew that he just had to see it, touch it, and admire the extraordinary plane. After viewing a few dozen planes inside of their hangars, they finally stumbled upon the magnificent P-51 Mustang. Mack had a most memorable experience, and a feeling of complete exhilaration when he first laid eyes upon the vintage warbird. He could only imagine how Felix must've felt when he'd first seen the P-51 Mustang. Mack spent at least 30 minutes walking around the plane, seemingly looking at every rivet, and touching nearly each piece of the plane. Although he wasn't allowed inside of the cockpit, he certainly took quite a few pictures of the Mustang. Mack was very inquisitive, and he loved reading the write-ups of all the planes there in the museum. As he read through the information about the P-51A, he noticed the serial number for the plane before him. Mack had a pretty good memory, and he thought that the serial number looked strikingly familiar. He pulled out his notes that had mentioned the details pertaining to Felix's fatal crash in his P-51A. The serial number for his plane was 43–6269, and the one in front of him was 43-6251. What an amazing coincidence! Mack quickly realized that this plane was nearly identical to the one that Felix had perished in, and it was certainly produced within days of each other.

After viewing the rest of the exhibits, Mack and Barbara made the 30 minute drive over to Corona for what he hoped would be a very special supper. Prior to beginning their journey to California, Mack began to wonder whatever happened to Felix's good buddy, Ray Simon. Armed only with his cellphone, and having a knack for playing detective on social media sites, Mack began digging to see if he could determine what had become of Ray. He had a few pictures of Felix posing with another man around the base, among airplanes, and on the beach. There was no writing on the backs of the pictures, so Mack wasn't sure if the gentleman was Ray or not. After having found Mr. Simon in the yearbook from Luke Field, he knew that Ray hailed from Napoleon, North Dakota. After scouring the internet with the very little information that he had, Mack stumbled upon a picture of a grave marker that he presumed might just belong to the Ray Simon that he was looking for. It turns out that Mr. Simon was buried in the Riverside National Cemetery, and since Mack knew that they were going to be in that vicinity, it was worth digging further. If he'd found the right guy, he was very glad to find out that Ray had survived the war.

Still unsure if he had a positive connection to the Ray Simon that he was looking for, Mack kept searching for more answers. He happened to stumble upon an obituary that mentioned many of Ray's family members. Mack took some of the crumbs that had just fallen into his lap, and he ventured onto his favorite social media site to see what he could find. He figured that if Ray was buried in Riverside, there was a chance that some of his family members might reside in a city near the cemetery. Mack felt lucky to have found some possible matches, and he immediately sent a message to those individuals whom he felt could be related to Ray. A few weeks had gone by, and Mack was beginning to feel that he wasn't on the right track after all. However, one day he received a text message from Debbie Simon, and it turns out that she just happened to be Ray's daughter-in-law. After reading her message, the hairs on Mack's arms were raised, and he felt a huge sense of accomplishment. Debbie went on to say that her husband, John Simon, was Ray's son. She also mentioned that her sister-in-law Sheryl DeJong and her husband, Nick DeJong, lived in the area as well. Debbie went on to state that Sheryl is Ray's daughter. What an amazing find, and what a terrific opportunity it was going to be for Mack and Barbara to meet these very gracious people. Could they have stories about Felix, pictures, or paperwork? Time would tell, but Mack went to bed that night knowing that Felix would be thoroughly impressed by what he'd discovered.

After pulling into the parking lot, Mack and Barbara proceeded to venture into the Lazy Dog Cafe for supper with his newfound friends. Although he had no idea what Debbie or Sheryl looked like, it didn't take long to spot them. They immediately greeted Mack and Barbara as if they were their own family members, and Mack could tell right away that they were very easy-going folks. After introducing themselves to one another, Sheryl commented with, "When you made a friend with Ray, you had a friend for life. He wouldn't have had it any other way." Mack and Barbara then greeted John and Nick who were holding spots for everyone at the table. The conversation was quite enjoyable, and Mack was elated as Debbie and Sheryl kept pulling out one thing after another from their bags. There were patches, training materials, a class photo from Felix and Ray's time at SAAAB, and they even had some of the very same pictures that Mack had saved on his phone. Amazingly, the family members were able to confirm that the man who was pictured in some of the photographs with Felix was indeed their Ray Simon.

Class photo of pilot squadron 47 from the Santa Ana Army Air Base taken in February of 1943. Photo provided by the Ray Simon family.

Although the family couldn't recall many stories about Felix, Nick mentioned that he remembered Ray talking about Felix on several occasions. The Simons and DeJongs provided Mack with some invaluable information about Ray, and in regard to his time in the service with Felix. It was an entirely fun evening, and Mack was pleased to know that Ray had come home from the war to become a successful dentist, and a loving husband. He'd been blessed with wonderful children, grandchildren, and even some great grandchildren. After enjoying a fabulous dessert, Barbara said, "It sounds like Felix and Ray were the best of friends, and I'm certain that they're smiling as they look down on us tonight. They're surely getting a kick out of us getting together, and Mack and I are delighted to be able to keep their legacy alive." John replied with, "Sitting around this table tonight, I can totally picture Felix with my dad shooting the breeze on a sandy beach or in the mess hall having a ball with all of their friends. I'm so glad that you folks reached out to Debbie, and I know that my dad would've enjoyed meeting you both." Mack then said, "Because of Felix, I'll be heading to school very soon to become an airline pilot. I know that y'all said that you love to travel, and it would be my honor to have you aboard a flight that I'd be piloting somewhere down the road." With that, they wrapped up the evening, but everyone planned to keep in contact with one another as time went on. After shaking hands with the men, and after giving a hug to the ladies, Mack said, "I'd rather not say goodbye since it seems so permanent. Instead, I prefer to say chow for now, and I hope that we'll meet again soon." On the way to the hotel, Barbara said to Mack, "You never cease to amaze me. I still don't know how you were able to track those folks down, but I must say that they were some of the nicest people that I've ever met. They were all just so friendly, and I really liked how Debbie and Sheryl were smiling and laughing during the whole conversation.

Early the next morning, Mack and Barbara began the four and a half hour trip to Lemoore, California. When they arrived near the downtown area of Lemoore, it was a little too early to check into their hotel. Therefore, Mack and Barbara decided that they'd walk around to explore the town. Although it was still a relatively small city, Mack imagined that it had changed quite a bit over the years. After enjoying a wonderful lunch at a nearby café, Mack and Barbara continued their walk until they reached the Lucerne Hotel. The historic building was no longer functioning as a hotel, but it appeared as though it was still in remarkable condition. Before continuing on, Mack pictured Felix and Elsie enjoying life while sitting out there on the second story balcony. After checking out of their hotel the next morning, they headed out along Route 198. Mack wanted to see what had remained of the former Lemoore Army Air Field, but when they arrived, he was rather disappointed that there wasn't much left of the base. However, it appeared that two of the original hangars, and a good chunk of the former parking ramp remained from long ago. Symmetrical blocks of farmland seemed to have replaced much of the former base, and the property wasn't that far from the Lemoore Naval Air Station. Mack quickly realized that the present-day base was very large, and he could tell that the city of Lemoore was still very much a military town. They then stopped by the Aviator Memorial, which was near the current base, to watch some of the aerial activity above and around them.

It was time for the young couple to head two hours west over to King City, California. There was plenty of daylight left, and they enjoyed the scenic drive as they wound their way through the curvy mountainous roads. Upon arriving in King City, they could tell that it was no longer the small town that Felix had visited back in 1943. They drove up and down Broadway, and then they cruised around some of the surrounding streets looking for any sort of building that might've been around back in 1943. The Hayloft, the King Bean Tavern, and even the El Camino Real Hotel had apparently been lost to history. However, Mack was glad to see that the former USO building was still standing although it now served as an ordinary office building. Even though the Reel Joy movie theater had now become a market, Mack could picture Felix standing out on the sidewalk, laughing with his pals while waiting to get in. He and Barbara enjoyed a nice supper at the Cork and Plough, and as they sat there eating, Mack could tell that the building didn't date back to 1943. Oddly enough, he had a nagging feeling that Felix must've spent some time near this property which was located there on Broadway Street. Before heading back to their hotel, they walked hand-in-hand around the downtown area, just like Felix and Elsie would've done so many moons ago.

The following morning, they proceeded to look for the train station that had played an important role to Felix and Elsie during his stay in King City. Mack asked around, and he found out that it had been moved from its original location over to San Lorenzo Park. They grabbed a pizza and a few cold drinks before heading over to the park for a fabulous afternoon picnic. A trip to King City wouldn't be complete without seeing the site of the former Mesa Del Rey contract flying school. Mack wasn't sure what to expect, but he knew that the grounds would be strikingly different from years past. While parked alongside the chain-link fence, Mack could see that the original Administration Building had stood the test of time. It was apparent that the building has been remodeled over the years, but he was glad that many of its exterior details had remained unchanged. Although Mack thought that it was unfortunate that the Administration Building, and several of the airplane hangars were now part of a produce company located next to the airport, he was happy that they were still standing. He gazed out towards the runway, imagining what a thrill Felix would've had as his PT-22 lifted off the ground for the very first time. Mack thought that it was pretty amazing that the airport had continued to operate as Mesa Del Rey. He then turned to Barbara, and said, "It's a real shame that the barracks buildings aren't here anymore, but it looks like at least one of the revetments remains over yonder." A kind man by the name of John happened to be walking by, and he overheard some of their conversation. He mentioned that a few of the barracks buildings had indeed survived, but they'd been moved to a location just down the street. Although Mack couldn't go inside any of the former barracks buildings, he was able to catch a glimpse of times past before they headed down the road, bidding so long to King City.

Barbara had been very supportive of Mack as he led their adventures in Lemoore and King city, but she was certainly thrilled to be finally on the way to San Francisco. She thoroughly enjoyed their drive along scenic State Route 1 as they headed north through Monterey, and on to San Francisco. They could've taken a shorter route, but Mack was equally impressed with the views as they traversed the winding road along the beautiful California Coastline. Mack and Barbara were glad that they'd been able to make a reservation at the Sir Francis Drake Hotel. Although they had no idea which room Felix and Elsie would've stayed in, the folks at the front desk were able to upgrade them to a fine room on the 14th floor. Just like Elsie had done many years back, Barbara peered out the window at the city lights beneath them. After changing into some warmer clothing, they headed out in order to explore the city by the bay. They had a hard time deciding what to do first since there were so many amazing things to see there in San Francisco.

Mack and Barbara set out on foot, and they eventually found a cable car that took them down to Fisherman's Wharf. There were plenty of fabulous smells emanating from the variety of restaurants, but they decided to purchase some sandwiches made with fresh sourdough bread at a nearby bakery. After finishing their meal, they made the two minute walk over to Pier 39. Barbara was excited to find the sea lion viewing area, and they enjoyed watching a large group of the wonderful creatures relax upon their wooden platforms. Barbara loved shopping, sightseeing, and sweet treats. She charmingly convinced Mack that ice cream was in proper order before heading back to the hotel.

Early the next morning, they made a return trip back towards the Fisherman's Wharf area. Mack and Barbara thought that it would be enjoyable to hop off the cable car near Lombard Street. They just had to walk up and down one of the craziest and curviest streets in San

Francisco. There was a long line of cars, so the decision to walk about the area seemed to have been the best choice. The flowers were beautiful, and it was an all-around enjoyable experience. Next, they headed over to Fort Mason, which happened to be the place where Felix's body had been received through the repatriation process way back in May of 1948. Although it was no longer an Army base, Mack could feel the energy and spirits of the many men who'd left for war off its docks. He could also visualize the processing of the great number of steel containers carrying the remains of fallen American soldiers. It was a very poignant moment for Mack, so Barbara decided to allow him as much time as he wanted to process the images of yesteryear.

Mack had finally seen enough, and he turned the reins over to Barbara. She decided that they ought to have lunch over at Pier 39. Afterwards, they grabbed some famous Ghirardelli chocolate before catching a cab over to Coit Tower. Chalk it up to poor timing, or just plum bad luck, the elevator happened to be inoperable when they arrived. Traversing the 13 flights of stairs, both up and down, certainly helped to work off their meal. The views of the bay and city from the tower were really impressive. They then decided to board a double-decker tour bus that took them to Chinatown and throughout much of the city. After crossing the Golden Gate Bridge aboard the bus, Barbara decided that it would be thrilling to walk back across the 1.5 mile bridge. There were plenty of places to stop in order to take in all of the magnificent views. Mack peered over the railing just enough to see the choppy water below. Upon reaching the center of the bridge, he pictured the Cardinal O'Connell passing beneath them before stopping at Fort Mason, which was located just up the coastline. Mack informed Barbara that the Cardinal O'Connell was the Army transport ship that had brought Felix's remains into San Francisco.

After their walk across the bridge, Mack and Barbara hopped back on the bus for a ride down to the Embarcadero. They headed over to Pier 3 to board the boat that would take them on a three hour dinner cruise around the beautiful San Francisco Bay. The views of the city's skyline were breathtaking, and the food was outstanding. Although Mack and Barbara were too young to drink, the amazing desserts were more than enough to satisfy them. To fully enjoy their final evening in San Francisco, they made sure to go onto the top deck as their ship passed underneath the Golden Gate Bridge. They certainly didn't want their extraordinary day to end. Mack and Barbara were exhausted, so the cable car ride back towards the hotel proved to be very relaxing. Unlike Felix, Mack looked out the hotel window before bed knowing what the near future held for him. There was to be an upcoming wedding, a new school, and the beginning of what he hoped would be an amazing career ahead of him. Mack felt sad that Felix had to spend his last night in San Francisco with so much anxiety and trepidation.

It took the better part of three days for the young couple to get back to Mustang, Oklahoma. They were in no real hurry to get home, so they saw some of the excitement that the Las Vegas strip had to offer, and they even found time to venture to the top of Sandia Peak on their return trip through Albuquerque. Mack really enjoyed all of the time that was spent with Barbara on the seat right beside him. There were plenty of laughs, and much debate about what the perfect wedding venue would be. Mack kept his eyes on the road while Barbara tossed out all kinds of ideas for their big event.

The time had come for Mack and Barbara to move to Norman for the start of their freshman year at OU. Mack had meticulously packed his '41 Chevy with all of their belongings that would be needed for their stay on campus. Before leaving home, Mack sorted and packaged all of Felix's belongings back into the cedar chest and footlocker. All but three of the items were stored for safekeeping in his family's garage. Mack was feeling nostalgic, so he thought that he'd take Felix's Texas AMC suitcase along with his regular luggage to school. However, once he made it onto campus, he planned to add an OU sticker to it at some point. Finally, Mack decided to bring a pair of Felix's silver wings, and a picture of him at his graduation from Luke Field. These items were very special to Mack, and they'd serve as a reminder of the goal that he'd set for himself.

Collection of items that belonged to Felix. The hat device in the upper left corner was used during his time as an aviation cadet. The hat device in the center was used on his officer's service cap. The small pin on the left with the propeller and the U.S. pins went on the lapel and collar of his service coat. Felix's pilot wings are in the upper right hand corner. The Scott family probably added the gold star to the bottom set of wings after becoming a gold star family following Felix's untimely death.

It was way too early to know if Mack would be successful at OU. However, he'd learned a great deal from Felix's college experience. Mack realized the importance of possessing a real passion for the classes that would be needed to obtain his pilot's license. He'd read about the courses that Felix had taken as he made his way through the Pre-Flight, Primary, Basic, and Advanced training classes. Mack reviewed the University of Oklahoma's course catalog, and he noticed some similarities to Felix's training regimen. An Introduction to Aviation, Aviation Safety, Aviation Law, Basic Air Traffic Control Regulations, Instrument Flying, and Advanced Flight Maneuvers were just some of the courses that Mack would be required to take during his time at OU. Many more classes would be needed as well, and he knew that there would be plenty of hands on training in multiple types of aircraft. Mack could tell from Felix's grades that he wasn't happy with what he was studying while at Texas AMC. He wished that the world would've been different at that time, so Felix could've had the opportunity to pursue a degree related to flying, which was something that he truly loved. Mack planned to get good grades, and he was going to do his best to become successful at OU. He realized that there wouldn't be any bombing or strafing runs, but he was hoping that he'd still have a blast as he pursued his adventure in the sky.

Mack was ecstatic when he climbed into the single engine Piper Warrior for the first time. As a freshman, he earned his private pilot certificate after regularly flying four to five hours per week. After a wonderful start at OU, Mack and Barbara were thrown a bit of a curve in the spring of 2020. The United States wasn't in the midst of a world war, but there were worldwide implications due to the outbreak of COVID-19. Suddenly, everyone's world had been turned upside down. Mack realized how the onset of war had affected Felix during college, and he vowed to not let this matter get in his way. There were clearly some delays and even a few challenges, but Mack and Barbara managed to carry on. At the conclusion of their freshman year, Mack and Barbara moved out of the dorm, and into an apartment of their own. They had a beautiful wedding in the summer of 2020, although it had to be held outside, and with less guests in attendance than they'd originally planned.

There were many months during the pandemic where interactions with groups of other people had to be kept to a minimum. Mack got a cat, and he just had to name it Felix after learning all about the famous cartoon series. Barbara got a corgi, and she named it Francisco. They were happy, and they were excelling in their classes. Mack was active in the Alpha Eta Rho aviation fraternity there on campus. He recalled that Felix had been active in several campus clubs, so he figured that it would be rewarding to join the Sooner Flight Club as well. Mack and Barbara would often meet up in between classes at the Campus Corner. They made it a point to reserve Monday evenings for date nights at Hideaway Pizza or at Fuzzy Tacos.

Mack continued to log many flight hours in the Piper Warrior each week. He went on to earn his instrument, commercial, and instructor certificates in that plane. Mack realized that his experience in the flight simulators, which were located on North Campus, was quite different than Felix's time spent in the Link trainer. Technology had changed quite a bit over the years, and Mack could only imagine what Felix would've thought of the modern day machines that were so critical to the training program. Countless hours were spent inside the different flight simulators, and Mack enjoyed every moment of it. As he advanced through the training program, he understood the real pleasure that Felix must've had as he flew each of the different airplanes en route to earning his wings. After mastering the Piper Warrior, Mack went on to get his multi-engine certificate in the Piper Seminole. Mack felt like a kid in a candy store when he was finally able to fly the King Air turboprop during his senior year. The King Air was no P-51 Mustang, but he certainly had the time of his life flying this advanced aircraft.

Mack's path to graduation was clearly different than Felix's path to earning his wings. However, Mack had a similar feeling after progressing through the private, instrument, commercial, multi-engine, instructor, and the air transport pilot certificate programs at OU. Having logged more than 1000 total flying hours, Mack was finally ready to graduate. Barbara had kept pace with her own coursework, so they were both able to receive their degrees in May of 2023. As Mack walked across the stage at his commencement ceremony, he pointed to the sky after receiving his diploma cover as a way to say thank you to Felix for being his copilot throughout his training at OU. Mack felt glad to have accomplished his goal, but he felt bad that Felix never got to experience graduating from Texas AMC.

In the months leading up to their graduation from OU, Mack and Barbara just couldn't decide where they wanted to go to celebrate. Should they travel to a faraway land, to some exotic beach, or to a place of historical significance? Although Mack was thrilled that he'd achieved everything needed to become a pilot with one of the major airlines, he had a nagging desire to go to India before beginning his career. Mack had become quite well-versed in Felix's life story over the years, and he'd always felt troubled that Felix wasn't able to complete his final training mission on that fateful day. Therefore, he felt the need to travel to the area where Felix had crashed his P-51A. Mack wanted to experience the beautiful scenery that India had to offer, but more importantly, he felt that he needed closure for both him, and for Felix. Barbara just couldn't believe that Mack wanted to go to India instead of going to Scotland with her, but she was very supportive of his decision.

Mack was very resourceful, and he felt that he was rather adept at networking. However, after running into nothing but roadblocks on his social media apps, he reached out to some folks at the Alumni Association there at OU. The staff was very helpful, and they found Mack's plan to go to India to be a wonderful idea. OU had a long history of training a great number of pilots over the years. Many of those pilots were proud to be alumni, and they remained as active members with the Alumni Association. Within a few days, Mack found it truly remarkable that he was communicating with an alumnus who was living in India. This gentleman wasn't just living in India, he was operating a business that provided folks with an opportunity to fly in an authentic World War II era airplane!

Numerous emails had finally turned into a video call. Mack was just chomping at the bit to meet the man who'd help him make his dream a reality. Barry Singh had graduated from OU many moons ago. He'd served for decades as a commercial airline pilot, and he'd traveled to hundreds of cities across the world during his career. Mack quickly realized that they had a great deal in common, and they shared many interests as well. He had a blast picking Barry's brain for his own career that was about to take off. Barry was fascinated by the research that Mack had done, and he thought that it was remarkable to find out that Felix had served so close to his place there in India. Barry extended an offer for Mack to come for a visit, and plans were finalized that he'd travel by plane to Dibrugarh, India.

Mack traveled with Barbara and her mother to Will Rogers World Airport over in Oklahoma City on 27 May 2023. Their flights were set to depart within a short time of one another, so they were able to hang out together for a spell before heading to their respective gates. The time had come for Mack and Barbara to say their goodbyes, and they gave each other a big hug and a kiss. For just a moment, he felt like Felix saying goodbye to Elsie. Mack wasn't overly thrilled that he'd be traveling through a total of five airports, and that it would take him nearly two days to get to Dibrugarh when accounting for the time zone differences. Nonetheless, he'd have quite a bit of time on the plane to think about whether he'd made the right decision to travel to India. The plane ticket was quite expensive, and he was going to miss seeing Scotland with Barbara and her mother.

Barry was waiting outside of the passenger terminal at the Dibrugarh Airport when Mack finally arrived. The men hopped into Barry's golf cart, and they proceeded to his hangar, which was located near the runway. Mack's jaw nearly dropped when Barry opened the roll-up door on the hangar to reveal the plane inside. Mack said, "Holy crap, you have an AT-6 Texan?" Barry quickly replied, "Not exactly. Although they are essentially the same plane, this is an SNJ-4 Texan, which was the Navy's version of the AT-6." Mack was practically drooling as he walked around the magnificent plane that featured a shiny aluminum fuselage and wings. There was a large white star inside of a blue circle on both sides of the fuselage, and on top of each wing. NAVY was painted in bold white letters next to the star on each side of the fuselage. Barry had chosen to deck out the tail in a red, white, and blue color scheme. Mack could see the yellow paint around the nose, and there were blue streaks running vertically down the wings.

After climbing up onto the wing walk, Mack slid into the cockpit thinking how much fun it would've been if Felix were in the rear seat. Mack's momentary mind drifting episode quickly faded, and he returned his full attention to Barry as he explained everything that was found inside the cockpit. The men spent the better part of that afternoon going over the functionality of the SNJ-4. Having never been inside of a World War II era fighter, Mack figured that his excitement most likely matched that of Felix when he first saw the remarkable AT-6 Texan. Barry was very encouraging, and giving with his time. He felt delighted to be able to share his knowledge, and passion for flying with a fellow Sooner. Barry was glad to take Mack under his wing for the week, all while running his airplane tour business.

Mack understood that Barry was a businessman, and that he'd only get an opportunity to fly when openings permitted. He was very grateful that Barry wasn't even going to charge him anything for the flights. For the first few days, Barry and Mack practiced takeoffs and landings, and all of the routine maneuvers in the SNJ-4. Mack sensed that a real friendship was developing, and he felt that Barry acted as if he were his own grandfather. Barry seemed to have reciprocal feelings, and he continued to show a genuine interest in what Mack was looking to accomplish while in India. By the middle of the week, Barry and Mack were flying over Dinjan. Mack thought that the experience was marvelous, and he could totally picture Felix climbing into his P-51A on the airfield below them.

There had been plenty of things to keep Mack busy during his stay in Dibrugarh when he wasn't flying. He seized the opportunity to visit several of the national parks in the area. Mack found the Jagannath Temple to be fascinating, and he visited the Jeypore Rainforest in the state of Assam near the end of his week. Mack couldn't have asked for a better experience during his time in India. Barry, and his wife, Chandy, had insisted that Mack stay as a guest in their home for the week. Mack was able to fully experience the Indian culture and food since Chandy prepared some of the most delicious meals that he'd ever tasted.

It was 3 Jun., and Mack was fully prepared to make his final flight with Barry in the SNJ-4. Before walking towards the plane, Mack pulled out a pair of Felix's wings, and he attached them to the upper left part of his flight suit. He then placed a map on the left wing in order to review their intended flight plan. Based on his research, Barry provided guidance as to the most logical training route that Felix would've taken on his final day in the sky. The coordinates for Felix's crash site were noted, and Mack began to finalize his pre-flight inspection of the aircraft. Barry thought that it would be appropriate for Mack to radio the tower for permission to take off. With clearance granted, Mack took control of the stick, and they were on their way.

They headed west over the Brahmaputra River until they reached the Pakke Tiger Reserve. Mack was hoping to see some exotic wildlife as they flew over the treetops, but unfortunately, the vegetation was too thick to see any animal activity beneath them. Mack continued west as they flew into the Sakteng Wildlife Sanctuary. After heading north for just a bit, they proceeded east, and flew over the Kameng River. Barry assured Mack that they'd keep a safe distance away from the Chinese border. Next, they passed through the Mouling National Park. There were plenty of rocky peaks below, yet the lush green vegetation of the forest made for a spectacular sight. It appeared that a river and streams had cut their way through the steep mountains beneath them. The final leg of their flight took them south towards the Dibru Saikhowa National Park. According to the crash report from Felix's accident, his flight officer commented that the area around Kobo is where he began his fateful Immelmann turn. There were clear skies, and the view of the farmland next to the divergent river beneath them was picturesque. Mack circled the area for about 15 minutes while taking in the whole experience. He was truly amazed that he was actually flying around the area where Felix had met his untimely death. The report went on to say that Felix had made several turns and flips as he began to spin uncontrollably over the rocky river below. It was evident that there was no way to tell the exact location of the crash site nearly 80 years later. There was no remaining wreckage to be seen, and there was certainly no memorial since his crash was just one of many during the war.

Mack was ready to begin his personal tribute to Felix, therefore he asked Barry to take control of the plane while he pulled a memento of sorts from his pocket. He'd ordered a few custom made dog tags with Felix's name and military information on them. The tags closely resembled the one that was back home that had actually belonged to Felix. Mack had attached one of the new dog tags to a keychain that was connected to a ribbon made of heavy fabric. There was an embroidered P-51 Mustang on one side of the ribbon, and Mack had sewn a Texas A&M patch onto the other side. Barry dropped down to an altitude of about 300 feet, and he then flew directly over the Brahmaputra River as Mack tossed his memorial to Felix into the rocks located between the fork in the river below. Mack then pointed to the sky, and said, "This one's for you, Felix!" He quickly regained control of the plane from Barry, and he proceeded to climb to an altitude of 6000 feet. Mack leveled out in the SNJ-4 before proceeding to complete an Immelmann turn above the area near the crash site. After successfully completing the maneuver, Mack circled the area one last time while Barry took some more pictures and another video. Before heading back across the river towards Dinjan, Mack wanted to pay one last tribute to Felix at the crash site. He repeatedly tilted the plane from side to side so as to wave goodbye to the fallen flyer. It was finally time to return to the airspace above Dinjan so that the mission could be considered complete. After flying over the former Dinjan Air Field, Mack successfully landed back at the Dibrugarh Airport.

With the SNJ-4 parked securely inside the hangar, Mack thanked Barry for a great week full of terrific flights. He then pulled a bottle of Canadian Club whiskey from his vintage B-4 bag, which of course happened to be Felix's brand of choice. The men proceeded to raise their glasses to celebrate the successful mission, and Mack knew that he'd made a friend for life. Barry vowed to keep in touch, and he told Mack to be sure to let him know if he was ever to pilot a plane to his neck of the woods. The time had come for Mack to place all of his belongings into the golf cart. Barry grabbed his keys, and he began the short trip to drop Mack off over at the terminal. The men exchanged a final handshake as they bid farewell to one another.

Mack settled into his seat on the plane to begin the long journey home. During his flight, he had plenty of time to reflect on how his life had changed forever simply because of what he'd won at an auction, and for a man named Felix E. Scott. Mack felt bad that Felix didn't get to see the end of the war with the Japanese after the atomic bombs were dropped on Hiroshima and Nagasaki. Felix had also missed Hitler's suicide, and the fall of Berlin, which ended the war in Europe. Mack thought that it was sad that Felix wasn't given a chance to earn the Air Medal, and that he hadn't been given an opportunity to be awarded the Distinguished Flying Cross. He never achieved his dream of becoming a flying ace either. To make matters worse, Mack couldn't find any record that Felix was even awarded a Purple Heart, all because he was killed in a training accident versus having been killed during combat. Mack had become entirely familiar with all of the challenges that Felix had faced before arriving in India. What if he hadn't been sick so that he could've made it in the service much earlier? What if it had rained on that fateful day, causing a delay so that he wouldn't have been able to fly? What if Captain Edwards had assigned him to a different P-51 Mustang? Mack figured that he could play the what if game all the way back to Oklahoma, but he realized that it wasn't going to change the fact that Felix had been killed in the crash.

After his evening meal on the plane, Mack decided to compose an email to Ruvonne to let her know about the successful completion of the mission there in India. He felt that she'd be proud of his accomplishments, and that he was following in the path of Felix's footsteps as a pilot. As the sun faded completely out of view, Mack stared down the aisleway towards the cockpit, knowing that he'd soon be flying an airplane full of passengers to locations all around the world. Before powering down his laptop for the rest of the flight, he stumbled upon a quote from Leonardo da Vinci that said, "The sky is home to the dreamers of the earth." Mack hoped that there would be a future filled with endless opportunities, and that a wonderful career lay ahead of him. As Mack prepared to begin the next chapter in his life, he felt that Felix would continue to be his wingman. He was committed to make Felix proud, and to live the life that he didn't get to fully live.

Bibliography

Adams, Jr. John A. *Softly call the muster: The evolution of a Texas Aggie tradition.* Texas A & M University Press. College Station, TX. 1994.

Army Air Force Training Command Visual Training Dept. *Aircraft and Principles of Flight-Preflight.* Conners-Joyce Associates 1944.

Army Air Forces West Coast Training Center. *Lemoore Army Air Field.* Army & Navy Publishing Co., Inc. Baton Rouge, LA.

Casualty report—Felix E. Scott. United States Army Human Resources Command. Fort Knox, KY.

Class 43-I graduation yearbook. The *King's Log-Mesa Del Rey.* Produced by the Third Army Air Force Flying Training Detachment Primary Pilot Academy. King City, CA.

Class 43-I graduation yearbook. *Luke Field.* Phoenix Arizona Engraving and Lithographing Company. Phoenix, AZ.

Griset, Rick. *Images of America: Luke Air Force Base.* Arcadia Publishing. Charleston, SC. 2020.

Jacobs, Harold A. *Topstick: With Some Help From A Guardian Angel.* 1st Books Library. Bloomington, IN. 2002.

Leftwich, Bill J. *The Corps at Aggieland.* Smoke Signal Publishing Company. Lubbock, TX. 1978.

Loupot, Sr. J.E. *Aggie Facts & Figures.* Printed by Loupot's Bookstores. 1989.

Miller, Edrick J. *The SAAAB Story.* Tri-Level Inc. Santa Ana, CA. 1989.

Palo Alto Airport, Inc. *Army Pilots in the Making-Mesa Del Rey.* King City, CA. 1942.

Pasco, John O. *Fish Sergeant: Aggie Tales for Generations to Come.* CreateSpace 2018.

Redon, Pere. *North American T-6 Texan.* Schiffer Publishing Ltd. Atglen, PA. 2014.

Strohn, Howard P. & Jernigan, John R. & Vanderwall Jernigan, Karen. *Images of America: King City.* Arcadia Publishing. Charleston, SC. 2022.

The Office of Air Force History. *The Army Air Forces in WWII. Volume Six "Men and Planes."* 1983.

Walker, Jr. James Knox. *Over At College: A Texas A & M Campus Kid in the 1930's.* Texas A & M University Press. College Station, TX. 2016.

War Department. *Pilots' Information File.* Headquarters-Army Air Forces. May 1, 1943 edition.

Watry, Charles A. *Washout! The Aviation Cadet Story.* California Aero Press. Carlsbad, CA. 1983.

Wright, Cynthia J. & Cox-Finney, Judy. *Images of America: Lemoore.* Arcadia Publishing. Charleston, SC. 2010.

Wynne, Nick & Moorhead, Richard. *Florida in World War II: Floating Fortress.* The History Press. Charleston, SC. 2010.

July 27, 1943–October 1, 1943. *The Arizona Republic.* Phoenix, AZ.

September 1938–January 1942. *The Battalion. College* Station, TX. https://newspaper.library.tamu.edu

May 27, 1943–July 22, 1943. *The Lemoore Advance.* Lemoore, CA.

Tax, Al. March 1943–May 1943. Flight Lines from Mesa Del Rey Airport. *The Rustler-Herald.* King City, CA. https://cdnc.ucr.edu

January 1942–June 1949. *The San Saba News and Star.* San Saba, TX.

January 1942–June 1949. *The San Saba News.* San Saba, TX.

December 1942–March 1943. *The Santa Ana Cadet.* Santa Ana, CA.

"Aviation Cadet Regulations Santa Ana Army Air Field Santa Ana, CA." www.aafcollection.com

Elebash, Clarence C. "Was it the Air Corps or Army Air Forces in WWII?" www.AAFHA.org

Crash reports. www.afhra.af.mil

"Charles Lindbergh—An American Aviator." http://www.charleslindbergh.com

Marshall, Norman S. & Denger, Mark J. "General James Harold "Jimmy" Doolittle." www.militarymuseum.org

Morgan, Lesa. "Lindbergh's Cat." www.greatermoundcity.org

O'Brien, Pamela. "Amelia Earhart—A Timeline." https://www.ninety-nines.org

"Pearl Harbor Attack." "Battle of Midway." "Doolittle Raid." www.history.navy.mil

"1938–39, 1939–40, 1940–41, 1941–42 football schedules and results." www.12thman.com

About the Author

Greetings. I'm so glad that you picked up a copy of my book. I'm a first-time author, and it's my pleasure to bring you a heartfelt story about my Great Uncle, Felix Ernest Scott.

I've spent the last four years researching as many details as possible in an effort to be able to fully tell the story of a little Texas farm boy who dreamed of being a pilot. While growing up in the 1980s, I never heard much talk about Uncle Felix, but nevertheless, I was always fascinated that he was a P-51 fighter pilot, and I often imagined that he must've died in a horrific, yet heroic, battle in the sky. For me, he was a great uncle who made the ultimate sacrifice while serving our country during WWII. I didn't know any of the actual details of his life, and, like the rest of his family and friends, I wondered how he had ultimately died while piloting his P-51 in the faraway land of India.

I was playing my favorite WWII Call of Duty video game one day in March of 2020 when I felt Felix's spirit asking me to tell his story. He literally described the concept for the book, and I even wrote ten chapter titles right there in my chair. It was an extraordinary vision, and I immediately shared it with my family. I have a passion for military history, and through meticulous research, I believe that I've crafted a touching narrative that brings Felix's story to life. A very special thanks to my Wife, Michelle Bass, for her support throughout this project. My Mother, Mary Jane Bass, and my Uncle Mack & Aunt Barb Stephenson, along with my cousins Wayne Blanton and Ruvonne Underwood Dennis, provided me with various personal recollections, pictures, or personal belongings of Felix, all of which proved to be extremely helpful in putting together the information found within the pages of this book. The scope of this work was quite daunting when I began the first chapter, since I wasn't the best student in English class during my school days. I had no idea how many rabbit holes that I'd need to dive down, but I can proudly say that I left no stone unturned in my quest to complete this project.

The visions with Felix continued throughout the last several years, and he provided me with a great deal of guidance along the way. I've uncovered many details, tidbits, coincidences, and some inspiring, and even hair-raising details while working on this book. Of course, there are some fictional pieces that were added to the story which helped to fill in some of the blanks for the time that Felix spent here on earth. There were many long days with a sore neck as I worked to make Felix's story come to life, but in the end, this was a labor of love. Many thanks go to my mother for the countless hours that she spent proofreading this work, and for the valuable insight and suggestions that she provided along the way. I would also like to give a shout out to my Nephew, Kevin Hickey, for assisting me with the initial concept for the cover of my book.

I'm a Southern California resident with deep Texas roots, and military service has been a big part of our family for generations. As a youngster, I stood in my grandparents' living room with awe as I looked at the medals that my maternal grandfather had earned for his service before, during, and after WWII. I can undoubtedly say that, he too, was an inspiration for me to want to embark on this wonderful journey. I'd like to give a tremendous thank you to Lynn Blankenship at the San Saba County Historical Museum, and to Lisa Kalmus, curator at the Sanders Corps of Cadets Center at Texas A&M University. Many thanks to John and Karen Jernigan for all of their help with my questions regarding times past in King City, CA. A special thank you to Eric Wydra for his help with my questions pertaining to the University of Oklahoma. Bill Beigel, WWII researcher and author, was instrumental in finding many things about Felix that I couldn't even imagine. Mary Ellen Goddard, a volunteer at the Costa Mesa Historical Society, was also very helpful with my research pertaining to Felix's time at the Santa Ana Army Air Base (SAAAB). Heartfelt gratitude goes out to Bobbie and Phillip Morris for providing me with a place to stay during my research visits, and for sharing their boundless knowledge of San Saba County. Finally, this work would've had some holes if it weren't for the invaluable help of John and Debbie Simon along with Nick and Sheryl DeJong. John and Sheryl's father, Ray Simon, went through training, and served with Felix up until the time of his death.

I hope that y'all enjoy my narrative pertaining to the life of an uncle who has been long gone, but never forgotten.

Fly high, Felix, you'll always be in the hearts of our family.